Crimson City

A Muzaffar Jang Mystery

MADHULIKA LIDDLE

First published in 2015 by Hachette India
(Registered name: Hachette Book Publishing India Pvt. Ltd)
An Hachette UK company
www.hachetteindia.com

SRD

ISBN 978-93-5009-786-1

Hachette Book Publishing India Pvt. Ltd
4th & 5th Floors, Corporate Centre
Plot No. 94, Sector 44, Gurgaon 122003, India

Typeset in Sabon 10/13
by Ram Das Lal, NCR Delhi

Printed and bound in India by Manipal Technologies Limited, Manipal

Crimson City

Madhulika Liddle is best known as the author of the Muzaffar Jang mystery series (*The Englishman's Cameo, The Eighth Guest and Other Muzaffar Jang Mysteries* and *Engraved in Stone*). Madhulika lives in New Delhi and also writes fiction in other genres, including humour. In 2003, her short stories won the top prize at the Commonwealth Broadcasting Association's short story competition. Her other passions range from history to classic cinema, travel and food: writings on all of these can be found at www.madhulikaliddle.com.

Praise for *The Englishman's Cameo*

'The mystery is intriguing, but it is Liddle's historically accurate portrait of Shahjahanabad, complete with the moonlit Yamuna, the paandaans, the palanquins, the noblemen's parties and bustling market places, that make the novel come alive. The plot will intrigue you and the narrative will enthrall you.'

– *Hindustan Times*

'*The Englishman's Cameo* is a genuinely promising debut. Its originality and freshness [are] its strongest point[s], and – after the dramatic resolution – one shuts the book hoping that Madhulika Liddle will continue with her literary project and act as a path-breaker for other history-mystery writers in order to build this fabulous genre's South Asian avatar.'

– Zac O'Yeah, *Deccan Herald*

'The writing style is vivid and descriptive... With the young and hot-blooded Muzaffar Jang following the trail to help his friend from being executed we have an Agatha Christie style plot in hand.'

– *The Hindu*

Praise for *The Eighth Guest and Other Muzaffar Jang Mysteries*

'The writing is crisp and taut, just the way a good mystery tale should be told. At the same time, the essence of the book is not lost... *The Eighth Guest and Other Muzaffar Jang Mysteries* still stands as a testimony that Indian writers can write a good mystery. Madhulika Liddle is a writer to watch out for.'

– *IBN Live*

'It is vividly descriptive with attention to detail and it is simply delightful to read the way the words just flow with no attempt to flummox the reader... Where others would be lost for being too commonplace, Liddle has been ingenious in creating a detective who is set in a time which places him far ahead in any competition.'

– *Asian Age*

Praise for *Engraved in Stone*

'The language is contemporary and fresh; the way of thought and movement is too. The narrative style is casual, the stuff of which young urban linguistic India is made.'

– *The Hindu*

'*Engraved in Stone* is a historical whodunit, racy and engrossing. Liddle painstakingly adds details from the period to make the story as authentic as possible.'

– *Time Out*

'...[I]t's the whodunit and adventure sequences that make up for the niggling irritations of the unlikelihood of someone like Muzaffar Jang actually existing, and that make *Engraved in Stone* such a pleasurable read.'

– *Sunday Guardian*

For Lara

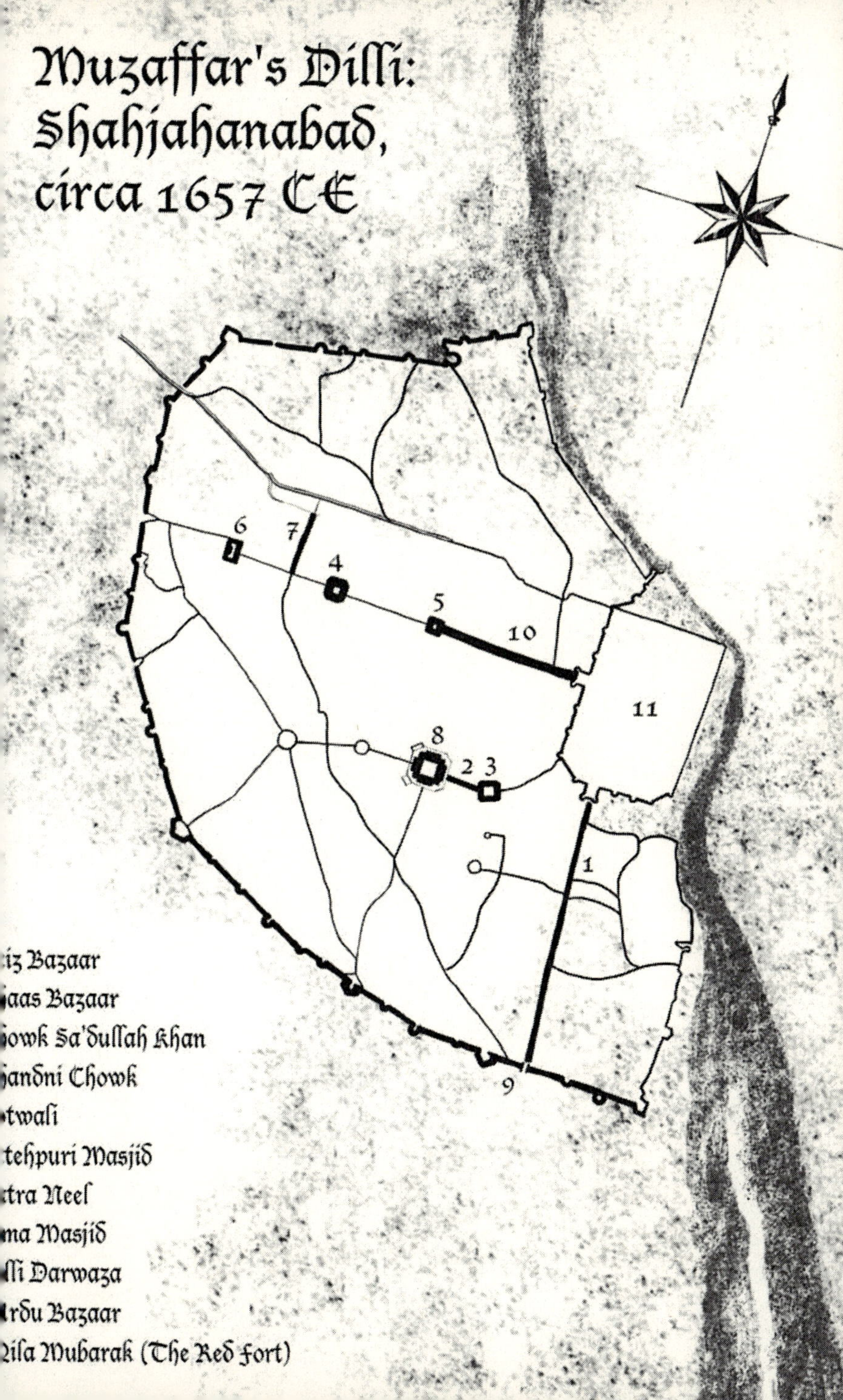

Muzaffar's Dilli:
Shahjahanabad,
circa 1657 CE
6
7
4
5
10
11
8
2 3
1
9
iz Bazaar
aas Bazaar
owk Sa'dullah Khan
andni Chowk
twali
tehpuri Masjid
tra Neel
ma Masjid
lli Darwaza
rdu Bazaar
ila Mubarak (The Red Fort)

CHAPTER 1

Dilli, Jumada Al-Awwal, March, 1657 CE

'Jahanpanah, Baadshah Salamat! Refuge of the world, lord of all! This insignificant creature trembles to come into your dazzling presence, my lord. My mind and my tongue cannot begin to find words adequate to express a millionth of the gratitude I feel, Jahanpanah – '

'If this is how long-winded he is when he's so dazzled,' whispered someone standing behind Muzaffar Jang in the Diwan-e-Aam, 'I shudder to think what he's like when he isn't overwhelmed by his feelings.' Ahead of them, past the red-lacquered wooden railings that separated the riffraff from the high nobility, past even the silver railings that separated the cream of the land from the Emperor, stood a nobleman, bent almost double in front of Shahjahan.

The Baadshah sat, white-bearded and stooped, his face wrinkled, his eyes impassive. High up on his white marble throne with its curved roof, with only his eldest son and heir, the Shahzada Dara Shukoh, and two guards, each bearing lances and swords, within arm's reach. Behind the Emperor was the back wall of the Diwan-e-Aam; on three sides, in front of him and on either side, stretched the hall, its red sandstone columns disguised with polished white plaster, its floor covered with rich carpets, and a heavy crimson canopy stretching out from the edge of the building, the Hall of Public Audience.

Muzaffar Jang, twenty-six years old and a notorious non-conformist, had never been a regular at the imperial court. As a member of the minor nobility, he had been easily overlooked and his absence rarely commented upon. His recent activities, however, had made him a more recognizable figure: the cream of the court now were aware that the young brother-in-law of Dilli's Kotwal, Farid Khan, was no ordinary young man, but one with an uncanny ability to sniff out the truth in matters criminal.

And Khan Sahib was not merely married to Muzaffar's elder sister Zeenat Begum; ever since Muzaffar had been born, this man – now standing across the hall, his hands clasped loosely below his waist, his face tense – had been the only real father Muzaffar had known. His own mother had died in giving birth to Muzaffar; and his father, the general Burhanuddin Malik Jang, had been too busy fighting battles for his Baadshah to be bothered with bringing up a young child, even if that child was his sole son and heir. Zeenat Begum, twenty-five years older than her infant brother, had picked him up, swaddling clothes and all, and brought him up along with her own children. For the sake of her honour, and that of her husband, Muzaffar was making an attempt to be rather more the responsible courtier he was expected to be. Not by Khan Sahib, who had accepted Muzaffar's maverick ways years ago, but by those finicky enough to judge Khan Sahib by the demeanour of his brother-in-law.

'These Hindus,' said another voice. 'They make a fine art out of licking boots.'

'They have to,' murmured the man who had initially spoken. 'It is the only way they can hope to make any progress in court. A worthless lot.' The derision was undisguised.

Muzaffar glanced back over his shoulder, searching the crowd behind him. Ahead, the Emperor had risen from his throne, and had started moving away, heading back for the royal chambers. His departure had caused the massed courtiers to begin moving too, like a series of ripples spreading out from a stone tossed into a pond. Behind him, Muzaffar saw only shifting figures, men moving away here and there, turning to talk to neighbours, beginning to take their leave. He frowned.

Despite the burgeoning buzz of conversation as the assembly disintegrated, Muzaffar heard a voice call, clearly but not too loudly, his name. It was Khan Sahib, making his way through the crowd towards his brother-in-law and sometime foster-son. A stocky man, almost a head shorter than Muzaffar's own impressive height, with a neatly trimmed grey beard and moustache, his eyes sharp.

Muzaffar's earliest memories from his childhood had been of Khan Sahib, a Khan Sahib who had fashioned Muzaffar's first bow and taught the little boy to hook his thumb in the drawstring, aim, pull, release. A Khan Sahib who had taught Muzaffar his first letters. Who had seated him on his first horse, given him his first lessons in riding, brushed away his tears when he had suffered a fall. Scolded him when he had been found guilty of a misdemeanour, and comforted him when a beloved pet squirrel had been killed by a stray cat.

He had changed little, thought Muzaffar with a private smile. Khan Sahib was still as solicitous of Muzaffar as he had been when Muzaffar was a boy. More respectful, of course, and accommodating of the fact that Muzaffar was now a grown man, but still.

'Why the frown, Muzaffar?' Khan Sahib said, by way of greeting. 'I could see you across the hall. That scowl does not suit you.'

Muzaffar had started walking towards the arches that led out; ahead of him, slaves stationed beside the columns were pulling aside the quilted curtains that hung at the arches, blocking the spring breeze, still a little too cool for comfort. Beyond a green-printed chintz curtain tugged back, Muzaffar saw a glimpse of the broad crimson canopy that stretched out from the sandstone overhang of the Diwan-e-Aam. The sunshine was weak, the sky cloudy.

'Someone said something disparaging about Hindus,' he replied. When Khan Sahib lifted an eyebrow in query, Muzaffar recounted the incident.

'And that distresses you, Muzaffar?'

'Should it not?'

The Kotwal shrugged. 'You are not naïve. When two different streams of thought – two different beliefs, and that too so diametrically different – are forced to live in close contact, their differences are bound to be accentuated. To be the cause of further differences. There is nothing surprising in that.'

Muzaffar walked on, hands clasped behind his back, chewing at his moustache, for a few paces more, until the two of them had exited the Diwan-e-Aam. 'You are wrong, I think, Khan Sahib,' he said eventually. 'In thinking that I am not naïve. It seems to me as if I have been naïve after all.' He glanced sideways, meeting Khan Sahib's gaze. 'I was under the impression that, at least at court, at least among the nobility, there was harmony between the Hindus and the Mussulmaans. Tolerance, if not more. Do the Hindus not furnish the empire with some of its best warriors? Its treasurers, its clerks, its bankers? If it were not for the Rajputs and the Khatris and the many others who handle its battles and its finances, the empire would never have succeeded.'

A small group of courtiers, their turbans bobbing, the hems of their woollen chogas flapping about their pyjama-clad legs, walked past. Muzaffar held his tongue, letting the men go well ahead of them before continuing. 'Was not the Baadshah himself inclined to look favourably upon the Hindus? Did he not buy the land for the Empress's tomb in Agra from a Hindu? Did he not – '

'Muzaffar,' Khan Sahib interrupted. 'There will always be people who will be prejudiced, to whom it will make not the slightest difference that their homes are being protected or their revenues earned because of a Hindu. Or a Mussulmaan, or whoever. Prejudice is prejudice, and it is invariably selfish. Let it not bother you so much. What you overheard was a chance remark; most men at court do not hold such views.'

They had walked through the painted gatehouse of the Naqqar Khaana, named for the kettle drums that were traditionally used here to play music – throughout the day on auspicious days like Eid and the Baadshah's birthday, at regular intervals to mark the passage of time on ordinary days. Right now, the Naqqar Khaana was silent but for the murmur of voices as courtiers passed through it on their way out of the Laal Qila, the red sandstone fortress that formed the focus of the city of Shahjahanabad.

The city that was Kotwal Sahib's domain. A restive, uneasy city, one that had been established with great pomp and show after the Baadshah had shifted his capital from Agra north to Dilli a few years earlier. It was still a grand city, fashionable and busy and glamorous. But, like every other city – even the most beautiful – Dilli had its underbelly, and keeping that clean was Kotwal Sahib's job.

They walked through Chhatta Chowk, the long arcade that ran all the way to the gate of the fort, the Lahori Darwaza, named for the faraway city that it faced. From here, Lahore could not be seen, but through the open gates of the fort, past the moat, could be glimpsed the spires of the temples, the shops of Chandni Chowk. Khan Sahib's face clouded over with worry.

'Let it be,' Muzaffar said quietly. 'Tell me, Khan Sahib. How is it with you? You look worried.'

☙

Khan Sahib said nothing for a moment or two, just staring straight ahead as if he had not even heard Muzaffar speak. Then he tilted his chin forward in a quick gesture, indicating the buildings, the long stretch of bazaar-flanked canal that lay beyond the walls of the fort. Through the grey clouds lowering over the city, a stray shard of sunlight lit up the spire of the Jain temple at the very head of the street.

'Look at that,' Khan Sahib said. 'It looks so peaceful, does it not? Quiet. You and I know that it is not.' He hunched his shoulders. 'She is like a child, this city. A spoilt child, unruly and obstreperous. So terribly difficult to control.'

'A child?' Muzaffar smiled. 'I wonder.' They had stepped out of the gloomy shadow of the Chhatta Chowk, and a slave – one of many stationed there to help courtiers with fetching horses or palanquins – came up to receive instructions. As the man sprinted off towards the stables, Muzaffar turned back to Khan Sahib. 'Do you remember that courtesan who used to live here in the fort, near Hayat Baksh Bagh, Khan Sahib? Mehtab, her name was.'

'And quite a woman, I believe.' Khan Sahib's voice was dry. 'I never had the pleasure of making her acquaintance – Allah be thanked – but you did, did you not? You seemed fascinated by her.'

Muzaffar shrugged. 'She was a fascinating woman,' he conceded. 'But what I meant was that this city reminds me increasingly of Mehtab. A coquette, scheming and ruthless, but also beautiful. Alluring, charming men into coming to her. And, when they are within her grasp, she winds them round her little finger and proceeds to milk them dry of all they have. Without any compunctions. And the men themselves are happy to give up all they have; such is the magic she weaves.'

Khan Sahib grimaced. 'You make her sound like an enchantress, a hoor of Paradise itself. Dilli is pure evil; there is nothing alluring or mysterious about it. Just undiluted evil, grime.' He squinted into the distance, looking towards the city. His gaze flattened as if he was looking further, staring into space.

'It is not just the city, Muzaffar,' he murmured, in a barely audible voice. His next sentence revealed to Muzaffar the reason for the sudden drop in pitch and volume. 'When the empire is tottering on the brink of collapse, it is hardly to be expected that its capital city will flourish. Do you remember what I had told you, when the winter was starting – about four months back, was it, when news had arrived that Bijapur had a new Sultan? When the man's legitimacy was in question, and the Baadshah ordered Shahzada Aurangzeb to lead a campaign into Bijapur?'

Muzaffar nodded cautiously, aware of all that had happened since, but unable to remember what Khan Sahib had said all those months back. Much had taken place in the interim, not just in Muzaffar's life – he had investigated several cases of crime; he had met and married Shireen; he had become a little wiser – but also in the life of the empire. It had acquired a new prime minister, the ambitious and ruthless Mir Jumla, who had come north from the Deccan, bearing gifts of precious stones and news of a kingdom ripe for an invasion. This very same Mir Jumla, as the Diwan-i-kul of the Mughal Empire, had been ordered south at the head of a massive army, to rendezvous with Aurangzeb's forces and invade Bijapur.

'I had said then that I feared the consequences of the campaign,' Khan Sahib said. 'At first glance, it would seem lucrative; nothing but wealth to be had from it, and territory to add to the empire. Not to mention the almost sure chance of a victory.'

'The Diwan-i-kul's and the Shahzada's massed armies far outnumber anything Bijapur may raise up against them,' Muzaffar agreed. 'But what is to prevent a repeat of the Golconda fiasco? Aurangzeb lead his army there too, ready to annex Golconda – and all that happened was that Golconda begged Dara Shukoh to have the Mughal armies withdrawn. And because the Baadshah loves his heir far too much, it was done. What if that should happen again? What if this expedition too should prove futile?'

'Aurangzeb will be furious.' The slave had arrived with their horses. Muzaffar took the reins of his handsome chestnut stallion, and mounted on his own while the slave held the other horse for Khan Sahib to mount.

'I fear,' Khan Sahib added as they moved off, 'that something is going to go wrong with this campaign too.'

Muzaffar grinned as he glanced over at his brother-in-law. 'That old adage of yours, Khan Sahib? "You may net trouble if you fish in troubled waters"?'

Khan Sahib did not nod or say anything, but his expression turned even grimmer than before.

'I hear,' Muzaffar continued, 'that the troops under the Diwan-i-kul and Aurangzeb have already besieged the fort of Bidar. Bazaar gossip has it that Bidar will fall any day now and the troops will return to Dilli loaded with plunder.' Off from the left, a group of young men – none of them more than seventeen summers old – burst into sudden laughter, clapping and shouting as they sprang apart. One of the boys, backing sharply away and laughing all the while, nearly collided with Muzaffar's horse. He whirled, red-faced and apologetic when he saw the annoyance in Muzaffar's face. Muzaffar stroked his horse on the neck, soothing the animal. He and Khan Sahib were well past the moat and nearing Faiz Bazaar when Khan Sahib said, 'I doubt if this is bazaar gossip you should pay much heed to. The garrison at Bidar is commanded by a certain Sidi Marjan. He is a doughty warrior; Aurangzeb will have a hard time breaking down his defences.'

'The Diwan-i-kul will no doubt find other ways to get

around that problem. The Diwan-i-kul's penchant for offering bribes first and exploring other methods later may work.'

'Not in this case. Sidi Marjan is also said to be fiercely loyal to his Sultan. The Diwan-i-kul may well find his bribes flung back in his face.' They had reached the head of the stretch popularly known as Chandni Chowk, the central artery of Shahjahanabad. Down its length flowed the Nahar-e-Bihisht, the 'Stream of Paradise', the canal which flowed through the fort before being diverted into the city. Its glittering waters cool and tree-shaded, flanked on either side by broad streets and rows of shops, selling all that the empire produced and imported. You could buy a carpet from Isfahan here, or a handful of saffron. A dancing girl or a glass hookah. A midget, a horse, or a garland of jasmine for a beloved's tresses. It was an intoxicating place, colourful and rich and noisy.

Khan Sahib reined in his horse. 'All we can do is wait and see,' he said, dismissing the topic. 'Where are you headed, Muzaffar? Home to Shireen?'

'Home, yes. Whether Shireen will be there or not, I do not know. I believe Zeenat Aapa was to call. And whenever my sister and my bride get together, they invariably choose to spend their time outside the haveli. Zeenat Aapa will probably have taken Shireen to introduce her to some friends, or to buy her something.' He smiled, half-sad, half-indulgent. 'Shireen has lived all her life in Agra; Dilli is far too exotic, too exciting for its charm to be over so soon.'

'We are not immune to its charm, either, are we?' Khan Sahib remarked, with a trace of sarcasm in his voice. 'Just like the courtesan you spoke of, this Dilli. Anyhow, if you are headed home, I shall ride alongside. I have to go to a neighbourhood near the Dilli Darwaza. Quite close to your haveli, actually.'

'Visiting someone, Khan Sahib?'

'Hardly. A man was killed nearby, in one of the lanes near Dilli Darwaza. The thanedar reported it to me this morning, just as I was setting out for court. And then, as he was stepping out of my office, he stumbled over the threshold and went down like a sack of potatoes. He's broken his ankle, I think.'

Muzaffar tut-tutted in sympathy. He was slightly acquainted with the thanedar in question, since Muzaffar's own haveli lay in the jurisdiction of the man's thana. A conscientious man when it came to his work, and not inclined to shirk his duty.

'A hakim was sent for. He must have arrived while I was at court,' said Khan Sahib. 'The ankle was swollen and painful. I would think it's a minor crack, but one that will need time to heal. Meanwhile, I'd better go and have a look at his thana, talk to the chowkidars who report to him, and appoint someone to carry out his duties in the interim.' Khan Sahib turned his horse to the left. 'And I need to see this murder for myself.'

'Do you mind if I come along, Khan Sahib? Just out of curiosity. And if it's somewhere near where I live, perhaps I will know something that may be of help.'

Khan Sahib looked hesitant, as if he were debating the question. It surprised Muzaffar; Khan Sahib, on previous occasions, had never refused a similar request. Muzaffar could even recall instances when Khan Sahib himself had – of his own accord – sent for Muzaffar. This reluctance to let Muzaffar assist in an investigation was uncharacteristic.

'Very well,' Khan Sahib said, with a sigh. 'If you wish. But try and remember that I am the law. I am the official here.'

And on that ambiguous and somewhat ominous note, he moved off.

☙

Dilli Darwaza squatted, grey and formidable, at the end of the straight broad road known as Faiz Bazaar. This was one of the nine gates that pierced the city walls, and like Lahori Darwaza, Kashmiri Darwaza, and Ajmeri Darwaza, was named for the direction it faced. In this case, the old city of Dilli, south of the grand capital Shahjahan had built. Just south of Dilli Darwaza could be seen the ruins of the 200-year old Firoz Shah Kotla, the citadel built by the long-ago Sultan Firoz Shah Tughlaq. Shahjahan's teams of builders had plundered Firoz Shah's fortress ruthlessly, stripping it of its red sandstone and its marble, leaving behind only the rubble they did not care to reuse.

The lane Khan Sahib turned his horse into led towards the Kalan Masjid, the 'large mosque'. Built around the same time as Firoz Shah's fort, it was aptly named, though the magnificent Jama Masjid next to Chandni Chowk now surpassed it in size and grandeur.

Past the Kalan Masjid and a few dozen yards into the lane, the road went the way of most of Shahjahanabad's inner area. The lane split into narrower lanes and alleys, branching off like an unpruned tree. Cul de sacs and dead ends, dingy little hovels and old deserted tombs where passing mendicants sometimes stopped for a night's rest: one could easily get lost in this maze.

Muzaffar, however, was familiar with the area. Khan Sahib, from having visited his young brother-in-law's haveli countless times over the past years, knew it well enough too. 'Heading for the chowki?' Muzaffar asked as Khan Sahib guided his horse between a small well and a row of vegetable sellers.

'Not just the chowki, but the scene of the crime,' Khan Sahib replied. 'The murder was committed a couple of houses from the chowki.'

'The criminals of Dilli grow audacious.'

Khan Sahib turned his head and directed a look of weariness at Muzaffar. Muzaffar dipped his head by way of apology; the inadvertent hit had struck a sore spot. Taken in conjunction with Khan Sahib's recent reluctance to have Muzaffar accompany him, it seemed to suggest that the Kotwal was – what? Muzaffar wondered. Had crime in the city really become so rampant that Khan Sahib and his men were finding it difficult to deal with it? Had all his many duties taken their toll on Khan Sahib? Was age catching up with him? Or had someone made a snide remark – Allah forbid – that Khan Sahib was not competent enough? Muzaffar was well aware that the post of the Kotwal of Dilli was a coveted position, and yet one to be feared too. It was a post that could be exploited by the corrupt; a previous Kotwal had been hounded out of the city, disgraced publicly and flogged, for having misappropriated funds and accepted bribes. On the other hand, it was a post that came with a barrage of duties, all the way from preventing and investigating murders and thefts to registering the entry of outsiders, to ensuring shopkeepers used correct weighing scales, to organizing festivities and illuminations at Eid and Diwali. To making sure women did not ride horses, slaves did not abscond, and workers were paid fair wages for their work.

It was a ludicrously long and complex list of duties. If it made Khan Sahib occasionally grumpy, Muzaffar should not be surprised. He mumbled a brief 'I beg your pardon', but Khan Sahib did not react.

☙

Muzaffar's haveli was less than a quarter of an hour's leisurely stroll from the chowki. It was not the most fashionable part of town; the elite mostly had their havelis nearer to Chandni Chowk – but it was a comfortable neighbourhood. Compared to the immediate surroundings of Muzaffar's home, the area just before the chowki lacked both charm and comfort. Mud huts made up most of the dwellings around. Recent rains had caused cracks to appear in the less expertly constructed, and fire – a hazard that perpetually hung over much of the city – had left an entire row of huts roofless, their thatch burnt, their walls blackened and partly collapsed. The smell of decay hung on the air.

'The house is right ahead, huzoor,' the chowkidar said when they dismounted at the chowki. A young soldier from the chowki hurried forward to take charge of the horses. The chowkidar himself, a man with a grizzled chin and bags under bloodshot eyes, was already beginning to move in the direction he had been pointing. 'It is just a few yards, huzoor,' he explained. 'The horses will be safer here – '

'Yes, yes. Lead on,' Khan Sahib said with a touch of impatience. 'I want to get this over and done with. This is Muzaffar Jang Sahib, by the way. He lives nearby.'

'I know of Jang Sahib,' the chowkidar acknowledged, with a swift look towards Muzaffar. 'You are well-respected in this neighbourhood, huzoor.'

Muzaffar ducked his head, embarrassed.

'And here is the place,' the chowkidar added, stopping at the barred wooden door of a small house. While the area east of the chowki had been one of hovels, this section appeared to be occupied by a somewhat wealthier class of people. True, there were no grand havelis and no expansive gardens – but there was more than the thatch-roofed mud huts of the poor. These were small houses, but built of baked brick, some with their roofs tiled, others thatched. A dirt road, packed hard by thousands of feet, human and animal, over many years, formed the thoroughfare. Occasionally, when it rained hard – as it had on the previous night – the earth was loosened and churned up into a muddy mess that clung to soles and hems.

Outside the second house beyond the chowki stood a man, lance in hand and an expression of ludicrous fierceness on his face. 'Thanedar Sahib told me to put a man on duty,' the chowkidar explained. 'The people in the neighbourhood have been curious.' It appeared that the presence, even of such a formidable representative of the constabulary, had not daunted the more persistent. An old woman stood a few feet away, one gnarled hand bunching up the rough brown fabric of her skirts just high enough to raise them above the mud of the lane. A poor woman, from the plain, unadorned look of her – and the mere fact that while a bright blue dupatta covered her head and shoulders, her face was uncovered. A noblewoman would not venture unveiled out of her house, possibly not even outside the women's quarters of her house. And she would certainly not stand thus, gawking in the street.

Or hurry forward in this impetuous fashion. The guard tried to stop her, but she shrugged off his hand on her arm as nonchalantly as if brushing off a fly. She ducked her head in the semblance of a salaam to Khan Sahib and Muzaffar, recognizing them as members of the nobility, even if she did not know their identities. But it was the chowkidar to whom she addressed her query. 'What has happened, huzoor? He' – a swift tilt of her head towards the guard indicated whom she meant – 'will not tell me. Is Aadil Sahib dead?' Her gaze, bright as a bird's, darted towards the shut door beyond.

'And why should you think so, Ameena Bibi?' The chowkidar asked in a dry voice.

'Why else would you have a man standing guard, huzoor? And if it were a simple affair of burglary, Aadil Sahib would be here too, would he not?'

She's a sharp one, thought Muzaffar.

'Have you seen anything, Ameena Bibi, that you suspect he is dead?'

For a moment, the old woman looked as if she would prevaricate. Then she shrugged, as if it did not really matter whether the chowkidar knew of how she had come by her information. 'I was up on the roof,' she said, gesturing towards the terrace of the house next door, 'sweeping the floor, when I saw you and your men milling around inside. In the courtyard. There was a body there, wasn't there? I couldn't see his face.

Was it Aadil Sahib?' She was excited now, her head jutting out, her free hand clutching the chowkidar's arm.

'Ya Allah, Ameena Bibi!' The chowkidar made no attempt to disguise his disgust at the woman's macabre interest in the crime. 'Yes, he is dead. Now please go and let us get on with our work.'

'But how did he die? He was perfectly well till yesterday – '

'He was killed. Now, please. Go.' He glared at her. Then, as if realizing that he might be shooing away a possible witness, he softened. 'If you saw or heard anything that could be of help, come to the chowki in half an hour's time. Or, better still, I will send a man to fetch you. But let us be now; we cannot keep Kotwal Sahib waiting.' He removed her hand from his arm firmly, and taking advantage of her momentary awe at the discovery that the nobleman before her was the Kotwal himself, pushed the door open and ushered Khan Sahib and Muzaffar in.

He pushed the door shut behind them. The voice of the guard could be heard beyond, telling the old woman to take herself off.

'I beg your pardon, huzoor,' the chowkidar said. 'These people – '

'Yes, yes. I know. Let's get on with it. Talk to her later, though. She seems enough of a busybody to perhaps know something, even if she doesn't realize it right now.' Khan Sahib moved forward, away from the wooden threshold. They were in a courtyard of packed earth, and there, flat on his back with his bony feet pointing towards the door, lay the dead man. Muzaffar noticed the edge of a muddied white pyjama, and the sleeve of a white jama from which a thin hand protruded. The rest of the man's body was enveloped in a large brown shawl, soaked in rainwater.

Khan Sahib turned to the chowkidar. 'When was this corpse found?'

'Just after sunrise, huzoor. A passerby noticed it.'

'Where is he?'

'I have his name and address, huzoor. I can send a man to fetch him.'

'Do so. I'd like to question him myself. And this man – the victim – the thanedar told me he was a cloth merchant. What was his name? Aadil?'

The chowkidar nodded.

The dead man looked to be in his mid-thirties, thin-cheeked and with grey strands in both his beard and the hair on his head – which was bare. The voluminous brown shawl that had pooled about his gaunt figure also spread about the rest of him, making him look like a collapsed angel, its brooding wings spread from knee to shoulder.

An angel made grotesque by a burst of crimson over its chest. A dagger had been plunged here, and withdrawn after it had done its work. Khan Sahib bent, easing away the edge of the shawl to expose the cotton jama underneath. The jama was wet, clinging in pinkish-red folds to the man's ribs. Muzaffar touched the shawl; his fingertips came away reddened. 'It's drenched through and through,' he said. He hefted the shoulder slightly, and bending till his cheek almost touched the ground, looked under.

'Wet as the earth he lies on, Sahib,' said the chowkidar. His face wore an expression of faintly amused patience, like a man humouring a child who insisted on poking its fingers into matters that were none of its concern.

Muzaffar glanced at him. 'Yes,' he said. 'What with the rain all through the night, I'm not surprised.' He looked around, his gaze searching the courtyard. 'I do not see a lamp or a candle around. He must have come to answer the door in the dark, then. Because it was raining, I suppose.'

'Come along,' Khan Sahib said, when the chowkidar did not comment. 'Let us go inside the house and have a look.

Perhaps there will be some clue there. Tell your man to keep an eye, here.' The chowkidar stepped out, and Khan Sahib turned on his heel. Muzaffar followed as the Kotwal walked through the small courtyard, to the two rooms beyond. Instead of a set of thin sandstone slabs sloping from the edge of the roof to form a dripstone, here was a row of kiln-baked tiles. Rainwater still dripped from the edge, forming a neat row of dimples in the earth below. A trail of mud, smudged and blurred but still recognizable as footprints, led into the larger room.

This was obviously a chamber meant for outsiders. It lacked the silken cushions, the Persian carpets and elegant Chinese porcelain that would have decorated the dalaans of Dilli's wealthy, but the sheet haphazardly spread on the mattress – where it had not been soiled by the footprints – was white and clean. The lime plaster on the walls was still creamy, the niches in the walls cleanly cut. There was no stone, carved or inlaid; no silk and finery; no sign of wealth. Just a lack of grinding poverty. A man who could afford a proper house, with a tiled roof and brick walls, was wealthy enough.

'There isn't much, is there?' Khan Sahib remarked. His eyes were still bleak and his expression shuttered, but at least he was not completely blocking Muzaffar out. That was reason enough to feel grateful.

☙

Muzaffar shook his head in wordless agreement. He was looking around, searching the room for signs. Of what, he did not know himself. Perhaps even the person who had preceded them into the room, leaving that trail of mud, had not known. His footprints meandered all across the room, from one niche to another, from the hookah to the single window with its plain wooden leaves. From the old brass paandaan and along the mattress, its sheet pulled out on one side, to the curtained doorway that led into the second room.

'This was where he lived, I suppose,' said Muzaffar as he held the curtain aside for Khan Sahib to step over the threshold and into the other room. There had been no need for the statement, but the silence of the house – punctuated only by the gurgle of water swirling along a drain somewhere outside – had begun to unnerve Muzaffar. From beyond the courtyard came the voices of the chowkidar and the guard. Mere snatches of conversation. The news had begun to spread in the neighbourhood. People had started coming by, eager to discover what had happened. It might be useful to fetch another man from the chowki to keep off the crowd of curious neighbours. 'Stay here,' Muzaffar heard the chowkidar say. 'I shall inform Kotwal Sahib, and then go and fetch someone.'

In the brief moment before he followed Khan Sahib, Muzaffar heard a sudden, sharp exclamation from Khan Sahib. 'Ya Allah! What is this?!' Muzaffar was already moving in behind him, looking over his brother-in-law's shoulder. Khan Sahib's reaction had prepared Muzaffar for something out of the ordinary. Even so, he was so taken aback by the spectacle before him that he did not say anything, just stood and stared.

This, as Muzaffar had correctly surmised even before he had entered, was the room where the cloth merchant had done most of his living. Under the small window was a sheet-covered mattress, with quilts and bolsters. There was a low, broad stool, and two large chests, one iron-bound, the other less formidable. A long, narrow niche in the wall held – or had held, thought Muzaffar – an array of odds and ends. Rolled-up papers, a reed pen, an inkwell, a small waterpot crafted from brass, once bright but now tarnished. The remains of a small bottle of attar. A somewhat cloying fragrance which combined lemons and jasmine and something else that eluded Muzaffar's generally sharp sense of smell.

The vial of attar had been smashed. Its stopper, with its little collar of glass still clinging around it, was all that remained in the niche. The inkwell, the waterpot, and the reed pen had been thrown to the ground, the inkwell shattered so that it lay in shards in its own congealing pool of black. The papers – some of them torn and mangled, one burned to a fragile black leaf that shivered in a sudden draught of air – lay scattered about.

A similar fury seemed to have been vented on the contents of the two chests. Both had been smashed open, the smaller one viciously enough to leave its lid half-broken. From both erupted a froth of cloth: silks, wools, muslins, brocades. These were not the usual garments one would have expected in a household, but a cloth merchant's stock in trade. Here was a bolt of crimson silk moire, its surface shimmering like water, probably from faraway Yazd. There, torn savagely, was a length of pale green qatifah-e-purbi, a plain silk that reminded Muzaffar of a peshwaaz he had gifted Shireen at their wedding. There were gold- and white-striped doriyah muslins, printed chintzes, heavy brocades and delicate muqqaishes, threaded through with fine hairs of silver. They lay spread across half the room, the cloth pulled and torn, muddied in places and bloodied in others. Beside the smaller chest, a small wickerwork basket had been ripped open to reveal skeins of gleaming filoselle silk threads, popular for embroidery. They spread in tangles and knots, emerald and scarlet, purple and orange and yellow, over the sea of cloth around.

Over it all hung the stifling smell of the attar. It made him feel nauseous.

ൽ

'I had thought the man was murdered by someone who meant to rob him,' Khan Sahib said, bending to move aside a length of deep blue silk. 'But I wonder. There is a fortune in fabrics here. If the murderer killed the merchant in order to rob him, he was a foolish man to have not taken at least some of this.'

'It might have been all too bulky and heavy to carry away in his arms,' Muzaffar pointed out. 'But yes, even one length of a brocade like this' – he indicated a richly embroidered piece, all gold thread and pearls, with a fringe of gold – 'and he could have lived in comfort for many years.'

Khan Sahib, already at the larger of the two chests, murmured, 'Unless he has taken away something. There is so much here, a man could decamp with the choicest pieces and we might never know.'

'This merchant seems to have lived all alone,' Muzaffar observed. 'I wonder who would know if there is something missing or not.' He was moving slowly around, his gaze wandering across the mess at his feet. Out of sheer habit, he stepped around the swirls of cloth, or moved aside fabric, even when it was too damaged to be of any use to anyone.

'There will probably be an assistant or a clerk of some sort,' Khan Sahib said, now bent over the chest with arms elbow-deep in a moss-green wool that would have made a fine winter choga. 'I will get the chowkidar to find him.'

'Hmm?' Muzaffar blinked. 'Yes. That might be useful... look at this, Khan Sahib.' He proffered a cream silk shawl, woven in a pattern of large red paisleys. One corner had vanished; it had been consumed by the same fire that had charred some of the remaining cloth. Brittle, blackened threads crumpled and fell even as Muzaffar watched. He handed the shawl to Khan Sahib and bent, lifting a small brass lamp – a chiraghdaan – from the floor. Its greasy bowl was empty of both wick and oil.

Muzaffar held the little chiraghdaan in his palm and gazed speculatively at it. 'It's the same pattern as the waterpot there,' he said, tilting his chin towards the companion vessel, which still lay on the floor. 'Either Aadil was still awake and with the lamp lit when he was interrupted. Or his murderer was cold-blooded enough to kill his man and then come in and examine the loot carefully, using his victim's lamp for it.' He placed the chiraghdaan on the shelf, then lifted the waterpot, before starting to pick up, one sheet at a time, the papers that were scattered all about them.

'And the lamp fell? Knocked down accidentally, or thrown down in a fit of rage?' asked Khan Sahib. He was absent-mindedly folding the ruins of the shawl. 'It set fire to this shawl, and that bit of paper there – but it was put out before it could cause further damage.' His fingers, swollen by the cold, caressed a still-intact paisley. 'I wonder if it was put out,' he murmured. 'Or did it die out of its own accord when there was no more oil left to feed it?'

'It certainly had enough cloth to feed it, Khan Sahib.' Muzaffar glanced up from the sheaf of paper he held. 'Look at this,' he added, extending the pages to Khan Sahib. 'He leafed through these. His fingers have left bloodstains here and there.'

Khan Sahib frowned as he looked through the pages, instinctively reading, too, what was written on them. 'They're not especially interesting,' he observed. 'The everyday accounting of the merchant's business. Dry as matchwood. Why would another want to read them? And that too at such risk to his safety? Any man in his right senses would have gathered up whatever loot he could and taken to his heels. Standing around and reading irrelevant documents like this – it's incomprehensible.' He shook his head in exasperation as he placed the pages in the niche, on top of the folded shawl.

'There is also the fact,' said Muzaffar, 'that he was a literate man. That in itself is an unusual thing, is it not? He cannot be a petty thief, Khan Sahib. There is more to this murder than a theft gone awry.'

CHAPTER 2

'Doesn't that seem to point to someone connected to the merchant through his trade? Perhaps that clerk Khan Sahib talked about? Who else would be interested in reading about the transactions he carried out?'

Shireen's excitement had made her voice rise. Muzaffar, looking on with affection in his gaze, said nothing as his wife put another stitch in the seam she was mending. There was no need for him to speak right now; he had discovered, in the few weeks he had known her, that the greatest compliment Shireen could pay anyone was to allow herself to become garrulous in their presence. To strangers and those she did not care for, Shireen was the very picture of dignity and decorum. A woman of relatively few words, though those words were invariably kind or sensible, or both. It was only in the presence of a very select few that she let herself relax and say whatever came into her head, without weighing it beforehand.

She was doing it now. Thinking through the puzzle Muzaffar had presented, and trying to find her way through it.

'Come to think of it,' she said, 'why would even his clerk want to look through those papers? Wouldn't he know, anyway, what was in them?' She had been focussing all her attention on the garment in her hands. Now she paused, and switched her gaze to Muzaffar. This was a question for him.

He shrugged. 'One cannot assume that Aadil shared every detail of his business with his clerk. It may even be possible that there was something in those papers that could have indicated a' – he groped for a word, spreading his hands, palms up, in a gesture of helplessness, ignorance – 'a discrepancy, perhaps.'

Shireen, who had turned back to her work while Muzaffar spoke, had reached the end of the row of neat stitches. She tied off the end into a double knot and bit the thread off. 'You mean embezzlement?'

'It is possible. Looking at the fabrics Aadil kept in his home, I am inclined to think he must do a lot of travelling to source his wares. If he was gone for long periods at a time, his clerk in Dilli might have spent weeks, even months, handling the business in Dilli by himself. Enough time to squirrel away something from the profits. One daam here, one rupee there. It would hardly even be missed.'

Shireen nodded as she spread the cloth – it was a jama of thick white cotton, suitable for the winter – on the mattress. Her fingertips ran swiftly down the seam, from waist to hem, smoothing the stitches. 'There,' she said, with a fleeting smile of satisfaction as she straightened her shoulders and looked into Muzaffar's eyes. She coloured up the next moment, and gave a self-conscious giggle as she added, 'I beg your pardon. I am being smug, am I not? No? But I must ask for your forgiveness in any case, for the cavalier way in which I have ignored what you said.'

Muzaffar trailed a fingertip down her temple, pausing to wind a stray silken lock around his finger, then dipped the fingertip into the dimple that had appeared in Shireen's cheek. 'I have even forgotten what I had said,' he admitted in a low, hoarse voice.

ᴂ

'I think I shall have another look at that merchant Aadil's house,' Muzaffar said to Shireen the next morning as they walked in the garden after breakfast. The sun had come out, a pleasant change from the bleak greyness of the previous day.

'Has Khan Sahib asked you to be there?'

Muzaffar's brows drew together. 'No. Why do you ask?'

Shireen shook her head. Muzaffar could sense a certain awkwardness in her demeanour; a few moments went by in silence, while she bent to pick up a dry twig from the lawn, twirl it about in her hands, and throw it over the wall – she would make a good archer, with that arm, thought Muzaffar, as he waited for her to respond.

'It is perhaps my imagination,' Shireen said. 'But from what you told me yesterday, it seemed to me that Khan Sahib was not happy to have you around. Perhaps he does not like you to – um – help?'

'He's always been happy enough to have me help before. I think it's just the sheer strain of these past few weeks. Dilli gets more unruly by the day, and Khan Sahib is worried, too, about how matters in the Deccan will affect the empire. He's anxious, not just as a subject of the Baadshah, but as an important official of the empire. Naturally he will be brusque at times.' Shireen was not looking convinced. Another worrier, this one.

'Believe me, Shireen,' Muzaffar said, wrapping an arm around her slim shoulders and pulling her into his side for a quick embrace. 'All is well. By the time we emerged from Aadil's house yesterday, Khan Sahib and I had discussed the incident thoroughly. He would hardly have done that if he resented my being there. That initial reluctance must have been a result of anxiety. Khan Sahib will not mind.'

When Muzaffar reached the doorstep of the murdered merchant, it was to find the house shut and barred, a stout rope knotted round the heavy iron lock on the door.

The armed soldier who had been on duty at the door of

Aadil's house the previous morning was gone now. There was no need for a guard here to deter inquisitive neighbours. They had, no doubt, seen all that was to be seen from the surrounding roofs or even from the street itself: the taking away of the corpse, the more intensive inspection of the house. Some would probably have been questioned, too, regarding whatever they knew of the dead man.

Muzaffar walked over to the chowki in search of someone who might let him into the house. The dingy little room that functioned as the chowki was deserted, but for a pimpled youth who was sweeping the floor. He knew nothing of where the chowkidar might be. Possibly out patrolling the street. And the men usually on duty had been sent out on various errands. Muzaffar left the boy to his work and ambled back, disappointed, to the merchant's house.

There was, he realized, not much to be gleaned from just standing outside the house and looking at the front door, or the mud-plastered brick wall that enclosed the dwelling. It was exactly like a dozen other houses of not-too-wealthy but not impoverished citizens in the neighbourhood. The house next door, for instance.

Muzaffar glanced involuntarily towards the house beside Aadil's, and stiffened. Standing outside the house, looking out into the street, stood a figure draped in drab grey and brown. A shapeless, hunched figure, its head covered and a wrinkled, thick-knuckled hand gripping a tall, sturdy stick.

'Ameena Bibi, I believe?' Muzaffar asked. He had crept up on her quietly, and she had apparently been so intent on whatever she was thinking of, that the old woman gave a violent start. She backed away instantly, turning to look at Muzaffar with frightened eyes. He noticed, though, that she had lifted her stick as if preparing to hit out. An old woman, but not one who would yield without a fight. He smiled at her and hoped that the gesture would prove reassuring.

'I was here yesterday morning with Kotwal Sahib,' he reminded her. 'When he came to first see the body next door.'

Recognition had dawned in the woman's eyes even before he had finished speaking the first sentence. A smile, wary and nervous, appeared on her face. She bobbed her head. 'Yes, huzoor, yes. I remember. You went into poor Aadil's house with Kotwal Sahib.'

It was an opportunity too good to resist. Muzaffar leaped at it. 'Aadil, yes. You knew him, I take it?'

The hesitant friendliness in Ameena Bibi's sharp old eyes turned to instant suspicion. She recoiled, mouth agape and eyes wide. 'I? Know Aadil Sahib? No, huzoor, no. Absolutely not.' She gave a half-hearted croak which Muzaffar interpreted to have been meant to be a light-hearted laugh gone awry. 'I am a poor maidservant, huzoor, and that too not of his household. How would I know Aadil Sahib? He was a wealthy merchant. There was no connection between us. Why would there be?'

'You seemed to be very interested in what had happened to him,' Muzaffar pointed out.

'Who would not be, huzoor?' Ameena Bibi lifted one shoulder in an expressive gesture. 'Had you stayed here for an hour or two longer, you would have seen that there were more people interested in what had happened to Aadil Sahib than had ever been there when he had been alive.' She sighed, shifted her stick to her other hand, seemed to relax a little, as if the presence of a nobleman no longer intimidated her. Muzaffar, watching her, wondered if anything did have the power to intimidate Ameena Bibi. She must surely be at least in her sixties, if not her seventies; and a doughty old woman she seemed to be. Fragile, perhaps, if one looked only at the thin body and the stick she clutched. But the eyes showed the steel within.

'Besides,' she added, 'he was, after all, our immediate neighbour. And we had lived in that house. Does that not create a deeper bond? With the house? With whoever lives in it now?'

ꟹ

Muzaffar's interest was aroused. 'You lived in Aadil's house? When?'

'It was not Aadil Sahib's house then, huzoor,' Ameena Bibi said in a patient voice. 'My Begum Sahiba's husband and his brother owned it. We lived there till – let me think – the rains had still not ended, but...' her eyes narrowed, as if trying to see more clearly into the past. 'Ah, the month of Dhul-kadah; how could I forget? I was not in Dilli then; I was in Surat. They moved houses while I was away.' A note of mild irritation had crept into her tone. Ameena Bibi, thought Muzaffar, probably prided herself on her standing as an old and trusted servant in the household; it had probably come as something of a shock to her to discover that the family could have undertaken a task as tedious and strenuous as shifting house – even if only to a building a few yards away – without her presence.

'And why did they decide to leave this house? Is Aadil related to – um – your Begum Sahiba's family? Was that why he took it over?'

'Parvez Khan Sahib is my lady's husband. His brother is Basharat Sahib,' Ameena Bibi said, with a smile of condescending patience. 'They are merchants too, like Aadil Sahib was, but no relations of his. I do not know why they took into their heads to move; this was a perfectly good house' – she glanced towards Aadil's house, looking at it with an abstracted sort of affection, reliving perhaps in her mind all her fond memories of the house – 'and I would have tried to persuade them to stay on.'

She suddenly seemed to realize that she was being unnecessarily garrulous. With a quick shake of her shoulders and a resettling of her thick brown shawl about herself, she added, 'But who would have listened to me? And Aadil Sahib probably paid them a good price for it, too.'

'Bibi,' said a male voice, calling from the narrow lane that separated Aadil's house from that of his neighbours. Ameena whipped around, and Muzaffar turned to look as well. A man, wearing a grubby white jama and pyjama, his head and shoulders wrapped in a threadbare black blanket, was standing a few yards from them. The edge of the blanket was pulled down so low over his head that it hid all of his face except the very bottom of a chin with a ragged beard.

'Bibi,' he repeated, in a more plaintive voice. 'A single coin, bibi, please. Allah will bless you. Feed a poor man, bibi.'

☙

Ameena Bibi had scurried off with a haste, thought Muzaffar with a wry smile, that made it seem as if that beggar was the answer to her prayers.

She had probably realized that she had been overly chatty with the young nobleman; would she get into trouble for it? Not, surely, for talking to a strange man, given the fact that she was probably old enough to be Muzaffar's grandmother. But for gossiping about the family? For neglecting her work?

Muzaffar sighed and turned back to face Aadil's house.

He stiffened. Approaching the house – almost at its doorstep, now – was a familiar figure: the chowkidar. With him was a stranger, but a man whom Muzaffar could quickly sum up from his very appearance. A wiry man, a thumbprint of sandalwood paste flaring up between his brows, his jama's strings tied up on the left in a column of neat knots. A chakdari jama, the distinguishing mark – like the tilak on his forehead – of a Hindu. As Muzaffar watched, the man reached under the shawl he wore draped over his shoulders. His hand emerged from it, clutching something. He reached forward towards the lock. The chowkidar looked on. A twist of the hand, the sound of ill-greased levers moving, and the man was removing the lock, handing it to the chowkidar to hold while he himself drew back the bolt and pushed the door open.

'I assume this gentleman is Aadil's clerk?' Muzaffar asked, stopping right behind the two men. They had been absorbed in conversation – the Hindu saying something about how Aadil had never really bothered to lock his house properly, despite the fact that he stored some merchandise here – and had not noticed Muzaffar's approach. The chowkidar jerked away, so startled that he almost dropped the lock he still held. The other man, while surprised, recovered in a trice.

He tilted his head in acknowledgement. 'Yes, huzoor. I was Aadil Sahib's clerk. Suraj Bhan, that is my name.'

Muzaffar introduced himself. 'I thought you seemed familiar with the house,' he added, 'going by the ease with which you unlocked the door – it catches, does it not? I saw you heft the lock a little to get it to open. A stranger would not know that that was the solution to that particular stuck lock.'

Suraj Bhan nodded. 'I have been familiar with this lock for years now.' He had retrieved it from the chowkidar, and now, having rehung it on the opened bolt, turned the key. 'Shall we go in, huzoor?' he asked the chowkidar, though his gaze rested briefly on Muzaffar too, as if acknowledging that Muzaffar – since the chowkidar had greeted him with a courteous salaam – may not be entirely unwelcome.

The clerk had been tracked down the previous day itself, Muzaffar was told as he followed the two men into the merchant's house. In the evening, early enough for him to come rushing quickly to his late master's home, before going to take a formal look at the murdered man, whose corpse had been temporarily transferred to the chowki. The sun had set and darkness had begun to descend by then, so Suraj Bhan had begged permission to return the following morning. He had come now to examine Aadil's house and give his verdict on whether or not anything was missing, whether or not there was a clue somewhere in all the mayhem that might point to a possible suspect.

ꕥ

A meticulous man, this, thought Muzaffar, watching approvingly as Suraj Bhan walked systematically through each room of the house, his gaze switching from one object to another, bending now to see something more closely, or lifting something to examine it against the sunlight streaming in through the windows which he had opened. The chowkidar, looking on, was silent, attentive.

'Hey Ram,' Suraj Bhan breathed when he entered the room in which the merchant's stock of cloth had been scattered so freely and carelessly. 'I saw this last evening too, but it looks even more horrifying in daylight.' He heaved a sigh and reached into the pocket of his jama, pulling out a sheaf of papers as he did so. 'Well, it is time I got down to work. This can be a tedious business, and it may take an hour or more.' He glanced, as if warning, first at the chowkidar, and then at Muzaffar. Muzaffar nodded. The chowkidar, taking his cue from the nobleman, nodded too, but a trifle reluctantly.

And long it was, as well as tedious. Muzaffar, waiting patiently next to the threshold so as not to get in the clerk's way, found himself impressed at Suraj Bhan's efficiency. The man had obviously brought along lists of all he expected to find in Aadil's house as merchandise. Now, having cleared half the room by piling up the cloth in the other half, he began taking an inventory of all the fabric, both whole and ruined, saleable and not.

ꕥ

The sheaf of papers he had placed on the shelf, along with a new reed pen and an inkwell. One glance at the topmost page, then he would bend down, eyes darting quickly through the cloth pooling all about his bare feet – he had removed his shoes at the door. Then, having found whatever cloth he was searching for, he would gather it up, fold it or roll it up into a neat package, and deposit it on the sheet that he had spread out in the other half of the room. Back to the paper, Suraj Bhan would lift the pen, dip it in the ink and make a mark on the page before getting back to searching through the cloth all over again.

'Would it be faster, do you think,' Muzaffar asked after a few minutes of watching this procedure, 'if I were to read out the contents of the pages to you?'

The man looked up at him with pleased surprise. 'If you would, huzoor,' he said, and handed over the pages, along with the reed pen. 'This,' he said, indicating the widest column of written matter on the page, 'is the list of items. If you would read out one at a time, and then place a mark here, as I have done for the others – that will be of immense help.'

Even with the two of them working together on it, the inventorying of the cloth took nearly two hours. The chowkidar, having stood by the door with increasingly obvious impatience for half an hour, had finally mumbled something about having to check on the chowki, and had made himself scarce. Muzaffar, as he gradually became more familiar with the task he was helping with, began to talk to Suraj Bhan. The task, after all, from the finding of the cloth in question to its folding, was more mechanical than anything; and the clerk seemed not averse to conversation.

'No,' he said, as he examined – with a sad expression – a piece of fine embroidered muslin, which had caught on the hasp of the chest and ripped, 'Aadil Sahib had no relatives in this part of the world. He was from Kashmir, huzoor, and that is where his family still lives. He is – was – never even really happy here in Dilli; was always yearning for home and wanting to go back. He told me, several times, that if he were able to find a good associate here, someone with whom he could build business ties, he would hand over his trade in Dilli and go home to Srinagar to run his end of the business there.'

'I assume he did not find someone?'

Suraj Bhan shook his head. 'No. It would have required a man willing to make frequent trips between Dilli and Kashmir. And Aadil Sahib, to be blunt, did not offer a share of the profits large enough to tempt any but the most desperate. A desperate man is not often the best man for the job.' He folded the muslin, leaving the ripped section of it clearly visible on the surface, and put it with the rest of the damaged wares at one end of the sheet.

'Who, then, inherits this trade? Whatever profits Aadil had made till now? This house?'

'His brothers, I suppose. In Srinagar. I shall have to write to them to let them know, and to ask them what is to be done with this.' Suraj Bhan's hands were busy, placing the intact cloth in a tidy pile on the sheet, the edges carefully aligned. He moved around the sheet, gathering up its corners. 'There is this house, and this material. There is more cloth at a small warehouse that Aadil Sahib had rented. There is a consignment due to arrive from Persia sometime in the early summer. I will need to know what is to be done with it all.' He leaned over the cloth, knotting the corners of the sheet into a secure double knot, tucking in the loose ends.

There was nothing missing from what he had expected to find at Aadil's home. Every last item on the sheets of paper he had carried had been matched with a corresponding length of cloth. Some of it was damaged, burnt or torn or muddied. But it was all there. Nothing had been stolen. 'Not even the papers,' said Suraj Bhan, having perused the documents that had been found in the room. 'It is all there.'

'I suppose you could say that I was the closest he had to a confidant here,' Suraj Bhan said as he shook out a length of unbleached cotton that had charred here and there. He proceeded to pile the damaged cloth onto it, bundling it in and tying it. There had been no real friends, just some business acquaintances, he said. And those not men whose company Aadil liked. 'I believe he was too homesick for anything,' the clerk said, putting the finishing touches to his tidying of the room. He glanced around one last time, taking in the two neat bundles of cloth, the closed chests, the things on the shelf now set to rights.

'No, huzoor,' he said, even though Muzaffar had not put a question to him. 'I cannot imagine any reason why anyone would have wanted to murder Aadil Sahib. He had no enemies in this town. No friends, even, if one were to be truthful. Why kill a man who is of no significance to you?'

Yes, thought Muzaffar as he made his way home for a late lunch. Suraj Bhan had proved as efficient, as wise and canny as Muzaffar had first guessed him to be. More. Muzaffar was reminded of the conversation he had overheard at the Diwan-e-Aam. He wondered what those men would have thought of Suraj Bhan.

'Does prejudice ever see virtue, though?' he muttered to himself as he turned the corner and came in sight of the wall surrounding his haveli.

And with that disheartening thought, he went in, only to find that there waited for him a tersely worded note from Khan Sahib. The local chowkidar had obviously reported Suraj Bhan's visit to Aadil's house, and had mentioned that Jang Sahib had not just been there, but had taken on the task of helping with the inventorying of the merchant's stock. What the chowkidar had thought of Muzaffar's intervention and assistance, Khan Sahib did not say. What he did say was that he did not like Muzaffar interfering in the kotwali's work. Muzaffar surely had other business to occupy himself with.

Muzaffar should, wrote Khan Sahib, refrain from poking his nose where it was not required.

ᴄᴕ

Muzaffar's memories of his childhood were a complex, sometimes confused, mass of events, sounds, sights and smells that seemed to encompass much of the land, all the way from Kabul to Patna, Srinagar to Gwalior. Khan Sahib, who had been in the service of the Baadshah – and before that, the Baadshah's father, Jahangir – had lived a primarily nomadic life. A year in Lahore, six months in Agra, another half-year in Gwalior. Sometimes as a kotwal, sometimes as a military commander, once even as the adviser to a commander who had received his command as a royal favour and knew next to nothing of the work he was supposed to be doing.

Their lives – Khan Sahib's, Zeenat Begum's, their children's, and Muzaffar's – had often been spent in on the road, travelling sometimes for weeks. Muzaffar remembered dusty roads in Rajputana, flowering orchards in Kashmir. Rivers in spate and streams dried to a trickle, narrow enough to be crossed on foot even by a child. Forests and cities. Crowded sarais and long-abandoned ruins.

And he remembered a particular excursion from when he had been about thirteen years old and the family had been living in Agra. Khan Sahib had received orders to travel to the town of Bahraich, in the subah of Awadh. It was an assignment of considerable importance, and it would take time. Zeenat Begum had flatly refused to accompany her husband, devoted wife though she was. Her eldest daughter, also living in Agra, was due to give birth, and Zeenat Begum was determined to be by her daughter's side through the ordeal. Muzaffar, when asked if he would rather stay on in Agra or go north with his brother-in-law, had jumped at the chance to travel to the hills.

The journey to Bahraich had been hurried, for Khan Sahib had been eager to get to his destination. On their way back to Agra, though, their pace had been more relaxed. They had taken the time to ride slowly through the forests beyond the town of Bahraich, and had camped beside the Sarayu river for a night and a day.

On that first evening, a local hunter had taken them through the fringes of the forest on foot. Muzaffar had, since early childhood, been interested in plants and animals. Khan Sahib had been an indulgent foster-father, and proud too, of Muzaffar's knowledge – 'He perhaps knows more about the animals of this land than the Baadshah Jahangir did,' he had been known to say, much to Muzaffar's embarrassment. They had been intrigued by all that the hunter showed them and told them, of the local plants and trees, the animals and birds and their intertwining lives.

'That flat rock, there,' he had said, pointing up at a boulder among the many along the riverbank, this one half-hidden by bushes. 'On chilly mornings, you can sometimes see a leopard sunning herself there. She had cubs this past winter; I have seen her with them several times on the rock.'

They did not see the leopard or her cubs that evening. The next morning, however, when Khan Sahib expressed a wish to go duck-hunting – 'just enough for lunch' – the hunter showed them fresh spoor near the marshes. The leopard was on the move, he said, peering into the pug marks imprinted in the soft, wet mud. On the move, and not too long back. She was in the vicinity. She may even be watching them as they walked on towards the duck.

But she was not; she was too busy keeping an eye on a herd of spotted deer. Khan Sahib, Muzaffar, and the hunter had crept up slowly on the scene, their vantage point shaded by the sal trees on the ridge above a bend in the river. At the base of the ridge spread a narrow strip of grassland, and here the deer grazed. 'Look, huzoor,' the hunter had whispered, a few moments after they had settled down. 'Look, down there – on that dying tree.' He had pointed west, and though it had taken Muzaffar's city-dweller's eyes some time to penetrate the camouflage, he had eventually seen it. The leopard, crouched in the lightning-shattered bole of the tree, its dry leaves and brown trunk disguising her pelt, keeping her hidden from her prey.

Muzaffar had looked at the deer, then back at the leopard. He had slowly reached back into his quiver and pulled an arrow from it. He was fitting it into the bow, pulling back the bowstring, when Khan Sahib had whispered in his ear, 'Why kill the leopard?'

Muzaffar had looked up into his brother-in-law's eyes. 'The deer are' – beautiful, he had nearly said, but had bitten back the word just in time, fearing it would sound effeminate, weak – 'with their young. Fawns.' He had swallowed, and the bowstring had slackened. 'A fawn that dies does not grow into a deer.'

Looking back, he winced at that statement. He should have had the courage to say 'I like deer. I do not want the leopard to kill them'. Khan Sahib had not smiled or shown any sign of amusement. 'The leopard too has cubs,' he had merely whispered back. 'Should they not grow up to be leopards?'

Muzaffar had lowered his bow, replaced the arrow in the quiver, and even gone so far as to remove the archer's ring from his thumb. Khan Sahib had said nothing until they were headed back towards their camp.

'It is not always wise to assume that the predator is always guilty or the prey always the victim,' he had said. 'This world moves in strange and unpredictable ways. Each of us, human or animal, can be the prey and the predator by turn. Now this, now that. And there is often little one can do about it. The wise man does not interfere unless he can foresee every outcome of his actions.'

'Surely that is impossible,' Muzaffar had mumbled. 'To foresee what may happen?'

'Exactly. Which is why it is better to remain aloof.' Khan Sahib had looked up, squinting at a bird of prey that wheeled slowly overhead in ever-expanding circles. 'And remember one thing, Muzaffar: just because I say something, it does not necessarily mean that I am right.' He had glanced back down at him and smiled, a rare smile of genuine affection. 'Let no one dictate your every action. And,' he had added, as he moved on again, 'stand by your decisions, whether they turn out to be right or wrong.'

ଓ

He looked down now at the note in his hand, and wondered. If time could be turned back and Khan Sahib and he were again to be there, on the bank of the Sarayu, but with this decision before them, what would Khan Sahib advise? This was not a question that did not directly affect them. Not a question of a leopard and her cubs surviving, or a herd of deer living to see another day. But a man, intelligent and confident of his ability to solve a crime, withdrawing from it because his investigation offended the keepers of the law? Or carrying on, regardless?

Regardless, too, Muzaffar thought with a stifled groan, of causing hurt to a man who had been a father to him.

It was a dilemma, and one he did not relish.

CHAPTER 3

Muzaffar was sitting in his room, poring over the accounts sent from his estate. For a mansabdar who was conscientious and not merely devoted to himself, it could be a tedious task. Muzaffar believed in involving himself – even if it was from a distance – in the problems that the people of his estates faced. There were many, and they ranged all the way from untimely rain to marauding jackals, cuckolded husbands to disputes regarding the boundary between one field and the next. Muzaffar feared that his compassion and sympathy, expressed during his infrequent visits to his jagir, had encouraged at least some of the complaints that had landed in his lap. Some had been filtered by the munshi or clerk who had forwarded them; some had apparently been considered too pathetic to be withheld. Or perhaps the complainant had been too vociferous to be fobbed off.

And all of them, munshi and village headmen and villagers back home, knew well enough that Jang Sahib would patiently read through and give due consideration to each plea and each complaint.

There was the sound of footsteps outside, followed by a discreet clearing of the throat. Muzaffar called out, without looking up from his work, 'Yes, Javed? Come in.'

The steward of his haveli drew the curtain aside and peered in. 'You have a visitor, huzoor. He introduces himself as Suraj Bhan, the clerk. He says' – there was a pause, as if Javed struggled to accept the assertion – 'that huzoor met him yesterday.'

Muzaffar had straightened up, surprised. 'Suraj Bhan? How did he – oh, send him in, Javed. And send for some refreshments.' He stopped, shook his head. 'No. I suppose, being a Hindu – he may not eat or drink anything here. I will call if he is willing to partake of something.' Javed left and Muzaffar gathered up his documents, hurriedly putting them away and wondering why Suraj Bhan should have come to call on him. Had he remembered something about Aadil that might indicate why the cloth merchant had been murdered?

The merchant's clerk looked a little embarrassed when he entered the room. Muzaffar's instinctive rising to his feet to greet the man seemed to discomfit the man even more. 'Huzoor,' he said, with a gulp, 'I beg you – do not inconvenience yourself –' and, for no reason that Muzaffar could see, he flushed a dull scarlet. 'I took the liberty of asking the chowkidar for huzoor's address,' he explained, even though Muzaffar had not asked.

Muzaffar gestured his guest to a seat on the mattress beside the one on which Muzaffar himself had been sitting. 'Some refreshment?' He asked, before checking himself. 'If you would want to, that is. And if it is not abhorrent to your religion,' he added, feeling as embarrassed as his guest had been a few moments earlier.

Muzaffar's words seemed to have put Suraj Bhan at ease somewhat. He lost some of this awkwardness, and when he replied, it was with a hint of a smile in his voice. 'The more hidebound of the keepers of my religion may find it objectionable, huzoor,' he said. 'I, however, hold to my own opinions about how I live my life.' His features, so grave the previous day, softened slightly. 'Thank you, huzoor, but no thank you; I am honoured that you should have thought of offering me refreshment – but I am in a hurry, and need to leave as soon as I possibly can.' He had, despite his graciousness, not accepted Muzaffar's offer to seat himself.

Muzaffar realized that he still did not know why Suraj Bhan had come calling. He hazarded a guess. 'Did you happen to remember something that might be a clue to Aadil's slaying? Someone, perhaps, who might have harboured an enmity towards your master?'

Suraj Bhan's discomfiture came surging back. 'No, huzoor; I regret not. No. I am here not in connection with Aadil Sahib's death, even though I am right now on my way to the kotwali. Kotwal Sahib has summoned me. I was expecting it,' he added, in a resigned tone. 'My late master's death is not the reason I am here. Instead' – he swallowed – 'I appear here for a selfish reason of my own.'

Muzaffar, still standing, in solidarity with the guest who had declined a seat, nodded, curious. 'Go on.'

'Yesterday, after I had left you, huzoor, I went to the chowkidar to tell him all that I had discovered. Or not discovered. The chowkidar told me about you, huzoor. Of your wisdom, your ability to get to the root of the matter and solve even the most baffling of crimes...'

'He flatters me.'

'I think not, not from what I have seen and heard for myself. And I am a man inclined to make judgments based on my own assessment of a man, not merely what I have been told by others.' He sighed. 'Huzoor, a friend of mine is in deep distress. You are the only one I could think of to ask for help. That is why I have come.'

ଓ

Muzaffar squared his shoulders and looked up at the door,

large and wooden, that shut the world out from the house in front of him. Muzaffar had never been in this street before, though he could guess that it was somewhere near Katra Neel, the street of the indigo-dyers. He had been in the vicinity often enough – this lane was not, as the crow flew, very far from the Kotwali, which sat bang in the middle of Chandni Chowk, Dilli's most glittering and busy market. One of Muzaffar's favourite qahwa khanas, where he would indulge himself in some of the black, bitter, coffee that made his senses sing, was probably within a stone's throw of this house. The sarai built by the Princess Jahanara Begum was close enough for Muzaffar to hear the sounds of carts trundling along towards it.

But he had never been to this house before.

Suraj Bhan reached out and knocked on the door, an urgent staccato. He paused, his ear pressed to the wooden leaves of the door, listening for sounds of someone approaching. Then he drew back and knocked again, this time louder. 'I hope nothing had happened,' he murmured, in a worried voice. 'Lakshminarayan would surely have left word with one of his servants – '

But at that moment, the door swung open, and Suraj Bhan, with a terse nod to the grizzled, bull-necked servant who stood there, ushered Muzaffar inside. 'Call your master, Ratan,' he said to the servant. And when Lakshminarayan – already bustling forward, his dhoti flapping about his legs – came, Suraj Bhan made the introductions more quickly perhaps than etiquette would have demanded. 'I have told Jang Sahib something of what has happened,' he finished, addressing his friend. 'But you must tell huzoor everything. And answer every question he puts to you.' Even as a flustered Lakshminarayan nodded, Suraj Bhan was dipping his head in a salute, stepping back towards the door that led from the courtyard onto the street outside. 'I beg your pardon, huzoor; I fear I am already late. I will come and pay my respects to you later today, if I may. Or tomorrow.'

And before Muzaffar could tell the clerk that he did not believe in the formal obligations society deemed it necessary to impose on itself, Suraj Bhan was gone.

Muzaffar turned back to Lakshminarayan. The two men looked at each other, both suddenly at somewhat of a loose end. Muzaffar finally said, 'If it suits you, shall we go in? I would like to sit and discuss this matter. And see the letter for myself.'

'Yes, yes. Of course. Do come in – Ratan, close the door behind us. Bolt it well, and stay here, within earshot. Come, huzoor.'

Muzaffar, following his host over the threshold and into the house, mentally riffled through all the information Suraj Bhan had given him on their way to Lakshminarayan's house. The man, Suraj Bhan had said, was a sahukar, a moneylender. Not an exceptionally wealthy man, but far wealthier than most of Dilli's population, which led a hand to mouth existence, far removed from the opulence of the court and the aristocracy.

Muzaffar knew – as did most – that there were two main categories of financiers in the land: the sarafs or the bankers, and the sahukars or the moneylenders. The sarafs were the big men, wealthy dealers who loaned lakhs of rupees. They did not use their own money in the transactions; they simply acted as astute intermediaries. It was to them that the princes and the nobility, and the wealthy merchants who traded with Persia and China and Europe went. The sahukars, while also dealing with the lending of money, dealt with the small fry. With the peasantry, the soldiers and shopkeepers, the riff-raff of Shahjahanabad. These were the men who loaned their own money, sums that would be as chaff to the fat sarafs of Dilli.

ꞵ

'Lakshminarayan has received a threatening note,' Suraj Bhan had explained as they had hurried through Chandni Chowk. 'Demanding a large sum of money. It comes with a threat; if Lakshminarayan does not pay up, his child's life is in danger.'

'And where is the child?' Muzaffar frowned. 'At home? Or has he – her, whatever – been kidnapped?'

'No. He's safe and well at home; at least, he was when I met Lakshminarayan this morning. But Lakshminarayan is very worried. Nothing like this has ever happened before. And his child is his very heart, his life. Should anything happen to Nandu, Lakshminarayan may well decide life is no longer worth living.'

That had sounded melodramatic, but it had also given Muzaffar a sense of what Lakshminarayan was like. A devoted father, imagined Muzaffar, a family man. Affectionate. A worrier.

Now that he had met the man and had entered his house, Muzaffar wondered how much of what he had imagined was true. Some, definitely.

☙

Lakshminarayan was a tall man, as tall as Muzaffar himself, and with a similar breadth of shoulder, but it was meagre flesh rather than the solid muscle of Muzaffar's own frame. He was in his late thirties, his hair already half grey, his eyes tired and his face drawn. This moneylending must be a tiring and stressful business, thought Muzaffar as Ratan shut the front door. And the situation in which Lakshminarayan found himself would have worried any man a few steps closer to the grave. Or the cremation pyre.

He looked about him. This was a small, comfortable town house, the house of a man who could look after his own but had no desire for pretension. There was, for instance, no sharp division of public and private space, save through the privacy offered by the walls between the rooms and the curtains at doors and windows. There was something quietly charming, contented, about this house.

'I fear it is a poor house,' Lakshminarayan said. 'But come in, Jang Sahib. You are welcome.'

The house was built as a series of rooms around a square, stone-paved central courtyard. A neem tree stood in one corner of the courtyard, the shade of its feathery-leaved branches spreading over almost half the yard. There was a small well at the other end. A rope-bed spread with a thin quilt of printed chintz stood beside the well, where the daytime sun would probably be the most abundant. A warm, sunny place to keep a toddler amused.

The toddler was there, but not quite in the courtyard. As the two men stepped into the courtyard, one of the doors looking on to it opened, and a girl emerged with an infant on her hip. She was perhaps fifteen or sixteen years old, a girl with large and watchful eyes, obviously a servant. The baby she held was, just as obviously, not a servant, if the little gold earrings in his ears and the neat, well-tailored clothing was anything to go by. Lakshminarayan's son and heir, and one much doted upon.

'Subhadra, stay inside,' Lakshminarayan said testily. 'I don't want you coming out here and getting Nandu hurt. What if someone were to throw another brick in?'

'He's been getting irritable and restless,' Subhadra explained, shifting Nandu to her other hip. Nandu let out a wail of protest, as if in support of her remark.

'Play with him inside the room, then. No, wait' – he turned to Muzaffar. 'Would you like to ask Subhadra any questions, Jang Sahib?'

Muzaffar wondered privately if he – or Subhadra, for that matter – would be able to make themselves heard above

Nandu, who had started crying in earnest. 'No,' he said. 'Not now. I would like to talk to you first, hear everything about this affair from you. If, after that, I have any questions that you do not know the answers to, I can talk to the others of your household.'

'Go on, then,' said Lakshminarayan, dismissing the girl with a perfunctory nod as he ushered Muzaffar into a room overlooking the courtyard.

☙

In a haveli, this would have been a dalaan, the traditional place to receive guests: a pillared room, opening on to the courtyard. In Lakshminarayan's relatively modest establishment, it was a cross between a dalaan and an office. Instead of scalloped arches and finely fluted columns, there were two large windows on either side of a door. Instead of a rich Persian carpet, there was a thick, serviceable rug, smart but not delicate or expensive. There was a chiraghdaan – a brass lamp, well-polished and with seven little bowls of oil, each with its own wick, standing atop a small pillar-like stand. There was a small brass vase full of marigolds, their powerful fragrance crowding the room. But instead of pretty lamps and porcelain vases in niches, there was a shelf crowded with ledgers. There was a small but strong-looking brass chest. And there was a small slope-topped wooden desk, the sort that sat on a mattress at a height just right for a man to sit comfortably cross-legged on a mattress as he worked. On it, and beside, were neatly stacked sheets of paper, some plain and some covered with writing. There was a ledger, and a stoppered inkwell with a reed pen laid across the stopper. On the flat space at the top of the desk was a brick.

'Sit, huzoor,' Lakshminarayan said. 'Will – will you have something to eat or drink?' Muzaffar caught the note of tension in the man's voice; he was being polite, Muzaffar guessed, in offering his guest food and drink. But his religion knocked as loud as his duty as a host. If Muzaffar were to accept the offer, a separate set of vessels – kept aside for the rare Mussulmaan who happened to come by here – would be used. Stored separately, washed separately, kept scrupulously apart from anything that may be touched by the family.

'No, thank you. Perhaps we had better get down to the matter at hand. What happened? Suraj Bhan told me that you received a threatening letter that demanded money in exchange for your child's safety.'

'Nandu is all I have in the way of family,' Lakshminarayan began. 'I mean,' he broke off to amend his statement, 'he is my only offspring. I do have other relatives, but Nandu is my only child.' He hesitated, as if waiting for a reaction from Muzaffar. When his guest only nodded encouragingly, Lakshminarayan continued. 'My forefathers belonged to Prayag. My mother still lives there, with my elder brother. But I am the only one here in Dilli.' He shifted uneasily.

There was no wife, it emerged.

'She died giving birth to Nandu,' Lakshminarayan said in a sombre voice. His fingers tugged absently at the short fringe of the plain brown shawl he wore draped over his jama and pyjamas.

'Who looks after the child, then?'

'There is the girl, Subhadra, whom you met with Nandu just now. She used to be my wife's maid; now she looks after my son.'

'Who else is part of the household?'

'There is an older woman who does the cooking and the cleaning. There is Ratan. He runs the errands and helps with the heavier work.'

'And that is all? The cook, the manservant and this maid – Subhadra?'

Lakshminarayan began to lower his head in a nod, then

stopped. 'For all practical purposes, yes,' he conceded. 'But I suppose if one were to be absolutely precise, there is another. Girdhar, my late wife's younger brother. He lives here too, although he is hardly ever to be found here. He usually comes home only to bathe and sleep.' The disgust in Lakshminarayan's voice was palpable; this Girdhar, thought Muzaffar, had not endeared himself to his brother-in-law. 'Occasionally for a meal or to play with Nandu. But, other than that, he treats the house like a sarai, only meant to cater to his needs.'

He fumed in silence for a few moments, then wagged his head like an angry bull trying to shake off a swarm of buzzing flies. 'That is all. There is no one else.'

'I see. Well, then let us get down to the immediate details, shall we? What did the note say?'

Lakshminarayan pushed his shawl up and burrowed inside his cummerbund. His hand emerged from the cummerbund, clutching a thick sheet of paper folded into a square. He unfolded it on the sheeted mattress on which he sat, smoothening out the paper. It was rough, the kind that was easily – and cheaply – available. No delicate parchment, this; no finely painted borders to reveal the identity of the writer. It was durable paper, if not good. Durable and commonplace. Indistinguishable from a thousand other such sheets of paper.

Lakshminarayan pushed it towards Muzaffar. 'This is it.'

Muzaffar picked it up. Four sentences – written in Devanagari, in black ink – had been scrawled across the middle of the page. Muzaffar winced slightly. 'My Hindi is not so good, sahukar sahib,' he said. 'I can spell my way through this, but – '

'"You have more money than is good for you. Ten thousand is all you need give to preserve the wellbeing of your child. Leave the money in a sack behind the shrine at the end of your lane. No later than noon tomorrow, or your child will perish." That is what it says, Jang Sahib.' Lakshminarayan had not taken the letter back from Muzaffar in order to read it. He had not even glanced at it; his eyes stared straight into Muzaffar's.

Muzaffar looked down at the paper. Of course, now that he knew exactly what was written on it, he could make sense of the letters. He had learnt to write Devanagari when he was a child, but since the bulk of his correspondence happened to be in either Persian or Urdu, his written Hindi had grown rusty with disuse. Now the letters sprang into instantly recognizable forms: the exaggerated bowl of the u; the sharp, straight downward strokes; the precisely placed vowels and conjoined consonants. The long-ago tutor who had taught a young Muzaffar his letters would have been pleased at this penmanship.

'This would be a well-educated man, I think?' Muzaffar hazarded. 'Or a diligent one.'

'He is certainly diligent enough to have discovered the exact amount I have acquired,' Lakshminarayan said bitterly. '"Ten thousand is all you need give"! As if I had lakhs stashed away in my coffers, just waiting to be distributed to every beggar in Dilli! And how much do these people – these leeches, preying on others – how much do they know of what it takes to build up what little money I can lay claim to? They are not the ones who gamble on what could well ruin them! They are not the ones who neglect even family and friends, just so that there may be something to pass on as an inheritance!' His face had paled with his agitation. Now, as he drew in a deep breath, trying to regain control over his emotions, his cheeks were suddenly suffused with blood. He blinked and reached up a hand to wipe his forehead. 'I beg your pardon, Jang Sahib. I am not myself.'

Muzaffar waved aside the apology. 'You said something about the writer having discovered the exact amount you had acquired. Why do you say that? Have you recently come into possession of ten thousand rupees?'

'And after much effort. A lot of my time is spent in keeping track of those who borrow money from me – there is always the chance that one of them will decamp. They try to stall me, put me off with excuses or assurances that the debt will be paid up... this was one such case.' Lakshminarayan's agitation had not completely died down yet; it kept revealing itself in the way he rattled on, barely pausing for breath. 'I had been chasing after a man who had borrowed a large sum two years ago. He was supposed to have paid me back a fixed amount of the principal, along with the interest, every month ever since. None of that have I seen over the past two years. Only over the past few months, because I have been constantly pursuing the man – reminding him, coaxing him, even threatening him, now – it is only as a result of that, that has he finally agreed to pay me back. The money arrived three days ago.'

ꕤ

'Who knew about it?'

Lakshminarayan shrugged, an eloquent lift of his wide shoulders. 'The neighbours, I suppose, might have guessed. The man came to my house to deliver the money, bringing it in a small chest. Anybody standing outside a nearby house, or up on a rooftop in the vicinity, might have noticed.'

'But they wouldn't have known it was ten thousand rupees.'

'There are merchants in the neighbourhood, and other sahukars. Men who deal in money. They can look at a chest or a sack and guess quite accurately the value of its contents. I wouldn't be surprised if one of them could tell how much it contained.' He heaved a pause, deep in thought. 'And there could be others who might know. This man – my erstwhile debtor, Jagannath – did not have the money till a week ago. He had said he was busy making arrangements to gather the money to pay me. Who knows how he got it? Perhaps he sold land. Perhaps he pawned his wife's jewellery. He couldn't have done it without the knowledge of another man. He must have got it from some source, either because he sold something, or because someone helped him out. Perhaps he borrowed from his friends, a little from one, a little from another.'

'From what you tell me,' Muzaffar said, 'I would think there would be others too, who owe you money. Are there any others to whom you have lent such large sums and who have not paid you as yet?'

'Such large sums? Very few. A handful of merchants who deal in leather, weapons, things the army needs. One man who needs funds to arrange for a Hajj. I am a sahukar, Jang Sahib. It is the poorer class who come to me. And yes, there are always those who delay. Few people can pay on time. I am used to it.'

Muzaffar bit his lip and went back to his scrutiny of the letter. 'And who delivered this?'

'We don't know. Nobody delivered it, exactly – someone threw it into the inner courtyard from outside the house, this morning. It was wrapped around a brick, tied with a bit of thread.'

'Ah. Was that why you told Subhadra there might have been a possibility that someone might throw another brick in?'

Lakshminarayan nodded, the crease between his eyebrows deepening as he did so. 'She is a fool. And disobedient.'

'So this was wrapped around a brick,' Muzaffar muttered. 'That accounts for why the paper is so crumpled. And why a man seemingly well-educated – and therefore possibly wealthy – should use such inferior paper. Inferior, but sturdy enough to withstand rough handling.' He turned the paper over in his hands, glancing momentarily at the side opposite the written face. He had half-turned the page back to look at the writing, but whipped it back and looked closely at the blank surface of the page. There were smudges of dirt here and there, and one corner was frayed.

'Look at this,' Muzaffar muttered, gesturing to Lakshminarayan to move closer. 'Here,' he indicated with a forefinger. 'Along this side.' He moved the page closer to the window, allowing the sunlight to fall on it directly. 'There's a thin, very faint line of blue there. Do you know how that might have happened? Did that mark appear on it while it's been in your possession – perhaps a stray stain from something? Or was it there when the brick was thrown into your house?'

Lakshminarayan shook his head in puzzlement. 'I did not notice,' he murmured. He glanced down inadvertently at his palms, as if searching for any traces of blue that may have transferred themselves to whatever he had handled. 'It may have been Subhadra, though I don't see how. Her hands looked clean enough to me.'

'She found this?'

'Yes. She was in the courtyard, playing with the baby, when the brick fell in.' He nodded in silent, quick acknowledgement of Muzaffar's soundless wincing at the realization that the child or the girl – or both – may well have been injured by the heavy object landing in their midst. 'It dropped almost in the centre of the courtyard, she said, well away from where they were sitting. I heard the thud from my room; I never realized what it was until Subhadra brought this in.'

Muzaffar reached for the brick and looked more closely at it. It was the common lakhori brick, kiln-baked, reddish-brown, thin and compact. These were what created the fabric of most buildings – havelis, pavilions, tombs, mosques. Over a solid structure of lakhori bricks, architects and builders would lay plaster, or a thin cladding of stone, depending upon the money the person who had commissioned the building was willing to pay. There might be paint, fine inlay work, carved stone – but beneath all that, there were these: lakhori bricks. Ubiquitous, and easy to pick up anywhere, at any construction site. Or even easy to pluck out of a loose wall.

Muzaffar heaved a silent sigh of disappointment as he

finished his examination of the brick. There was nothing to distinguish it from millions of other bricks.

As he put it back on the desk, however, he noticed the coiled length of thick thread that had lain hidden beneath the brick. 'What's this?'

'It was knotted around the note, holding it in place.'

Muzaffar picked up the thread and ran it through his fingers. There was nothing exceptional about it. Just a thick thread of unbleached cotton, a pale creamy-yellow in colour. One end – Muzaffar's eyes narrowed – was about an inch of deep blue. He moved closer to the window, peering at the blue, rubbing it between the tips of forefinger and thumb. 'It leaves no mark,' he said softly.

'Should it?'

'I don't know,' Muzaffar said as he placed the thread back under the brick. 'I thought it might.'

Outside, the sound of the baby's crying had stopped. Perhaps he had been soothed by Subhadra's cooing. Perhaps he had fallen asleep. At any rate, the house was relatively silent.

'Well, Jang Sahib,' Lakshminarayan said. It was an unfinished remark, but it was also a question. More a question, realized Muzaffar, than anything else. This was an anxious man. His worry had reverberated in every syllable when he had scolded the girl for taking the child out into the courtyard. It showed now in the tense lines of the man's face.

'I noticed your manservant acts as a guard at the front door,' Muzaffar said. 'Is that his usual post? Or have you deputed him to stand guard after you received the note?'

Lakshminarayan shook his head, but whether in affirmation or negation, it was impossible to tell. 'I told all three servants what the note said. They had to know. I couldn't afford to have any carelessness as far as Nandu is concerned. I told them I was going to fetch help, perhaps from the thanedar, and that they should keep a strict eye on Nandu until I came back.'

'Why didn't you go to the thanedar?'

Lakshminarayan looked disconcerted, embarrassed. 'I know I should have, Jang Sahib,' he replied, after a moment. 'That had been my intention. But I had barely gone out into the street when I realized that it may not be the best course to adopt. To report a matter such as this to the thanedar would result in everybody getting to know within the space of a few hours. He would send out the chowkidar to question people, and if the man were overzealous, there might be a man sent out with a drum to announce it to the neighbourhood – '. He shuddered visibly. 'For a businessman like me, reputation is everything, Jang Sahib. If people come to know that Nandu is so much my weak spot' – he shuddered – 'it will spell disaster for me.' He looked up into Muzaffar's eyes. 'And fate appeared to have a hand in it, too. Suraj Bhan arrived just as I was standing there, wondering what to do. And when I confided in him – well, he told me about you, and that he thought, from what little he had seen of you, that you may take pity on me.' He ducked his head. 'Thank you for coming here, Jang Sahib, to listen to me. To help me save my child.

'That was why I never went to the thanedar. Also, I wondered if the thanedar would even entertain me. After all, Nandu is safe and sound. Kotwal Sahib's men have enough to do trying to catch criminals; I doubt if they would even listen when no crime's been committed yet.'

Muzaffar nodded. 'And Ratan? Did you put him at the door only now, after you received the note?'

'It is his duty to attend to the door and receive any visitors. Or repel them. I have merely impressed upon him the importance of particular vigilance now that this has happened.'

The man at the door had certainly looked as if he would be a formidable doorman, one who could put up a good fight if called upon to stop intruders. He may have once been a wrestler; the broad, bulging shoulders and chest and the solid neck suggested a great deal of physical training.

Muzaffar frowned, a sudden thought striking him. 'So was he at the door when the brick was thrown in?'

'Yes, of course' – the sahukar began to say, before he realized what Muzaffar was implying. 'Oh, you think he would have seen someone throw the brick in through the doorway? No, no; that wasn't how it was. We keep the front door shut and latched at all times. It's Ratan's task to open it if we have any callers. Or, if the door is open, he sits outside and keeps an eye on it. The door was closed when the brick was thrown in. It didn't come through the door, you see; someone pitched it over the rooms, from outside the house.'

ᘓ

Muzaffar raised his eyebrows. 'Ah. I see.' He nibbled at his lip. 'And how are the houses around yours arranged? I think the two houses on either side – overlooking the lane – are flush with your own house? This house shares walls with them?'

'With the house on the right, yes. On the left, no. On that side, there's a very narrow lane, just enough for a man to squeeze through.'

'In front is the main street. And behind?'

'There is a patch of open ground. A washerman uses it to dry his laundry, and children play there sometimes. In the winter, the older men of the neighbourhood sit there during the day. It's sunny and warm, and secluded enough – nobody to disturb them.'

Muzaffar mused, staring down at the letter, then out of the window into the stillness of the courtyard. It was empty now; all he could see was the bulk of Ratan sitting on his haunches near the door, picking at his teeth. 'Might they be there now?' Muzaffar asked. 'The old men?'

'Very likely.'

'Perhaps we should go and talk to them, then,' Muzaffar said, rising to his feet. 'If someone threw a brick into the courtyard earlier today, it's possible one of them saw something.' But as he trailed behind Lakshminarayan, out of the room and through the courtyard, Muzaffar wondered if there was really any chance of one of the old men possibly witnessing something as odd as someone throwing a brick into a man's house. Would a man doing something so antisocial do it in full view of another? Muzaffar thought not. But there just might be a possibility that something had been seen.

CHAPTER 4

The sahukar led Muzaffar to the yard behind his house by way of the lane between his house and the next. The lane was as narrow as Lakshminarayan had described it – a bulkier man than Muzaffar might have had to walk sideways – and it was claustrophobic, a suffocating, too-long stretch of narrow path between the looming walls of the two houses. Muzaffar winced audibly as his shin caught on something hard. He glanced down; it was the roughly carved end of an earthen pipe meant to drain away rainwater from the neighbour's terrace.

'I beg your pardon, Jang Sahib.' Lakshminarayan, realizing his guest had paused, halted in his tracks and half-turned. 'We've become so used to that protruding bit of pipe, we take it in our stride. I should have warned you.' He sounded concerned, contrite. 'Are you all right?'

Muzaffar gave his shin a last rub. 'I'm all right. Whoever designed your neighbour's house deserves to have his shins banged against that. Again and again, until he learns his lesson.' He grinned. 'But there is no harm done. Let's go.'

The large quadrangle at the end of the lane was open and awash with warm, inviting sunlight. The ground must be grassy during the rains; now, the winter had reduced the grass to little more than scrubby sparse patches of yellow.

On four sides loomed the backs of houses, all more or less similar to Lakshminarayan's own. The alley through which Lakshminarayan had brought Muzaffar was the only way in or out of the yard.

No children were playing here at present. There was no washerman in sight, though drying clothes hung on three clotheslines stretched between two trees. Near the centre of the ground, where there were no trees to block the welcome warmth of the sun, a thick rug had been spread. On it, clustered around a pachisi board, sat four old men. A game was in progress.

They listened with widely differing levels of interest, when Muzaffar told them why he had come and explained what he wanted to know. One of the men stared at him, wide-eyed and attentive to the point of being embarrassing. Another, lying on his side with two old bolsters tucked behind him, seemed to have not even realized there had been an interruption. The remaining two seemed to neither hang on Muzaffar's every word nor be indifferent.

One of them, a mostly-toothless man, was the one who had just gathered up the cowries to fling them down on the board. 'No,' he said, confidently enough when Muzaffar asked if they had seen anyone throwing a brick – throwing anything, he clarified – over the rooftops and into Lakshminarayan's house. 'Nobody.' Next to him, his sprawling teammate shifted against the bolsters and grunted, urging the man to throw the cowries.

'Did you happen to see anybody up on any of the roofs? This side, especially?' Muzaffar asked, nodding towards Lakshminarayan's house and the two houses flanking it.

The old man flung the six cowries down on the embroidered board. All four men peered at the shells, looking for the number of shells with their open ends facing up. Muzaffar and the sahukar had been forgotten for the moment. Two men grumbled; the other two – including the man who had been answering Muzaffar so far – chuckled with obvious glee. He moved his piece forward, inching it closer to the charkoni, the four-cornered goal in the centre of the board. 'Not that I remember,' he said as one of his opponents gathered up the cowries to play his turn. 'What do you think, Gopal?' he asked his team mate.

Gopal tilted his head up, looked at the roof and then squinted into Muzaffar's face. 'When? Now?'

'Any time today.'

But no; they had not seen anybody up on the roof. Not Lakshminarayan's, not his neighbours'. Muzaffar and Lakshminarayan stood about for a while, Muzaffar hoping that his presence – an irritant, certainly, for even he could see that he was an unwelcome distraction for the pachisi players – would jog the memory of one of them, encourage them to remember something.

They did not, and after a few minutes, Muzaffar glanced towards Lakshminarayan and shook his head, indicating that they should return to the house.

He did not, however, enter the house this time; he stopped at the threshold, hanging back. 'I cannot see the way forward right now,' he admitted, a little-shamefacedly, to Lakshminarayan. 'Even the fact of the brick being thrown into your house – how it was done, from where – eludes me.' He hesitated, Lakshminarayan's crestfallen expression mirroring his own disappointment, making him feel even more at a loss. He cleared his throat, thinking rapidly. 'I think it might be useful to visit your neighbours. Talk to them, and if you trust them, take them into your confidence.'

'I do trust them,' Lakshminarayan said. 'They are good people.'

'Then tell them what has happened. Ask them if they or anyone in their households saw anyone suspicious. In the meantime, I will – ' Muzaffar fished around frantically, trying to think up a useful, profitable task for himself, one that would reassure the sahukar – 'I will take this letter home and see if I can make out anything further from it.' It sounded lame, and seeing the light die down in Lakshminarayan's eyes made him feel like a heartless brute.

'And din it into the heads of your servants that no outsider is to be let into the house. Nobody you do not trust. And the child is not to be allowed out, unless in your own company. The least we can do until we find out who is behind this, is to keep Nandu out of reach of any possible kidnapper.'

ꕥ

As he rode back home, Muzaffar brooded over the matter. It was easy to see why anyone would pick on Lakshminarayan as a victim; he was prosperous, yet not wealthy enough to command a small army of servants to guard his child. And not influential enough to get the machinery of the law working on his side, rounding up all the known and suspected criminals of the thana in an attempt to pin the blame on one man.

His thoughts ran on, from the thana to the kotwali, and from there to Kotwal Sahib, and to Kotwal Sahib's blunt little letter of the previous day. Stay away from the work of the kotwali, Khan Sahib had written. And, by extension, stay away from the work of the thanas that formed the network at the apex of which sat the kotwali. Khan Sahib would not be pleased if he knew that Muzaffar, far from obeying his order, had gone off the very next day and got himself involved in an investigation.

But it was not, really, he told himself. No crime had been committed. Nothing had been stolen, no one killed. The child was safe. A threatening letter, that was all. Perhaps it had been written in a fit of anger by a debtor unable to pay back what was due from him. All wind, empty words that would not be followed by action. All Muzaffar had done was to listen, to reassure, to prevent – possibly – a crime.

He was not convinced.

ᴓ

'A Hindu?' Shireen's eyes widened. The dupatta, a pale pink dotted with tiny flecks of gold, had slid off her head and lay pooled about her shoulders, spilling over the edge of her plain creamy-white pashmina shawl. 'You – you actually went into the house of a Hindu? And a Hindu came here?'

She had not been at home, Muzaffar remembered, when Suraj Bhan had called in the morning. An elderly noblewoman known to Zeenat Begum had been ailing for the past few days, and Shireen had gone that morning, in her palanquin, taking dried apricots, almonds, walnuts, raisins and many good wishes for the old lady's health. Javed would have informed her of Muzaffar's going out when she had returned; but he may not have thought it necessary to mention Suraj Bhan.

Now, listening to Muzaffar recount all that had transpired during the day, she seemed to him to be not merely surprised, but even horrified.

'Why?' Muzaffar asked, puzzled. 'Should a Hindu not have come here?'

She lifted her hands to her shoulders, adjusting the errant dupatta, putting it back over her hair. 'Who am I to say who may come or not,' she said in a prim little voice brimming with disapproval. 'It is your haveli, Jang Sahib; you are the master. Whom you entertain is your business, not mine.'

Muzaffar frowned. 'You do disapprove,' he murmured. 'Why, Shireen?'

She had not been expecting him to confront her so directly, perhaps. It may even have been that she had not been expecting him to try to find out why she held the views she did. Most other men would have agreed with her assertion – even if it was sarcastic – that the husband was the lord and master of the house, and that his wife's opinion did not matter. Most other men, if their wives had expressed – even in a roundabout way – a disapproval of things as they were, would have ignored them. Muzaffar, by probing, threw her into confusion. She blinked, her hands trembled as she lowered them from her head, and the dupatta slipped down once again to settle about her shoulders.

'Well? What is it, Shireen? Surely you are not one of those who believe that Hindus are inferior beings?' He said the last two words with a slight sneer; he could not help it. It was a term he had once heard someone use – in full earnest – and had never quite been able to forget it. Or forgive the speaker. He had forgotten who it was, but he had not forgotten the astonishment and the revulsion he had felt.

'Inferior? No, of course not,' Shireen said. Her eyes were very wide. Muzaffar could tell that his accusation had come as a shock to her. It comforted him; it had come as a bolt out of the blue for him to discover that his wife – always so wise, her thoughts and her views so in harmony with his own that it made him marvel – could have harboured prejudices such as this.

But there was still the matter of her not liking Suraj Bhan's visit to their haveli.

'Not inferior,' Shireen was saying. 'Different.'

'Different?' Muzaffar frowned. 'And that is enough to make it horrifying for you that a Hindu should have come to this house?'

Shireen looked up, her eyes flashing so brilliantly that for one dumbstruck moment Muzaffar believed she might actually hit him. She stared, though, silent and unmoving, and the fire in her eyes gradually died down. 'I was not horrified, Jang Sahib,' she said. Her voice was still stiff; she had not forgiven him. He was not sure he had forgiven her either. 'Perhaps I was too shocked to be polite in my reaction. I – I do not hate Hindus; it is just that I have never really known any. A maid here, another servant there, but no one else.' She nibbled at her lower lip. 'Nobody whom I could really talk to, to find out how much like us they are. Or not.' She glanced up, the expression in her face hesitant. 'They aren't, are they? I mean, they worship so many gods? How can they? And they bow their heads before stones, and revere cows and elephants and other animals. And they drink cow's urine to purify themselves, do they not?' She made a face.

'Not all of them do.' Muzaffar let his gaze wander to the window, looking out, trying to put his thoughts into words. Somewhere outside, he could hear the mad chatter and flapping of a flock of babblers, probably hopping about the garden, pecking for insects.

'And if you think Hindus are a strange lot, then try looking at us from their point of view. To bury our dead, leaving their corpses to feed the earth, instead of being cleanly burnt and disposed of. To eat the flesh of animals. To – ' he broke off at the sight of her face, which had gone very white. 'It is a question of difference, Shireen,' he added, making a deliberate attempt to be gentle. 'But difference need not necessarily mean that one is worse than the other. Mussulmaans have been living in this land only for a few centuries now. In the beginning, perhaps, our ancestors were outsiders, looking down on the infidels. We, you and I, are no longer foreigners. We are part of this country, sons and daughters of this land. If we do not think of Hindus – and all the others, of other faiths – as equal to us, this land will wither up and die.'

௸

It was a long lecture, and left Muzaffar feeling embarrassed at the thoughtful look on Shireen's face. He would have been elated if she had admitted to being converted to his point of view. He would have been taken aback, too. So, while he felt a twinge of disappointment, it came as no surprise when his wife, after a few moments of cogitation, merely nodded. 'I suppose so,' she said. There was doubt in her voice.

'Is the land not already withering up, Jang Sahib?' she added, startling him. 'This campaign in the Deccan – surely it cannot be good for the empire? Even if the Shahzada's armies win, will the Baadshah be able to stem the rot? I hear the treasury is under great stress, as it is. And such a campaign – so far, and so many men, such a large army – is that not expensive?'

It was, and Muzaffar, no matter how much he would have liked to protect Shireen from the harsh realities of life, could not help but agree. Word had trickled into Dilli as it was; Sidi Marjan, the commander of the garrison at Bidar, still held the fort. He was well entrenched, and all Aurangzeb's cannons and war elephants and many thousands of men did not seem to be making much progress. A protracted campaign, its expenses rising with every passing day. And who knew whether it would succeed or not, anyway?

There was no point in discussing it; they, sitting here in Dilli, a minor nobleman and his wife, were helpless. All they could do was worry and fret about something that would affect them, but whose outcome they could in no way influence.

Shireen appeared to have come to the same conclusion. With a shiver, she pulled her shawl closer about her shoulders, tucking her hands well into its folds. 'But tell me,' she said, 'what did you discover? Who threatened this sahukar?'

Muzaffar admitted he did not know. 'I have instructed Lakshminarayan to go and meet his neighbours, to find out if they saw anyone suspicious. I doubt that he will learn anything valuable.' He reached into the pocket of his choga and pulled out the thread, one end of it stained blue, that he had brought home from Lakshminarayan's house. 'And I will go to Katra Neel tomorrow morning.'

Shireen leaned forward, taking the thread from him, examining it. 'This was what was tied around the brick, you said. Around the note.' She tilted her head towards the page, now smoothed out, which too Muzaffar had brought back, and shown her. 'Why do you go to Katra Neel? Who lives there?'

'Look at the end.' Muzaffar caught the dangling end of the thread and stretched it out to its fullest length, exhibiting the rough creamy-dirty colour of the thread.

'It's blue,' Shireen observed. 'So? Because it's blue, it must be indigo, and because Katra Neel is the street of the indigo dyers, this thread would have come from there?' She had carefully coiled the thread into a neat little ball as she spoke. She handed it back to him now. 'Isn't that a somewhat tenuous connection? Anybody can have a bit of blue thread in their house.' She looked around, eyes searching the room. 'Look at that cushion there, or the bolster – there's blue in that embroidery, and in that piece of printed cloth. Even your turban has blue in it. Pull out a loose thread and use it to tie a piece of paper around something, and you might just have used a bit of blue thread without thinking twice about it. One doesn't have to be a dyer to do that.'

This was what he liked about her, thought Muzaffar, with affectionate admiration. She was clever.

'Yes. But most of the thread we, the buyers, get is fully dyed. You're unlikely to find thread that's blue at one end, with the rest left undyed.'

'But – '

Muzaffar lifted a hand, palm outward, stemming his wife's question. 'Yes, but. In a bit of dyed cloth, you may well find one like that. Look at the note, though,' he prompted. Shireen picked up the paper from the mattress, her expression dubious.

'I don't see – '

'Turn it over. Not the side on which there's writing. The other. Look at it closely. What do you see there?'

'There's a faint blue mark here.' Shireen sounded thoughtful.

'A straight faint blue mark. It's about the same width as the thread, perhaps a little thinner. It was left by the thread; you can follow the faint crease that has been left by the thread on the paper where it was tied fast round the brick. If the thread left a blue mark, it means that the dye ran. It hadn't set in yet, it was still wet.'

Shireen looked up from the note, curious.

'But when I first felt the thread – pressed it between my fingers – it left no mark. It had dried by then.' Muzaffar took the paper from her and folded it into a neat square, replacing it in his pocket along with the thread. 'You and I, we who use cloth in our houses or on our bodies – we don't get thread like that, even if we were to find a loose thread hanging. By the time it reaches us, the thread, or the fabric into which it is woven, is dry.'

'So that was what made you think of a dyer? You think a dyer from Katra Neel sent the note? Why?'

'Greed? I do not know, Shireen. But perhaps tomorrow morning, if I explore Katra Neel for myself and ask around a little, I might find something. Let us see.'

☙

He had been, thought Muzaffar with a surge of self-disdain, unduly optimistic. Foolishly optimistic. Katra Neel was mayhem. Busy, industrious, but chaotic, a katra – which, like all other katras – was both home and workplace to its inhabitants and their families, all of them dyers. At night, the gates at each end of the katra would be barred and locked, securing the dyers and their goods inside, making this an enclave separate from the world outside.

In daylight, the katra bubbled and seethed with activity. Much, thought Muzaffar wryly as he made his way through the lane, like one of the many dyeing vats here. There was dyeing, of course, though not all of it in full view of passersby. Through an open door here, an ajar window there, could be glimpsed steam rising from a vat, a wiry arm stirring a bubbling, coloured liquid, the smells – metallic, mineral, vegetal, depending upon the source of the dye – permeating the air.

Neel, indigo, was what gave the street its name, for it was the purest, richest, most precious colour here. But Katra Neel did not dye fabric only with indigo. There was much else here. The red of madder, the yellows of everything from everyday turmeric to expensive saffron. Carbon black and safflower, pungent cow's urine and brown catechu. They left their stains everywhere, from the bodies of the dyers – nearly each of the men here would go to his funeral pyre with his skin wearing the colours of his trade – to the houses, the stones, the trunk of the lone peepal tree at the entrance of the katra.

Muzaffar, emerging from the katra at the end near the sarai of Jahanara Begum, harrumphed. It had been a fruitless exercise, and a frustrating one. Nobody really had the time to speak to him, and those that had been polite enough – or in awe enough of a nobleman – to stop their work long enough to answer his questions had not been able to help. There were dozens of men in the katra, he was told. How were they to know who had borrowed how much money from which sahukar? Or who had dealings with whom? No, they had not heard of Lakshminarayan. They apologized. They dipped their heads, and went back to their work.

'Jang Sahib? What are you doing here?'

Muzaffar turned, and there was Suraj Bhan, by now a familiar figure. Inclined to plumpness, but with an energy animating him, as if he could not wait to get down to doing some useful work. A good man, Muzaffar thought, and a man he was beginning to like. Suraj Bhan was probably a likely suspect in Aadil's death, and a man guided more by his mind than his heart than Muzaffar might have baulked at the idea of befriending a possible killer. Muzaffar merely turned the thought over in his mind, decided he liked the company of Suraj Bhan, and greeted the man with a smile.

It emerged that Aadil's former clerk – still looking for employment – had come to Katra Neel on business. He had written to Aadil's brothers in Srinagar and awaited their instructions. 'From what I have come to know of the family over the past few years, I suspect they will not want to come to Dilli to dispose of Aadil Sahib's goods. They will probably tell me to sell off what remains, wind up the business, and send the proceeds to them.'

And so he was preparing: by going through Katra Neel, talking to the dyers and sellers of cloth from whom Aadil had bought goods. Telling them of the merchant's death, of the cloth that may need to be returned, if it could not be sold elsewhere. Feeling about, checking if there was a chance. 'And trying to see if there might be anybody here who could offer an explanation for Aadil Sahib's death. I doubt it, but there seems to be no harm in asking.'

They fell into step and proceeded down the lane, turning from Katra Neel on to the street that ran perpendicular to it, the wall of Begum Sahiba's sarai on its right.

Muzaffar told Suraj Bhan of his mission in visiting Katra Neel. The man listened sympathetically to his tale of one vain hope dashed after yet another. 'I was a fool; I should have asked Lakshminarayan first, found out from him if there was anybody in Katra Neel who would want to cause him harm,' Muzaffar said. 'It occurred to me only last evening, long after I had come home. And you know how it is with ideas that come when the sun has gone down: they seem so very bright, so very brilliant, as if to compensate for the darkness of the night. It seemed, last night, a very good idea indeed to come searching in Katra Neel for the writer of that letter. Now all I have succeeded in doing is to let most of Katra Neel know that I suspect one of its inhabitants of a crime.' He grimaced. 'What a hare-brained thing to do!'

Suraj Bhan shook his head. 'Do not blame yourself, huzoor. It can happen to all of us. And I do not believe you have cause for worry; men who work as hard as they do here have little time for gossip. Those you questioned will probably have forgotten about it by now.'

Cold comfort, thought Muzaffar as they walked on. His experience told him that men at work were as liable to gossip as anyone else. And talk such as this – suspicion, a potential crime, a culprit amongst their midst – that was not easily forgotten.

But what was done could not be undone. He chastized himself mentally one last time, before deliberately changing the topic. 'And what about you? You had been summoned to the kotwali yesterday. What happened?'

Too late, Muzaffar remembered that he had promised himself that he would not interfere in that particular case. Not after the way Khan Sahib had put him down, not after that curt little note that had told him to mind his own business. He was curious, which was why he had not stopped Suraj Bhan from talking about the direction Aadil's trade might be headed now that the merchant was dead. He should not have questioned Suraj Bhan, though. That was more than taking a polite interest in affairs that did not concern him.

But it was too late.

'What I had expected,' Suraj Bhan replied. 'Kotwal Sahib questioned me. Asked to see those papers, the inventory you so graciously helped me compile the other day' – he was too busy watching where he was going, and so missed seeing his companion wince. Muzaffar could well imagine Khan Sahib's reaction on discovering that Muzaffar Jang had been there, at Aadil's house, helping the dead man's clerk take stock.

'And he asked me for details of every man with whom Aadil Sahib traded, every man I knew of whom he knew.' Suraj Bhan walked on in pensive silence for a few moments, then sighed. 'It is baffling, Jang Sahib. Utterly incomprehensible. I do not boast when I say that I knew the ins and outs of Aadil Sahib's life. I know there was nobody who would gain from his death. Not a soul. Surely it must have been a thief – but then why come and knock on the door? And why not steal anything?' He turned to gaze, as if seeking answers, from Muzaffar.

Muzaffar gazed back, equally helpless. 'I do not know,' he replied. And Khan Sahib will not be happy if I poke my nose in this affair any more, he thought of adding.

They parted ways a little short of Fatehpuri Masjid. Suraj Bhan had to make his way through the market surrounding the Khari Baoli – the saline step well, its water now used for bathing or for animals, though when it had been completed a century earlier, it had been built for the express purpose of providing drinking water. Suraj Bhan had to meet a trader in the vicinity; a man dealing in spices, but scheduled to join a caravan headed for Kabul in the spring. 'I hope he shall be able to carry some cloth to sell. He has done so in the past,' Suraj Bhan explained. 'I think we shall be able to get better prices in Kabul than here.'

Muzaffar walked on till the Fatehpuri Masjid, the quietly elegant mosque constructed by one of the Baadshah's wives, Fatehpuri Begum. A few steps beyond the arched gate, well outside the sanctified ground of the mosque, was a makeshift stable where he had left his horse. He mounted up and turned towards the direction of Lakshminarayan's house.

If he could do nothing about finding the murderer of Aadil, the least he could do was prevent the kidnapping of Nandu.

CHAPTER 5

Muzaffar met Lakshminarayan in the street outside the sahukar's house. Lakshminarayan was standing outside the house of one of his neighbours, talking to another man. From the way the man stood, one hand resting on the door post of the house, the other resting on his hip, Muzaffar guessed that this house was his. One of that large family Lakshminarayan had told him about.

'Narasimha knows nothing,' Lakshminarayan said, having bid a hurried farewell to his neighbour and come forward to greet Muzaffar. 'I asked him; I got him to ask everybody else in the household, too, down to the lowliest of the sweepers and the youngest of the children. There are perhaps thirty of them in that house, what with him, his brothers, and their families. Nobody saw anything suspicious.' They had reached the door of Lakshminarayan's own house; he rapped on it with his knuckles, a staccato sound. 'Open up, Ratan!'

The house looked as serene as it had the day before, though with one difference: the maid Subhadra was in the courtyard with Nandu.

Lakshminarayan's infant son, standing on very shaky legs beside the cot, was bawling and Subhadra was holding him around his chubby waist. She was saying something to him, her words too soft and too distorted by the child's crying for Muzaffar to make sense of. Baby talk, he assumed.

She looked up as the two men entered the courtyard. It was a quick, curious glance; then she was scrambling up, reaching for the toddler and sweeping him up into her arms as she rose to her feet. The child wriggled, still wailing.

'What are you doing outside, Subhadra?' Lakshminarayan snapped. 'I told you not to bring him out into the courtyard. Take him inside. And keep him there.'

The girl was trying to keep a hold on Lakshminarayan's son – he was a strong child, Muzaffar could tell – and right now he was fighting back as best as he could. 'He doesn't want to go in, babuji,' Subhadra replied, her voice strident. The infant was now pummelling her with one small fist. In the other, he clutched something – something that crumbled and fell, leaving grains of bright yellow on the odhni draped around Subhadra's shoulders.

'What's that he's got in his hand? Is he eating something?' Lakshminarayan asked. He moved forward, hands extending towards the baby in an instinctive gesture of paternal affection. The baby reciprocated, turning to his father. His crying came to a sudden, welcome stop. An endearing two-toothed smile lit up his round little face as he stretched out his arms towards his father. 'What is this, Nandu?' Lakshminarayan asked. 'Eating something, and not even sharing it with your baba?' His voice had changed, now brimming with love. 'Come, give me a taste – '

'Don't, babuji,' Subhadra said, removing the last crumbs from the child's tiny hand. 'It was a laddoo. He's put spit all over it; you mustn't eat it. I'll tell Gangu to fetch you some fresh ones.' She wiped the baby's mouth briskly with the end of her odhni.

'No, that's all right. I don't want any,' Lakshminarayan said quickly, looking a little embarrassed as he drew away from the child. Nandu burst into tears again, distressed at being separated from his parent. 'Go, Subhadra. Take him inside. Keep him inside.' He stood, hands clasped behind his back, watching as she took the child away.

'I do not suspect my neighbours, Jang Sahib,' Lakshminarayan said, seating himself on the charpai, the rope bed that stood in the courtyard. It had been pulled into the centre of the yard, where the sun shone down on it, benign and warm. Muzaffar sat down, perching himself on the edge of the bed. He did not care for charpais; they tended to sag and pull one down.

'Of course, it could always have been that they might have seen something but not thought it of any importance, since they would not have known that I had received this horrible letter,' Lakshminarayan continued. 'But I told them about it, and they did not know. They are good people. Good neighbours. They have stood by me in bad times, when my wife died and Subhadra did not know how to handle Nandu yet.'

'And your other neighbour?'

'Vidyacharan. He's an old man. Used to be a saraf, once upon a time, but he's fallen on evil days. Most of his money is gone, along with his family and his health.'

'His family is gone? What do you mean? Did they desert him?'

'Not intentionally. His sons died, one of cholera and one in an accident – he was gored by a runaway bull. Vidyacharan is a frail, withered old creature now. More or less a recluse. But I met him, too, before I went to Narasimha's house. Neither he nor his servants saw anything.' He lifted his head, looking towards the houses flanking his own, Narasimha's house sharing a common wall, Vidyacharan's further away, the narrow lane separating it from this house. 'No, Jang Sahib; I would wager my life on it. These people have nothing to do with it. Narasimha does not need the money; it would be a pittance to him. And Vidyacharan could not be bothered. He's a good man, and not' – he searched for a word – 'worldly.'

There was a despondent silence. Muzaffar broke it with a question. 'Do you know anybody in Katra Neel?'

☙

That too, thought Muzaffar, as he followed Lakshminarayan through the narrow alley beside his house, had ended nowhere. Lakshminarayan knew no one in Katra Neel. Even after Muzaffar had explained his theory, he could not offer any reason for why anybody from Katra Neel would write him a letter such as the one he had received. He had stared helplessly up into Muzaffar's face, and Muzaffar – staring back, feeling as much at a loss as Lakshminarayan, had racked his brains, searching for a possible clue, something that might lead somewhere. The only thing that had come to mind might well prove to be as dead an end as the others, but for want of anything better, it would have to do. 'Let us go back to that yard behind your house,' he had suggested. 'Perhaps the children might be there, or the washerman. Perhaps one of them saw something.'

There were no children in the stretch of ground behind Lakshminarayan's house, though Muzaffar saw signs of play: a little patch of clay had been watered down and churned up, and inept hands had tried to fashion a lopsided and roofless little hut and an unidentifiable four-legged creature next to it. Someone else had left a kite, tattered and useless, its bright pink paper flapping on the ground.

The washerman was there, though, taking down dried laundry. He glanced at Lakshminarayan and Muzaffar as they stepped into the yard, but carried on with his work. 'Yesterday?' he asked, in response to Muzaffar's question. 'In the morning?' His hands worked of their own volition, forming neat, precise folds in the jamas and pyjamas, the odhnis and ghaghras and whatnot he was gathering up. 'No. I did not see anybody around. Not here. But then, I'm not always here, huzoor. I have to go wash clothes at the diggi. And then deliver them to my customers. I come and go. The old men who play pachisi here may have seen something.' He bent to straighten the pile of folded clothes on the sheet he had spread on the ground.

He was already knotting up the ends of the sheet, preparing to hoist the load of laundry onto his shoulder, when he suddenly frowned. 'Not yesterday. No. But today – just a little while back – I did see a shadow pass by.'

'Where? And when?'

'There, up there on Sahib's roof,' the washerman, his hands still busy, tilted his chin to indicate the roof of Lakshminarayan's house. 'There was someone there. I did not look up to see; I was too busy' – his expression turned an odd combination of sheepish and defiant, as if ready to defend his lack of curiosity, and yet ashamed that he had not shown more of an interest in his surroundings – 'but I did see the shadow as it fell on the ground. Someone was hurrying across your roof, Sahib.'

He had finished tying his bundle, and pulled it up onto his shoulder. 'Twice. Once from there' – he gestured towards the narrow lane separating Lakshminarayan's house from his neighbour's – 'and back again.' He inclined his head by way of farewell. 'That was all I saw, huzoor.'

'And when?' Muzaffar repeated his question.

'Oh, shortly after I arrived here. Perhaps half an hour ago, though it may have been a little more. May I go now, huzoor? I have clothes to deliver.'

'What do you think, Jang Sahib?' Lakshminarayan asked in an anxious voice, after the washerman had taken his leave and departed. Muzaffar and he stood alone in the yard, looking on at the barren clothesline, the blank walls surrounding them, the remains of the children's play.

'It could have been someone from your household. One of the servants, up on the roof on some chore. Sweeping the roof, perhaps.'

'It was swept two days back. And I know Gangu does not do that task more than once a week, not at this time of the year, when we sleep in our rooms instead of on the roof. And nobody goes up on the roof otherwise. We have our courtyard to dry clothes in, or spices, or whatever we need.'

'Perhaps we had better return to your house, then. Confirm it for ourselves.' Muzaffar saw disappointment cloud Lakshminarayan's eyes, but carried on regardless. 'It is best to make sure that it was not actually anybody with a legitimate errand. Shall we go?'

But before they had moved more than a couple of yards towards the lane through which they had entered, out of it came hurtling a brawny, bulky figure. It was Ratan, Lakshminarayan's servant.

He came running, his speed such that Muzaffar feared the man would come barrelling into them. But Ratan, it seemed, had no intention of stopping; he slowed only long enough to shout out something, and then swung, gesturing, urging them on to follow him back to the house. The sound of the man's words echoed in Muzaffar's ears as he raced after Ratan and Lakshminarayan. 'Babuji! Come quick – Nandu has disappeared!'

Muzaffar, still uncomfortable and a little disoriented in the suffocating confines of the lane, ran doggedly on, following Ratan and Lakshminarayan. He was trying hard to keep his balance and not go barrelling into the men ahead of him, but he stumbled once again on the end of the pipe projecting from Vidyacharan's house wall. He cursed, glancing down involuntarily as he did so. There was a smudge of fresh red blood on his pyjama where it had come in contact with the pipe.

Muzaffar frowned. Then, heedless of the fact that his host, and the host's servant, had run on ahead, he bent and pulled up the lower edge of his pyjama. The skin underneath was smooth, unbroken. But on the edge of the pipe was a smear of red that mirrored the one on his pyjama.

ଓ

The story took a long time emerging, because those who told it were incoherent, interrupting each other and punctuating their accounts with weeping, curses and mutual accusations of neglect. The curses came from Ratan. The weeping was courtesy Gangu. She was a stout woman, greying hair spewing out untidily from a loose bun and her hands wringing her cotton odhni as she tried to hold back her tears. Subhadra was rubbing the older woman's plump forearm absently, consolingly. It was to her that Muzaffar finally turned, when he thought he had gleaned whatever he could from the emotional ramblings of the other two servants.

'So, you put Nandu down to sleep, and then you went to the kitchen to help Gangu?'

Subhadra swallowed, nodded.

'Then what happened? What made you come back to check on Nandu?'

'I had been away from him too long.'

'And you found him missing. Where is this room?'

Like puppets on a shared string, Lakshminarayan, Subhadra, Ratan and Gangu all turned to indicate – or glance at – a room almost diagonally across from the office where Lakshminarayan had seated Muzaffar the previous day.

Not much could be seen of the room under the shadow of the wide dripstone that hung out from it and all the other rooms, separating them from the roof above. It was a room conveniently located for a nursery: the well and the kitchen nearby, to fetch water and food for the child at a moment's notice; the courtyard outside, an inviting playground. The staircase to the roof right beside the door, easy to climb up to on a sunsoaked winter day.

'I – I looked all over for him,' Subhadra was saying. 'I thought he might have woken up and crawled off the mattress. But he wasn't in the room. He wasn't in the rooms next door, either. So I hurried back to Gangu, to tell her Nandu was missing – and if she would help me look for him.'

Muzaffar cast a sideways look at the doorman. 'And when did you tell Ratan?'

'Just after. When Gangu and I came out of the kitchen.'

'She told me Nandu had vanished,' Ratan butted in. 'That maybe I should look outside in the street, if he had crawled out.'

'But if Ratan is in charge of the door,' Muzaffar turned to Lakshminarayan for confirmation – 'and if the door is kept shut all the time, that would hardly be likely, would it? Nandu is too small to unlatch a door and let himself out.'

Ratan bristled. 'I was not careless, if that's what you – '

'Ratan,' Lakshminarayan said warningly.

The big man reined himself in with difficulty. 'Babuji, I saw the girl take Nandu inside the room; I knew he was asleep. Where would he go? And I was sitting on the platform outside the door, looking out all the while.' Muzaffar knew what the man meant. Each of these large houses had, on either side of the main entrance, a small platform, just large enough for a man to sit on comfortably. Fringing the platform on its outer edge would be the outside arch of the doorway, with either sconces built into it, or decorative niches to hold lamps and illuminate the entrance at night.

Ratan went on, hurrying to offer up proof of his innocence. 'Even if Nandu had woken up and come crawling out, he could not have extended a foot over the threshold without me seeing him. And nobody could come in. I promise you, babuji.' – his voice turned fervent, and Muzaffar was surprised to see tears spring into the man's eyes – 'I swear, on all that is dear to me, Nandu did not go out through this door, and nobody came in. Believe me, babuji. I tell the truth.'

Muzaffar looked out, through the open door, into the street outside. It was busy; there were hawkers and vendors of everything from vegetables and fruit to clothing and utensils. There were mendicants, ear-cleaners, barbers, masseurs walking along and advertising their trade – Muzaffar could hear the voice of one calling out, even now. There were servants from the neighbouring houses, many of whom would no doubt be known to Ratan. It was not unthinkable for him to have been distracted long enough for a mischievous toddler to have crept out.

It did not seem likely, though. Ratan could hardly have been so distracted. And other people in the street would have noticed and alerted him.

'Did you go into the room and see for yourself?' Muzaffar asked, looking first at Gangu, then at Ratan.

'Subhadra said she had looked all over,' Gangu said. Ratan nodded mutely in agreement. 'The room is almost bare now – there is nowhere a child can burrow in and hide. Just a mattress, and a couple of takhats, those low stools. Nothing else. How could Subhadra miss seeing Nandu there?'

Ratan nodded again, more vigorously this time. Muzaffar had sensed a growing indignation in the man. Ratan had given the impression of being a man with a highly developed conscience. Muzaffar could well imagine that he would blame himself, even if he did not say it, if there were the slightest chance that any dereliction of duty by Ratan had allowed Nandu to be spirited away. This man would do his hardest to assert his innocence. And he was not above trying to point out the shortcomings of others.

He did so now.

'Well, she certainly doesn't strike me as being too devoted to the poor child!' Ratan barked suddenly, his chin jutting out at Subhadra. 'Her! Standing out there – out in the street, not even in the safety of the doorway! And with the child in her arms, too. Isn't that being careless? What if someone had whipped Nandu out of her arms and made off with him?'

'Stop shouting, Ratan,' Lakshminarayan turned to Subhadra. 'What is he talking about? Were you standing in the street with Nandu? Today?'

She dipped her head slightly, acknowledging the fact. 'Only for a little while. Nandu was restless, cooped up inside the house. He likes to go out for a little while every morning. I was very careful; I didn't put him down for a moment. He was in my arms all the while.'

'You were chatting with someone!' Ratan interrupted. 'I saw you. Holding the child within a hair's breadth of a stranger. Offering him up, almost. What if – '

'It was just a passing mendicant, babuji,' Subhadra cried out, turning to Lakshminarayan in her own defence. 'He said he hadn't seen such a pretty child for many years. He blessed Nandu, nothing more!'

'I saw you put your hand into his begging bowl!'

'So?! Is it a crime to give alms to a mendicant?' Subhadra lashed out at Ratan, and then whipped around towards Lakshminarayan. 'It was just a laddoo, babuji. Gangu had given me some for Nandu, more than he could possibly have eaten. Where was the harm in giving one to a holy man? He had blessed Nandu, after all.'

'And all of this happened while your babuji was away, is it?' asked Muzaffar.

The girl nodded. So did Ratan. 'Nandu was perfectly all right,' Subhadra added. She looked up at Ratan. 'You saw me bring him back in after the mendicant had gone. And you did, too, Gangu, didn't you? You pinched his cheek and told him not to eat all his laddoos at one go.'

The older woman nodded, her gaze flicking from Subhadra to Lakshminarayan to Muzaffar.

There was a silence, broken only by Ratan's agitated

breathing, and the chirruping of a sparrow in the branches of the neem tree.

Outside, from the street beyond the shut door, came the sound of many voices. Not raised or angry voices; but voices nevertheless. And then someone began pounding on the front door. 'Ratan!' shouted a man's voice. 'Where are you? Open up! What's going on? Open up, you fool! It's me!'

ଔ

Lakshminarayan's brother-in-law Girdhar was barely twenty years old, a wiry young man with a blotchy face and angry eyes. He burst into the courtyard through the door when it was opened. 'What is this all about?'

'Close the door, Ratan,' Lakshminarayan said quietly, looking beyond Girdhar's shoulder to the curious crowd of onlookers – Muzaffar spotted two of the pachisi players among them – outside. 'There is no need to involve the world and his wife in this.'

'In what? What has happened? Everybody in the street is saying there were women screaming in here and Ratan rushing around outside like a madman. Has there been a theft? What?!' He whirled about, staring wildly at everybody, until his gaze came to rest on Muzaffar. 'Who are you?'

The door shut with a thud, to the murmured protests of the crowd gathered beyond. Ratan pulled the heavy metal bolt into place.

'There's no need to make an exhibition of ourselves,' Lakshminarayan said. The strain in his voice was evident, but he was calm. Muzaffar was impressed. This was a man who obviously doted on his child. Yet, while Gangu had wailed and Subhadra and Ratan had come close to fisticuffs and Girdhar looked ready to burst – Lakshminarayan had remained in control of himself. He could not completely hide the worry in his eyes or suppress the fear in his voice, but he was making an effort to do so. And he was managing admirably. 'And Jang Sahib is not just a guest in this household, he is also helping us. If you cannot behave yourself and show him at least the respect due to a man older than you and of an infinitely higher rank, it is best that you go back to wherever you have returned from.'

The contempt in his voice was thinly veiled. Girdhar had the grace to flush, and muttered an almost inaudible apology. Muzaffar nodded, embarrassed at being the inadvertent cause of friction, and embarrassed even more that attention had been drawn to his rank. Among the nobility of Dilli, Muzaffar Jang, son of the late general Burhanuddin Malik Jang, brother-in-law of the Kotwal, and a man of surprising investigative abilities, was also regarded as an eccentric for not boasting of his rank and the privileges to which it could entitle him. A maverick, said an indulgent few. Others, less kind, called him a madman and merely graced him with a nervous smile and passed by quickly if they encountered him in the street.

'Perhaps,' he suggested in a quiet voice, 'it might be appropriate for us to go into your room and acquaint your brother-in-law with all that has transpired. He needs to know, too.'

Girdhar concurred with alacrity. Lakshminarayan, torn between annoyance at his young relative and anxiety for his missing child, led the way into the office. Behind them, in the courtyard, Muzaffar saw Gangu and Subhadra seat themselves on the charpai, the girl murmuring consolingly to the older woman. Ratan took himself off, to sit on his haunches beside the bolted door.

'This is how well you take care of my sister's only child!' Girdhar exploded when he was told all that had happened. 'First, you killed her off with your neglect of her! And now you can't even shell out a few rupees to keep her child safe!' He spat in an exaggerated, theatrical way which might have been amusing had the circumstances been less serious. 'Rolling in wealth, but without the slightest fatherly feeling – I am ashamed my father ever gave my sister to you in marriage!'

For the first time in the course of the day, Muzaffar saw Lakshminarayan lose that laudable self-control of his. His eyes flashing, he spat out: 'And you? What about you? Do you think your father wouldn't have been ashamed of you? When he was dying, he gave you over into my charge so that I could look after you until you could stand on your own two feet. And what have you done to honour his memory? You've been squandering away all your inheritance, gambling and going to cock fights and patronizing the whores of Chawri Bazaar – oh, don't think I don't know!'

Girdhar had turned red. 'I never – '

'Don't interrupt,' Lakshminarayan snarled back, his face now as flushed as his young brother-in-law's. 'I know exactly what you've been up to. I don't say much because you're hardly ever here. And because my wife wouldn't have wanted me scolding you. But let me tell you this: you've turned out a disgrace. A disgrace to our clan, a disgrace to our community. You can't even' – he was now spluttering in his rage – 'you can't even manage the few tasks I set you! I've never seen a poorer excuse for an apprentice!'

Girdhar bridled, suddenly changing from angry to indignant. 'Me?! Me, a bad apprentice? This, when I've been doing every single task you've set me to do! You told me to visit that man in Mehrauli; I did it. You told me to pester those peasants to pay up; I did it. I even brought back one instalment. Do you remember? And what about that cloth merchant?! I've been going to him every other day for the past two weeks, following him about and nagging him to clear the debt. He'll do it one of these days, see if I'm not proved right – '

'Cloth merchant?' Lakshminarayan asked irritably. 'Who?'

'That Jagannath, who else? How many other cloth merchants have we been awaiting payments from?'

Muzaffar, sitting silently on the sidelines all this while, spoke up, addressing himself to Lakshminarayan. 'This Jagannath is the man who paid you three days ago, isn't he?'

The two brothers-in-law appeared to have completely forgotten Muzaffar's presence. They jerked around and turned to him with faces bearing almost identical expressions of bewilderment. Lakshminarayan, older in years and experience, was the first to pull himself together. Literally, with a shake of his head and a straightening of his shoulders. He licked his lips. 'Yes, that was him. He's the cloth merchant.' He frowned as he turned back to Girdhar – but the frown was a puzzled one, not an angry one. 'When did you talk to him last?'

'The day before yesterday. I had to trail him all the way from Urdu Bazaar to Katra Neel. He said he was trying to gather the funds. That he might be able to pay us soon.'

'Why should he say that?' Lakshminarayan murmured, forefinger rubbing his chin. He blinked, then turned to Muzaffar, wagging his head wearily, as if to shake away all memories of the embarrassing family tirade that Muzaffar had witnessed. 'I beg your pardon, Jang Sahib. All this has nothing to do with why you are here. We are simply wasting your time – and are nowhere close to finding my child.'

'We just might be,' Muzaffar said briskly. He did not wait for Lakshminarayan to express the astonishment on his face; instead, he turned to Girdhar. 'You found this man – Jagannath? – in Katra Neel? And was he alone?'

Girdhar had far from overcome his initial suspicion of Muzaffar; the furrowed forehead and the disapproving twist of his turned-down lips were proof enough of that. But he did, after a moment or two of thought, reply grudgingly: 'No. He wasn't. He was with a supplier – one of the dyers of Katra Neel.' Muzaffar nodded, egging the younger man on.

'That was it? Just a dyer?'

The obstinate look was fading from Girdhar's face as he thought back. 'No-o,' he said eventually. 'No. There was another man there. Kanhaiyalal. He's also a sahukar. He was there on the same errand as I was, trying to recover a debt from Jagannath. A few thousand rupees.' He glanced towards Lakshminarayan. 'Kanhaiyalal sends his respects.'

'Oh.' Understanding dawned in Lakshminarayan's eyes. 'I see.'

Muzaffar could guess at what was passing through Lakshminarayan's mind. 'I think Jagannath would have made quite sure that he kept very quiet about paying back your money, if there was the chance of another of his creditors discovering the fact. What do you think? If Kanhaiyalal came to know that Jagannath had paid back what he owed you, he would probably complain and press for his own money to be paid.' Lakshminarayan was nodding, and Muzaffar continued. 'So Jagannath chose the easy way out. Your brother-in-law didn't know that Jagannath had cleared the debt; it was safe to lie to him. And to keep Kanhaiyalal appeased. Or at least secure in the thought that even if his debt was not being cleared, neither was anyone else's.'

'He certainly meant to pay Kanhaiyalal back,' Girdhar said. 'I had stepped out back into the lane when I overheard him telling Kanhaiyalal that he would clear his debt too, in two days' time.'

Lakshminarayan shrugged. 'All right. So maybe Jagannath has come in for a fortune from somewhere. But we still don't know where Nandu is.' He looked out of the window, and into the courtyard outside, misery in his eyes.

Muzaffar stared out, too, his eyes blank. There were things here that were beginning to appear suspicious. The cloth merchant, visiting a dyer in Katra Neel – that tied in with his, Muzaffar's, errand of earlier that morning. But that errand had led nowhere. And, from what Girdhar had said, there seemed no reason to point the finger of suspicion at Jagannath, a man acting as any other man would, if short on cash and having to pay off one impatient sahukar after another.

There was something. Something, hidden amongst all the many things, large and small, trivial and momentous, that he had heard and seen in the past day. Muzaffar could feel it in his bones. But he could not see the way forward. And he could not see which clue to follow.

'Lakshminarayanji,' he said. 'A crime has been committed. Your child has been kidnapped; there is no doubt of that. I think it essential that you inform the local thanedar at once. The law needs to know.'

A few minutes later, riding slowly back through the crowded and narrow alleys of Lakshminarayan's neighbourhood, he cursed himself. The disappointment in Lakshminarayan's eyes on hearing Muzaffar's words had been like a physical blow. Or worse, actually: a blow that should have been struck, ought to have been struck, but which had been controlled, held back. Not because punishment was unwarranted, but because the man entitled to deal that blow was too kind, too proper.

It did not make Muzaffar feel any better. It only served to deepen the guilt that gnawed at him.

Yet what else could he have done, he asked himself for the hundredth time. There was the memory of Khan Sahib's note still in his mind, telling him to keep his nose out of the kotwali's business. There was the fact that this, now that Nandu had actually been abducted, was no longer a case merely of a threat, but of an actual crime. Certainly the domain of the keepers of the law. Lakshminarayan would possibly even face some terse questions about why he had not informed the officers of the law when the letter had first arrived.

There was the matter, too, that Muzaffar had absolutely no idea where to begin looking for the missing child.

Above him a flock of pigeons – released from a rooftop in the vicinity – flew up into the blue sky, wings flapping, circling and flowing as one body. Muzaffar watched them, mesmerized. Then, when the pigeons wheeled, heading back for home, he turned his horse too. It was time to go back home. He had not been out a long time today, but he was beginning to miss his haveli. It was, he thought, because he now knew that Shireen would be home, waiting for him.

☙

As it was, he was not destined to get back home quite so soon. He was nearing the imperial mosque, the Jama Masjid, when his horse cast a shoe, and Muzaffar was forced to dismount. It was not difficult to find a blacksmith to shoe the horse; there would certainly be some in Khaas Bazaar, the 'choice market', which lay along the stretch of road connecting the fort to the Jama Masjid. Muzaffar led his horse along, jostled by the crowds that thronged the market. It did not take him long to find a blacksmith, but the man, his face gleaming with sweat and his brawny arms hammering out a piece of metal on his anvil, shook his head when Muzaffar approached him. 'Busy, huzoor,' he grunted. 'I will be free in a quarter of an hour's time, but not before. If you wish, you can leave your horse here – tie him up there; my boy will make sure it remains safe. Wander around, buy something. Come back in half an hour. I'll have him ready for you.'

His words, half of them obscured by the constant banging of hammer on anvil, were not rude. Simply matter of fact. Muzaffar, with no option but to search for another blacksmith – who may turn out to be even busier than this one – agreed.

As he walked away from the blacksmith, into Khaas Bazaar, Muzaffar smiled to himself, remembering Shireen's telling him of what Zeenat Begum had to say about the market. "Khaas

Bazaar is not a place for delicately nurtured ladies to go, Shireen. The men go there, to eat kababs at the food stalls, or to buy falcons and hunting dogs. Or to watch dancing girls. There are astrologers there too, and story-tellers."

'It sounds very interesting,' Shireen had murmured, when she had mentioned this to Muzaffar. Her husband had noticed the faintly wistful note in Shireen's voice, as if the delicious impropriety of visiting Khaas Bazaaar had made it even more attractive. 'Khaas Bazaar does not merely offer all those delights,' he had said, by way of clarification. 'There is much else that is sold there. Mundane things. Weapons. Clothing. And fruit, flowers. Potions and medicines, though some say that three-fourths of the physicians who set up shop in Khaas Bazaar sell bags of dirt in place of medicine. Believe me, my love, contrary to what my sister may have led you to believe, Khaas Bazaar is far from being the highway to iniquity.'

He had reached Chowk Sa'adullah Khan, the square in the middle of Khaas Bazaar. A heaving, busy mass of people, animals, and their concomitant smells, sounds, and colours. Muzaffar paused, wondering whether to just stand there and look around. There was nothing he could think of to buy, and he was not a man to go throwing his money about, impulsively buying things that he had no need for. But it was impossible to stand still here; the crowd surging around him would not let him do so. It caught him up and swept him on, pulling and tugging. But some twenty yards into the mass of humanity, and he found himself pulled up short because a hand had reached out and gripped the corner of his choga.

It was a hakim, wearing a vivid blue choga and seated on a Persian carpet that had seen better days. His stock in trade lay spread all about him: pouches, large and small, guarded by a skinny youth with a wart on his nose.

'Huzoor,' began the hakim, his voice ingratiating. 'A fine young gentleman such as you – ah, but I fear you will not require my services. The elixirs I offer! The ecstasies that can be yours!' His grip on Muzaffar's choga had not slackened, and Muzaffar, from previous experience, knew what was coming. Offers of purified mercury and borax. Of fine pastes made from the finest cow dung, mixed with butter and the juice of the thorn apple, and who knew what else. A wool-like product obtained from an insect called a jalshuk – Muzaffar had never in his life seen one, but he had heard it praised to the skies by hakims such as this – which was meant to be mixed with mustard oil.

'I have no need for aphrodisiacs, old man,' Muzaffar said, and with a sharp tug, pulled his choga free and went his way.

Next to one of the fountains, he passed a small knot of people clustered around a daastaango, a story-teller who was in the middle of recounting the adventures of Amir Hamza. The Daastaan-e-Amir Hamza had been derided by the Baadshah's illustrious ancestor, the Shah Babar, but with little effect; this fantastic story of romances, pranks, magic and adventure had become perhaps the most loved of all narratives in Dilli's streets. The daastaango was describing Amir Hamza's friend, Amar Ayyaar, now. 'His eyes were like cumin seeds, in size and shape; his ears were like apricots, and his cheeks had the soft look of yeasty bread – '

'He sounds more like a dinner than a man!' shouted a wisecrack, and the daastaango's voice was drowned out in a wave of laughter. Muzaffar smiled, amused, and turned to go on. He had heard this section of the story several times already, besides having read it so often that every word was imprinted on his brain. Part of the charm was, he mused, in forgetting, enough to be absurdly pleased when one's memory was jogged into remembering it all over again.

He was walking past a food stall, the aroma of roasting meats and spices washing over him, when he felt a hand on his shoulder. 'Huzoor!'

Muzaffar turned, ready to stave off yet another seller of

quack remedies, stories, or other wares he had no need for – and blinked. The man standing beside him had a face that was vaguely familiar, but to which Muzaffar could not, offhand, put a name. A thickset man, leaning on a crutch, its wood still fresh and new. He favoured one foot, the toe of its boot resting only very gingerly on the ground. A foot, then, that had only recently been injured.

'Ah. You are the thanedar of our area, are you not?' Muzaffar asked, with easy affability. 'Khan Sahib told me you had injured yourself. Are you better now?'

'Back at work, huzoor, though still a little hindered by this ankle of mine.'

Muzaffar glanced down at the man's foot. 'Should you be moving around?'

'The hakim pronounced it unbroken, huzoor. Merely badly sprained.' The thanedar looked over his shoulder towards a lad who was standing behind him. 'Here, Qasim; I do not pay you to stand around gaping. Come and lend me your arm.' He shifted, heaving a sigh of relief as the youth's sturdy young back took the weight of one arm – and its accompanying half of the thanedar's considerable bulk. 'I beg your pardon, huzoor,' he said to Muzaffar. 'I would have stayed at home and kept off my feet; but who will do my work for me?'

Muzaffar tut-tutted in sympathy, and with a murmur of commiseration, was turning to leave, when the thanedar said, 'Huzoor, do I keep you from your business? I hope I am not in the way – '

'No. But I thought you would rather be getting back to your work.'

'This is work, huzoor. I am here on work.' He made as if to step closer to Muzaffar, then seemed to realize that it would entail dragging young Qasim along. 'May I beg a favour of you, huzoor? If you can spare a few moments of your time, perhaps we can sit there' – he indicated, with a tilt of his chin, the nearby fountain – 'and talk a little.'

Muzaffar stiffened, suddenly wary. 'What about?'

The man was already hobbling towards the fountain, supported by Qasim on one side, the crutch on the other. Muzaffar hesitated, then, because it would seem churlish to argue with a man temporarily crippled, he followed. Ahead of him, the thanedar reached the edge of the shallow rectangular pool. He bent to grasp the wide stone rim, and swung himself down slowly and carefully onto it. He stretched out his leg and balanced the crutch on the edge of the stone slab on which he sat. 'Some matters that concern us, huzoor,' he said, squinting up into the sunlight at Muzaffar's face. He kept looking up at Muzaffar, but added, 'Qasim, take yourself off. But stay within earshot; I don't want to have to go hunting for you.'

'Thanedar Sahib,' Muzaffar said, still standing. 'What is this about?'

'The chowkidar at the chowki nearest your haveli told me that you accompanied Kotwal Sahib the other day, huzoor. To the house of the cloth merchant who was murdered. And that you were there, too, the other day, when Aadil's clerk took stock of all the wares at the merchant's home. I believed you helped him.'

Muzaffar nodded. He was seized by a sudden dread. Had Khan Sahib sent word down to his minions, telling them to warn Muzaffar off? No, surely not. Khan Sahib would not be so lost to what was proper. He might reprimand Muzaffar – the more fitting term would be, perhaps, to flay his hide – but it would be done in private. In public, Khan Sahib would uphold Muzaffar's dignity.

He was proved correct by the thanedar's next words. The man leaned forward, his hands resting on his knees, his eyes squinting up at Muzaffar. 'It is regarding that murder that I would like your opinion, huzoor. We all know how acute you are – '

Muzaffar cut him off. 'Please do not drag me into this affair. This is an affair of the kotwali. I have nothing to do with it.'

'You were there, huzoor. You saw it all.'

'As did Kotwal Sahib. And I am sure he has conveyed all his instructions, as well as all he observed, to your chowkidar. It would not be seemly for me to interfere in the matters of the kotwali, Thanedar Sahib,' he said. 'You know that.'

'If you were being meddlesome, huzoor, or merely eager to satisfy your own curiosity,' replied the thanedar, 'I would agree with you.' He winced as a sudden, raucous shout of laughter burst from the steadily increasing throng surrounding the daastaango. It subsided almost as quickly as it had risen, leaving behind the odd giggle, the occasional comment. From further along the market came the tinkling of a dancing girl's ankle bells and the dhum-dhum-dhum-dhumm! of a dholak being used to drum up enthusiasm for an upcoming performance.

The thanedar had looked away briefly towards the sound; he now looked back at Muzaffar. 'But, huzoor,' he said with a small smile, 'even you cannot deny a thanedar the right to question a witness. That is why I am asking you to sit down and talk to me. Will you?'

CHAPTER 6

'A witness?' Muzaffar spluttered. 'You think I know something about that man's murder?'

'I did not say that, huzoor. But' – he lifted a hand to the back of his neck, and massaged his nape – 'if it would not be a bother, huzoor, could you do me the honour of sitting down? It is difficult to question someone as tall as you when he is standing and you have no choice but to sit.'

Muzaffar glowered at the man by way of response, but sat down. Nearby, the daastaango had been forced, by the loudness of the dance that had commenced, to bring his tale to an end. The more generous of his listeners had dropped money into the upturned bowl of the turban he held out. Others, less driven by their consciences, had simply wandered off. The thanedar's helper, Qasim stood leaning against the outer wall of a nearby shop, watching the two dancing girls twirl and whirl, their gauzy orange dupattas floating like sunset-hued clouds on the breeze.

'Well? What is it?'

'This.' The thanedar reached inside his cummerbund and drew forth a slim, narrow packet wrapped in rough unbleached cotton and tied with string. He undid the knots on the string and pulled out, from the folds of the cloth, an object a little shorter than a man's forearm. It was flattish, mostly straight but with a perceptible curve at one tapering end. The other end revealed a hollow interior: this was an envelope of some sort.

'A dagger sheath?' Muzaffar took it from the thanedar, who had proffered it to him. He looked it over, running his fingertips along the worn brown velvet covering the wood that formed the body of the sheath. The top, against which the hilt of the khanjar – the dagger – would rest, was held in by a band of steel, a collar carved with rough flowers. It was a pattern echoed on the steel tip at the other end of the sheath.

'What does this have to do with the murder?' Muzaffar asked, handing the sheath back to the thanedar.

'It was discovered by the chowkidar on the very day the murder was discovered,' he replied. 'Long after you and Kotwal Sahib had left Aadil's house. The chowkidar sent a man off to question the neighbours and another to find that clerk, and he himself did a cursory search through Aadil's house. This was what he found.'

'Where, exactly?'

'In the room where the fabrics had been stored. Lying near that welter of cloth on the floor, just inside the threshold. That was why he noticed it in the first place.' He stopped, seeing the stony look that had come into Muzaffar's eyes at the implication – even if unintended – that something as significant as this had escaped the eye of both him and Kotwal Sahib. 'Oh, huzoor. I did not mean to imply – this was covered by cloth; it was just that the chowkidar tripped over the threshold as he entered the room, and in doing so, he slipped on a bolt of silk. This was under that.' He gulped, his face apologetic. 'I do beg your pardon, huzoor. I would not dream of – '

'There is no need for apology. What matters is that this was found. I hope it can be useful as a clue.'

The thanedar looked relieved that the nobleman seemed to not have taken offence. 'The chowkidar showed it to Aadil's neighbour. The man knew the merchant slightly. He used to live in the house that is – was – Aadil's.'

Muzaffar nodded. He remembered his conversation in the street with the maidservant, Ameena.

'Till six months back,' he remarked.

The thanedar's eyes widened. Muzaffar told him about the conversation with Ameena.

'Ah. I see. Yes. Well, the chowkidar showed this to the man – his name is Basharat, I believe. He could not recall ever having seen this in Aadil's possession. Or a dagger that might match this. We wondered if perhaps on your visit there that morning, you or Kotwal Sahib may have dropped it there.' He looked down at the dagger sheath, regarding its shabbiness with a sheepish eye. 'I doubt it, though. Surely such a neglected piece would not belong to you, huzoor, or to Kotwal Sahib.'

'It isn't mine,' Muzaffar agreed.

'And it is not Kotwal Sahib's. I have just been to him at the kotwali, and he confirms it.'

He had rewrapped the dagger sheath. He now put the last knot in the string around the packet and was sliding it back into his cummerbund when Muzaffar said, 'It seems rather a coincidence that you should have come looking for me in Khaas Bazaar. Would it not have been far more convenient to have come to my haveli?' He raised an eyebrow, more sarcastic than questioning.

'I was not in Khaas Bazaaar on your trail, Jang Sahib,' the thanedar said comfortably. 'I am here because I wanted to visit some of the shops where weapons are sold. I wondered if one of the shopkeepers may be able to recognize it and tell me whom it could have belonged to.' He saw the dubious look in Muzaffar's eyes and gave an embarrassed chuckle. 'Yes, huzoor; I know. I was being stupidly optimistic. But even if nobody could recognize it, I hoped that some shopkeeper, just by examining this sheath, may be able to tell me more about the dagger it may have housed.'

'Which is missing, I assume? You mentioned that the chowkidar found only the sheath. No dagger?'

The thanedar nodded. 'No. No dagger.'

'And of course there was no khanjar in the dead man's body,' murmured Muzaffar, half to himself. 'Whoever killed him had pulled out the dagger after doing the deed.'

Again, the nod.

'Have you been to a shopkeeper yet? Have you shown this khanjar sheath to anyone?'

'Not yet, huzoor. That was where I was headed when I noticed you.'

Muzaffar stood up. 'Then perhaps you had better go on with your work,' he said. 'I shall not delay you.'

The man stood up, with some difficulty, though Muzaffar extended an arm to help. A shout from the thanedar brought Qasim running. The thanedar draped his arm heavily along the young man's shoulders, hitched up the crutch – which Muzaffar had handed him – and looked at Muzaffar with narrowed eyes. 'Will you not care to come with me, huzoor?' he asked. 'I would have thought it would have been of interest to you.'

Muzaffar shrugged noncommittally. 'It is official work,' he said. 'None of my business.' And, with a curt nod to the man, he strode off in the direction of the Jama Masjid.

☙

The thanedar would no doubt go, thought Muzaffar, to one of the more experienced makers of weapons who had their shops in Khaas Bazaar. Muzaffar could even guess which men he would go to. Men who dealt in everything from khanjars and kataars, with their distinctive curved blades, to the bichhwa, its wavy blade imparting to it a marked resemblance to the scorpion for which it was named. Men who could supply a beautifully damascened blade worthy of a prince, or a sturdy, practical poignard that was all strength, little beauty.

It was no concern of his. At least, thought Muzaffar, with a sigh of frustration, it should be no concern of his; Khan Sahib had expressly forbidden it. He should be grateful to not be involved in matters of the kotwali.

He made his way back to the blacksmith, using a roundabout way that allowed him to skirt Chowk Sa'adullah Khan. He had no wish to run into the thanedar again. At the very least, it would be an embarrassing encounter, after the curt way in which Muzaffar had cut short their recent conversation.

The blacksmith, however, had not yet shod Muzaffar's horse. Someone who outranked Muzaffar – one of the salatin, the many distant cousins, nephews, and other relatives who lived in the imperial palaces by virtue of a shared ancestry with the Baadshah – had arrived in the interim. His stallion, a magnificent grey, had a shoe loose. Not off, just loose, Muzaffar observed with annoyance. But the man had elbowed his way in, using sheer rank to make the blacksmith abandon what he had been doing. The man was now bent over the horse's hoof, hard at work.

For want of anything better to do, Muzaffar walked away towards the wide steps of the Jama Masjid, and seated himself there. He was aware of the surprised looks he drew from the motley crowd that milled about the entrance to the imperial mosque. A nobleman, sitting on the steps, was a novelty. There were jugglers here, and petty magicians who performed simple tricks for the amazement of the easily pleased. There were beggars and sellers of kababs. There were travellers, staring up in awe at the most magnificent mosque in the city. But the noblemen who came here arrived on horseback or in palanquins, made their stately way up to the mosque itself, and thought it beneath their dignity to sit among the riffraff.

A quarter of an hour had passed. Surely the aristocrat – whoever he was – was gone by now. The blacksmith would be free. At any rate, it would be better to stand there, beside the man, and ensure that it was his horse that got attended to next. Muzaffar surged to his feet. Surely the thanedar, what with his aching ankle, would have left Khaas Bazaar by now.

So intent was he on reaching the ramshackle little smithy, he did not even realize that he was walking past a row of shops that specialized in weaponry. Striped red and green awnings stretched out from dripstones, offering shade to the men – mostly amirs – who came by to examine the wares. Displayed on beds of velvet, like prized jewels, guarded over by a watchful servant, were rows of weapons. Swords, mostly, and some lances. A few shops even had odds and ends, ranging from fearsome maces to battle axes to matchlocks and powder horns. And there, half-shaded by a red awning, was a shop that dealt only in daggers. Daggers, large enough to pass for swords, and with protective steel guards to shield the wielder's arm. Tiny daggers, thin and vicious enough to be pushed through the rings of a mail shirt. Delicately deceptive little knives that looked no more dangerous than a needle, but could kill.

'Huzoor?'

Muzaffar glanced up the short flight of steps that led to the shop, expecting to see the shopkeeper. Or possibly an assistant, positioned there to keep an eye on the daggers displayed outside the shop.

But it was neither the shopkeeper nor his assistant; it was Qasim, and beyond his shoulder was the smilingly triumphant face of the thanedar.

ɞ

'I could not shake him off,' Muzaffar admitted to Shireen that night, as they sat at dinner. 'I suppose it was kismet; no matter how much Khan Sahib may rail against me for getting involved in the matters of the kotwali, there is nothing I can do. It is predestined.'

Shireen's eyes twinkled. 'Perhaps it is the mere fact that you have made yourself indispensable to the kotwali and the thanedars who report to Khan Sahib,' she said. 'That is why they trust you and turn to you for advice.'

She saw the look in his eyes, the indecision and the hesitation. Muzaffar was not convinced. Shireen offered him the bowl of mixed greens – mainly spinach, with plenty of dill, cardamom, pepper, cloves and ginger, all tossed in hot fragrant ghee. It was a favourite dish of her husband's, as she had discovered in the few weeks she had been married to him; and she had especially ordered the cook to make it for this meal. Muzaffar, she could see, needed cheering up.

He shook his head, refusing the dish. Shireen sighed. 'If it is kismet, as you insist on calling it, then there is no point fighting it, is there?'

He raised an eyebrow.

'You may as well tell me what happened,' Shireen said. 'What did the thanedar have to say?'

Muzaffar tore a scrap of naan in half and used it to aimlessly push around a morsel of haleem, ground meat cooked long and slow with crushed wheat and spice till it was smooth as the finest velvet. Observing her husband's disinterest in it, Shireen was inclined to think the haleem had as much flavour as a fold of velvet too.

He pushed the morsel to the rim of his plate – the rim was littered with bits of uneaten food, an odd thing for Muzaffar, who was too conscientious to waste his food. 'Let me wash my hands,' he said. 'Then I'll tell you.'

'He pushed the shopkeeper forward to explain it all to me,' Muzaffar said, after the servant bearing the sailabchi and the ewer of water had withdrawn and they were alone. 'The man said he had examined the dagger sheath well. Very well; he had even peered into it, and pushed in a bit of cotton wool on the end of a wire to try and ascertain the usual contents of the sheath. Nothing there, except some unidentifiable grime.' He saw the look of interest in Shireen's face, and shook his head. 'Grease and dust and Allah knows what else, accumulated over the years. There may be some dried blood in there, but it's impossible to tell.'

'It was a rich man's dagger' he continued. 'The velvet covering on the outside of the sheath, and the steel used for the bands around the tip and at the top – all of those, he told me, pointed to it holding a very fine dagger indeed. But no dagger, sadly. No sign of it at all. After Suraj Bhan had taken stock and tidied up the place, the chowkidar had his men search the house. They looked in every nook and cranny, but to no avail. '

Shireen's forehead crinkled in puzzlement. 'I wonder what happened that night.'

'Yes. I wonder. I can only assume that, after he had used the dagger to kill Aadil, he did not return it to its sheath. Perhaps he kept it ready in his hand, just in case someone else emerged from the house.' Muzaffar reached forward to pick a couple of almonds from the bowl that lay between them. 'And there is the fact that whatever clues we've managed to find so far seem to suggest that the man is not a common thief. A man, in fact, who is literate enough to have looked through the papers Aadil kept in his room. And a man who carries a dagger sheath that belongs with an expensive dagger.'

'He could have stolen the dagger,' Shireen pointed out.

'That is a possibility. I suggested it to the thanedar, and he said there had been no reports of a stolen dagger in the recent past.' He tipped the cracked, empty shells of the almonds onto a saucer. 'Not that that matters. It could have been stolen years ago – after all, the velvet on that sheath is so worn, a wealthy owner would have had it redone a long time back. And it's always possible that it wasn't stolen in Dilli, anyway.'

Shireen moved the bowl of almonds closer to Muzaffar. She did not smile when he helped himself to a few more nuts and continued to talk. 'The thanedar has kept the sheath but I suspect it will end up just being an artefact, nothing more.' He cracked an almond – a paper-shelled one, as they were known, the shell brittle and thin – and shook the bits of shell onto the saucer. 'He was headed back towards the chowki to see what the chowkidar had unearthed in the meantime. Since I had run out of excuses, I agreed to accompany him.'

'And?'

'He had set the chowkidar on checking up the records for the thana.'

Shireen nodded. She was aware that among the many and multifarious tasks of the Kotwal and his minions – thanedars and chowkidars included – was the maintaining of records for the inhabitants of the areas under their jurisdiction. Along with his task of maintaining law and order – extending all the way from apprehending criminals and meting out justice, to preventing newly widowed Hindu women from being dragged off forcibly to be burnt on their husbands' pyres – the Kotwal had to fulfil a wide range of administrative duties. It was his and his officers' duty to keep track of the inhabitants of each house: the number of people, their relationships with each other, their means of income. They were to make sure that births, marriages, and deaths were duly noted, and that every man who came to stay in a neighbourhood – or left it, for that matter – was recognized as being present or absent, as the case may be.

'Did the chowkidar find anything?'

'Nothing that could give us any hope.' Muzaffar grimaced as he looked down at the shrivelled almond in his hand.

'What do you think, Jang Sahib?' she asked when he did not say anything for nearly a minute.

'It does not make sense,' Muzaffar admitted. 'The thanedar is of the opinion that a thief entered – perhaps pretending to be an acquaintance of Aadil, which would account for Aadil's having opened the door to him. Yes, it sounds flimsy, does it not? Especially as, from what Suraj Bhan tells me, Aadil had almost no friends. Who would call on Aadil at such an unearthly hour?' He discarded the almond shell and pushed the bowl of nuts away. 'The thanedar thinks the man entered, killed Aadil at the door itself, then went into the house and ransacked it, looking for valuables to steal. Perhaps he was startled by a sound – a night watchman in the street, something like that – which made him flee without actually stealing anything.'

'But he seemed to have had the time to examine the dead man's documents.'

'Not to mention the capability to do so. And the desire.' Muzaffar glanced up. 'There must be something in those documents, mustn't there? But Suraj Bhan looked through them all, in my presence and the chowkidar's, that day when we took an inventory. There was nothing there, he said, that would interest anyone. Or benefit anyone.'

'The thanedar is wrong, then,' Shireen murmured. 'Have you pointed it out to him? Told him what you think?'

'No.' Muzaffar leaned back against the bolster, his fingertips moving over its velvet cover in a repetitive, absent-minded caress. 'It is the kotwali's work. I shall not intervene.' He had told her – though in a deliberately offhand way, as if it were just another occurrence, nothing of any import – of Khan Sahib's note. His pretended indifference, he could tell, had not fooled Shireen. He knew now, even as he spoke the words, that his refusal to involve himself in the investigation of Aadil's murder did not fool Shireen. She was getting to know him too well to accept that Muzaffar was not interested in solving the crime. Or that his conscience did not plague him to point out something the officers of the law might have overlooked.

There was an awkward silence. Shireen fiddled with her dupatta, pleating its edge into narrow strips, folding them over, then undoing them.

Without looking up, she asked, 'And what about that – that Hindu, the sahukar? That was not a crime. It would not be wrong for you to help out there.'

'It is now a crime. The child Nandu disappeared this morning.'

Shireen's head jerked up, her eyes huge in a face gone white. 'Allah,' she whispered. 'The poor child. The poor father.' The dupatta had fallen, forgotten, from her hands. 'Why did you not tell me earlier, Jang Sahib?'

'I did not think you would be interested,' Muzaffar said quietly. 'You did not seem to like my associating with the man because he is a Hindu.'

The paleness of Shireen's face turned from that of shock to that of anger. 'It is one thing to keep one's distance, and quite another to spurn simple humanity,' she said, in a stiff voice that surprised Muzaffar. 'I know you think I am incorrigibly provincial in my outlook, Jang Sahib. So be it. That was the way I was brought up; there is nothing I can do about it. My parents, when they were alive; my uncle, who has been my guardian in the past few years – all believed firmly that Hindus and Muslims and Buddhists and whatever other faiths there are, are there because there are inherent differences in the way they regard life.' She had been so vocal in her indignation, she had barely drawn breath. She paused, gulped, and carried on before Muzaffar could get a word in.

'They taught me that there were differences, and because I know no better' – this, a direct barb at the husband who had implied that she perhaps fell short of his expectations – 'I see the differences, too. And I agree that it is perhaps all for the best if distances were maintained. But I do not agree that acknowledging differences is tantamount to being inhuman.'

She came to a sudden stop, out of breath, and now looking a little red-faced as well. 'I beg your pardon,' she mumbled. Then, with a swift but brief return of her defiance, she added, 'Please remember this, Jang Sahib. I may not be friends with Hindus, but that does not mean I cannot sympathize with a man whose only child – and motherless too, poor waif! – has been kidnapped. What must be happening to that man?! What have you discovered there? Surely you will do something there.' Her gaze had turned beseeching.

And Muzaffar, though he cringed at the thought of telling her that he had instructed Lakshminarayan to report the abduction of Nandu to the local thanedar, had no alternative but to tell her the whole story.

'You really cannot tell who might be responsible, Jang Sahib?' Shireen asked, in a subdued whisper, when he had finished.

Her husband shook his head.

'But if you cannot tell who might have kidnapped the baby, how is the thanedar to say?!'

It was a flattering endorsement of his abilities, but Muzaffar, lying in bed, tossing and turning about under the quilts, cudgelled his brains to think of a possible clue. There seemed none. Not Katra Neel, where Lakshminarayan had admitted he knew no one; not the letter, which could have been written by anyone. Not the brick, which could have come from anywhere. Not the ransom demanded. Not a whisper of hope. Not a thread that led anywhere...

Muzaffar went still. Beside him, he could hear the low, regular breathing of Shireen, feel her warmth through the clothes. But his mind was far away, in another part of the city, racing madly, trying to link one fact to another, one idea to another.

CHAPTER 7

'Salaam,' Muzaffar said, when an astonished and suddenly hopeful Lakshminarayan came hurrying into the courtyard from his room. It was early in the morning, barely an hour after sunrise, and the city was still waking up. Lakshminarayan however was, hardly to Muzaffar's surprise, already dressed and ready for the day. To go, Muzaffar could wager, to the local thanedar or the chowkidar. Ratan, who had opened the door to Muzaffar, had given him the news that there was no news. The thanedar had taken cognizance of the fact that Nandu had gone missing, and that the child's father had received a threatening letter, but whether or not an investigation had been launched was anybody's guess. It was obvious that Lakshminarayan, the absence of any news reducing his previous anxiety to something close to panic, had decided to go and camp at the doorstep of the chowkidar in charge.

His first words after an abstracted namaskar were, 'Huzoor, I – I hope' – he fell momentarily silent, then carried on – 'I hope you are here because you have thought of something. Anything, huzoor. Anything to bring my child to me. I am ready to give whatever the kidnapper asks for. Ten thousand, fifteen – if only I could have my Nandu back.' Tears had come into the man's eyes as he spoke.

'I believe I know what may have happened,' Muzaffar said. 'If you would call your servants together, here in the courtyard, we may find the solution to this mystery right here.' He saw puzzlement in the sahukar's eyes, and hastened to add, 'And we may be able to get Nandu home before noon. Hurry, Lakshminarayanji. There is not a moment to lose.'

Ratan, hovering in the background, not close enough to overhear Muzaffar's words, but near enough to understand that the visitor bore possibly glad tidings, was sent off to fetch Gangu and Subhadra. They came within moments in response to the summons, Gangu wiping wet hands on the end of a turmeric-stained odhni, Subhadra trailing along behind. In their wake also came Lakshminarayan's young brother-in-law, Girdhar, his hair still tousled and his eyes bleary from sleep. This man might be worried about his nephew, but it had not, seemingly, bothered him enough to make him either forego his sleep or rise early to head for the local chowki. But he was curious. Or was he scared? Had he come out to see if he was going to be accused of trying to extort money from his own brother-in-law? Muzaffar had sudden misgivings.

But it was too late now, and he did think his deductions would prove correct.

'Jang Sahib would like to speak to all of you,' Lakshminarayan said, his glance moving from Ratan to Gangu and then on to Subhadra. He ignored Girdhar.

'Just one question, and that is all,' said Muzaffar. He strolled around to where Ratan was now standing, in line with the closed front door. 'Where were you when the brick fell into the courtyard that morning?' He was looking up into the manservant's face. Ratan blinked. Perhaps he had been expecting an interrogation about the thoroughness of his search for the missing infant. Muzaffar's question seemed to catch him by his surprise.

His lips pursed in thought as he looked at Muzaffar, who

stood waiting, with an expression of patient calm that he did not feel. 'I – ah,' Ratan's face cleared. 'Yes, I remember. I had gone to the end of the street to buy flowers from the woman who sits there. Babuji had said he meant to go to the temple, and wanted fresh flowers'. Muzaffar directed a quick glance at Lakshminarayan, who nodded, confirming Ratan's testimony.

'And you?' Muzaffar turned to Gangu. 'Where were you at the time?'

'In the kitchen.' The woman's voice had turned hoarse; her eyes were swollen, red with all the tears she had shed. 'Making laddoos. Nandu and Babuji like them a lot.'

'Yes, of course. I remember,' Muzaffar looked over his shoulder, towards his host, and smiled gently. 'Did you get to eat any of those laddoos, Lakshminarayanji?'

Lakshminarayan started, caught offguard. He looked peeved too, when he shook his head. As if I would have bothered about sweets at a time like this, he seemed to be thinking. But he said nothing of what might have been passing through his mind.

'But Nandu was eating one, wasn't he, when I came here later?' Muzaffar asked, addressing his question to Subhadra as he turned to her. 'When Lakshminarayanji brought me home with him, we found you feeding Nandu a laddoo.' It was a rhetorical question, and Subhadra stared back at him, her face expressionless. 'Where were you when the brick fell in here?'

'There.' She pointed, to the charpai, now standing near the well. 'I was playing with Nandu.'

'You were both lucky it didn't hit either of you.'

She shrugged, a quick lift of her shoulders accompanied by a dismissive half-nod.

Muzaffar had moved closer to the girl; she came up to below his chest, so he was looking straight down at her when he asked, in a very soft voice, 'What did Jagannath promise you in exchange for your help? Money?'

He had thought Subhadra would start crying. On the heels of that thought had come another: that all the crying and screaming since the discovery of Nandu's disappearance had been done by Gangu. Subhadra had not shed a single tear.

She did not even – and this he had expected her to do – turn indignant or begin trying to plead her innocence. She did not make a dash for the door. It would have been useless, anyway; Muzaffar and Ratan were standing ranged across the door, which was of solid wood, bound with bands of iron and secured with a heavy iron bar and bolt.

Instead, without a word, and with only one wild-eyed look into Muzaffar's face, Subhadra whirled and went sprinting across the courtyard, heading for the staircase that led up to the roof. Muzaffar stretched out an arm to grab her, but his hand closed on thin air, missing the edge of the girl's billowing odhni by a hair's breadth. He was already turning, racing after her along with Ratan, when Girdhar – closer to the centre of the courtyard – sprang forward. He was lithe, strong; but even he was panting by the time Muzaffar and Ratan between them caught hold of Subhadra.

ଓଃ

'Uff,' Girdhar grunted, pressing a hand to his jaw, where Subhadra, flailing wildly, had hit him. 'She loosened a tooth there, I'm sure. I hadn't known she was such a wildcat.'

Gangu, bending over him as he sat in the room with Lakshminarayan later that day, firmly moved his hand aside and pressed a pad of faded cotton cloth, old, soft and warm, to it. 'Keep it there,' she said as she moved back to pull the brazier closer to Girdhar. 'Warm it again on that once the cloth starts cooling.' She had been fussing around with turmeric and warm milk and other concoctions for the past few minutes, cooing over an embarrassed Girdhar.

'Yes, yes,' he said. 'It's all right, Gangu. You can go now; I will manage.'

So Gangu, still clucking like a worried hen, gathered up some of the things she had brought into the room with her – a couple of spoons, a small brass waterpot, a pair of tongs for the brazier, and a dishcloth – and went out, leaving the men to themselves. They heard her talking softly to Nandu out under the neem tree, where he had been left in the care of Ratan.

They sat inside the room, the young Mughal nobleman, the sahukar and his brother-in-law, and listened to the sounds filtering in from the courtyard. The giggling of the toddler, the man saying something in a voice made deliberately high and squeaky, the woman murmuring soothingly.

The household, still bearing scars of all that had happened in the past two days, was limping back to normal. It had been a hectic, dramatic morning, with Muzaffar, Lakshminarayan and Girdhar rushing to the local thanedar's, and persuading him to depute a chowkidar to go along with them to Jagannath's place of business. The thanedar, both aware of Lakshminarayan's complaint as well as Muzaffar's reputation, had complied with easy alacrity. The credit for this victory, after all, would be added to the thanedar's account. He would be the one claiming the arrest of the guilty party. So enthusiastic was he that he had insisted on accompanying them. Subhadra, the only woman among them, had been dragged along, as a key witness and accomplice, but had maintained a stoic silence through it all.

Jagannath did what Muzaffar had expected him to: he had protested his innocence. He had refused to admit that he knew Subhadra, had insisted that he had nothing to do with the note, or with Nandu's kidnapping. But if Jagannath could be obstinate, so could Muzaffar. Especially with a belligerent Ratan and an injured (and therefore even more belligerent) Girdhar to back him up. And the thanedar, who could not bear the thought of possible victory sliding out of his hands. He, however, had been as much at sea as the rest of them – barring, of course, Subhadra – and had allowed Muzaffar to do all the talking, all the accusing, all the confronting. He had merely stood by, arms folded imperiously across his chest, assuming the semblance of a seasoned general who has graciously stood aside to allow a callow captain to lead the charge.

Muzaffar was, despite the cases he had investigated, not yet exactly sure of how matters would proceed. He had gone prepared to spend a good while pushing and prodding, goading and bullying; but it had taken only a few sentences from him to make Jagannath give way.

'I followed your trail till here, Jagannath,' he had said. 'How long do you think it will take me to find out where you have hidden Nandu away? Your accomplice is a dyer, is he not? A man who works in indigo, and who left his mark on the message you sent. A careless man. His neighbours in Katra Neel may not yet have seen the child; but how long will it be before someone notices? And I have been down Katra Neel, asking everybody about a kidnapped toddler. Someone is bound to realize, as soon as they see a strange child, that something is wrong.' He had paused, and had cast an eye towards the thanedar. The man had simply given a supercilious nod, encouraging Muzaffar to continue. 'Well, Jagannath?' Muzaffar had asked. 'Of course, if you refuse to say where Nandu is, Thanedar Sahib need only collect his men and seal off both ends of Katra Neel before he goes searching through every house, one by one, from threshold to back wall. I do believe your accomplice will be happier to give up his little hostage rather than be arrested. What do you think?'

It had not taken long for Jagannath to buckle under and tell them the name of the dyer in whose home Nandu had been temporarily incarcerated. The thanedar, spurred on by a gentle suggestion from Muzaffar, had sent one of his men, along with Lakshminarayan himself – by now weak with relief and impatient to be reunited with his son – to Katra Neel.

Now Lakshminarayan drew in a deep breath. 'We would never have got Nandu back had it not been for you, Jang Sahib,' he said in a voice that quavered with emotion. 'You have said you will not accept payment, but even if you would, I would never be able to repay you sufficiently.'

'Let him be,' Girdhar said gruffly. 'You're embarrassing him.' There was a hint of humour in his voice, though, and Muzaffar, glancing at the young man, saw a twinkle in his eyes. A pleasant change from the surliness of Girdhar when Muzaffar had first made his acquaintance. 'Satisfy our curiosity, Jang Sahib, please. How did you do it?'

'Yes.' Lakshminarayan added. 'I was too agitated to think about it before, but I cannot imagine how you solved the mystery. I would never have suspected Subhadra. Jagannath, yes; perhaps. He's a – a trader, a hard-headed merchant. But even him, no; I would never have guessed – not when he had just paid back my money.' He knitted his fingers together and leaned forward, his eyes keen. 'Tell us, Jang Sahib.'

Muzaffar remained silent for a while, gathering his thoughts. Then he reached across to Lakshminarayan's desk and picked up the brick. 'This,' he said, hefting it. 'It's a brick, not a stone. If you throw it any distance, it will show signs of that throwing. If somebody had thrown the brick from one of the houses next door, or from the yard behind your house, or even from the street in front – it would have required force to loft the brick over the rooms that ring your courtyard. The force would have been enough to shatter the brick.' He looked up from the brick, first at Lakshminarayan and then at Girdhar. Both men were watching him intently.

'Even if someone had somehow climbed up onto your own roof – let us say, from that narrow lane between your house and your neighbours – and dropped the brick from your own roof down into the courtyard, the brick wouldn't have remained intact. It may not have been completely broken, but would it have remained thus?' He indicated the brick: it was clean, intact; only the corners were worn somewhat, but there were none of the sharp edges or the relatively brighter red one would expect of a piece broken off recently.

'No, it wouldn't,' Muzaffar said, answering his own question. 'So if nobody threw the brick into your courtyard, but Subhadra brought it in to you, saying that somebody had – she must have been lying. And the only reason I could see for that was that she had done it herself.'

ଓ

'Write the note? Subhadra isn't even literate.' Girdhar, the arrogance of his youth never too far from the surface.

'No, not write the note. She must have been given the note, wrapped and tied around the brick, and just told what to do with it. She must have dropped the brick on the floor of the courtyard – from a height loud enough for the thud to be heard – maybe just from waist high. That would have alerted you, and anyone else who was close enough to hear, that something had dropped, that Subhadra wasn't simply making it up. She had made sure beforehand that there was nobody around. Gangu was busy in the kitchen, Ratan was out on an errand, Girdhar was not at home, and you were at work in here.'

Lakshminarayan's eyes had widened.

'And, do you remember what the old men, playing pachisi, had said when we spoke to them? That they had seen nobody up on the roof. The washerman did say he saw the shadow of someone going across your roof – back and forth – but that was not on the day this brick was thrown in. It was on the day after.'

'And I saw something else when we went on that errand, talking to the washerman. Do you remember that bit of drainpipe sticking out at the lower end of your neighbour's house wall? I hit myself against that – and I saw a smudge of fresh blood on it. That blood was not from me, even though I had stumbled against the pipe. But someone else had come or gone that way – down that lane, sometime not much before we were there. Recently, enough, for the blood to be still wet.'

'Tell me,' he said, turning to Lakshminarayan, 'Who are the people who frequent that yard? The old men, the washermen, the children. Who else?'

Lakshminarayan looked doubtful. He exchanged a glance with Girdhar, who merely shrugged, as if to deny any knowledge of the neighbourhood and its comings and goings. Then, clearing his throat, Lakshminarayan said, 'Nobody else, I suppose. It is not a thoroughfare; there is just this one alley leading into the yard, and few outsiders would even guess at its existence. The only people who use it – even if only occasionally – are those who live around it.'

'And they would all be familiar with the alley? With the drainpipe that must be avoided? They would know that you have to step carefully, or you will very likely injure yourself?'

Lakshminarayan nodded, his eyes now alight. Girdhar too had sat up, his face wearing an expression rather more suited to his years than the cynicism he tried to don. He looked as interested as a four-year old who had discovered where his mother kept her store of jaggery, but who was trying very hard not to let his excitement show for fear of the treat being whisked away before he could lay his hands on it.

'That smear of blood suggested two things. One, that someone who wasn't very familiar with the lane had bumped into the pipe. Two, that person had come into the lane but not till the end that opened onto the yard.'

'Why? Why the assumption that he did not go till the end?'

'Because the blood was fresh when I touched it; no more than a few minutes had passed. And, because the washerman had been in the yard beyond for the past half an hour. He would have mentioned it if a stranger had appeared in the yard. Remember, too, that the washerman said he saw that shadow – passing twice – and that too shortly after he had arrived.'

Girdhar's brows knitted. 'What do you mean?'

'That a man came down the lane and climbed up the wall to the roof of this house. He went along the roof, and down the stairs – to take Nandu, who was sleeping in the room next to the stairs. He then went back the way he had come; that was the second time the washerman noticed the shadow.'

'That would have been dangerous,' Lakshminarayan observed. 'What if one of the others in the house saw the intruder? Gangu, or Ratan? Gangu, of course, is almost always to be found only in the kitchen – she even rests there, when she's free. But Ratan? He invariably sits right next to the main door, and the staircase is in direct sight. He would immediately see anyone who came down it, or went up.'

'Unless Ratan was in on it,' Girdhar remarked.

Muzaffar looked at him with respect. 'True. But I already suspected Subhadra because of the brick. And Ratan said something that made me think he really had no idea what was going on, because he unknowingly revealed how Subhadra had worked it all.

'When we were talking to the three servants, an argument sprang up between Ratan and Subhadra. Each of them accused the other of negligence. Ratan said that Subhadra had taken Nandu out into the street and was talking to a wandering mendicant.'

'Yes, that annoyed me,' Lakshminarayan said. 'My wife, when she was alive, had indulged Subhadra too much. She is a wilful girl... but this? I hadn't expected this of her.'

'We never do, Lakshminarayanji,' Muzaffar said gently. He returned to his story. 'The inadvertent revelation of that incident out in the street explained a couple of things. You see, when you brought me into your house that day, Nandu was eating a laddoo, and when you tried to have some of it too, Subhadra stopped you. Very deliberately, saying he'd put spit all over it. Then, just a short while later, Nandu fell asleep – so that Subhadra could leave him in that room, go off to the kitchen, and be well away from the child when he vanished.'

'I don't understand, Jang Sahib.'

'This. That something had been mixed into the laddoo. Opium, perhaps, in a dose small enough to not injure the child, but to put him to sleep for a good while. Trying to make away with a child who is merely asleep naturally is too risky; he could wake up at any moment and start howling. He had to be kept quiet for him to be kidnapped.

'I didn't know who was behind it all, but there were other, smaller details that puzzled me too. Why did the culprit send you a note demanding the money and threatening to kidnap the child if you didn't pay, if he intended to kidnap Nandu anyway? Why bother to inform you beforehand? And if his original plan had been to wait for you to pay up, then why did he change it? And how did he manage it? Lifting Nandu right out of a house that at least had Gangu and Ratan in it, even if we were not there and Subhadra was on his side?'

A silence fell. It was broken by a ripple of childish laughter from out in the courtyard. Ratan, playing with Nandu, was tickling the child. Nandu was curled up in the big man's capacious dhoti-clad lap, clutching with plump fingers at the shawl Ratan wore.

'It was the mendicant whom Ratan mentioned,' Muzaffar said. 'You' – he looked at Lakshminarayan – 'mentioned that you told your servants what had happened, and gave them instructions to keep a close watch on Nandu. Then, the morning Nandu was found missing, you had gone out, to call on your neighbours, to try and find out if they might suspect someone. You must have been gone for a while, I suppose?'

The sahukar nodded. 'Yes. An hour, I think, at Narasimha's house, because there were so many people to be called in, to discuss the matter. Perhaps a quarter of an hour at Vidyacharan's house.'

'Ample time for Subhadra to have made her report and received fresh instructions on what to do.'

'From the mendicant?' Girdhar butted in.

'The man disguised as the mendicant. Perhaps our friend Jagannath himself. Or a henchman, sent with orders on what course to adopt in what circumstances. Subhadra was given the brick and the note at a time when all of you were unaware of what was about to happen. I assume she was allowed to go about just wherever she pleased, in and out of the house' – he glanced questioningly towards Lakshminarayan, who nodded silently. 'She must have been told, back then, perhaps a few days ago, that the mendicant would come by at so-and-so hour, and she was to tell him what had happened. Whether or not you seemed inclined to pay the ransom.'

'But after a threat like that, it would have been logical enough to bar the house and shut everyone in,' Girdhar pointed out. 'Any man worried about safeguarding his only child would be expected to take some measures to prevent a kidnapping. Wasn't there a chance that Subhadra wouldn't be able to make it out into the street in time to meet the mendicant?'

'I suppose she had already been told what to do if she had been told to keep Nandu inside at all costs. First of all, she needn't have taken Nandu out into the street at that time; she could easily have handed him to Gangu or Ratan and pretended to go out on an urgent errand by herself. Or – since Jagannath knew about the lane between your house and your neighbour's – the mendicant could have climbed up onto your roof and had a word with Subhadra there. He certainly shinned up later.

Whether still disguised as a mendicant or not, I don't know.'

Lakshminarayan pondered over what Muzaffar had said. 'It does make sense. And since Subhadra came back into the house with Nandu safe and sound after her meeting with the mendicant in the street, Ratan would not suspect her. My child was still safe, after all.'

'And when she met the mendicant, she must have told him that you had been agitated, and that you had gone out – did you tell your household where you were going?'

'No one except Ratan. I saw no need for it. If someone came, Ratan knew where I was to be found; that was enough.'

'Jagannath's plan must have been to wait and see what you would do,' Muzaffar said, after a moment. 'He must have hoped that, when you received the letter, you would be frightened enough to yield up the money without any further ado. But then I arrived. Still not the law, of course, but Subhadra noticed that I was asking questions, investigating the affair. When she reported that back to Jagannath, he adopted the next course of action: to actually kidnap Nandu. Perhaps he meant to follow it up' – he hesitated, not wanting to say what he knew would surely distress Nandu's father – 'with another note, possibly threatening even swifter action should you delay any longer. That would make even a fairly stingy man take the matter seriously, I think.'

Lakshminarayan looked grim, but he said nothing.

'Either she had already been given the opium beforehand just in case Jagannath's hand was forced – or the mendicant passed it to her then, when she put his hand into his begging bowl. Remember? Ratan mentioned it. Whatever it was, the mendicant went his way, having whispered to her what she was supposed to do next. And she came back inside, broke up a laddoo and mixed it with the opium before feeding it to Nandu.'

'That was why she wouldn't let me eat any?'

'Even a dose small enough to put a baby to sleep might have some effect on an adult. They couldn't risk you feeling dizzy or sleepy and putting two and two together – or, worse still, you being able to taste the opium. It hadn't been really cooked into the laddoo; there would be a definite hint of it despite the sugar and the ghee and everything else. An odd taste. Perhaps that's why Nandu was crying so when we arrived – the laddoo was probably quite unpalatable. Unpleasant, at the very least.'

Lakshminarayan nodded slowly, his face sombre.

'And when he was asleep, all she had to do was carry him into the room next to the staircase and leave him there for Jagannath – or his minion, whoever the kidnapper was – to carry away.

'Gangu was busy in the kitchen; there was no fear of her suddenly emerging. You were away, gone out. And Ratan, by his own admission, was sitting outside the main door, on the platform. Keeping a simultaneous watch on the front door and the street. Because one did not expect that a kidnapper would come in through the house itself, down the stairs.

'An agile man, picked especially for the job, could easily scale the outside of your house from the seclusion of the lane beside. He crouched on the roof, I think, waiting to see if he could get a good opportunity to creep downstairs. And he got it, easily enough, with nobody around Nandu, since everybody assumed he would be safe inside the room. All the man had to do was slink down the stairs and gather up the sleeping child. He descended from the roof – this time with Nandu – the same way he had come up. Perhaps the burden of the child made him slip, or perhaps it was just the mere fact that he was in a hurry; he scraped against that jutting pipe and left blood on it. But he hurried on, down that alley and out on to the main street. Nandu had no doubt been securely wrapped and concealed in his shawl. Nobody would look twice at a man walking along with a sleeping child in his arms, anyway.'

'And that was it? So – so simple?' Lakshminarayan whispered, his eyes wide. 'Done while we were standing in that yard at the back, talking to the washerman.' He wagged his head, as if marvelling at the evil genius that had hatched the plot. 'But how did you guess it was Jagannath behind it all?'

'It seemed likely. Just the mere fact that the demand came for exactly the same amount that Jagannath had paid up. It seemed too much of a coincidence. Yes, I know you said that there are neighbours around who are in the same trade and who may well be able to gauge how much money you'd have received just the other day – but who better to know exactly the amount?

'And the demand came for that specific sum. No more, no less. No less would be understandable; you are a man of means.' Muzaffar gestured vaguely, indicating the house, the undeniable if understated comfort of the place. 'And – I'm assuming – a man well capable of paying much more than ten thousand for the safety of your child. I am right, am I not?'

'I would bankrupt myself for Nandu.'

'Yes. So why ask for just ten thousand? If one is demanding money, then why stop at just that sum?' Muzaffar stretched out his arm again, lifting the brick from Lakshminarayan's desk and putting it on the mattress with one hand, while he picked up the coarse thread with the other. 'And there was this thread, used to tie the note around the brick.'

He explained it, repeating what he had told Shireen, pointing out the connection between the thread and the presence of a dyer in the conspiracy. 'Jagannath, after all, is a cloth merchant. It is hardly surprising that he would know dyers; possibly even know one of them well enough to have him agree to help. The man was probably – no, certainly – promised a part of the proceeds as an incentive to help.'

'There were other things, too, that made me begin to suspect Jagannath. There was, for example, the odd lie

Jagannath told Girdhar: that he would return the borrowed money soon. Perhaps he thought that later, when you and Girdhar compared notes, Girdhar might think he had heard wrong. Or perhaps he said it simply because the other sahukar, Kanhaiyalal, was present, and Jagannath did not want him to know that he had cleared your debt, but not his.

'The real reason, I think, was that Jagannath really did intend to clear Kanhaiyalal's debt. After Girdhar had gone – or so Jagannath thought – Jagannath did tell Kanhaiyalal that he would pay Kanhaiyalal back within two days.'

Girdhar's eyes had narrowed as he tried to follow Muzaffar's train of thought. Lakshminarayan simply sat back and listened, looking a little flummoxed, but not asking any further questions.

'And – from what you told me,' said Muzaffar, 'you have spent the past few months pursuing Jagannath to get him to pay you. And with no success until now, when he suddenly seems to be flush with funds. But even if he finally does have the money to pay both you and Kanhaiyalal back, why try to hide that fact from both of you?' He paused, and because neither of the two men said anything, he went on after taking a sip of water from the goblet placed near his elbow.

'Because he didn't have the money to pay you both. Who knows where he managed to lay his hands on the ten thousand he paid you? Perhaps it was honestly gained; perhaps it was not. But pay you he did. If someone tried to extort that money from you soon after, the blame couldn't be laid at Jagannath's doorstep.'

'But he made the mistake of asking for exactly the same amount he'd paid up,' Girdhar said. 'That was stupid.'

'And he was unlucky enough to use a newly dyed thread to tie the note,' Muzaffar added.

Lakshminarayan sat back, eyes shut, his back leaning against the bolster behind him. He drew in a deep, shuddering breath and opened his eyes, his face breaking into a radiant smile. Muzaffar realized that he had not seen Lakshminarayan smile all day long, except when talking to Nandu. The smile transformed his face, erased the dark shadows under his eyes and wiped away the worries stamped across his features. 'And I was fortunate enough to find my way to you, Jang Sahib,' he said softly. 'Thank you.'

CHAPTER 8

It was well into the afternoon by the time Muzaffar got back to his own haveli. The arrest of Jagannath, followed by Nandu's rescue, and Lakshminarayan's insistence on hearing every detail of how Muzaffar had traced the letter to Jagannath, had all taken time. Muzaffar, having set out so early from home – with barely a kabab and a roti to keep body and soul together – had begun feeling the pangs of hunger while explaining the logic of his investigation to Nandu's doting father. Even as he spoke, he had begun to recognize the signs of a meal being cooked in the vicinity. The aroma, wafting in the air, of spices being fried, the earthiness of simmering lentils, and the warm, pungent smell of asafoetida. The splutter of vegetables being added to hot oil, the clang of metal as a spoon was used to stir a pot. More clangs and much clatter as utensils were washed. The sound of water being poured.

Gangu even came, once the clattering had died down and the aromas had settled into those of a cooked meal – to stand at the door, and peek in. She had looked meaningfully at Lakshminarayanji as she had asked, 'Shall I feed Nandu, then, babuji?' As if to say, when will you get rid of your guest, babuji? This guest who has given us back our little darling, but whom we dare not feed in our house?

Muzaffar had wondered, for the brief moment before Lakshminarayan had answered, what the sahukar would do. His praise of Muzaffar, and his gratitude, had been sincere. Muzaffar had no doubt that Lakshminarayan did regard Muzaffar as something akin to a saviour.

Would a man grudge a meal – even if only a few morsels – to his saviour?

'Yes,' Lakshminarayan had replied. 'Feed him, Gangu. Girdhar and I will eat later.'

Yes, thought Muzaffar, as he made his way home later. Yes, he had been a fool to imagine, even if only momentarily, that he, a Muslim, would be invited to partake of a meal cooked in a Hindu household. No matter how highly Lakshminarayan would think of Muzaffar, when it came to more personal matters – the sharing of food, for instance – Muzaffar would always be the outsider.

It was odd, he thought, that a man could be on the one hand praised to the skies, and on the other, not even considered human enough to share food with. He wondered what Lakshminarayan's reaction would have been if Muzaffar had been crude enough to ask for food. He would probably not have refused; that would have been far too impolite. There would have been a compromise, perhaps. The sahukar and his brother-in-law might have sat and watched their guest eat, saying all the while that they would eat later, an exaggerated form of hospitality; but they would not have eaten along with him, even if hunger was gnawing at their insides. And, when Muzaffar had taken himself off, the dishes he had eaten in would be thrown away, the terracotta dishes broken, the shards pitched into the street. Gangu would bathe and go to the temple to purify herself.

It would have been excruciatingly embarrassing.

Even though it was closer to sunset than noon, he had therefore eaten lunch at his own home. Half his appetite had already vanished by then, but the mere act of sitting down at the white sheet spread on the carpet before him, of talking to Shireen as he ate, was balm to a somewhat bruised soul. He should not be hurt, he thought, at Lakshminarayan's behaviour. Being cordial, even deeply grateful, did not come in the way of religion and traditions that were too far rooted in one's life to be easily cast aside.

But hurt it did, even if he told himself that Lakshminarayan himself might have felt guilty about it.

'I see,' said Shireen, when he told her – as casually as he could, in response to her question of why he had remained hungry through much of the day. Her voice was soft, subdued. 'It is a double-edged sword, is that what you mean to say? If we regard the Hindus as different, they regard us as different, too. Too different to be even humane to.'

Muzaffar shrugged, sitting back after he had eaten. 'There are men of all faiths who cling too closely to their faiths to let humanity get in the way. And there are men who remember that faith is a personal thing, something that should raise you above petty things like whether or not a man shares the same beliefs as you do. That is what I believe religion should be: a way of making ourselves better human beings. Not self-righteous, not standing in judgement over others.'

Shireen was looking solemn. So solemn, indeed, that he felt sorry for her. What he had said could be construed – had been construed, he was sure – as an ungentle slap on the wrist for her. 'Well, then,' he said, in a deliberately affectionate tone, 'I have told you all that happened to me today. It is your turn now; tell me. How have you spent your day?'

'Ah.' Shireen lightened, the gloom dissipating as a slow, somewhat triumphant smile appeared on her face. Muzaffar, looking into her face, saw the twinkle that had come into her eyes. 'While you have been away investigating an abduction, someone here has been abducted.'

ଓ

'Do you remember an old woman called Ameena?', Shireen continued. 'She is a servant in the household of the merchant Basharat.'

For a moment, Muzaffar's eyes narrowed, confused – it had been a long day, and there had been too many occurrences, too many names, too many thoughts pulling his brain in different directions. Then it dawned on him. 'Ah. The old woman who had come to Aadil's house the morning we found him murdered. Yes, I remember her.' He stared, his mind beginning to race again. 'She has been kidnapped? When? How?' A sudden thought came into his mind. 'And how did you come to know?'

'The entire mohallah knows of it. Sometime, just around noon, the news began to spread in the neighbourhood. It seems nobody had seen her since late last night, after the household retired for the night. Then, this morning, nobody missed her till quite late – I believe she occupied somewhat of an exalted position among the servants; nobody dared question her, whether she came or went, or when and where.'

'If not the other servants, at least Basharat and his family? Would they not ask after her? Would not they have wondered over her absence?'

'They did. Or, rather, the lady of the house did. Ameena was her personal maid, who had accompanied her to Dilli after she was married.'

'Basharat's brother's wife, I believe.' Muzaffar remembered his conversation with Ameena the day he had met her – the day they had been interrupted by the beggar. He recalled the old woman telling him that her mistress was married to a merchant named Parvez, brother to this Basharat Shireen had mentioned.

Shireen nodded. 'Yes. The woman – this Ameena's mistress – is called Nilofer. The neighbourhood, by the way, is abuzz with rumours about Ameena's disappearance. I would think even the rats that infest the drains would know about them by now.' Her lips curved in a small, sudden flash of humour.

'Everybody has been talking about them,' she continued, with a chuckle. 'I have had a bangle-seller come by who was more interested in telling me all she knew about Ameena and her mistress than she was in selling bangles. I have had a seller of carpets, another of silks, and even a woman wanting to sell me love potions – and all of them had something or the other to say about Ameena's disappearance.'

'And what did you get to hear?'

'Mostly a lot of rumours. One school of thought seems to be that she has been murdered – perhaps by Basharat, perhaps by his brother. Or maybe even both of them, working together. And that her body has been thrown into the household well.'

'Hardly likely.'

Shireen nodded. 'Or tucked away in the tehkhana.'

'To begin stinking within a few days? That would not be a very intelligent way of ridding oneself of a corpse. Not to mention the question of hygiene – '

'I am merely recounting what I was told, Jang Sahib,' his wife interrupted, in a tone that was distinctly tart. 'I do not subscribe to these views, myself.' She had looked up at him sharply, and seeing the contrition in his eyes, she added more mildly, 'There were some, though, that had more plausible things to say. The bangle-seller had actually visited Basharat's house this morning. She was there when Ameena's absence was first noticed, and she made it a point to loiter about until she had gleaned enough information to make her the chief gossip-bearer of the mohallah.'

'And?'

Shireen stretched an arm out for the slender-necked, round-bottomed glass pitcher of lime-and-orange flavoured sherbet. 'Ameena seems to have vanished, but not all that she owned has vanished with her. Yes, she has taken most of her clothing, and the little knickknacks that she held in affection. Mostly gifts bestowed by Nilofer.'

'Those have all vanished with her,' Shireen said, pouring out the sherbet for Muzaffar. His goblet, a beautiful one made of rock crystal, enamelled in red, green and gold, was a very fine piece gifted by a wealthy nobleman whom Muzaffar had helped in finding the killer of his father. The man had been lavish in his praise and his munificence; there had been goblets such as these, a Persian carpet, a pearl necklace, and – what appealed to Muzaffar far more than the rest – a finely painted copy of the Razmnama, a Persian translation of the epic Mahabharat, originally commissioned by the Emperor Akbar.

At the moment, though, Muzaffar was more interested in what Shireen had to say.

'Most of the other things she possessed – blankets, heavier clothing, and so on – have been left behind. The chowkidar has been questioning everybody in the household. Who knows what conclusions he has reached?' The sherbet had left a little droplet of stickiness on her thumb; she rubbed it absently against the tears of condensation that had run down the outside of the cold pitcher. 'Perhaps,' she added, 'you might learn something if you were to go and meet him. After all, you did meet Ameena that day, even spoke to her.'

'I have already been told off once by Khan Sahib,' Muzaffar replied. He swirled the sherbet – now only halfway up to the rim of the goblet – and took a long, slow sip from it. 'And why should I want to learn anything, Shireen? It is none of my business, as Khan Sahib said.'

He had expected acquiescence, a quiet acceptance of his will. At the most – considering this was Shireen, and not a woman to back down without a fight, even if the weapons she carried into battle were disguised as tact and charm and gentle persuasion – some gentle resistance. But he had not expected the sudden outburst that came his way. 'How can you sit back and disclaim any – any interest, even? – in the sufferings of people around you? One man is dead, and now the woman who may have had some knowledge of his death has gone missing, and you say that you wish to know nothing of it!'

Muzaffar was staring at her, his handsome face frozen into unyielding lines, but his eyes narrowed as he watched her. All Shireen's vehemence was directed at him, but she was not looking at him. A deaf man watching her would have thought her to be venting her frustration on the napkin that she had pulled into her lap from its position beside the pitcher of sherbet. She was rubbing her thumb – now long-clean – on it in a frenzy of activity. 'What if something should happen? What if – '

'Shireen,' Muzaffar said, in a voice dangerously low. 'The question is not what may happen or what may have already happened. The question is whether Khan Sahib will tolerate any more interference on my part. I have already crossed that line once today in the case of Nandu's kidnapping. It is possible that the thanedar there will claim all the credit for himself. On the other hand, he may not. If – or when, I should say – Khan Sahib comes to know that I interfered yet again in a case that was the domain of the thana, he will be furious. I dare not even allow myself an interest in this.' He drank down the rest of the sherbet and wiped his lips with the back of his hand. 'What do you want? That Khan Sahib should publicly disown me? That he should declare me a vigilante? Have me clapped into prison or fined?'

To his surprise, she snapped back, 'And what if it so happens that none of his men are able to see what you can? What if the chowkidar and the thanedar cannot see that there might be a connection between the death of Aadil and the disappearance of Ameena?' She drew in a big gulp of air, trying to still her agitation. When she spoke again, it was in a calmer, slower tone. 'I have seen you at work. I know how you observe things other men do not. I know you are far more capable than all of Khan Sahib's thanedars put together – '

'No,' Muzaffar said, with an air of finality. 'That is the most shameless flattery I have ever heard, and it is not true, either. No, Shireen; don't try to convince me. I may be indecisive at times, but on this matter my mind is made up. I have already probably got into trouble with Khan Sahib about the Nandu business; if he discovers that – on top of that – I have poked my nose into an affair I had already been warned away from, he will not spare me. I will not go poking my nose in this business of Aadil and Ameena and what might have happened. Let it be, Shireen. I am not interested.' He put the empty goblet aside, and got to his feet. 'As it is, I have enough to occupy myself with.'

He rose to his feet, and bowed formally to his wife, startling her. 'I shall return to my papers. I have work that still needs to be done.'

Having said which, he left the room and returned to his work. He sat down, pulled out the fat ledger he had been leafing through, unrolled and unfolded the myriad documents that had come for him. He read and re-read. And read once again. It made no sense at all; the words did not go beyond his eyes.

Finally, with a sigh of exasperation, he flung aside the papers and sat back, leaning against the cool plastered surface of the wall behind.

He was caught in a dilemma, and saw no way out of it.

A soft clearing of a throat outside the door heralded the arrival of the household steward, Javed. When he stepped in, it was with a folded sheet of paper in hand. 'This has come for you, huzoor,' he said, holding it out. 'From Kotwal Sahib. Shall I ask the man to wait, huzoor?'

'Let me read this first, Javed.' Muzaffar took the letter from Javed. It was a short message, so short that he had barely started reading it before he had finished. Muzaffar pursed his mouth, wincing at what he read. 'No,' he said to the steward. 'The man need not wait. And – get a horse saddled for me, Javed. At once. I have to go to meet Khan Sahib.'

ꟹ

'I beg your pardon, Khan Sahib,' Muzaffar said to his brother-in-law, after he had been shown into the dalaan where the older man sat. Khan Sahib's steward had retreated, a servant had brought a bowl of fruit and placed it in front of Muzaffar, and had, in turn, gone from the room. Khan Sahib had, in a few choice words, indicated to Muzaffar that his exploits with reference to the kidnapping – and subsequent rescue – of Nandu had been reported at the kotwali.

'I had not intended to trespass on the jurisdiction of the kotwali or the thanas,' Muzaffar continued. 'Believe me, Khan Sahib. That was why I had Lakshminarayan report the matter to the thanedar – '

'After you had already investigated it in part!' Khan Sahib exploded. 'If you were truly determined to keep your nose out of our affairs, you would have told Lakshminarayan – no, not even him, but his friend, that clerk – that he had better bring the matter to us. You should never have gone to Lakshminarayan's house in the first place!'

'Why ever not?' Muzaffar retorted. 'It wasn't as if a crime had actually been committed. Lakshminarayan had only received a letter threatening consequences if he should not pay up. What would have happened if he had gone to the thanedar with that letter? Nothing! It would simply have been pushed away, and he would have been warned not to waste the thanedar's time. No, Khan Sahib' – he had seen the Kotwal's face growing increasingly red with indignation – 'you cannot hope to fool me into thinking that your thanedars can spare the time to investigate every single would-be crime that is reported to them. When even murders and thefts have gone unheeded, where the victim was not an influential man – why, a letter such as this would simply be ignored.

'Besides,' he added, before the Kotwal could interrupt, 'You were the one who's always taught me to take my own decisions, to choose the path I will follow. Do you remember that day, years ago, near Bahraich? The leopard? The deer? This is the path I care to take. To come to the aid of people who need my help. Lakshminarayan needed my help. That is all.'

Khan Sahib's face had turned crimson with rage as Muzaffar had continued to speak. When the younger man stopped, however, Khan Sahib remained silent. Beside him, half-forgotten all this while, stood a goblet of sherbet. He reached out for it, and gripping it, brought it up, stopping short of his mouth. Over its rim, he looked at Muzaffar, his eyes cold and hard as twice-frozen ice. His knuckles, noticed Muzaffar, had turned white.

'And what happens as a result of this?' he asked, his voice low and hoarse; dangerous. 'Lakshminarayan emerges thinking that the thanedar – the entire administration of the law in Dilli – is useless. That the next time one comes up against a crime, the solution is to go to Muzaffar Jang.' His voice turned sarcastic. 'Muzaffar Jang, the brilliant mind. Muzaffar Jang, the man who can sniff out criminals better than the best hound in the Baadshah's menagerie. Muzaffar Jang, whose very name inspires fear in the murderers and thieves – '

'I did not – '

'No!' Khan Sahib thundered. 'No, you did not, and you never will! You cannot think beyond preening your feathers and basking in the glory of your successes!' He banged the goblet down, its contents untouched, down on the carpet beside the mattress on which he was seated. He had been, too, leaning further and further forward as he spoke. Now he suddenly fell back against the bolsters, as if all the frantic energy of his fury had drained him. 'Get out of my sight,' he said quietly, looking fixedly at the polished chiraghdaan, with its seven wicks, each flame still dancing in the aftermath of the storm. 'Get out, and don't show your face again. Not here, and not at the kotwali.'

ꕥ

Zeenat Begum, her grey eyes huge and full of pain, came to visit Muzaffar at his haveli the next morning. She had sent a servant earlier, to check that her brother would indeed be at home. When she emerged from the palanquin – which had been carried into the mahal sara, where Shireen waited to greet her – Zeenat Aapa was her usual composed, dignified self. She gave brisk orders to the maid who had accompanied her to wait outside. Her greeting to Shireen was kind and sweet.

They walked together down the corridor, Zeenat Begum's pearl-grey pashmina shawl in stark contrast to Shireen's coral pink one. A maid – Shireen had turned down, much to her husband's relief, the offer of having a eunuch preside over the mahal sara – followed them to the guest chamber. The Kotwal's wife was seated near the only window through which the warm sunlight shone into the room. Shireen ordered refreshments and was about to send the maid about her work when Zeenat Begum said, 'Where is your husband, Shireen? If he is not busy, can we have him join us here?'

Shireen blinked, caught offguard. This was an awkward moment; she did not know how to respond. Muzaffar, she knew, would be busy going over the documents that had arrived from his estate. Not busy enough to refuse to meet his sister. But this sister was wife to the very man who had thrown Muzaffar out of his home the night before. Muzaffar had supplied Shireen with an abbreviated version of all that had transpired between him and Khan Sahib, and though he had not expressed it in so many words, she had sensed the deep hurt and resentment in her husband.

Mindful of the maid still standing in the room, waiting for instructions, Zeenat Begum forced a smile. 'Call him, anyway,' she said, addressing Shireen, but loud enough for the maid to hear. 'I am his sister, after all; surely he can find the time to talk to me when I come visiting.'

'There is nothing to be said,' a gruff Muzaffar said when he came into the room a while later. 'All that had to be said, Khan Sahib said yesterday.' He was tight-lipped, as he had been since he had left Khan Sahib's haveli the previous evening.

She watched him askance. In Shireen's limited experience, men did not like women prying into their affairs. Both her father, and her uncle – who had been her guardian after the death of his brother – distanced themselves from their womenfolk when it came to anything that could be expected to cause distress. Attempts to probe would be laughed away. Offers to share the burden would be scoffed at. She squirmed, unsure. 'I wonder where the maid has disappeared,' she said, when a few moments had passed by in an uncomfortable silence. 'Perhaps I should go and check – '

She had risen even as she spoke, but was pulled up short by a simultaneous 'No,' from both Muzaffar and Zeenat Aapa. Shireen chose to look at her husband, a question in her eyes.

'There is no need for you to leave, Shireen,' he said. 'This is a family matter, and you are family now. Sit down.'

He had already turned back to his sister by the time Shireen reseated herself. 'Why have you come, Aapa? Won't Khan Sahib be furious when he comes to know of this disloyalty? Surely he cannot countenance this rebellion?'

'Stop it. You know he did not mean all that he said – '

'Really?' Muzaffar's eyes blazed. Shireen, mute spectator though she was, flinched. Zeenat Begum did not so much as let an eyelash flutter. 'Aapa, sometimes the things one says in the heat of the moment are what matter the most, are they not? It is only when we are carried away by our emotions do we let our guard down and say what we really feel, not what propriety or humanity or petty considerations for feelings obliges us to say.'

'And what about you?' Zeenat Begum shot back, her temper flaring. 'Was it as undeserved as you make it out to be, Muzaffar?'

'I did what was best at the time. Lakshminarayan was close to panic. Who would not have been, with their child missing? Would you or Khan Sahib have sat back and waited patiently if – Allah forbid – one of your children had been kidnapped? I only did what I had to, Aapa. Perhaps if the thanedar had shown more resourcefulness, if it had seemed to me that he was doing something to discover Nandu's whereabouts, I might have refrained. But what was he doing? Nothing!

When Zeenat Begum merely glared at him without speaking, he leaned back against the bolster with a sigh. 'Why have you come, Aapa?' he asked. 'To apologize? Or to get me to apologize? Or to add to Khan Sahib's recriminations?'

Zeenat Begum did not answer immediately, her gaze moved to Shireen, as if seeking support. Or perhaps asking Shireen if she knew how to handle this recalcitrant man. But Shireen was looking studiously down at the deep orange-red flowers painted in henna on her hands. She had stayed in the room, as she had been instructed to; but, wise woman that she was, she was not letting herself get dragged into a quarrel that she had never been part of. Zeenat Begum's lips curled up in amused appreciation. She looked away from Shireen, and back at her younger brother.

'I will not add to what my husband has already said. But I will not apologize. Not on his behalf, and not on yours. He is my husband; you are my brother. Both of you are equally dear to me, and my loyalty is to both of you. Do not tell me to choose, Muzaffar.' She placed a hand on Muzaffar's. 'Your quarrel is with Khan Sahib. Do not drag me into it.'

ᨓ

Muzaffar had returned to his room and to his work even before Zeenat Begum had left the house. He had taken his leave of her in as polite a voice as he could muster, giving as an excuse – legitimate though it was – the fact that he had to get back to work, because the man in charge of his lands was expected to arrive in Dilli three days later. 'I would like to have all my decisions ready, all my questions prepared, for when he comes. It is best that I discuss everything with him and send him back without further delay. There are matters connected to the land that we dare not postpone, not if the fields have to yield a good harvest this year.'

Neither of his womenfolk had made any demur, though Muzaffar sensed that both Shireen and Zeenat Begum knew full well that Muzaffar might have spared a quarter of an hour to sit with them. He had bowed, stepped over the threshold, and made his way back to his papers, but his mind had refused to focus on the reams of paper before him. The sense of injustice, of being misunderstood so grossly, was too strong. The bile rising in his throat was too bitter to be ignored. It had not let him sleep till nearly dawn, and Zeenat Aapa's visit, though probably with the best of intentions, had only made him feel worse.

Muzaffar woke with a start, the raucous cawing of a crow somewhere outside jolting him out of his sleep. Warm golden sunlight, split into star-shaped shadows by the stone filigree of the screen, poured in through the window opposite. It poured in at a high angle; it was well into the afternoon. Muzaffar blinked, looking about him. The scattered papers were proof enough that he had gone to sleep over his work.

Someone, however, had entered the room while he had been asleep. On a low rosewood stool inlaid with mother of pearl now sat a large salver with a covered plate, with two matching bowls of blue and white ceramic, both covered. Beside the salver was a pitcher, its curving glass belly full of sherbet. Someone in the household – Shireen, he suspected – had thought of him at lunchtime, and having discovered that he had fallen asleep, had decided to have food and drink brought for him and left within easy reach for whenever he should wake. He straightened up, wincing as muscles gone stiff cried in protest.

His belated lunch over, Muzaffar stepped out of his room, feeling more than a little sheepish. He had, after all, excused himself from the company of his wife and sister on the pretext of work. It was embarrassing to imagine that one of them – or worse, both – might have come in and found him asleep instead of at work.

But Shireen was not to be found in the rooms of the mahal sara. He looked inside their bedroom, in the room where she had been entertaining Zeenat Begum, even in the little baradari – the four-sided pavilion – that adjoined the room. She was not there.

'Is Begum Sahiba in the khanah bagh?' Muzaffar asked of a maid who had emerged from the corridor that led to the khanah bagh, the inner garden of the haveli. Shireen was fond of flowers. Going out into the garden and gathering fresh blooms to be placed in the rooms, both public and private, was her favourite way of spending a sunny spring afternoon.

'Begum Sahiba is not at home, huzoor,' the maid said.

She must have gone out on one of her visits to an acquaintance, thought Muzaffar. He nodded to the maid to go about her work, and headed back to his room, feeling somewhat at a loose end. There was work to be done, true, but he would have liked to see Shireen, and perhaps to apologize for the cavalier way in which he had spurned her company – and that of his sister – earlier that day. Zeenat Aapa he had known all his life; she knew him well enough to overlook his cantankerousness. She would have, without his having to apologize, forgiven him, knowing that he had not meant to insult her. With Shireen, much as he loved her, his relationship was still new. He had known her only about three months. He had been married to her less than a month. Gentle and sweet and wise as she was, he could not be sure that she would forgive him quite as easily.

It made him feel guilty, eager to see her, tell her that he was sorry for having been offhanded.

But she was not around, and he had no option but to go back to his work.

Half an hour passed in a slightly abstracted perusal of the papers at his desk. Another quarter went by in pacing about the khanah bagh, glaring at the lone gardener turning over the earth in one of the rose beds. Finally, when he could stand it no longer, Muzaffar retreated to his room and sent for Shireen's chief maid. Ruqayya was a level-headed and reliable woman who had been part of Shireen's dowry. She, thought Muzaffar, would know where Shireen had gone. And, more importantly for his peace of mind, when she could be expected to return.

'Ruqayya Aapa is not at home either, huzoor,' said the maid who came from the mahal sara in response to his summons. 'She has gone with Begum Sahiba.'

'Gone with Begum Sahiba?' Muzaffar echoed. 'In the palanquin?'

'Begum Sahiba was in her palanquin, huzoor. Ruqayya Aapa was on foot.'

Muzaffar chewed at his upper lip, puzzled. Nearly every place Shireen visited – the homes of noblewomen she had been introduced to, the bazaars, the gardens, the little zenana mosques, all the places a lady might frequent – were not within easy walking distance. Certainly not for a woman like Ruqayya, a far from sturdy specimen. Shireen, to his knowledge, had never taken Ruqayya as an escort anywhere. 'It would be too cruel to make her walk such long distances,' she had explained. 'The kahaars who carry the palanquin – well, it is their work; but Ruqayya is not used to walking so much. And why should she?'

Shireen had consented, however, to have an armed manservant escort her palanquin whenever she did venture out.

'Did Rashid go out with them, as usual?' Muzaffar asked. 'With his lance and dagger?'

'Yes, huzoor. He was there, walking in front of the palanquin.'

Muzaffar nodded to the woman in dismissal. When she was gone, he hunched over his desk, elbows leaning on its sloping top, his fingertips massaging the base of his skull, which had begun to ache.

Shireen must have gone somewhere within walking distance, if she had made Ruqayya accompany her on foot. But why had she taken Ruqayya along? Shireen was not one of those fragile noblewomen who would summon a maid to flick away a fly that had settled on her wrist. Shireen was also, while perfectly aware of the proprieties expected of an amir's wife, not obsessed with remaining within the rigid confines of purdah. She would sit, discreetly veiled, in her curtained palanquin, and call for the manservant to stand beside the palanquin, close enough at hand for him to be able to hear any instructions she had to give.

Outside, the shade of the mango tree on the lawn had begun to stretch as the sun began its slow and inexorable descent towards the horizon.

Muzaffar, torn between annoyance at Shireen's unexplained absence and impatience to have her back so that he could apologize, slowly began to become aware of the change in the atmosphere. Beyond the tree was the wall; and, beyond the wall was the main street of the neighbourhood. The sounds that drifted from it throughout the day were predictable enough: hoof beats, the rhythmic creak of cartwheels, the cries of vendors hawking their goods, an occasional song, the laughter of children at play. When he had first entered the room in the morning, he had heard those sounds – he was sure of it – but now they were gone, silenced or changed sometime in the course of the day.

He straightened up slowly, ears pricked, paying closer attention. Yes, he had not heard children's voices out there for a long time. Earlier, there had been a kaan-mailiya, an ear-cleaner, offering his services. And another vendor, calling out something in a singsong voice so indistinct that Muzaffar had failed to grasp what the man was selling, whether vegetables from the riverbank or silks from Isfahan.

There were no vendors now. Instead, there was a strange hush. It had fallen sometime in the past half-hour, the usual hubbub of the day abruptly and unnaturally stopped, as if a palm had been slapped across the collective mouths of the neighbourhood.

Muzaffar rose, and in that very same moment, a man began calling in the street outside. Shouting, loud and clear, and in a voice that throbbed with panic. 'Hurry! Hurry, we have very little time! The city gates will close in another few hours! Then – ' the rest of the sentence was drowned out in a sudden bubbling up of noise. A child was crying, a woman shouting to someone, the sound of a cart's wheels turning on the stones of the street outside.

Muzaffar was hurrying out of the room and down the corridor even as the noise outside swelled. More voices were added to the hubbub, along with odd thuds and clangs. By the time Muzaffar had sprinted down the main path and to the small gateway of the haveli, it seemed to him as if half the neighbourhood had gathered outside the house.

His steward, Javed, was standing at the gate along with the doorkeeper. A few other servants – Muzaffar recognized a stablehand and the chief gardener – were hovering about, curiosity written all over their faces. They drew aside and Javed turned just as Muzaffar arrived on the threshold of the gate.

'What is it?' Muzaffar asked, looking out onto the street, now a surging mass of humanity. Confused humanity, too, seething and simmering, rushing about aimlessly in a near-panic, shouting and weeping. He stared, flummoxed. At the gate of the haveli opposite stood two bullock carts along with a palanquin and three horses. Servants hurried about like ants, lugging out wooden chests, large bundles, and odds and ends – a massive silver urn, an enamelled platter the diameter of a man's arm, a carpet rolled into a long floppy cylinder. The carts were already piled to the brim. Muzaffar watched with increasing bewilderment as the servants slung the carpet across the back of one of the horses.

'What on earth is going on, Javed?' Muzaffar repeated.

'I beg your pardon, huzoor – I do not know. I have sent Nazir to find out.'

But the hustle and bustle was not confined to the house opposite them. It was reflected, in varying degrees, in the surrounding area. Here came a small family of obviously poor people, the father rushing on ahead, carrying a large and heavy sack – the tools of his trade, perhaps. Behind came his wife, veiled and carrying a sack that nearly doubled her up. Its contents clanged and bulged. Beyond her, hurrying to keep up, came seven children, ranging in age from a boy barely adolescent, to a toddler who could not have been more than three years old. Each carried something: pots, pans, clothing. Muzaffar would have wagered anything that they held all their worldly belongings in their arms.

There were others, too, not quite so loaded down with possessions, but with much to gossip about. Men stood about here and there, collecting in knots under the nearby banyan tree or at the well in the square halfway down the street. Men who put their heads together and talked animatedly. Men who looked up every now and then, glancing furtively – or was it fearfully? – around. Men who shuffled and fidgeted, breaking away from the groups they formed, regrouping within minutes.

'Here comes Nazir, huzoor.'

The servant, a youth barely eighteen years old, had emerged from the house opposite. He pushed his way through the people around – the family had now started exiting their mansion, the women heavily veiled, the children moving in a wide-eyed, excited gaggle. Muzaffar stepped down from the threshold of the gate into the street below, and grabbed Nazir's arm before he even reached the gate.

'There's been a murder, huzoor,' Nazir replied in a whisper.

CHAPTER 9

Muzaffar stared at his servant. 'In that house?' He indicated, with a tilt of his chin, the house opposite, emptying so rapidly of both occupants and accoutrements. 'No, but it can't be,' he murmured, without even pausing to let Nazir speak. 'There would have been at least the chowkidar here, and he wouldn't have let anyone leave until the investigation was over and done with.' His gaze, travelling from the carts – now rolling steadily forward – to the horses, snapped back to Nazir's face. 'Where? And who?'

'Near the chowki, huzoor. I have not been able to discover who it was, but he was found murdered late this morning. It has driven people into a panic. They' – he gestured over his shoulder, at the house which he had just left – 'think they could well be next. There are others too, terrified that they will be murdered in their beds. First that cloth merchant, then that old woman who disappeared. And now this.'

But Muzaffar had stopped listening. He had whirled about and gone bounding back up to the gate, scattering his servitors like a flock of pigeons trying to escape a stone flung into their midst. 'Which way did Begum Sahiba go this morning?' he asked, looking at each face in turn, his own anxious.

The stable hand looked as if he knew, but it was the

doorkeeper – long enough in Muzaffar's service to be aware that he would not be punished if his answer was not to the liking of his master – who answered. 'That way, huzoor,' he gestured. The stable hand, watching over his shoulder, encountered Muzaffar's eye and nodded.

Muzaffar's gaze moved across the street, his glance taking in the now milling crowds. A man on horseback would be slowed down in traffic such as this; a man on foot would go much faster. He sent Nazir off at a sprint, into the haveli and Muzaffar's own room, to fetch his dagger. While the young man was gone, Muzaffar gave Javed some quick instructions: to keep the house in order, to ensure that the servants stayed in and did not take it into their heads to desert – and, if any official from the chowki or the thana came visiting, to get them to wait. 'In any case, I am going in the direction of the chowki,' he added as an afterthought.

Then, with his dagger now firmly tucked into his cummerbund and his face set, he moved off at a brisk pace, weaving his way between the crowds.

☙

Closer to the chowki, things were worse, as Muzaffar had feared they would be. There were more families bundling up their belongings – few or abundant – and fleeing. There was more shouting, and more panic. There was more jostling, more pushing and shoving in an attempt to get away.

Muzaffar paused, trying in vain to look over the sea of heads, curving cart-roofs, and the occasional palanquin. It was useless; there were too many obstructions. He stood on tiptoe, but even with his impressive height, it did not help. A few paces ahead, though, he could see the spreading canopy of a banyan tree. He knew that tree; he had passed it often enough to know that built around its trunk was a high platform of packed earth.

Muzaffar set off, determined to climb the tree if he had to, to get a better view.

He did not need to climb the tree, after all. Not even one of its lower branches; the platform elevated him sufficiently. Once up on it, Muzaffar began systematically to examine the scene before him, his gaze moving steadily from east to west, zigzagging north and south as it swept the area, searching for something familiar. Right at the end of the street, on the periphery of his vision, was the solid little stone hut that served as a chowki. That seemed to be the centre of considerable activity. A mob had congregated outside it, and Muzaffar could see that a couple of soldiers, instantly recognizable by their brown leather tunics and their lances, were struggling to keep the crowd at bay. They were heavily outnumbered, and Muzaffar wondered how long they would be able to prevail. The apprehension in him was fast turning to panic. If – and the very thought filled him with dread – the fear and anger of the crowd overcame their fear of the law, a riot may ensue. Where was Shireen?

At the chowki, a sudden hubbub broke out. A well-placed thrust with the flat end of a lance, and a soldier managed to push back. A small knot of particularly obstreperous young men scattered, stumbling and toppling over each other in their attempt to get out of the way.

In the window that seemed to open momentarily through the crowd, Muzaffar glimpsed a palanquin, borne by four harried-looking kahaars. A palanquin, painted deep blue. Beside it, leading a horse and making very slow progress, was a man Muzaffar knew well enough. It was his servant, Rashid.

ଓ

'What possessed you?!' Muzaffar asked, with a fierce glare that would have wilted Shireen had she been looking at him.

But she was not looking at him. She was sitting, head bowed, on a white-sheeted mattress in the main chamber of the mahal sara. Deep within her domain, a feminine figure swathed in a crimson-embroidered pashmina shawl that covered most of her, revealing only the neckline of her moss-green peshwaaz and the hem of her crimson-and-white striped pyjamas. She had dressed up, in the very height of fashion, for her visit. At any other time, Muzaffar might have been more intent on admiring her. At the moment, his anger, brought on by fear of what might have happened to her, had swamped every other emotion.

'Well?'

She did not move a muscle.

Muzaffar had been pacing the room all this while, hands clenched into fists behind his back. 'Shireen,' he said, his voice low and ominous.

She looked up at that. But, instead of answering his question, she asked one of her own. 'Why were you not surprised that Basharat had been killed?'

Muzaffar paused in his pacing, thrown offguard by her question. It was a momentary lapse, however. 'I am the one asking the questions, Shireen. Not you,' he snapped back.

'I shall tell you the answer, Jang Sahib, to your question. But that is not what you want, do you? You already know why I had gone, and where. Otherwise you might not have been able to find me.' She lowered her chin again, looking down at her henna-tinted hands. 'How did you know what had happened? How did you know where to find me?'

Muzaffar looked at her with a mix of admiration and frustration. Finally, having concluded that Shireen could not be domineered and pushed into admitting what she did not consider a mistake, he gave way. 'I was told that you had taken Ruqayya with you. And you did not have her sit in the palanquin with you; she walked alongside. When you first arrived in Dilli, we had discussed that. You had said you did not want Ruqayya to have to walk long distances – so I deduced that this time, you were not going a long way.'

Shireen nodded, following his reasoning.

'But you are not used to taking a maid along with you even on other visits. Even when you call at a haveli nearby, you manage with the help of the manservant who escorts you. So if you took Ruqayya along, it must have been with a definite purpose in mind.'

Shireen glanced up, her eyes keen and bright.

'And you left while I was asleep, in my room. Had I been up and about, I might have asked where you were going. I might have – no, I would have, even you know that – stopped you. With me asleep, you could slip out. And not tell anyone, except the kahaars who bore your palanquin, where you were headed. It seemed obvious that you had slunk off somewhere I would not have approved of your going.' He heaved a sigh, and as if drained of his will to keep standing, seated himself on the mattress opposite her.

'The house from which that maidservant Ameena vanished. Next door to the house where the cloth merchant Aadil lived before he was murdered. You've been trying to persuade me to poke my nose into that case, and when you realized I wouldn't do it, you decided to take matters into your own hands. That's why you took Ruqayya along, didn't you? You could introduce yourself to the lady of the house, and be solicitous without appearing meddlesome. Your maid, as is the way with servants, would find herself almost certainly taken away into some other corner of the mahal sara, to be entertained by the servants there.'

Shireen flushed.

'You must have instructed her, of course. To keep her ears and eyes open for anything she might hear about Ameena, or even Aadil. Anything suspicious. Well? Did your assistant prove her worth?' He snapped out the last sentence.

'I beg your pardon,' Shireen said, in a small and contrite voice. 'I did not' – she hesitated, swallowed, and then shook her head. 'No, I will not pretend I did not mean to go behind your back. Khan Sahib may have put you off investigating this case – '

'Any case.'

She gave him a baleful look. 'I should hope not. But. No matter what Khan Sahib may have made you do – whether of your own volition or because you really do not wish to incur his fury – that has nothing to do with my curiosity. I wanted to know what had happened. It seems too much of a coincidence that two adjoining households should be struck by two murders and what looks like a kidnapping, all in the course of a few days. Surely there is something amiss there.'

'And what would you have done had you discovered the truth? Gone to Khan Sahib?'

Shireen reached up and tucked behind her ear a stray tendril of hair that had escaped from under her dupatta. Her earrings, dangling paisleys studded with pearls and enamelled with green, shimmered with the movement. 'I would have come to you. As I have now.'

'You did not come to me. I brought you here.'

She glared back at him, the defiance in her gaze unmistakable. 'Jang Sahib, I was headed back home when you found me. Had I been meaning to go to the kotwali – or to visit Khan Sahib and Zeenat Aapa's haveli – that is not the direction I would have taken.'

'So you did find out something. What?'

Shireen blinked, caught off guard by the sudden change in Muzaffar. She gaped in what her very proper aunt would have referred to as an unladylike way, and even went so far as to gulp. 'Do you mean,' she mumbled, when he continued to gaze steadily at her, 'you – you do not mind?'

'Ah. Now who is the one to ask questions to which the

answers are already known?' Muzaffar's eyes twinkled as he gave her a quick smile, an indication that his sense of humour, suppressed ever since Khan Sahib had ticked him off so roundly, had resurfaced. 'I would have thought you would have flung this at me, but perhaps it is up to me to remind you. "Those who are guiltless are brave in speech; only he who gives false weight has fear of the inspector."'

'Sa'adi's Bostan? You quote my favourite back at me, Jang Sahib?'

'I could not resist the temptation,' Muzaffar admitted. 'I would think you would have sprung that on me to convince me of your guiltlessness.'

Shireen looked discomfited. 'I do not think I could have mustered up the courage to spout Bostan at you when you were angry.' She paused, giving herself – and him – time to get over the awkwardness of the disagreement that had sprung up between them. After a moment, she said, 'but you still haven't told me why the news of Basharat's murder did not surprise you.'

ଓ

'Somebody had been murdered, that much I knew; Nazir had told me that. The closer I got to the chowki, the thicker grew the crowds, the worse their panic. I had already been told, too, that the man had been found murdered late this morning. If it were a complete stranger – somebody you did not even know about, somebody unconnected to this affair – I think you would have come straight home. After all, there are dozens, even hundreds, of men in this mohallah. If, while you were away visiting, you had heard that there had been a murder, I would imagine you would have returned at once. Even if only to beat me over the head with your assertions that I should be doing the chowkidar's work for him – '

'Jang Sahib! I do not beat you over the head!'

– 'but if something sensational had happened at the very same household,' Muzaffar continued, pointedly ignoring the interruption, 'you might have stayed back both out of curiosity and courtesy. Or you may have been asked to stay back while the chowkidar carried out a preliminary investigation and asked questions.'

'The chowkidar did come,' Shireen admitted, 'but he did not ask to speak to me. I stayed on because I was curious, and because Nilofer – that is Basharat's sister-in-law, Ameena's mistress – was very insistent that I should wait and be by her side. Not that she allowed the chowkidar to question her, but...' she broke into a mischievous smile. 'She is quite a character, that one. You would find her intriguing, Jang Sahib.'

Khan Sahib's words came back to Muzaffar. No; he had promised – in a fit of pique, yes, but he had promised nevertheless – that he would not interfere in the work of the kotwali. It was none of his business. Ameena's disappearance was none of his business, and the slaying of her mistress's brother-in-law was no business of his either.

And yet, because he was incorrigibly inquisitive, he could not bring himself to tell Shireen to hold her tongue, to not tell him any more. He wanted to know, even if he could do nothing about it. The thought crossed his mind that if he did deduce something of any importance – something that could possibly throw some light on any of these recent happenings in the neighbourhood – he would not be able to rest easy unless he had informed the thanedar. Which, of course, would be tantamount to informing Khan Sahib.

Shireen was watching him with mounting impatience. She was obviously eager to tell him, even if he showed no signs of wanting to know more. Muzaffar shrugged. 'If you say so.'

She looked crestfallen at that noncommittal remark. Then, as if deciding that she would tell him whether he liked it or not, Shireen went on. 'She is very beautiful. By far the most beautiful woman I have ever seen. And, oh, so very aware of it, too. Henna on her hands' – she looked down fleetingly at her own palms, and winced – 'and not fading atrociously, like mine is.' She continued. 'Kohl on her eyelids, her cheeks reddened, and her lips red with paan. She even wears missi, you know.'

Muzaffar grimaced. He had seen the occasional fashionable woman – a dancing girl at a party, or a wealthy lady too vain to consider it improper to allow her face to be seen in public – using missi. It was a black powder, ground from a dried herb and rubbed liberally into the gums and on the inside of lips to turn them an inky hue. The better to highlight the evenness, the whiteness and the beauty of a woman's teeth, it was said. Muzaffar privately thought it looked grotesque.

'And her clothes. Her jewellery. Bangles up to her armpits. Everything of the finest money can buy – her pearls must have cost a fortune in themselves. Five strings, and each perfectly matched. With a massive pendant,' Shireen held her forefinger and thumb apart, about an inch and a half separating the two, 'consisting of a diamond set in gold, with little diamonds and rubies studded all around the edge.' Shireen heaved a sigh that was halfway to a shudder. 'Can you imagine? Wearing all of that, and clad in garments finer than what I got married in – and she assured me that she had not been intending to go anywhere, and had not been expecting visitors! Just to sit at home, all dolled up.'

She shook her head, as if doubting her own recollection of the woman she had met. Or, and Muzaffar understood the emotion, marvelling at the vanity of this Nilofer. Or pitying her for having nothing better to do with her time than to spend it in something as futile as decorating a body that would eventually be nothing more than dust.

He privately agreed with her. This all-absorbing fascination with decorating oneself, while leaving the mind blank and unadorned, did not appeal to him, either. That – the importance of the intellect, the love for books and learning, of widening one's horizons – was what had first attracted him to Shireen, and he continued to be grateful that he had found a woman so different from most of her contemporaries.

But to agree at this stage, to say that he did think Nilofer seemed like an utterly vain and unlikeable creature, would be to make Shireen think he was interested in the tale she had to tell. It would be safer, by far, to remain silent.

Shireen looked at him, injured. 'Do you really not desire to know any more, Jang Sahib?' she asked, when he did not speak. 'Truly?'

'What would be the use of it, Shireen? I have already promised that I would not take an active interest in anything that is the domain of Khan Sahib and his twelve thanedars. What, then, is the use of my curiosity in this matter? If I were to know, I would still be powerless to act. That would be even more frustrating.'

Shireen's gaze was steady. He could almost imagine the wheels of her mind turning, fitting one fact to another. Recalling his resentment against Khan Sahib's admonitions. Weighing that against the innate curiosity of the husband she now knew somewhat. Realizing, perhaps, that he was torn between wanting to know and putting up a front for the sake of it.

'Ah, well,' she said finally, with an affected sigh. 'I doubt if you will find anything at all interesting in what happened today. Nothing, to be sure, that could cast a light on the disappearance of that maid, Ameena. Or the murder of Basharat.'

And, before he quite knew what she was doing, Shireen had begun telling him about how she had arrived at the house of Basharat and his brother Parvez.

ʘ

She had, by getting the servant Rashid to ask a vegetable-seller sitting near the chowki, found the house of Basharat and his brother Parvez – the glamorous Nilofer's husband. 'It is not a very large haveli,' Shireen explained. 'And not lavishly appointed. Fine enough without being luxurious. I think Parvez must spend all his money keeping his begum in style.'

On their arrival at the house, Rashid had told the doorkeeper who the visitor in the palanquin was. A servant had been sent rushing off to the mahal sara to announce Jang Sahib's Begum Sahiba's arrival. Another – a woman – had come, bearing on a small salver a glass of sherbet and a paan, which she had offered to Shireen through the parted curtains of the palanquin.

A few minutes later, a more self-assured maid had arrived, to bid Shireen welcome. Rashid had been whisked away to another part of the house. Ruqayya had followed the maid into the mahal sara, with the kahaars bearing the palanquin, which they left outside the women's quarters before retreating. Shireen had been assisted out of the palanquin by the maid, and had come face to face with the beauteous Nilofer, who had emerged from the mahal sara once the kahaars had departed.

'It all sounds very proper,' Muzaffar remarked, though a little grudgingly. It seemed churlish to continue to maintain a stony silence when Shireen was so obviously intent on telling him all that had transpired. And yet, he dare not sound too encouraging. It was like trying to keep one's balance on a bowstring.

From the expression on Shireen's face, Muzaffar could tell that his unenthusiastic response had disappointed her. She had hoped to have caught his attention by this point in her narrative, and she had not. Rather, she was too new a wife, too new in his life, to be able to recognize the very subtle signs that Muzaffar Jang, for all his lackadaisical demeanour, was actually deeply interested.

She persevered, however. 'It was. Very much what one

would expect in the household of a petty nobleman. Not that Basharat and Parvez are noble – not from what I could gather. Wealthy, certainly, but not noble, even if Parvez's wife behaves as if she were Shahzadi Jahanara herself.'

'Where did the wealth come from? Trade?' The question had slipped out before he could stop it. Muzaffar saw the gleam of triumph in Shireen's eyes. It was too late, however, to withdraw the question or to pretend indifference any longer. She knew it now, knew that he was listening to every word she said.

With a straight face, and without drawing attention to that lapse in his supposed disinterest, she replied. 'And in very varied commodities, too. It seems the two brothers deal in anything that is likely to bring in a profit: textiles, gemstones, carpets, all those fancy things the Europeans bring on their ships. Those clocks and coats and hats. Parvez used to live in Surat till a couple of years back,' she added. Of course, thought Muzaffar; Surat was the city for an ambitious merchant to set up shop. It was the major port on the western coast, and ships from across the world – as far east as China, as far west as England – stopped here to offload and take on cargos of everything from silks to spices, wood, gold, and diamonds. He remembered, too, what Ameena had said, that morning when he had met her in the street. She had mentioned that she had been away in Surat when Parvez and Basharat had sold off their home to Aadil and shifted into the house next door. And Ameena was the maid of Nilofer, Parvez's wife.

Muzaffar wondered if Nilofer hailed from Surat. Had the marriage been contracted in that port city? Perhaps Nilofer was the daughter of a wealthy Surat merchant; that would account for her expensive tastes.

Shireen had reached for the pitcher of water next to the mattress and poured some for herself. 'They had originally been living in Agra,' she said, after a sip, 'but when the Baadshah decided to move to Dilli, Basharat and Parvez thought a shift to the new capital would be more lucrative for them. So they moved as well. Some years back – six or seven, Nilofer was not very clear when – they decided that they would do even better for themselves if one of them moved to Surat.'

'And Parvez was the one chosen?'

She put down the goblet. 'Yes. Nilofer is from that city too. Ameena had looked after her and her brother Shamsuddin all their lives. She brought them up, really. So when Nilofer got married, she brought Ameena with her.' Her brow crinkled as she thought back to her conversation with the other woman. 'She appears to have been very fond of Nilofer – or so I gathered from what Nilofer told me.'

'And?'

'And Nilofer does not know where Ameena could have vanished,' Shireen admitted. 'I tried to prod her, to ask if Ameena could have had some pressing business that could have required her to suddenly leave – even without informing Nilofer – but no, there was nothing she could think of. All she said was that Ameena had seemed rather more excited and nervous than she had been the past few days.'

'Ameena had been "excited and nervous the past few days"? And why? Did your friend know?'

'She is hardly my friend, Jang Sahib,' Shireen pointed out. 'She said Ameena had been jittery and fidgeting since the past few days – since their neighbour, the cloth merchant Aadil, was found dead.'

'She would be. She had seen his corpse, even if only briefly.'

'No. I mean, she had, but why should that have kept her all excited and tense for so long? She had, from all Nilofer told me, lived a long and eventful life, by no means secluded and protected. She had seen dead men before. She had seen family members die or be dragged off to prison. She would be shaken by a murder in the house next door, but she would not let it prey on her mind for days altogether.'

'How do you know that? Is that an arrow shot into the night, Shireen, just because you know Ameena was old?'

'Of course not. I am repeating what Nilofer said.' Shireen gave her husband a look of reproach, and he gave her an apologetic shrug in return.

'And she hardly seemed tense about it, now that I think of it,' he said. 'Excited, certainly, but not scared. More curious than anything else.' His eyes narrowed suddenly as something occurred to him. 'She had seen family members dragged off to prison? Who?'

Shireen looked shamefaced. 'I didn't ask. Nilofer was talking, and I didn't want to interrupt her, for fear she would lose the thread of what she had been saying.'

Muzaffar was tempted to tell Shireen to visit Nilofer a second time and glean that bit of information. He restrained himself with difficulty and, keeping his voice as level as possible, asked, 'What else did she tell you?'

Shireen's eyes brightened at this implied admission that her husband was at least ready to begin an investigation. 'No, Shireen,' Muzaffar added, quick to see her reaction. 'I am not plunging into this. Since you have already begun digging yourself in, we might as well see what we can glean from it. If I find anything of value that may help the thanedar in his investigations, I shall tell him. But, as Allah is my witness, I shall not step into the thanedar's territory.'

His wife nodded, deflated, but not entirely. Muzaffar supposed she felt that this was better than nothing; that Muzaffar should imply he was interested, even if he continued to insist that he would report everything to the law.

'Nilofer did not have much to add,' Shireen said. 'She last saw Ameena the night before the maid disappeared. Ameena had attended to her, helping her undress and remove her jewellery before she went to bed. The next morning, Ameena was nowhere to be found.'

'So Nilofer was the last person to see Ameena in the house?'

'No. One of the other maids said that she had seen Ameena around midnight. Perhaps a couple of hours after she had left Nilofer's chamber.'

'Midnight? That's late, indeed.'

'At any rate, that was the last anyone saw of her. The next morning, when she didn't come to Nilofer's chamber long past the usual time, Nilofer sent another maid to check. That was when they discovered she had disappeared.'

'Along with those few precious belongings of hers? You mentioned that her blankets were still there? And some other things?'

Shireen nodded. 'That was what Nilofer said. Blankets, a few old clothes, a worn quilt. A small stool that Nilofer had gifted her. Nothing of great value.'

'What could an old servant have possessed that could be of great value?' Muzaffar asked. 'No matter how wealthy the mistress, I doubt if the maid could have had anything more than a few strings of beads – or, if this Nilofer Begum is exceptionally generous, a gold bangle? You know better, Shireen, tell me. What do you think? Did Nilofer say what was missing?'

'She just said "trinkets". Beads, I suppose, but I did not ask. She did say, though, that not one piece of jewellery had been left behind, no matter how small.' Shireen's forehead furrowed as she thought back to the conversation. 'And, yes. A shawl, and a pair of leather slippers. A couple of dupattas.'

'Which one may assume she might even have been wearing when she left the house.'

Shireen looked at Muzaffar sharply. '"Left the house"?' she echoed. 'Do you think she went of her own accord? I thought she was abducted.'

'It seems unlikely. Would she have been wandering about the house, or even sleeping in her own room, wearing all the trinkets she possessed? And I doubt a kidnapper would give her time to go about gathering up all her jewels before dragging her off.' Muzaffar reached forward to pull the pitcher of water towards himself. 'No, Shireen. I think Ameena left of her own accord, and did so on foot, I think, carrying nothing that would be too heavy or bulky, or would slow her down. Or was not strictly essential.'

'The blankets?' Shireen looked dubious. 'The quilt? In this weather?' She shivered involuntarily. 'It is too cold to leave behind things like that.'

Muzaffar chewed at his moustache. 'Which would mean that wherever she was going, she was sure someone would provide shelter and warm quilts.' He squinted out of the window, to where the shadows had begun to lengthen perceptibly. A squawking flock of green parakeets, long tails streaming behind them, flew noisily overhead and into the trees behind the haveli. The day was waning.

ঙ

'No one saw her going,' Shireen volunteered. 'They have a manservant who acts as doorkeeper during the day and sleeps in a small room next to the main door at night. If she went out that way, she was quiet enough to not disturb him.'

Down the corridor outside came the sound of footsteps. The steward, Javed, appeared in the doorway, his eyes carefully averted from Shireen, who had quickly veiled herself and pulled her pashmina shawl into place, covering her hands. 'Huzoor,' he asked, 'shall I have someone light the lamps here?'

Muzaffar nodded. 'How are things outside, Javed?' he added. 'In the street? The noise has lessened, I think.'

'There are fewer people about, huzoor. The chowkidar went around the mohallah and talked to several of the householders. Most have gone back to their homes.'

Javed lifted the two chiraghdaans that sat in the room, one on the floor near Muzaffar, the other in a niche next to the door. With a bow made clumsy because both his hands were occupied, he left the room. Somewhere in the back of the house, perhaps outdoors, where a mess of spilled oil or soot would make little difference – or could easily be covered up with loose soil – a lamp man would get down to work. He would clean the lamps and place oil-soaked wicks in each of the little brass bowls that formed the chiraghdaans. He would add more oil to each bowl, and light the wicks before the lamps, now illuminated, were brought back to the room.

'Was Ruqayya able to find out anything?' Muzaffar asked, when Javed had gone.

Shireen shook her still-veiled head. 'I have not had a chance to talk to her yet. Shall I send for her?'

'In a while. Tell me the rest. You still haven't told me about Basharat's death – when was that discovered?'

'Ah, yes.' Shireen sat up, pulling back the dupatta from a face suddenly animated. 'That came as quite a shock. Nilofer and I were sitting and talking. I had been trying to get her to talk about Ameena, and about Aadil – though Nilofer did not seem to know anything about Aadil, or to be even mildly concerned that their neighbour had been murdered. She was more intent on finding out where I had bought my earrings from, and whether it was true that the best zardozi was to be bought in Agra.

'I must have been there about three-quarters of an hour when we heard a commotion in one of the further rooms – in the mardana, the men's quarters. Nilofer did not pay much attention at first,' she broke off, her forehead crinkling into a frown as she recalled the morning's events. 'She doesn't seem to be even especially interested in what goes on in her own home, you know,' Shireen said, 'almost as if she had detached herself from the rest.'

'Who are the rest? Her husband, of course. And Basharat, may Allah grant peace to his soul. But who else?'

'No one else. That is all the family there is, in this house. There are servants, of course. But I got the impression' – she nibbled at her lip – 'that Nilofer did not much care about anyone. She seemed so completely absorbed in her own little world of clothes and jewels and cosmetics... and when that hubbub broke out, she simply made a face and said, "Some quarrel, no doubt. They are always quarrelling". It astonished me. Not just what she said, but the way she said it. With so much disdain.'

She shook her head, as if shaking off the distasteful memory of Nilofer. 'Shortly after, a maid came rushing in with the news that Basharat had been found dead in his bedchamber. To give her credit, Nilofer did look shaken. But not shaken enough to lose her presence of mind, or her selfishness. All she said was that she did not want to be pestered by the chowkidar or his men. That if any of them sought an audience with her, they should be told that she knew nothing, and did not like to be disturbed.'

'As if that would keep them from questioning her. She could be ordered to come forth for questioning. In purdah, of course, but she could not refuse a direct order.'

There was a discreet cough outside the door; Javed had returned. With him came a servant, bringing the lit lamps. Muzaffar waited for the lamps to be placed, for Javed to ask if Begum Sahiba had any special instructions to be passed on to the cook for dinner, and for Shireen to give whatever orders she had. When the steward and the servant had gone, he turned back to his wife.

She did not wait for him to ask a question. 'The maid who brought the news said that Basharat's servant entered his bedchamber late this morning, when Basharat had still not arisen. He found the room empty, and Basharat's bed as it had been the previous evening. He hadn't slept in it.'

'Where was he found, then?'

'In the room that he and Parvez use as an office. It's in the public part of the house.' All havelis were segregated into private and public areas, and Muzaffar, from the mere mention that the office was in the public part of the house, could guess that it would have been frequented by visitors. Business acquaintances, traders, men from whom the two brothers had bought goods.

'The steward of the household had seen the lamp burning in the room around midnight. Basharat and Parvez, it seems, were in the habit of often working late into the night. He had stopped by, seen that Basharat was still at work, and had been told that nothing was needed; Basharat still had much to do, and would work an hour longer. Perhaps more.

'So, when one of the servants was heading towards the office to clean it this morning, the steward cautioned him. There had been instances in the past when Basharat had dozed off against the bolsters, amidst his papers. And, sure enough, when the servant peeped in, carefully, he found that Basharat was slumped over his desk, seemingly fast asleep.'

'But dead?'

Shireen's face was sombre as she inclined her head. 'They did not discover that until much later. Perhaps the steward and the rest of the servants were too caught up in their other duties; perhaps they did not think it proper to disturb Basharat. But his personal servant did go in, and discovered that the man was dead. He had been stabbed in the back, and the dagger pulled out and taken away.'

'Stabbed? There would have been blood. Enough of it to be seen. The servant who had looked in earlier must have been extremely near-sighted, to have overlooked a detail like that.'

'I heard that the dead man had been clad in a dark choga. Black, perhaps. The blood did not show. And he was sitting at the far end of the room.'

'I suppose the curtains were drawn and the lamps had all burned out,' added Muzaffar. 'It would have been dingy in a room like that.'

Shireen nodded.

'What else did you learn?'

'Nothing. I sat around, keeping my eyes open and my ears pricked for any titbit that might come my way, but that was all I could learn. Eventually, when I saw it was futile, I decided to head back home.'

Muzaffar sat staring into the flickering flames of the chiraghdaan in front of him, his eyes brooding. 'Perhaps your maid Ruqayya may have learned something more,' he said finally. 'Not merely about Ameena, but possibly also about Basharat. Let us have her sent for, shall we?'

☙

Ruqayya, entering the room a few minutes later, looked apprehensively towards Muzaffar. She had been present, after all, when he had come upon Shireen's entourage on its way home, and she could not have failed to notice that he had looked furious. Whether that fury had been directed only at a recalcitrant wife, or whether it was also going to be vented on those who had accompanied her on that expedition, was a moot point. Muzaffar could understand her fear, and motioned to Shireen to speak.

'I have told Jang Sahib why I took you along with me to Nilofer Begum's house, Ruqayya,' Shireen said. Now that none of the menservants were in the room, she had unveiled herself. Her very expression – carefully schooled to look unperturbed and kind – was calculated to put the maid at her ease. 'Jang Sahib and I would like to know if you were able to discover anything.'

As far as the murder of Basharat was concerned, Ruqayya

knew as much or as little as her mistress; it had all been a whirl of conjecture, with rumours flying swifter than arrows in a pitched battle. There was nothing that Ruqayya could contribute on that topic that Muzaffar had not already heard from his wife.

On the subject of Ameena, however, Ruqayya had considerably more information. 'They all called her Ameena Bibi,' she said. 'She commanded a lot of respect. Some fear, too, I think.' Ruqayya's informants had been two maids, one of them the woman who had greeted Shireen on her arrival, the other a younger one, perhaps only fifteen years old. They had been, to start with, a little cautious, the girl even shy. But Ruqayya, well tutored by her mistress, had remarked that Jang Sahib had been at Aadil's house with Kotwal Sahib the very morning the cloth merchant was found dead. She had added that he had met Ameena Bibi, and that seemingly offhand remark had been enough to encourage the two others to speak up. Ah, Ameena Bibi. That was another mystery.

'Begum Sahiba heard that someone had seen Ameena the night she disappeared,' Muzaffar remarked, interrupting Ruqayya's narrative. 'Another of the maids.'

'The younger one who was talking to me, huzoor.' Ruqayya's head bobbed vigorously, both eager to please as well as nervous. 'She had seen Ameena Bibi that night. At around midnight, she said.' She hesitated, perhaps waiting for a sign from her master and mistress. Shireen murmured, 'Go on, Ruqayya. Tell us. What was Ameena Bibi doing at that hour? For that matter, what was this other maid doing, at such a late hour?'

'Nilofer Begum had given her a garment that had to be cleaned of a bad stain. It was a very delicate silk, and finely embroidered too. And Nilofer Begum had said she wanted to wear it the next morning, when she went to Chandni Chowk. Ismat – that is the maid, the girl – had no choice.'

Shireen inclined her head in understanding. Muzaffar, a

little puzzled, looked across at his wife and she gave him a barely perceptible smile.

'Yes, Ruqayya,' she said. 'I understand. So this girl, Ismat, was busy trying to get the garment clean and ready for Nilofer Begum to wear the next day. And how did she happen to see Ameena?'

'Ismat was on her way to the well in the courtyard at the back, Begum Sahiba. In the far wall of the courtyard is the door which looks out onto the lane behind the house. Ismat said she stepped out of the room, and was crossing the courtyard when she heard a low voice somewhere in the shadows.'

The story was told, with Ruqayya building up the suspense and keeping her two listeners both enthralled and, at least on the part of Muzaffar, somewhat impatient too. She would have made a good daastaango, he thought: one of those professional storytellers who made a fine art out of recounting a tale, embellishing it and drawing it out till the listener would pay gladly to know what came next. Muzaffar hoped Ruqayya was confining herself to drawing out the tale, not embellishing it.

Nilofer's maid Ismat may be young, but from Ruqayya's account, it seemed she did not lack intelligence. Ismat had concluded that at such an unearthly hour, when all the rest of the household was asleep, anybody cowering near the outside wall and conversing was doing so with the intention of not being discovered. So she too had immediately slid into the shadow of the nearest wall, had crouched and removed her slippers – which were inclined to squeak – and had edged forward slowly to listen. She had not dared to creep too close, because the moonlight was bright. The result was that even when she strained to listen, she could only catch snatches of the conversation. Worse, the intervening wall prevented Ismat from catching even the merest hint of what was said by the person outside.

She did, however, hear the voice of the person nearer to her, the person inside the courtyard. It was Ameena Bibi, speaking 'in that distinctive nasal voice of hers, even though she was whispering'. Ameena Bibi, wrapped in her large brown shawl, almost trailing to the flagstones, her ear pressed to the wooden door, one hand cupping it in an attempt to hear better. 'I told you! How could I have known? And it's your fault, too; you knew what he looked like – ' the rest of the sentence had been swallowed up, or she had been interrupted by the other; Ismat could not tell.

There was some more murmuring, and then Ameena Bibi had said, 'Yes. If the lamp burns even at this hour – then you can be sure. No, not tonight; they've retired. Tomorrow; try tomorrow.' There was silence. Ismat heard some muted sounds, indistinct murmurs which may have been expressions of assent from Ameena Bibi, or mere acknowledgment that she was listening.

Suddenly, Ameena Bibi stepped back from the door, and almost simultaneously, something flew over the wall, into the courtyard, landing with a soft thud on the flagstones. Whatever it was, it had been a blur of white in the moonlight, and it stood out against the relative darkness of the courtyard as Ameena Bibi hurried forward and picked it up, tucking it inside her shawl.

'Wait,' Muzaffar said. 'Before you go any further – did Ismat see what it was? Or could she make any guesses?'

Ruqayya looked shamefaced. 'I did not ask, huzoor. I think she would have told me if she had seen what it was.'

'Ameena Bibi picked it up and tucked it away. Then what?'

'There had been some more somewhat muffled whispering at the door. Ameena had seemed more hurried now – or perhaps the person outside had been eager to leave. The old woman, wrapped in her shawl, had nodded vigorously a few times, had muttered 'Yes, yes,' and had finally said, 'Allah keep you safe.' She had paused, and then had said, a little hesitantly, 'You have left instructions? I will not be turned away?'

The answer to that, of course, had not been audible to Ismat, but Ameena Bibi had murmured a soft word of thanks before bidding her unseen friend farewell. Then, huddling into her shawl, she had gone off towards her own room.

'And Ismat? Did she follow her to see what Ameena was about?'

Ruqayya shook her head. 'No, huzoor. She did not have the time – she had to finish cleaning Nilofer Begum's peshwaaz. She had already wasted time enough. Anyway, she said Ameena Bibi had been headed towards her own room, so she guessed the old woman was finally going to bed. Perhaps they would get to know what that was all about the next morning.'

That was all Ruqayya could offer by way of gossip gleaned. She had kept her eyes and ears open during the visit, but there had been no more information forthcoming. Not because the maids – Ismat, in particular – were reticent or suspicious, but because it seemed there really was nothing to be shared. Ismat, to her credit, said that she had gone the next morning into the courtyard to see if she could find any sign of whatever it was that had been thrown into the courtyard. But that had been late in the morning, long after a zealous sweeper had cleaned the courtyard well.

'What do you think?' Shireen asked Muzaffar after Ruqayya had left the room.

Muzaffar had sunk into a reverie, the frown on his face showing that he was deep in thought. 'Wh – what?' he mumbled, in absent-minded response to Shireen's question. When she looked on enquiringly, without repeating what she had said, he gave an embarrassed smile and apologized. 'I was thinking,' he explained. 'That conversation – even though we only have one side of it to go by – sounds interesting.'

Shireen waited, her eyelashes veiling the brilliance of eyes that sparkled with eagerness to know more. Muzaffar, too canny to be fooled by those demurely lowered eyelids, was not fooled. It did his self-esteem no end of good to know that his wife thought so highly of him that she assumed he was halfway to the solution, just based on what he had learned from Ruqayya.

On the other hand, there was the fact that the suspicion that had taken seed in his mind might well mean that he would have to go – as he had vowed to do – to the thanedar. As a concerned citizen, it would be his duty to report even his suspicions to the authorities.

'Shireen,' he said, 'I think Ameena Bibi had something to do with the murder of Basharat. She may not have killed him herself; she could not have, I believe, considering she was an old woman and he a man in his prime, almost certainly stronger than her – but she was involved in the conspiracy to murder Basharat; of that I am almost sure.

'That remark about the lamp burning – at midnight? At "this hour"? And that it would mean they were still at work? That sounds suspiciously as if she were talking about Basharat and Parvez working on in their office after the rest of the household had gone to bed.'

'And to come "tomorrow" – that would fit with Basharat's murder, the next night,' Shireen added, horrified. She swallowed, staring into Muzaffar's face with eyes wide. 'Ya Allah.' Her voice was a mere breath. 'Could it be true?'

'It seems to be,' Muzaffar said, drily. 'But it does not take us much further. There is the fact that Ameena has vanished. She will need to be found before she can be questioned. And to search for one woman, not a very noteworthy woman either, in a city as vast as Dilli, is an almost impossible task.'

'Surely not for the thanedar.'

'True. Then all we can do is hope that the thanedar arrives at the same conclusion that we have reached. And that he decides it is worthwhile to search for Ameena Bibi and ask her some questions. Like who the man was whom she was talking to that night in the courtyard. And what he threw into the courtyard, which she picked up. And why she – the maid of Parvez's wife – would want to help someone murder Basharat.'

'Perhaps,' said Shireen in a hopeful voice, 'Basharat had wronged Parvez in some way? Cheated him out of money? Treated him unfairly? Some of these old servants are very loyal indeed. I could imagine that Ameena's loyalty to Nilofer might extend to Parvez as well.'

'Perhaps.'

'You do not think so, Jang Sahib?' Shireen asked, in an accusing tone.

'Who am I to think anything?' Muzaffar said. His voice was bitter. 'Yes, I admit I am interested; it would be foolish to try to hide that from you. But what Khan Sahib said still rankles. Perhaps I am being overly sensitive. Yet the truth remains; what he said is correct. It is not for a man like me – with no authority, no power – to go about questioning people or trying to investigate a crime that is no concern of mine.'

Shireen looked as if she was going to protest, but after a glance at Muzaffar's face, she remained silent.

She sat there, eyes lowered, long curling lashes brushing her cheeks. A glossy curl had broken loose of its moorings under her dupatta and now lay on her shoulder. Muzaffar reached out and caressed it, letting his fingers curve through its silken length. Shireen looked up and smiled at him, a small but genuine smile of warm affection.

'You smell wonderful,' Muzaffar murmured.

'It's an attar,' she said. 'Of jasmine. Too often overpowering, I think – but this one is special: so delicate, so elegant, don't you think? Zeenat Aapa's friend, the wife of that nawab – brought it for me as a wedding present. It's from Kanauj. The best attars are made in Kanauj, you know. I didn't know,' she added, in a beguilingly naïve way. Muzaffar could not help but smile.

Shireen was all honesty, all openness. He could not resist the temptation to bend forward and kiss her.

'Come, my love,' he said, getting to his feet. 'Let us go and have our dinner. It is late, and we have both had a tiring day.'

ଓଃ

The munshi who managed his jagir, his estates, came to spend half of the next day in discussions, bringing with him the news of his master's lands, and taking back with him the decisions, the money, and the greetings that Muzaffar sent for those who lived and worked on his land. There would be some rancour, for Muzaffar had been forced by powers beyond his control to extract revenues despite a poor crop. He had tried to be fair by ensuring that the burden of paying those taxes was distributed in such a way as to be heavier on the relatively wealthy farmers. They would smart at it, but they – and the rest of the populace – would perhaps also be grateful, even if grudgingly, for the wells Muzaffar had ordered dug, the seed he had ordered bought and distributed, and the gifts he had sent: sugarcane, grain, jaggery, cloth. These were hard times, and the hardest hit were – as ever – the poor. Guilt weighed on Muzaffar even as he bade farewell to his munshi.

The next three days were days of ennui. Muzaffar loitered about the house, trying to find things to do. He took a round of the entire haveli, all the way from the dalaan where he entertained guests, to the stables and the storehouses, into the very private depths of the mahal sara. He noted down what needed to be repaired or refurbished, had long discussions with his steward Javed, and gave instructions for some plaster to be relaid, some sections to be painted, and some new sheets to be purchased for the mattresses in the dalaan.

He tried to read, but even this – one of his favourite pastimes – was unsatisfying, because he found it well-nigh impossible to concentrate. He would open a book and begin reading, but find after half an hour that he was still on the first page, and that too with no knowledge of what he had been reading. His mind wandered, trying to make sense of all that he had learned in these past days. Of Aadil, of Ameena, of the man most recently murdered. There was too much to mull over, too much to wonder about. Too many questions rose in his mind, and, because he had vowed to himself that he would not ask them, they fermented, creating possible answers, suggesting theories, maddening him.

Shireen, although she cast him a reproachful glance now and then, had not attempted any further persuasion. He respected her for it. At the same time, in the perverse way of a restless, obstinate man, he resented the ease with which she had given up. He wondered how long he would have resisted if Shireen had gone on insisting that he investigate the murders of their mohallah on his own.

In the late afternoon of the third day, fed up with sitting at home, Muzaffar went out. His intention was to visit his friend Akram, a man as conforming as Muzaffar was maverick; as fashionable and obsessed with his own face and figure as Muzaffar was disinterested in himself; and as woolly-headed as Muzaffar was sharp-witted. A year back, Muzaffar would never have imagined that he could be friends with someone as different from him as Akram. But Akram, for all that he was different, was also a man of undoubted sincerity, an honest man, unpretentious for all his foppishness. A good man.

But Akram, his steward informed Muzaffar regretfully, was not at home. His father, an influential old nobleman, had summoned his son, and Akram had gone off this very afternoon to meet his parent. The steward did not know when Akram Sahib would return. He may, perhaps, even spend the night at his father's haveli.

Bored and restive, Muzaffar made his way to Chandni Chowk

and a qahwa khana he was particularly fond of. An animated discussion was in progress behind him, and he eavesdropped shamelessly. It appeared that the fort of Bidar was still besieged, and the garrison commander Sidi Marjan still showing no signs of weakening. The general opinion among the coffee-drinkers seemed to be that it was a matter of mere time before the armies under the Shahzada Aurangzeb and the Diwan-i-kul managed to break the siege. Muzaffar heard not a word of dissent, not a whisper of anything that might be considered sceptical of the prince's chances of winning the battle. It was as if everybody was convinced that Aurangzeb would return victorious, that he would bring back to Dilli long processions of elephants laden with jewels from the Deccan. And that the annexation of Bijapur would suddenly bring the Mughal Empire back from the edge of the precipice it was so precariously perched on.

It was disgusting, thought Muzaffar as he drank down the last of his coffee. The conversation – even though he had merely listened to it, not participated in it – had left a taste in his mouth as bitter as the brew. That people could be so naïve, lead such utterly blinkered lives, was astonishing. He wondered, with growing despair, how people could fail to see that the Baadshah had ruled too extravagantly, spending the Empire's diminishing funds in ill-afforded projects. Yes, perhaps a century from now, people would still stare in awe at the Taj Mahal or the Jama Masjid or even the Qila Mubarak; but the money that had gone into them could have been used more wisely, to prolong the life of the Empire. To institute agrarian and revenue reforms, to improve the land, strengthen trade. There were so many things that could have been done. Should have been done.

Instead, there were these magnificent projects, these treasury-draining expeditions, these thousands of leeches sucking vigorously away at the life blood of the Empire.

Muzaffar paid for his coffee and headed back home. He rode his horse down the main artery of Chandni Chowk – the straight road, with the water channel running down its length, from Fatehpuri Masjid down to the Jain temple facing the fort. At the Darwaza Dariba, the gateway that led into Dariba, he urged his horse on through the gate and into Dariba.

Dariba, originally Dar-e-be-baha, 'the pearl of unsurpassed lustre', was the ostentatious name of this street, and perhaps fitting too, for it was the street of the jewellers. On either side of the street, shaded by canopies of red and green velvet were shops that sold every conceivable ornament a woman – or a man – could want. There were jewellers here who catered to the most exacting of the royalty and the nobility. They would go, the jewellers themselves, not their assistants, to the homes of the ladies they sold their wares to. Spreading out, on strips of deep blue velvet and red silk, the finest jewels money could buy. Heavy baazubands or armlets; delicate churin or bangles, worn in sets of several churin each; gajrah, bracelets of gold and pearls – and those, just for the arms. There were, in addition, an array of ornaments meant for just about every part of the body, from the forehead down to the toes. The ladies would try them out, spend hours looking over the jewels, buying some there and then, placing orders for others that they wished made to so-and-so specifications, to match this piece of clothing or that piece of already owned jewellery.

The only thing Muzaffar had ever bought from Dariba had been an archer's ring. Meant to protect the wearer's thumb from the sharp bowstring that cut into it when the string and arrow were pulled back, the archer's ring sat broad on the inside of the thumb. The most basic were crafted from a piece of wood or horn, whittled down and shaped into a circle, broad on one side and narrow on the opposite. The more fashionable – the type worn by Akram, for instance, who perhaps had last lifted a bow as a boy, when at play – were of equally durable, but far more expensive materials. Jade, or gold, enamelled, or inlaid with precious stones. Muzaffar's had been a simpler one, of rock crystal, plainly cut and undecorated. He had bought it from a small shop which specialized in archer's rings, and the jeweller, Muzaffar remembered even now, had been utterly shocked that an amir – a man well able to afford a jade ring, adorned with gold wire and enamel – should buy such a sorry little thing.

He rode on, past the shop – it still did brisk business, though it appeared the jeweller had also started crafting turras and sarpeches, the turban ornaments that men wore on the front or the sides of their turbans.

'Muzaffar!'

Muzaffar reined in his horse and, still in his saddle, turned. 'Akram. I didn't notice you. Buying something?' He smiled; it was good to see his friend.

Akram was stepping out of the shop, a brilliantly dressed figure in a deep maroon choga, its hems embroidered in shades of blue, ranging from turquoise to the colour of the sky at midnight. His turban was the blue of the purest lapis, and a string of perfectly matched pearls hung around his neck. He was a vision of sartorial perfection. Muzaffar privately wondered if he would ever be able to carry off anything half as flamboyant with Akram's panache.

'A turra. Do you know, that one I had – do you remember, the cluster of pearls and rubies, with that brilliant white feather? – well, the feather had become a little bedraggled. And, really, there are some colours red just doesn't look good with. I can't wear it with my brown choga, for one.' He noticed the glazed look in Muzaffar's eyes, interpreted it correctly as disinterest in the finer details of fashion, and changed the topic. 'But what about you? What are you doing in Dariba? You are hardly one to frequent the jewellers'.'

'I was just passing through Dariba, on my home way home from Chandni Chowk.'

'Ah. Visiting Kotwal Sahib at his office? Are you helping

him in an investigation? It's been so long since I saw you, Muzaffar. Three weeks, at least – or has it been more? What have you been doing? What crimes have you solved, what baffling puzzles have you unravelled?'

It was meant, even Muzaffar could see, not completely in jest, even though Akram's tone was light-hearted. Akram had been a part of several of Muzaffar's adventures, and had seen, at close quarters, how Muzaffar worked. Even Muzaffar knew that Akram's respect for his abilities was genuine, his faith in Muzaffar's powers of deduction sincere. It made him feel oddly humble.

He toyed briefly with the idea of telling Akram that Khan Sahib had told him off for his investigations. The thought was only fleeting; he realized, almost as soon as it passed his mind, that it might sound complaining, the whining of a fretful child deprived of its favourite toy. There was, too, no need for Akram to know right now.

'Nothing,' he said. 'Life has been mundane. And I was not visiting the kotwali; just a qahwa khana.'

Akram made a face. 'That horrible liquid. How can you bring yourself to drink – to enjoy! – something so bitter?' The moue turned into a sunny grin. 'But I am glad to find you here. I was meaning to visit you one of these days, to check on you. Are you over the excitement of being married? Have you settled in? Has Begum Sahiba been shown all the wonders of Dilli by her doting husband?'

Muzaffar dismounted. Akram seemed in no hurry to end the conversation, and a long chat between a tall man astride an impressive stallion and a man of average height, standing on his own two feet, was difficult. The horse, too, had been getting increasingly skittish and difficult to control. Muzaffar guided him away to the side of the street, away from the flow of traffic: the pedestrians, the many palanquins, other horses.

'Shireen is quite at home now,' Muzaffar admitted. 'Zeenat

Aapa has been a most affectionate sister-in-law. She has taken Shireen around to all the bazaars, has introduced her to all the ladies of her acquaintance, has helped her make friends. Left to my own devices, I would probably just have taken my wife on a trip down the Yamuna, showing her all the birds.' He grinned, a little self-deprecating. 'And, of course, opened my library to her and shown her all my favourite books.'

Akram grinned back. 'From what you've told me of her, I believe Begum Sahiba would not be averse to that at all.' He stroked the horse's neck, the magnificent topaz in his ring shining like a miniature sun as his hand moved along the glossy chestnut hide. 'Tell me, what are you doing tomorrow? Are you free for the day?'

Muzaffar nodded. 'Yes. I am free. Why? What do you intend?'

'Ah, good. Come with me, then, Muzaffar. Down towards Mehrauli. I have to find a site suitable for a tomb for my father.'

CHAPTER 10

Muzaffar gaped. 'Your Abba?' he blurted out, remembering the frail, white-bearded old gentleman, a well-respected courtier who was trusted even by the Baadshah himself. 'But – I did not hear – surely – '

Akram was looking at him with puzzlement. Now, he suddenly burst out laughing. 'Heaven protect us, Muzaffar! How very low you must think me, to imagine that I would be out shopping for a turra if my father – Allah give him a long life – were really gone. No, no. He is alive and well; do not worry. It is just that he has decided, as he is wont to do every few months, that it is time for him to choose a good site for a tomb for himself.' Muzaffar had relaxed, and Akram grinned at him. 'Any misdemeanour on the part of any of the younger members of his family troubles Abba enough to want him to embrace death. The last time it was a cousin of mine, who insisted on marrying a dancing girl. Marrying her, mind you, making her his Begum. Before that, it was my youngest sister. She decided she wanted to become a hermit, and spend all the rest of her days in a hut somewhere in the hills. Stupid girl; she would have driven herself mad within days... thankfully, that idea died a natural death, when she realized that hermits would probably have to do their own cooking and bathe in rivers.'

He shrugged. 'Every time something like this happens, Abba decides he's had enough of this life and wishes Allah would summon him. So he wants to get ready.'

'And this time?'

'An uncle of mine. Instead of marrying the young lady Abba had hoped he would offer for, he has gone and proposed to the old widow of that Nawab Imtiyaz Khan – remember him? Abba is distraught; he had hoped Uncle would start up a second family with a young bride at the helm, but Uncle has put his foot down. Even if he'll never be a father again, he insists he will marry this lady and none other.'

'A romantically inclined lot, your family.'

'Hmm. Abba hates it. He thinks we're all beyond redemption.' He sighed. 'All I can do is go off on yet another site-searching trip. I've already been – these past few times – to everywhere from Qutb Sahib's dargah to Nizamuddin Sahib's. Abba was especially keen on Nizamuddin Sahib's dargah. So much sanctity, he was sure some would rub off on him and perhaps be the salvation of the rest of his clan too. But no such luck. Do you have any idea just how many people are buried around Nizamuddin Sahib's dargah? Hundreds, Muzaffar, hundreds. From Humayun to Rahim, to plenty of no-accounts who probably didn't even deserve to be there in the first place.'

'And now you go to Mehrauli? But I thought you already said you had been to Qutb Sahib's tomb? That's in Mehrauli.'

'I have. But Abba wants me to explore Mehrauli further. He says I should look around the vicinity of Balban's tomb. Says if he can't be buried near a saint, he may as well be buried near a Sultan. I tell you!'

So Muzaffar found himself roped into accompanying Akram to Mehrauli the following day. And not a bad thing, either, he thought to himself, as he mounted up again and rode past the Jama Masjid, down Chitli Qabar, and towards home. It would give him something better to do than just stewing at home and driving himself into a frenzy wondering what the truth was behind the killings of Aadil and Basharat.

℺

Muzaffar dragged his palm down the length of his face and examined the result with distaste. When he wiped his palm on his horse's neck, it was to discover that the big chestnut was sweating. 'I must have been mad,' he snapped, 'to have agreed to come on this madcap expedition with you. Madcap and fruitless. Why do you listen to every man you meet who tells you that he will allow his hut to be razed for a thousand rupees and you can build the tomb there? Do you really think your father would be satisfied to have his tomb built on a plot of land the size of a handkerchief? He would balk, Akram. Balk, and in a way that would leave you – '

'You're just being irritable because you didn't get to eat lunch till three hours after noon,' Akram retorted. 'It's just the hunger speaking.'

'If it had been the hunger speaking, it would have started shouting long before.' Muzaffar glared at his friend. 'I wouldn't have minded anything – not the hunger, not the inconvenience, nothing – if you had just shown some common sense – '

'The hunger,' insisted Akram, in a tone that suggested he deliberately chose not to pay attention to anything Muzaffar was saying. 'And the tiredness. It has been unseasonably warm today, has it not? No wonder you have perspired so much.' Muzaffar, cut off in mid-sentence, had opened his mouth again to speak, but Akram barrelled on. 'What you need is a good bath. Hot water and cold. Steam. A massage at the hands of a man who knows his work.'

'Here,' he added, reaching out and tugging on Muzaffar's horse's rein, urging the horse to the right. 'This way.'

'Why on earth? All I want to do is go home – '

'Later, later. Let me take you to Hamaam Abdul Jabaar Khan. Surely you've been there before, Muzaffar? No? Allah! And here I was, thinking you knew this town – ' He had let go of the rein, confident now that Muzaffar was following him. 'You will like this, Muzaffar. You will like it very much, I think.' Akram grinned.

A quarter of an hour later, Muzaffar, lying on a warm marble slab and feeling the masseur's strong hands pummel away at his back and shoulders, had to agree. He did like it. He had enjoyed his bath – the water was hotter than the tepid kind he had found in a couple of other public hamaams in the city – and the massage was blissful. The first few prods and pressings had been painful, but after that it had turned magically relaxing. Muzaffar had sunk into a stupor, a sea of calm drowsiness that made time stop. He was in the chamber that housed the hot water bath. Besides him and Akram and their respective masseurs, there were half a dozen other men there. With his eyes closed, he imagined he was in his own home, sunk into the soft quilts, hovering on the edge of delicious sleep.

The public bath house of Abdul Jabaar Khan was a rare find indeed. It was smaller than some of the other public hamaams dotting the imperial city – primarily because this hamaam was an all-male one; there were no bathing areas for women – but it made up for what it lacked in size by being well-equipped, clean, and beautifully decorated. This, the hot water bath, had no pretty frescoes on the ceiling; the steam of the closed chamber would have ruined them in a matter of weeks. But the vestibule where Muzaffar and Akram had been received by an attendant had sported a beautiful vaulted ceiling, its lime-plastered squinches polished to an alabaster sheen and painted with tulips, poppies, and tapering wine-jars.

The dressing room beside it was smaller but equally lovely, and the attendant courteous. Akram had asked for new loin cloths – 'They know me here,' he had whispered when the attendant had gone, 'and, on the odd occasion when I've come by without a change of clothes, they've always obliged with a new loin cloth.' The length of muslin offered by the attendant was indeed fresh from the loom, clean and crisp.

In the hot bath, steaming water rippled down a sloping white marble chute set in one wall, and ran gurgling along a shallow channel cut into the floor. The channel emptied into the square tank used as a communal pool. Above the pool, in the centre of the shallow dome, daylight filtered through skylights of green and blue glass.

'Would you like to turn over, huzoor?' asked the masseur. 'And sit up, if you please. It will be more effective when – ' Muzaffar did not hear the rest of what the man said, because his voice was drowned out in a sudden outbreak of shouting from somewhere outside. Not out in the street, Muzaffar realized within the same instant. That pandemonium had emanated somewhere within the hamaam's buildings, in another chamber nearby.

The first discordant sound he had heard had been a scream. Not a scream of pain, of someone having slipped and fallen awkwardly, or someone accidentally brushing against one of the hot water pipes. No; what he had heard was a scream of fright, of panic. Something out of the ordinary had happened. His instinctive reaction was of curiosity, and he was already rising to his feet, reaching for his jama and brushing aside the masseur, when Akram, lying on the bench beside his, looked up groggily.

'What's happened? Has someone been murdered?'

Muzaffar, tying the strings of his jama on the right side of his chest, paused. He had not considered the possibility; it had not even crossed his mind. Or had it? He had to admit it, now that he thought about it, that he had imagined some crime, some misdemeanour. Perhaps something as seemingly trivial as a stolen lot of soap or fragrant oil. Or a hamaam slave found riffling through the contents of a patron's purse. Yes, a crime. That was what had piqued his interest.

It should not have. He had been warned, in no uncertain terms. Even if he were interested, he had to learn to suppress his curiosity. If a crime had been committed, the officers of the law would be sent for. It was not his business.

Akram had risen to his feet by now. 'Something's wrong,' he said, picking up his towel – a large piece of thin, absorbent cotton, lying on the bench – and beginning to rub himself briskly. His torso gleamed with the oil his masseur had been working into his skin. 'Why aren't you going to see?' he added with a frown, when he saw that Muzaffar was dawdling over the ties of his jama.

'Whatever it is, it's hardly any of our business.' It sounded idiotic, and Muzaffar winced even as he heard his own voice.

Akram's jaw dropped. 'Not our business? Why – something could have happened out there.' Around them, the room had emptied out; his voice echoed in the chamber, bouncing back from the vaulted ceiling. The other patrons had rushed off, one of them still in his wet loin cloth, leaving a trail of water from the pool. The two masseurs and an attendant who had brought in an armload of towels had also hurried away. Beyond the walls, somewhere not too far, they could hear voices. Busy conversation, many voices talking at the same time. Excitement.

'If it had been nothing,' said Akram, 'people would have returned by now. Come on, Muzaffar. Let's go.'

And because he could think of no believable excuse for staying back – and because deep down, curiosity was gnawing at him too – Muzaffar accompanied Akram out of the hot water bath and through the dressing room that lay beyond.

Outside the dressing room and connected to it by a short corridor was the central vestibule. It was a large chamber in the form of a half-octagon. Short corridors radiated out from it into the other parts of the hamaam: the cold bath, the privies, the storehouses, and what Muzaffar presumed was some sort of office. To a bird flying above, the shallow-domed buildings of the hamaam might look like a gigantic half-flower, its petals spreading out symmetrically around the chopped-off centre.

A small crowd had clogged up one of the corridors. There were bathers, some yet to use the hamaam, others half-clothed and tousled, a few partially damp, probably having abandoned their baths midway in order to satisfy their curiosity. The little corridor hummed with whispers and questions, rumours flying back and forth. One of the attendants of the hamaam – his white pyjamas and jama acting as a badge of office – came along from the far end of the corridor, pushing his way through the crowd, down towards the central vestibule. Akram, showing an unexpected presence of mind, reached out and grabbed the man's arm. 'What has happened, Altaf?'

The man pulled up short, trying to tug his arm away. Almost simultaneously, his eyes – strained and nervous – noticed who had intercepted him. 'Ah, Khan Sahib,' he said. Akram had not boasted when he had said he was known here. The attendant glanced over his shoulder towards the crowd in the corridor; nearly everybody had turned and was watching Akram and the attendant.

'Come into the office, Khan Sahib,' Altaf whispered. His gaze flicked towards Muzaffar, looking on over Akram's shoulder.

'It's all right, Altaf,' Akram said, his voice as low. 'Jang Sahib is my friend.'

'What is it?' Akram asked, when Altaf had ushered them down a deserted corridor and into a neat office. A sheet-covered mattress with a small desk sat under a window – the only window Muzaffar had seen in the hamaam till now. Bath houses were invariably well insulated; the precious steam that opened pores and cleansed tired, sweaty bodies could not be allowed to escape.

Besides the desk and its concomitant papers, reed pen and inkwell, the room was occupied entirely by wooden chests, shelves and niches. Muzaffar could guess what was inside the chests: towels; new loin cloths like the one he and Akram wore; possibly even a change of clothing for the odd emergency, the very privileged customer. On the shelves were neat, carefully-aligned piles of other, easily recognizable items: stiff brushes, mops, new twig brooms, candles, and jars of oil, the latter both for lighting lamps and for massaging stiff muscles. And there was the all-pervasive, sweet smell of khus, or vetiver, used to scent soap made from lye and vegetable oils. It was a quiet office, silent right now but a very important part of the hamaam. No doubt there were more store rooms like this, packed with enough to keep the hamaam going for days.

'It's Abdul Jabaar Sahib,' Altaf said with a weary sigh as he came to a halt next to the window. He turned to Akram, his face taut with tension. 'He's committed suicide. Sliced his wrists in the hot bath.'

❧

Akram's immediate reaction was to turn and stare at Muzaffar. Muzaffar's immediate reaction would have been to say something – to ask how Abdul Jabaar could have committed suicide in a bathing chamber that nearly a dozen other men had been present in till a few minutes back. He held back. Mulish, he realized, but so be it. Akram scowled, puzzled. 'Muzaffar?'

'They should send for the local chowkidar. Or thanedar,' Muzaffar said, dismissively. 'He will know what to do.'

'But – ' Akram looked about, his face a picture of frustration. 'But – how can this be?!' He turned back to the man, Altaf. 'We were in the hot bath. The two of us, and several other men. Patrons and servants. Abdul Jabaar wasn't – '

Altaf had begun to fidget, his weight shifting from one foot to the other, his fingers drumming on his arms, crossed over his chest. No doubt he had important and urgent business waiting for him; a dead master, a hamaam spilling over with curious patrons, with more riffraff coming in from the streets to see what had happened. Attendants and slaves to be controlled, the family to be informed and the law, too.

'No, no, huzoor,' he said, interrupting Akram. 'Not in the larger hot bath. Abdul Jabaar Sahib has a smaller, private room that he uses. It is reserved for him for this one hour every day. He comes in' – Altaf was still using the present tense for a man already dead, Muzaffar noticed – 'everyday, at about the same time. Nobody is allowed into the hot bath till after he has left. It is the same with the small cold bath in the chamber next door. That too is exclusively Abdul Jabaar Sahib's while he is here.'

The last few words of what he said were lost, trailing off into near-silence as four men entered the room. No, five; Muzaffar corrected himself. Five men, though one of them was dead. Abdul Jabaar Khan came into the office of the hamaam he had built, carried on a broad plank, his body covered decorously from head to toe with a white sheet. He was an exceptionally corpulent man; no wonder it required four men to carry him. Outside, the murmur of the crowd had died down. The other bathers, having seen the man's corpse carried away, had gone back to their interrupted baths. Some had had their curiosity sated for the time being. Others, the inveterate gossips or the more inquisitive, had probably gone unwillingly, feeling thwarted and dissatisfied. There would be gossip, speculation on why a man should suddenly commit the ultimate sin – worse even than taking the life of another – but there would be nobody poking around here in the office.

As the men lowered their burden to the floor, the plank tilted, letting a plump, naked arm drop lifelessly from it. The bleeding had stopped – or perhaps someone had done a quick job of cleaning up the dead man in his private bath chamber – but the ugly crimson slash on Abdul Jabaar's wrist told its own unpleasant story.

Altaf moved forward in the very same instant, arms reaching to steady the plank. The plank straightened, Abdul Jabaar's gruesome limb was snatched up and covered again, made decent. But someone, trying to retain a hold on the makeshift stretcher, must have tugged too hard on the sheet. Or perhaps Altaf himself had, with his sudden lunge, displaced the sheet. It slipped down over the dead man's face and up to his chest.

It was a face one would not forget easily. Heavy jowls and thick lips, half-hidden by a thick beard and moustache, the man's expression even in death one of imperiousness. Abdul Jabaar must have been a man with a short temper, thought Muzaffar. A man used to commanding others, never bowing, never compromising.

Though Abdul Jabaar was dead and swiftly cooling, the superciliousness still shone in his open eyes. Those eyes bulged obscenely, and froth, wiped none too carefully from his mouth, had dried into an ugly white crust around his lips. Below, his plump neck bore blotches of purple along the sides and across his Adam's apple.

Altaf pulled the sheet over the dead man's face. Akram let out an audible sigh of relief. 'Have you sent someone to his haveli?' he asked in a whisper.

'Yes, huzoor.' Altaf glanced around, abstracted, anxious. Muzaffar wondered if the members of Abdul Jabaar's household were as arrogant as the head of the family appeared to have been. If so, whoever had gone to inform them of the sudden death – by his own hand, too – of the head of the household, was not to be envied.

'Let us go, Akram,' Muzaffar said. 'There is nothing for us to do here.' He turned even as he spoke, and began walking. He had already stepped over the threshold and into the corridor beyond by the time Akram caught up to him and grabbed his elbow.

'What on earth is the matter with you?' Akram hissed, not bothering to hide his annoyance any longer. 'You're behaving as if – as if you weren't interested at all.' His frown deepened. He bit his lip, now looking unsure. 'Is everything all right, Muzaffar? You don't seem your usual self. Are you ill? Is something wrong?' He was worried now, Muzaffar could see.

He shook his head. 'There is no need for you to worry. I am well. Nothing is wrong.' He hesitated, wondering whether or not to tell Akram. Finally, seeing that the anxiety still clouded Akram's face, he added, 'It is not my place to be interfering in matters of the law. I have been told so, and by none other than Khan Sahib himself. It is no use,' he continued, hurrying to stall the objections he could see rising to Akram's lips. 'It is no use at all to try to persuade me. Or dissuade me. I – I am tired, Akram. I do not want to have anything to do with it. The very thought of it sickens me.'

Akram had let go of Muzaffar's sleeve. He was gazing at his friend, however, looking on with pensive eyes. For a few moments, he remained silent. Then, with an expressive shrug, he said, 'I see. Well, nobody can force you to do something you have decided against. I do not blame you. But would you mind coming with me? I want to see; I am curious.'

And Muzaffar, because he was curious too, nodded cautiously.

☙

The central vestibule was quiet now, deserted except for the doorkeeper standing at the entrance. He glanced over his shoulder at them, inclined his head briefly towards Akram in recognition, before turning his gaze back on the street outside. A grim bleakness had settled over the hamaam. Only a quarter of an hour earlier, the bath house had hummed with activity as patrons came and went, chatted and laughed, or indulged in lazy gossip as they relaxed in the baths.

There was silence now. Or near-silence. A low murmur drifted out of the bathing chambers – men discussing what had happened, no doubt – but it was muted. Not a single laugh punctuated the relative stillness of the building. The hamaam seemed to wait with bated breath. For what, only the Almighty knew.

Akram looked at Muzaffar with an expectant air. Muzaffar could guess what was going through his friend's mind: Akram was waiting for Muzaffar to put aside his reservations and lead the way. Muzaffar did nothing. He smiled benignly back at his friend and stood in the centre of the vestibule, looking at the depiction of a garden – flowers and fruit and birds in the trees – painted on the upper walls. He heard a muffled oath from Akram. Then, a question addressed to the doorkeeper: 'Altaf told me Abdul Jabaar was found dead in his private bathing chamber. Where is that?'

It was so laughably direct a question, so undisguised, that Muzaffar would not have been surprised if the doorkeeper had refused to reply. Or had returned an evasive answer. What he had not taken into account, however, was the fact that Akram was known and respected here, in Hamaam Abdul Jabaar Khan. The doorkeeper probably did not see any harm in telling Akram where the dead man had been found. He pointed the way, down one of the corridors radiating from the vestibule. 'They have not yet cleaned it, huzoor,' he warned.

And they had not. The supply of hot water from the water channel down into the tank had been turned off, but moisture still hung in the air. It was hot and humid enough to raise a sweat in a matter of moments – which was the entire purpose of the steam. This room was a good deal smaller than the main hot bath, and therefore perceptibly warmer, even with the hot water no longer flowing. The tank in the centre of the room – the pool in which the bather would immerse himself – still contained water, slowly draining away through earthen channels into the maze of pipes under the floors of the hamaam. The water that still remained in the tank was a deep, disturbing crimson.

'I wonder why he killed himself,' Akram murmured. Even though his voice was low, his words echoed in the empty room. 'I didn't really know him, but everything I'd heard about him – well, he didn't sound like the sort of man to take his own life.' He wandered aimlessly about the room, meandering in a haphazard circuit along the edge of the tank. Muzaffar followed, though in less aimless a fashion. He kept quiet, his eyes moving about the room, looking at the walls, the floor, the ceiling. Taking in the details of the place, pushing into the slots of his memory all that he was seeing.

'And why would a man like him want to commit suicide? You didn't know him, did you, Muzaffar?' Akram paused too briefly to allow Muzaffar to even respond; he probably guessed – and correctly, too – that Muzaffar would not have known the man. 'Extremely wealthy. Never knew want, I would think. Well spoken of. Well respected… but, that,' he conceded, with a shrug, 'is of course no reason for a man to not kill himself. I mean, who knows? Perhaps I'm wrong. There may have been things in his personal life nobody else knew about. Things that drove him to kill himself – but in public, like this?' He shuddered.

'He did not kill himself.'

ɞ

Muzaffar's words hung in the air.

Akram blinked. He had been too lost in his own thoughts, too busy analzying for himself whether or not Abdul Jabaar Khan could have killed himself, to notice Muzaffar's air of growing impatience. He stared at Muzaffar, and when he finally spoke, his voice was shaky. 'His wrists were slit, Muzaffar. Both of us saw that,' he said. 'A man does not lie back quietly and allow another to cut open his veins.'

'You saw the dead man as clearly as I did, Akram,' Muzaffar said, 'when that sheet slipped. You did, didn't you?'

Akram nodded, his expression almost comically miserable. He had known Muzaffar less than a year, but it had been enough.

'Yes,' Muzaffar continued. 'A man does not let another slit his veins without fighting back. And, as far as I know, a man who dies like that does not usually have discoloured patches on his neck. Patches which looked suspiciously like the marks of fingers, by the way. And did you notice the way his eyes bulged? Or the froth around his mouth? I'm no hakim, but I've spent enough time with them over the past few months to get some idea of how to read a corpse.' He moved forward, walking towards the white marble chute – carved with shallow scallops, to make the water ripple as it flowed over. 'Come and have a look at this,' he invited, indicating the chute and the channel into which it disgorged its water. When Akram reached his side, Muzaffar went down on his haunches and pointed to the edge of the chute. On it, half-hidden by the lip of the chute, was a small smudge of red. Muzaffar put the tip of his forefinger to it; the finger came away with a faint smear of crimson on it.

'Blood?' Akram asked.

'Blood.' Muzaffar stood up and looked around. Except for that swiftly-draining pool of scarlet water in the centre, the rest of the room was clean.

'And how does that make you so sure Abdul Jabaar was killed?'

'It seems unlikely to me that a man who had slit his wrists would wander around the room, dripping blood. That is the whole point of slitting your wrists while lying in a pool of water, isn't it? That the blood ebbs slowly – and supposedly painlessly – away. You sink gently into unconsciousness and then death. If Abdul Jabaar did indeed cut his own wrists, why did he get out of the water and wander all the way to the chute? Why did he drip blood only here, but nowhere else in the room? And remember, he must have been bleeding quite copiously, if he eventually died of it.'

'Eventually,' Akram pointed out. 'He may have been bleeding for a long time.'

'How long? That attendant – Altaf? – said that this was Abdul Jabaar's private bath for this one hour every day. An hour is not that much time.'

He rubbed his forefinger on the end of his turban. 'This man was murdered, Akram. I am sure of it.'

'What you say makes sense,' Akram agreed, 'but what I said still hasn't been answered. No man would lie still and let his wrists be cut. It's not as if the man was stabbed through the heart, that he was silenced immediately. Of course, the murderer may have gagged him, but still – '

'There's no point discussing this further, Akram,' Muzaffar said brusquely. 'Come, let us go. Abdul Jabaar's family will be arriving soon, I suppose. As will the thanedar. It would be awkward for me to be found loitering about here.'

It was not until they were outside the hamaam, walking towards the stables where their horses were tethered, that Akram said, 'If you're right – if Abdul Jabaar was killed – his sons won't rest until they've had the murderer executed.'

Muzaffar raised an eyebrow. 'Vindictive?' He glanced towards a passing trio of horsemen, their mounts galloping towards the hamaam. Some way behind them trailed a palanquin, carried by six kahaars, panting audibly and streaming sweat as they ran past with their load. Abdul Jabaar's kin, thought Muzaffar, come to claim their dead. 'But understandable, I suppose,' he continued, in response to Akram's remark. 'The grief for a loved one cannot be assuaged by revenge, but that doesn't stop people wanting to avenge a death.'

Akram too had turned to look at the passing entourage. 'That must be them,' he said, before looking back at Muzaffar. 'It isn't just that. Revenge, yes. But also prestige. "How dare someone kill Abdul Jabaar?" That's what his sons will say. They're an arrogant lot. Their father was like that, and his sons are cast in the same mould.' Akram looked down at his thumb, at the brilliant archer's ring he wore on it. He turned it around, once, twice, with the fingers of his other hand. He slipped it off, gazed at it, then slipped it on again. Muzaffar watched in puzzled silence; he could see that Akram, usually unflappable and calm, was agitated.

What came next shook Muzaffar. Akram clasped his hands behind his back, and his eyes were worried when they looked into Muzaffar's. 'If they suspect it was murder,' he said, 'and – Allah forbid – Kotwal Sahib is unable to discover who was behind it, they might get very nasty indeed.'

Muzaffar frowned. 'They may. But what can they do? Badmouth Khan Sahib? He is well-liked enough to be able to weather that storm.'

Akram shook his head. 'In the normal course of events, yes. But you don't know these people, Muzaffar. Abdul Jabaar and his family are well-connected; they have sympathizers and supporters amongst the highest echelons of the nobility. They can probably make their way to the Shahzada Dara Shukoh. They could – ' He broke off, his cheeks flushed at the realization that he had been on the verge of saying something he would sooner not have even imagined. He gave a forced smile, trying to lighten the impact of his ominous words. 'Don't worry. Kotwal Sahib can look after himself. Besides, he's too high up in the ranks for such an incident to really cause any damage.'

Muzaffar bit his lip. He gazed blankly at Akram's contrite

face. The man was probably wishing he had not said anything, but perhaps it was all for the best. To be forewarned was to be forearmed. Yet, the man who needed to be forearmed could not be forewarned, unless Muzaffar swallowed his pride and went to Khan Sahib. What would he say? Khan Sahib, I was a fool to interfere in the kotwali's affairs. But now I am here to tell you that there is real danger to you if you do not solve, quickly and correctly, the case of the murder of Abdul Jabaar. That was all I came to say, Khan Sahib. Be quick and be correct. Goodbye, Khan Sahib, and may Allah help you.

He shuddered at the thought of Khan Sahib's reaction to even a tenth of that.

And yet. He could not stand by. Khan Sahib was not just his brother-in-law; he had been more father than Muzaffar's own sire, Mirza Burhanuddin Malik Jang. Had Farid Khan, husband to Zeenat Begum, refused to take in the tiny scrap of humanity his mother-in-law had left behind, Muzaffar Jang might never have crossed babyhood. Or, if he had made it into childhood – even manhood – he doubted if he would have had half the education, the sense, and the values Khan Sahib had imparted to him in the fifteen-odd years Muzaffar had been part of his household.

He did not owe Khan Sahib a warning of what was to come if Abdul Jabaar's murder was not solved swiftly. He owed it to the affection he felt for the man.

ꟹ

He stopped in his tracks. 'Akram.'

His friend turned, looking questioningly at Muzaffar.

'I – I think I'll go back to the hamaam. You go back home if you wish; I need to ask people some questions.'

Akram smiled, a wry smile but one tinged with relief too. 'You do not know the people at the hamaam,' he said, 'and they do not know you. Oh, they may defer to your rank, but that does not always work, does it? I will come with you; I know most of the attendants there; they trust me. I would even go as far as to say that they like me.' He looked towards the domed silhouette of the hamaam, outlined against the orange and pink clouds of the sunset sky. The horsemen had alighted at the entrance – which by now was lit, torches stuck into the sconces on either side of the arched door – and a couple of servants were leading away the horses.

'Do you want to meet Abdul Jabaar's sons? Tell them what happened?'

'Of course not.' Muzaffar shuddered. 'No, I did not mean I want to barge in right now. When they've come out, when the coast is clear. If they are as keen on vengeance as you think they would be, I would rather they thought, for the time being, that their father did indeed do himself in.'

'A little harsh,' Akram remarked, as the two of them veered away from the stables and wandered over to a mud platform built around the base of a banyan tree. 'It is a shameful thing for a man to be thought to have killed himself. Especially when he did not.'

Muzaffar said nothing, and remained mostly silent over the next half hour as they sat there under the banyan tree, watching the colours of the sky fade and darken into a uniform blue-black. Lamps and torches came alight, twinkling in the shops and houses around. There drifted on the air the smells of the bazaar: of kababs cooking at a little eatery; of cheap perfume wafting from a palanquin headed towards Chawri Bazaar, where all the brothels were; of horse manure, from the nearby stables. The call to prayer rang out from a nearby mosque, and was echoed, far and near, by other muezzins in other mosques.

Muzaffar stared at the entrance to the hamaam, waiting, watching. Time passed. There was some activity at the doorway: servants scurrying about, carrying things – at this distance,

Muzaffar could not tell what, but he could guess. Cloth, perhaps, to shroud the body more decorously than it had been before. Incense or attar, to cloak the stench of death, though Muzaffar doubted that Abdul Jabaar would have begun to smell of decay yet. Not so soon, and not in weather still cold. He watched, trying to ignore the restlessness of Akram beside him.

Over three-quarters of an hour had passed before an entourage emerged from the entrance. The dead man, now covered over so completely that only the protuberant paunch indicated that the body on the wide plank borne by six men was that of Abdul Jabaar. Before him came the men Muzaffar had seen ride up to the hamaam. They walked now with heads bowed, solemn and sad. Or plotting vengeance, wondered Muzaffar bleakly.

He watched long enough to see them give instructions to the bearers of the body, before mounting and setting off themselves. He saw Abdul Jabaar being taken away, trailed for a short distance by a band of curious onlookers who were quickly shooed away by two servants of the hamaam, escorting their late master's body to the home which had been his.

'Come along,' Muzaffar said, when the excitement had died down. 'Let us go in.'

The clientele of the hamaam had been asked, in most cases politely, to leave. More persistent hangers-on had been evicted with less tact. Akram had been inclined to finally introduce Muzaffar as the brother-in-law of the Kotwal, and to announce to Altaf that this was the man most feared by the criminals of Dilli. 'I would rather we relied on your charm,' Muzaffar had said in a dry voice as they rose from their seat under the banyan tree. 'And you do know them very well, do you not? They will not mind you asking questions.'

'I will not be the one asking questions.'

'Well, you will just have to use your charm to convince them that it is perfectly natural for your friends to ask questions too.'

Muzaffar did not mean, however, to push himself forward as the curious one. By the time they reached the entrance of the hamaam, he had tutored Akram on what to ask and how to ask. There would be hitches, he knew: an answer often led to a question that had not even been envisaged till that very moment – and Akram, while no fool, was not skilled at work like this. Muzaffar would have to jump in and ask questions too. He prayed that he would succeed in being offhand about it. Or at least that people would not remember that the sombrely clad amir accompanying Akram Khan Sahib had asked a lot of very probing questions.

The attendant who had been on duty at the bathing chamber Abdul Jabaar used was a nervous-looking man named Ilyas. Muzaffar recalled him as one of those who had carried Abdul Jabaar's corpse into the hamaam's office. The man had been the one to lose his grip on the plank. He still looked dazed, his eyes wide with apprehension. Altaf – who, thanks to Akram, Muzaffar now knew as the man in charge of the daily operations at the hamaam – stood by, a mostly silent observer.

The four of them had gathered in the room where the dead man had been found. The bloodied water had drained away, leaving behind a stained marble tank. They would have to scrub it soon, thought Muzaffar; marble had a way of holding stains.

'So you found the corpse, did you?' Akram began, and Ilyas flinched. His gaze flicked to Altaf. 'Go on,' Altaf whispered. 'Tell huzoor.'

Ilyas gulped. 'I – I didn't find him, huzoor' he said. 'Another man did. He began shouting and calling for help.'

Akram exchanged a quick glance with Muzaffar, as if asking for reassurance. Muzaffar's left eyebrow lifted, almost imperceptibly. A man who did not know him might not even have noticed it. Akram noticed it, recognized it, and interpreted it correctly. 'Another man?' he asked Ilyas. 'Who was he? An attendant? A servant?'

Ilyas cleared his throat. 'No, huzoor. A patron.'

On their way back into the hamaam, Muzaffar had touched upon this possibility. A servant or attendant at the hamaam would not be difficult to interrogate, he had said, because in all probability the man would still be around. If Abdul Jabaar's dead body had, instead, been discovered by a visitor to the hamaam, Muzaffar had wondered if the man would have lingered on, or have slunk quickly away. Many men would have done that, none too eager to be interrogated repeatedly by the officers of the law. Especially when the dead man happened to have been one as well-connected as Abdul Jabaar appeared to have been.

Muzaffar had instructed Akram in the line of questioning he was to follow should it emerge that the corpse had been discovered by someone not at the hamaam.

'But how could that be? How did a patron happen to go into Abdul Jabaar's bathing chamber?,' Akram asked. His voice quavered slightly, not confident of his ability to carry off this subterfuge. 'It was a private one, was it not?'

'He was waiting – ' Ilyas began to say, but was interrupted by Altaf, who spoke up, louder and more confident. 'The chamber is reserved for Abdul Jabaar Sahib only while he is – was – here. After he had bathed and left, anybody who cared to do so, could use the chamber.'

He glanced towards Ilyas, as if asking him to confirm what he had said. Ilyas nodded, but said nothing. Altaf continued. 'It doesn't happen often, huzoor. Most people who come here prefer to bathe in the larger, communal chambers. Very few come into Sahib's personal bathing chambers. But some do, now and then.' He glanced at Ilyas, who muttered a barely audible affirmation.

'When did this man arrive?'

It was Ilyas who answered, but only after another hurried look at Altaf. 'Just as Abdul Jabaar Sahib's servant arrived.

Then, when Sahib sent his servant off, I saw this man'

Muzaffar, realizing that Akram had missed an important cue, and would probably never even notice the significance of what had just been said, interrupted. 'A servant? Did Abdul Jabaar Sahib bring a servant along with him?'

Both Altaf and Ilyas looked startled, Ilyas a little more so. Altaf, having already seen Muzaffar when Abdul Jabaar's body had been brought into the office over an hour earlier, had probably summed up the nobleman as a man as curious as the next. Ilyas had so far seen Muzaffar only as a silent spectator, standing by while the more flamboyant-looking Akram asked all the questions.

He hesitated, but whether that hesitation was out of reticence – a reluctance, perhaps, to answer this stranger – or out of a genuine need to pause, to think back, Muzaffar could not say. 'No, huzoor,' Ilyas finally said. 'The servant came later, when Sahib had already been in the bath for a while.'

'How long?'

Ilyas shrugged, his timidity now beginning to dissipate a bit. 'Perhaps a quarter of an hour, huzoor. A third. I don't remember. But Sahib had been in the water for a while.'

'Why did the servant come, do you know?' Muzaffar had left off any pretence now; there were emerging facts he had to probe. To leave it to Akram would be foolish, for Akram, well-meaning though he was, would probably never think of asking any of these questions. A swift glance at his friend's face told Muzaffar that Akram, far from looking affronted at this summary takeover of the duty initially assigned to him, had a triumphant gleam in his eyes.

'He told me there was an urgent message from Sahib's home,' Ilyas replied. 'He didn't wait for me to let Sahib know he had come; he simply barged right in.'

Muzaffar frowned. 'Did you go in after him?'

The man shook his head. 'I could hear Sahib, huzoor. He

sounded angry. I didn't want to interrupt.' From the look on his face, Muzaffar could hazard a guess: it had not been merely a desire to not interrupt Abdul Jabaar in his bath. It had also been, most likely, a desire to save his own skin that had stopped Ilyas from going in. Abdul Jabaar would probably have been angry, not just at the servant who had entered his bathing chamber unbidden, but also at the attendant whose laxity had allowed the intrusion.

'All right,' Muzaffar said. 'How long was this servant inside?'

'A very short time, huzoor. He went in, and I heard Sahib scolding him, just a couple of minutes later. Then the servant came out, to say that Sahib was calling for me. A little while, that's all it was.' His brow crinkled, then his face brightened as if he had struck upon an effective way of communicating the passage of time. 'The other patron, huzoor – the one who discovered Abdul Jabaar Sahib's body – he arrived almost at the same time as Sahib's servant. He had begun undressing when the servant was inside. Then Sahib called me in, and when I came out of the bath chamber, the man was already down to his pyjamas.'

Muzaffar pinched the bridge of his nose between the tips of his forefinger and thumb, squeezing his eyes shut briefly. When he opened them again, the gentle smile on his face was one that only those who knew him well would have recognized as forced. 'I see. So let us get back to what happened when the servant came. He entered the bathing chamber and said something to Abdul Jabaar, which perhaps displeased him. Then the servant came out and called you in too?'

'No, huzoor. He came out and told me that Sahib had summoned me. Then he went away, out of the hamaam.'

'Ah. And what had Sahib to say to you?'

'He said he was ready to get out of the hot bath, and that I should send a man to give him his massage. He also told me to go to his cold bath and ensure that it was ready. To have his fresh clothes laid out ready for him, because he had to leave soon.'

'He seemed all right to you then? Not depressed, or in shock?' Muzaffar let his voice trail off, hoping Ilyas would interpret that unfinished sentence correctly. Had Abdul seen Jabaar looking as if he intended to commit suicide?

'He was still a little annoyed, huzoor, I think. But he – he didn't look as if he was getting ready to kill himself.' Beside Ilyas, Altaf drew in a sharp breath, as if berating his subordinate for his bluntness.

'So you went off to obey his orders? And Abdul Jabaar was healthy and alive when you left the bathing chamber?'

Ilyas nodded eagerly. 'He was, huzoor. He was already climbing out of the bath.'

'And how long were you gone?'

'Longer than I had thought I would be, huzoor. I had to go looking for the masseurs all over the hamaam; nobody had expected Sahib to curtail his bath so soon. And then I had to go to Sahib's cold bath and tell the attendant there to have it ready.'

From somewhere in the hamaam, Muzaffar could hear the sound of a twig broom being used briskly to sweep a floor.

'Then what happened?' he asked.

'We heard screams,' Ilyas said. 'I didn't realize what it was, at first.'

'We came running, all of us,' Altaf interjected. 'I was in the office, closer to this chamber than Ilyas was. I, and the doorkeeper, and a couple of patrons who were just coming in – we all hurried over here to see who was screaming.'

Ilyas swallowed, licked his lips, and picked up the story. 'It was the man who had been waiting outside for Sahib to vacate the bath,' he said, addressing Muzaffar. 'He had peeked in and seen Sahib, dead.'

'Where is he now? This man who found Abdul Jabaar?'

Altaf and Ilyas looked at each other, as if searching for an answer – which neither could provide. 'There was a lot of confusion when Sahib was found, huzoor,' Altaf admitted, finally. 'Many people milling around, and the shock of the incident. He must have wandered off into some other part of the hamaam, or gone away. We did not think of him, really.'

Which was understandable, given the circumstances. Altaf and his men must have had enough on their hands without having to comfort a distraught patron. That he had taken himself off had probably been more a relief than anything else, at the time. As it was, everybody had assumed – still assumed – that Abdul Jabaar had killed himself. This patron, whoever he was, would have been considered an embarrassment. They would have been glad that he had not hung around, blabbing about the suicide to all and sundry.

'Where is the knife?' Muzaffar asked. His voice echoed in the room.

Ilyas blinked. 'Knife, huzoor?'

'Abdul Jabaar Sahib must have used a knife to cut his wrists. He could hardly have thrown it away and then come back to lie in the tank and bleed.'

Ilyas flushed. 'I beg your pardon, huzoor. I had not realized – that knife. It was found next to Sahib's body, lying in the water beside him.' An ordinary knife, he explained, small, wooden-handled, made of iron. No, he answered to Muzaffar's question, he had never seen such a knife in Sahib's possession before. Altaf concurred. The knife, they agreed, looked out of place. Such a wealthy man as Abdul Jabaar Sahib, and such a crude knife.

Muzaffar looked, his eyes hooded and brooding, at the tank with its ominous red stains. The metallic stench of blood hung in the air. He glanced back at Ilyas and Altaf only when the latter cleared his throat – a subtle but obvious indication that these two men had work to get back to, even if the noblemen had not.

'Was there anybody else around at the time?' Muzaffar asked, addressing Ilyas. 'Maybe out there, in the corridor? Someone who could have slipped past this other man – the visitor who found Abdul Jabaar?'

Ilyas's eyebrows drew together in an expression of concentration. 'No, huzoor,' he answered, after some thought. 'There was no one. Sahib likes – liked – his privacy. If he'd seen that man peep in, he would have yelled curses at him.'

'I wonder why the man did look in. Was he a regular patron? If he were a regular, would he not have known that he had no chance of entering until Abdul Jabaar had finished his bath?'

'I hadn't seen the man before, huzoor,' Ilyas acknowledged. 'But he seemed to know that Sahib was inside, and that the chamber would be for his exclusive use while he was there. Perhaps the doorkeeper informed him. I certainly told him, when he came this way. He said he knew, and that he would wait.'

'Apparently he got impatient after a while. Or did he hear something?'

Ilyas shrugged. 'We did not think of asking, huzoor. There was so much on our minds right then. It may be that he did hear something.'

Down the corridor outside came the sound of approaching footsteps. A man, his feet probably clad in sandals, walking hurriedly towards the chamber that had been Abdul Jabaar's hot bath. He arrived, a thin, excited-looking man dressed in the white jama and pyjamas of the hamaam's attendants, and holding – like a badge of office – a twig broom in one hand. Slung over one shoulder was a waterskin, the brown hide taut and bulging.

He stared, taken aback, at Muzaffar and Akram. His gaze switched, then, to Altaf. 'Abdul Jabaar Sahib's elder son ordered me to clean this chamber, huzoor,' he mumbled.

Altaf nodded. 'He is the master now.' He sighed. 'Huzoor' – he looked, in turn, at Akram and Muzaffar – 'if there are no more questions, may we?'

CHAPTER 11

'What do you think?' Akram said, as he walked towards the stables with Muzaffar. The night, by the standards of Chandni Chowk and its environs, was still young. The sun had set a mere hour ago, and there were chandeliers and lamps aplenty to light up the shops, the qahwa khanas, the palaces of pleasure. There were public houses here, and private ones too, where the musicians would just be beginning to tune their instruments, the dancing girls putting on their jewellery and making up their faces, the patrons setting out in their palanquins for a night of feasting and entertainment, even debauchery.

The area just around Hamaam Abdul Jabaar Khan was less refined, more mundane: the shops here sold commonplace things like cotton and woven baskets, grain and oil and rope. The entertainment was whatever one could eavesdrop on, if one had nothing better to do than listen in on the conversations of strangers discussing how many children they had or how high the price of grain would rise in the coming year.

'About what?'

'This, of course. Abdul Jabaar. You are convinced he was murdered, yet you did not protest when Altaf let that servant come and start cleaning the place. I would have thought you would have stopped it. After all, if it's a murder, the thanedar should be told. And if the thanedar is told, he would want to see the chamber as it was – '

'The chamber wasn't even as it was when we saw it. Abdul Jabaar had already been moved. So had the knife. In fact, we never even saw the knife.' A thoughtful look came into Muzaffar's eyes. 'I wonder what happened to it eventually. Did they throw it away? Or did Abdul Jabaar's sons take it with them?'

'Why didn't you ask?'

Muzaffar frowned, the expression of distaste directed not at Akram, but at himself. 'I did not want to get Altaf or Ilyas suspicious. As it was, I had asked too many questions. Morbid curiosity or a fascination for the macabre can only make a man so inquisitive. I had begun probing too deep.'

'What does that matter?' They had reached the entrance to the stable; a servant stationed at the wide arched doorway went off to fetch their horses. 'So what if Altaf and Ilyas should wonder at your asking questions? It doesn't make a difference.'

A man leading a string of mournful-eyed donkeys, each laden with a sack of sand, went by. The smell of sweat and manure followed them. 'It does make a difference,' said Muzaffar quietly. 'Have you realized, Akram, that Ilyas may well be the murderer?'

☙

'Ilyas?! But – but how could you imagine – that man couldn't hurt a fly. At least,' Akram qualified, 'I don't think he could. He looks so nervous. So frail. Come, Muzaffar, surely even you realize that. Abdul Jabaar was a big man, strong. If what you say is correct, then it cannot have been Ilyas. Ilyas could not hold down Abdul Jabaar by himself to cut his wrists.'

'But Abdul Jabaar was not killed by having his wrists slit. Don't you see? He was strangled, and shortly after that, even before the blood could begin to thicken in his veins, his wrists were cut open to make it appear that he had committed suicide.' The servant had emerged with the horses; Muzaffar took the reins of his chestnut and handed the man a coin.

'You are right about Ilyas's frailty, though,' he admitted, a little grudgingly, when he and Akram, now mounted, had moved off. 'One needs strength even to strangle a man.' He chewed his moustache, maintaining a pensive silence as their horses trotted down the street. 'Perhaps he had help. An accomplice? The patron who supposedly found the body? And then disappeared too, so very conveniently.' His mind was making connections faster than he could articulate them; he was getting excited, and yet there was a sense of dawning frustration too. 'And how am I to find that out?' he groaned. 'Ilyas is already wary of me; he will lie, I am certain, if I were to question him any further. If I had had the sense to think it over, I could have planned this better – '

Akram cut short the self-reproach with a snort. 'Don't be an idiot. You have always found ways to make enquiries when you've needed to, haven't you? Don a disguise. You're good at that. Maybe you can try and get a job at the hamaam; when you're inside, you can discover a lot more than you can as a mere visitor.'

Muzaffar shook his head. 'I don't have the time for that. It'll take too long; what if Abdul Jabaar's sons start suspecting that it was murder, and get after Khan Sahib?' He rubbed an agitated hand on the rough wool of his choga, where it draped over his thigh. 'But there is one thing: the motive. Why would Ilyas kill Abdul Jabaar?'

Akram had no suggestion to offer; all he did was look askance at Muzaffar. Muzaffar, seeing the glance, heaved a sigh. 'Khan Sahib would have my hide for forming a theory about a man's guilt without first finding a plausible motive. But Ilyas seems the likeliest culprit, does he not? He had the opportunity – there were no others around, neither customers nor attendants – except for that other patron. And that man may well have been Ilyas's accomplice.'

He manoeuvred his horse around a halted palanquin; the owner had stepped out to go into a qahwa khana, and the kahaars had seated themselves on the ground, resting their backs against the long poles of the palanquin. 'There is the case of the servant, too,' Muzaffar said, when they had passed the palanquin and its bearers, and left the qahwa khana behind. 'Ilyas said a servant had come from Abdul Jabaar's house. That man cannot be held responsible, since even Ilyas admits that Abdul Jabaar was alive and well after the servant had gone. But it might be worthwhile to find out who the servant was, and talk to him. He may be able to throw some light on this affair.

'Perhaps I shall go to Abdul Jabaar's haveli tomorrow,' he said.

☙

To Muzaffar's consternation, his resolve to visit Abdul Jabaar's haveli the next morning was foiled even before he could set off from home. He was in the process of tying on his turban – instructions had already been given for his horse to be saddled and fetched from the stable – when Javed entered with the news that a merchant, Parvez, had come to meet Jang Sahib. 'He asks that you be informed that he is the brother of the man Basharat, who was murdered the other day. He also tells me that Begum Sahiba visited his begum.'

The rest, the man himself conveyed to Muzaffar when ushered into the dalaan where Muzaffar received his guest. He apologized profusely for intruding on his host in so summary a fashion. He had passed by last night, but had not thought it polite to come calling at so late an hour. He would not have been surprised had Jang Sahib refused to entertain him.

Muzaffar waved away his apologies and asked, as tactfully as he could, the reason for this visit.

'Oh! I – I have been most remiss. I beg your pardon.' Parvez flushed. He was a burly man in his early thirties, but with a beard gone prematurely grey and a mouth that had not even curved into the semblance of a smile when he had greeted his host, even though his words had been effusive enough. 'I met Aadil's clerk yesterday, and he told me that huzoor was famed for his intelligence and his skill in unravelling the most tangled of puzzles.'

Muzaffar could not imagine Suraj Bhan using such flowery language, but let it pass. 'Suraj Bhan? You know him?'

'Only slightly. He was Aadil's only real assistant, you see, so I ran into him once or twice when I visited Aadil. Not that I visited the man much – just when we were finalizing the selling of our house to Aadil. Suraj Bhan struck me as a very capable man.' There was a pause, and then Parvez plunged ahead. Basharat had been very dear to him. As brothers should be, of course, but even so. His killing had come as a terrible shock to Parvez, and the thanedar seemed to have not been able to come to any conclusions regarding the culprit.

'Even though, between them, the thanedar and the chowkidar questioned everybody in the house. Their men turned the room upside down. As if the murderer had not already created enough of a mess!' – for a brief spell, disgust came into Parvez's expression. Muzaffar, imagining blood spilled on the sheets, was taken aback at the man's next words. 'All our papers – all of them, our ledgers, our letters, our records – everything that is kept in that room, was strewn about. There was something unholy about it. Jang Sahib, if you had seen that room, you would have thought the man had killed my brother and then danced all about the room, scattering every page in glee.'

It did sound eerie. Blasphemous. And familiar.

Parvez drew in a sharp breath, steadying himself. 'I beg your pardon, Jang Sahib. This has all been most distressing.'

'I can understand,' Muzaffar said in as soothing a voice as he could command without appearing patronizing. He did not know exactly why Parvez had come. He could conjecture, but it would be just that: conjecture. He waited, silent, waiting for the man to say something, give some indication of his reason for coming to meet someone he had only heard of.

It was not long in coming. Parvez suddenly burst forth: 'If you will only help me, Jang Sahib!' The plea came out as a high-pitched squeak, making him sound ridiculous, but at the same time strangely vulnerable, desperate. 'Help me, Jang Sahib. Help me find the man who murdered my brother.'

'Surely the thanedar is investigating the case?'

The man nodded, but with a miserable sort of resignation. 'He did come for a brief while. The chowkidar spent considerably more time in our house.'

'And?'

'They seemed to think it was an unsuccessful robbery. You may have heard, Jang Sahib, that there was a similar incident just next door, a few days back. Our neighbour was murdered and his house ransacked. In his case, though, I believe the intruder even tried to burn the place down.'

How rumour distorted the truth, thought Muzaffar fleetingly. 'I heard it said that nothing was actually stolen from Aadil's house,' was all he said.

'Nothing was stolen from ours, either. There was nothing to be stolen in that room,' Parvez said, his voice bitter. 'A foolish thief, I would think, to have blundered into a house, that too into the only room where a lamp was burning. Any man breaking into a house at night would have had the sense to enter a room that was dark. Either empty, or with its occupants fast asleep. Why go into the only room that was obviously occupied by a man likely to be still awake?'

'That makes you think it was not a thief?'

Parvez nodded, his beard wagging against his chest. He was a wealthy enough man, but it was not reflected in his clothing, which was sombre. His choga was brown, a dull plain colour unrelieved by embroidery or interesting weaves. His jama and pyjama were white, his turban as dull a brown as his choga. There was not a thread of gold or a single pearl by way of ornamentation on his person. No rings, no necklaces, not even a muted sarpech in his turban. A far cry, thought Muzaffar, from the extravagance Shireen had reported in his wife, Nilofer.

Belatedly, Muzaffar remembered that it might be because the man was in mourning for his brother.

But Parvez was already speaking. 'Also the fact that there was nothing in that room to steal. Papers? Who would want to steal papers? Documents that would be of use only to the two of us? There was nothing there that would interest anybody else. Just our own records, records of sale and purchase, letters to other merchants, letters to officials. Personal correspondence. What was there to steal?'

It had been the same with Aadil, Muzaffar remembered.

'Why would a man break in and then not steal anything?' Parvez continued. 'It seems so pointless.'

'Were there any signs of someone having broken in? There usually are, you know – a couple of panels smashed in on a door or a window, or signs of someone having climbed up onto the rooftop terrace. And, of course, if a door or window was smashed, it would have created enough noise to wake up someone in the house.'

Parvez frowned. 'There were no smashed doors or windows.'

'The terrace?'

'The staircase leading down has been newly plastered. The workmen left just yesterday. There would have been evidence of anybody passing that way. There was none.'

'Is there any other way in or out of the house?'

The man shook his head. 'Only the ways a legitimate visitor to the house would use. The front door, and the back one. That is not used much, except by the servants and by those who come by to sell wood or vegetables, things like that. Or so I am led to believe,' he added, making it clear that he, Parvez, was a man – and a wealthy one at that – and so could not be expected to know every little detail of the mundane daily routine of his household.

Muzaffar ran a fingertip along the rim of the goblet he held, mulling over what Parvez had said. It seemed, so far, to fit with what he already knew. Ameena, after all, had been acquainted with the murderer; the girl Ismat's recounting of the conversation she had eavesdropped upon had indicated as much. It would not be too much of a leap of imagination to believe that Ameena may have handed over a spare key, or surreptitiously loosened a couple of slats in a window, to allow the murderer to enter the house even after she herself had exited it.

But there was the motive to be considered. He placed the goblet on the salver beside him.

'Tell me about your brother, Parvez Sahib,' Muzaffar said. 'Who were his enemies? People who might have profited from his death?'

Parvez frowned. 'Enemies? My brother had no enemies, Jang Sahib. He was a good man.'

'So was Jesus Christ,' Muzaffar retorted, with some asperity. He saw the look of bafflement on his guest's face, and made an attempt to be less caustic. 'Being good is no guarantee that a man will not have enemies,' he explained, as patiently as he could. 'It does not matter how good a man is, but how good others are, too. I do not dispute the fact that your brother may have been a good man; but there will always be men who will fear the integrity of a good man. Or be jealous of his good fortune – and with the wealth you and your brother possess,

I should not think that impossible...' he paused, watching the expression change on Parvez's face. Realization was taking the place of indignation, and was, in its stead, giving way to thought. Parvez's mind was busy, now, even as his eyes gazed into space, trying to think of Basharat and the enemies he might have made. He frowned, nibbled on the inside of his cheek, picked out a walnut from the bowl in front of him, then discarded it uneaten, even unshelled.

'You are right, Jang Sahib,' he said, when a few minutes had passed. 'Yes, I can think of men who would have liked to see my brother dead.' He cleared his throat. 'Shall I – do you want to know?'

'Certainly. That was why I asked.'

It spilled out, a long list of men. Merchants, petty traders, shopkeepers, an owner of camels who had once supplied animals for a caravan Basharat had gone in, all the way to Isfahan. A drunken soldier who, on a dark night, had bumped into Basharat in an alley near Matia Mahal, had been knocked into the drain and had vowed vengeance. A beggar who had come to their doorstep on Eid when Basharat had been distributing alms to the poor – and had been turned away because the last of the silver coins and the last of the leaf-wrapped packets of food had just been given to someone else.

'I suppose not the beggar,' Parvez said with a nervous giggle. 'That would be too much. But the others – ?'

'Not the soldier, either. And not the camel trader, I think, considering – did I understand this correctly? – that he was in Kabul? Or was it Lahore?'

'Kabul.'

'Precisely. I doubt if he would have come all the way to Dilli to kill your brother because of a camel that had been returned with half its tail gone.' Muzaffar had battled between laughter and anger during Parvez's list of possible enemies for Basharat. That had been replaced by excitement: there were chances here, if one sifted through them, of possible clues. Of men, perhaps, who might actually have been driven to hit out at Basharat. Enter his home, it may be, for a surreptitious meeting, a forced meeting. Carrying a knife to reinforce an argument, to act as a threat. Such a meeting could get out of hand. It could end with a man dead.

Parvez was looking crestfallen. 'You do not think any of the men I talk of could have been responsible?'

Muzaffar was quick to reassure the man. 'Absolutely not. Business rivalries can ruin men, and ruined men can be desperate. There could well be among those men some who had reason to hate your brother enough to want to do away with him... that man, the Turani, I think you said he was? Yes? And the poet who had invested his all in a consignment of carpets? You said he had even attacked Basharat Sahib in the marketplace, is that right?'

There were a couple of others, men whom Parvez was certain had resented Parvez. Ghulam Mustafa, hopeful that Basharat, a widower these past seven years, would marry his sister – but who, after having convinced himself that the match was fixed, had been furious to discover that Basharat had no intentions of ever marrying again. 'Not that my brother ever so much as met Ghulam Mustafa's sister, or expressed any desire to make her acquaintance. But you know how men can delude themselves into believing just about anything.'

There had also been Bansi, a hot-headed young man, briefly employed as a clerk, whom Basharat had suspected of having embezzled money. 'We never did find conclusive proof of it,' Parvez said, a trifle regretfully. 'But Basharat was certain he had siphoned off at least two hundred rupees. He denied it till the end.'

'Was he turned over to the authorities?'

No, he was not. Basharat had not had any proof of Bansi's guilt; the thanedar would have laughed in his face and told him to get lost. Basharat had been certain, however, and had – as a result of that certainty – turned Bansi out. Bansi had been very bitter about it.

'I doubt he would have done anything,' Muzaffar said. 'What would he have gained by murdering Basharat? If he indeed were guilty of embezzlement, he should have been thankful that he had got off without being jailed or flogged. To kill Basharat would have been pointless. And if he were indeed innocent, why turn that innocence into guilt – and that too the guilt of murder, not just theft?'

Parvez was looking, as Muzaffar had guessed he would, as if all his hopes had been dashed. 'What about Ghulam Mustafa?' he persisted. 'And the others? Do you think they too – ?'

'I would not dismiss them lightly,' Muzaffar admitted. 'But tell me one thing: did all of these men know Ameena?'

☙

Parvez had been startled. His first reaction had not been to answer Muzaffar's question, but to ask one of his own. 'Ameena?' Confusion furrowed his brow. 'Who Ameena?'

Muzaffar had explained, and Parvez had looked even more bewildered than before. 'Ameena Bibi? But why would my wife's maid know any of them? Why would that make a difference, in any case?'

He had not known of what the young maid Ismat had told Ruqayya. Muzaffar gave him a brief account of Ismat's tale: of the surreptitious night-time conversation between Ameena and an unseen conspirator, of the package thrown in, of Ameena's damning advice that the man return the next night, and go to the room where the lamp burned, because it meant that he would still be at work –

'Allah!' Parvez had breathed in sharply. 'I had no idea – and this wretched woman has vanished, too. No doubt she knew suspicion would fall on her. Where will we find her, do you think, Jang Sahib?'

Muzaffar confessed he did not know, and repeated his question about Ameena's possible acquaintance with any of the men Parvez had listed as suspects. 'Whoever killed Basharat Sahib,' he pointed out, 'was the man, I think, who spoke with Ameena that night when Ismat overheard them. And from what Ismat said she had overheard, it seems as if Ameena knew the man well enough. So whoever you suspect should have had some opportunity to have met Ameena.' He paused, mulling over what he had said. 'There is, of course, the possibility that the man made his plans well and sought out a member of your household whom he could buy over. Perhaps he offered her wealth.'

Parvez, it seemed, had not really known Ameena. He had seen her around, of course, considering she was his wife's favourite maid. And he had known of her disappearance, though it had not jolted him too much. A minor inconvenience, he had thought, dismissing it all the while as an old woman's sudden whim to go off somewhere without telling anyone.

'I will ask my Begum,' he said, as he took his leave. 'She will tell me if there is a possibility that Ameena knew any of these men.'

Muzaffar, seeing him out of the dalaan, remembered something he had meant to ask the man. 'Parvez Sahib,' he said as he held the curtain aside, its quilted chintz heavy, 'why did you leave Surat and come away to Dilli? Is not Surat a far more lucrative proposition for a merchant? I have only been briefly to the city, but I was under the impression most traders considered it the best place to trade from.'

A wary, shuttered look had crept into Parvez's eyes. He looked away, at a maulsari tree that stood beside the path, its dark green glossy canopy studded with the tiny white stars of its blossoms.

'I had made my money in Surat,' he said finally. 'It was more important for me to return to Dilli. I desired it. My brother needed me; we had begun to miss each other.'

Muzaffar nodded. 'I see. And your Begum Sahiba is, if I am not mistaken, from Surat? I believe that was what my wife mentioned to me.'

Parvez inclined his head by way of affirmation. He still looked uncomfortable 'She is.'

'She must miss her family and friends, then. Would not that have been reason enough for you to stay on in Surat?' He knew he was being – as his salty boatman friend Salim would have called it – as tactful as a bullock within sniffing distance of a cow in heat. But he could sense something elusive about Parvez's reluctance to talk of Surat and his sudden shift from there to Dilli.

'My wife has no family in Surat.'

Muzaffar's eyes narrowed. 'I had heard there was a brother. Shamsuddin? Was that his name?'

Parvez did not reply at once. They had walked past the maulsari tree, and he glanced back over his shoulder at it. 'That is a fine tree, Jang Sahib,' he murmured. 'Do you know, some people use its bark to clean their teeth? And the ancient physicians of Hindustan claimed that it cured several diseases. Sushruta, I read, recommended using its fruit and flowers to heal wounds, and its leaves as a cure for snakebite. Imagine that!' He was patently hedging, trying to avoid answering Muzaffar's question. Muzaffar bided his time and said nothing. Parvez finally sighed. 'We do not know where Shamsuddin is now,' he said finally. 'We have not heard of him for the past several years.'

Muzaffar's eyes narrowed, but he did not comment. They walked on in silence until they reached the gate, where one of the stable hands was holding Parvez's horse. Parvez took the reins from the man, who went back to the stables, leaving Muzaffar alone with his guest.

'Jang Sahib,' Parvez said, turning to look up into Muzaffar's face. His own wore an expression of deep distress. 'My brother was very dear to me. I will do anything it takes to avenge his killing. Please help me.'

Muzaffar offered a few words of comfort, and of reassurance. 'When you have asked your Begum Sahiba about Ameena, let me know,' he added. 'And if anything comes to your mind.'

The man nodded. 'I will.' He stepped forward, getting ready to mount, and stopped in midstride, shaking his head vigorously, as if in self-deprecation. 'And to imagine,' he said, with a surge of emotion, 'that I might have saved my brother by my mere presence that night!'

'How do you mean?'

'We were sitting in the room till late that night, Jang Sahib. We often did, working even after dinner. Invariably, Basharat was the first to retire' – Muzaffar wondered at the irony, considering that Parvez was the one with the wife waiting for him – 'while I would spend another hour or so in the room. That night, I had a headache. A truly frightful one that made me dizzy and nauseous. Basharat insisted I go to my room and lie down.' He rubbed his jaw, looking despondent and relieved all at the same time.

'If I had resisted him, I would have been with Basharat when the murderer entered. I might have been able to save him.'

CHAPTER 12

He would drop a word in the thanedar's ear, thought Muzaffar as he watched Parvez ride away from the gate. A word, a gentle nudge in what he hoped was the correct direction. But first, he had to go and find out more about what had happened to Abdul Jabaar. Abdul Jabaar was dead, and so was Basharat; but if Muzaffar did not move fast and try to find the man responsible for Abdul Jabaar's death, Khan Sahib might find himself in deep trouble indeed.

Muzaffar hurried to Akram's house, but his friend was not at home. An urgent summons, explained the steward of his house, from Sahib's venerable father. Akram Sahib, he added as an afterthought – a cautious afterthought – had seemed to know what it was about, and had appeared certain that he would return within an hour's time. 'Perhaps if huzoor were to wait in the dalaan?' he suggested. 'Sahib will probably be back soon.'

It was nearly noon by the time Akram returned. A warm, beautiful day it was turning out to be, though it had started out with the crisp chill of winter still in the air. There was still a light breeze ruffling the feathery canopies of the neem trees and setting the peepal leaves rustling, but the breeze was a gentle one, refreshing but not chilling. A day on which to sit out on an open verandah, drinking coffee – if one were fond of the beverage, as Muzaffar was – or sipping sherbet, if one were not. A day on which to laze about, playing chess while watching the sun shine through the trees and onto a garden bursting with flowers. A day to savour the all too short season of Dilli's spring.

For the poor, a day like any other, though greeted with the appreciation that it was not as bitingly cold as the winter gone by had been.

Abdul Jabaar's haveli, on an occasion other than this, would perhaps have been the venue for a day of lazy enjoyment: it looked made for the tranquil and luxurious comfort of the very wealthy and powerful. It spread across spacious grounds, the buildings of the mansion surrounded by a grove of mango trees.

Mohallah Abdul Jabaar Khan, the neighbourhood that had mushroomed around the dead man's haveli and drew its name from him, had come to know of the death on the very evening his corpse had been brought home. The news had spread swiftly, cobweb-like, through the surrounding mohallahs. When morning came, with it came also droves of people. Some came to offer sincere condolences; the majority came to satisfy their curiosity or to find a juicy morsel of gossip for later. All through that day, and spilling over into the morning of the next day – by which time the dead man had been interred – had come visitors. Some had come in a group, uneasy, mumbling their condolences more out of a sense of duty than anything else. Others had been too loud, too vocal in their sorrow to seem sincere.

In the early afternoon on the second day after Abdul Jabaar's death, after the crowd of visitors had thinned somewhat, an elegant young noblemen came riding down the lane. He drew his horse to a standstill outside the gate of the haveli and dismounted. He was dressed sombrely, as befitted the occasion; but even though his choga was a muted brown, his turban bereft of any decoration, and his person free of all jewellery, it was obvious that this was an amir of both means and taste. The gatekeeper, suitably awed, made a hasty and deep salaam. Yes, he said in response to a curt question. Yes; the family were all at home. If huzoor would step in – he beckoned to a servant hovering just inside the gate – huzoor would be escorted inside immediately.

That left huzoor's companion, a tall and handsome specimen, as imposing as his master, though in a different way, far less wealthy yet impressive. He was dressed simply, in plain cotton jama and pyjamas, a thick, serviceable grey shawl wrapped around his shoulders and worn leather sandals on his feet. Obviously a servant. But the expression on that face was a self-assured one. Perhaps the master belonged to the highest strata of society, and his position had rubbed off on his servant. The gatekeeper was intrigued.

While calling to a groom from the stables to take the guest's horse inside, the gatekeeper regarded the guest's servant with interest. 'Why don't you come in and sit down a while?' he asked the man, once the horse had been led away. 'There is space in here.' He indicated the low stone platforms built into the inside walls of the gatehouse to act as benches.

'I would like that,' the visitor said, with a grateful smile that made him seem more approachable than he had first appeared. 'It's been a busy day, has it?' he asked, as he entered the gatehouse and seated himself next to the gatekeeper, who had carefully chosen for himself the one warm spot on the bench where the sunlight still slanted in.

'Not as much as yesterday. All of Dilli has been trooping in here since the night before last. Some have come more than once, even though they are neither relatives nor were ever close to the master when he lived.'

'Hmm.' The visitor lifted his shawl on one side and reached into a pocket in his jama. He withdrew a small pouch of worn blue velvet, almost certainly a hand-me-down. He pulled the drawstring apart, tipped out a small pile of areca nut shavings onto his palm, and extended it to the gatekeeper in an open invitation. 'There are some advantages of working for a man like my master,' he murmured with a half-smile while the gatekeeper subjected the contents of his palm to a close inspection. 'Not much in the way of brains, but he's a good man to work with. And generous.'

'If you can afford such luxuries,' said the gatekeeper, helping himself to a large three-fingered pinch of the areca nut, 'I would say you are a man to be envied. Who is your master, by the way? I haven't seen him here before.'

'Akram Khan Sahib,' said the visitor, picking up a relatively minute pinch of areca nut and returning the closed pouch to his pocket. He tossed the areca nut into his mouth and chewed silently for a few moments before he said any more. 'The son of Abdul Munim Khan. Surely you've heard of him? One of the Baadshah's most well-respected generals.'

The gatekeeper nodded vigorously. 'Yes, yes. Of course. So is your master – Akram Sahib, did you say? – also a military man?'

The other man burst out laughing. 'Akram Sahib? Military? Never! He would faint right away at the first glimpse of blood.' He sobered suddenly, leaning a little closer to the gatekeeper as he said in a near-whisper, 'He nearly did the day before yesterday, you know. We were at the hamaam when it happened. Akram Sahib was inside; I was outside, waiting for him.'

The gatekeeper's eyes had widened. 'So your master actually saw – ?'

The visitor made a face. 'Yes. He was with a friend of his. The friend was more curious than Akram Sahib was, but Akram Sahib had to go along with it. He cribbed all the way home, about how the smell of blood had got into his clothes and his hair, and how it would take many baths to get it all out.' With his tongue, he pushed the remains of the areca nut into one cheek till it bulged like an overfull sack. 'His friend was convinced it could not have been suicide, though.'

'What?!' The gatekeeper's eyes had widened in instant shock, and his voice had sunk to a whisper. This was gossip at its juiciest, and he was well aware both of the privilege and of the dangers attendant upon paying heed to it. 'But how? Everybody said Abdul Jabaar Sahib had cut his wrists.'

The other man shrugged. 'Who knows? Akram Sahib's friend thought otherwise. He said there was something fishy about it. That perhaps' – he was now almost whispering into the gatekeeper's ear – 'he was murdered.' The visitor sat back with a smug look on his face, as if it were not mere dry areca nut he had been eating, but a paan, laced with everything from saffron to sheets of fine silver. The gatekeeper looked on, but said not a word.

'I don't know,' the visitor said after a while as he looked around him, his gaze wandering speculatively over the grounds of the haveli and the mansion itself. 'Why should anyone want to kill Abdul Jabaar Sahib, anyway? From what I've seen of this mohallah – and all the staff at the hamaam – it seems your master was universally loved and admired.'

The gatekeeper gave a snort. Whether of derision or disbelief, or some other emotion, it was hard to tell. Just as he began to say, 'Fat lot you know – ' his eyebrows came together and he sat up a little straighter. He stood up hurriedly, gesturing to his newfound friend to rise as well. 'Someone's coming,' he muttered as he stepped out of the gate into the lane outside.

Sure enough, more of the gentry had turned up to commiserate with the bereaved family. This was a large group; two middle-aged men on horseback; an old man in a palanquin; and two well-curtained palanquins, with the womenfolk inside. The visiting servant, who had been chatting all this while with the gatekeeper, slipped away inside and stood in the lee of the gate, hidden behind the rose bushes that flanked it.

ꟹ

He waited while the guests were ushered in, their horses led away and a eunuch from the mahal sara summoned to accompany the ladies' palanquins into the house. Then, when all was quiet again, he emerged.

'Ah, there you are,' the gatekeeper said. 'I thought you'd gone.'

'Where will I go? My master's still inside.' He stood for a moment, still chewing on the acrid areca nut. 'May I sit?'

'Yes, of course. Come.' The gatekeeper seated himself too.

They sat in silence, the gatekeeper ruminating, his visitor surreptitiously keeping a sharp eye on the gatekeeper. The patch of sunshine shining into the gateway had been shrinking with every passing moment; it had been reduced to a mere sword blade of light when the gatekeeper spoke up. 'Your master didn't really know mine, did he? I have never seen him here before. And I have a good memory,' he added, with a touch of pride in his voice. 'I may not remember names, but I remember faces.'

The other man nodded. 'You're right; I don't think Akram Khan Sahib knew Abdul Jabaar Sahib well. Not to visit, no. But in court, I suppose. Akram Khan Sahib was distressed enough when he discovered in the hamaam what had happened.'

The gatekeeper nodded. 'Yes,' he said, his tone disdainful. 'He would be. That's what all of this is about' – he gestured towards the far stables, outside which the horses of the visitors could be seen tethered. 'All this coming and sympathizing and saying what a good man he was. That's how the nobility, are aren't they? They stand by each other.'

The other man maintained a respectful silence. The

gatekeeper continued, his voice now bitter. 'Their philosophy in life is a simple, self-serving one: you scratch my back, and when you itch, I will scratch yours. You be good to me, get me a hefty mansab, and I'll make sure you get your share of the profits. And the other way round.'

He spat viciously into the rose bushes, leaving a spatter of brown dotting the leaves. 'They're on their best behaviour with the rest of their lot, that's how it is. All courtesy and charm and hospitality. Of course your master would respect Abdul Jabaar Sahib; everybody at court did. And he went about being such a good man, didn't he? Getting baolis dug, building that sarai and that hamaam. Have you been to the garden he laid out near the Kashmiri Darwaza?' He paused long enough to draw breath and to note that his companion had shaken his head, no.

'You should. All very welcoming, even for the poor. He was the epitome of philanthropy. All who visited the hamaam or the gardens, stayed at the sarai or drank from the baoli – all of them, without knowing him, would say what a good man he was. How noble and kind. They even say that the imam at the Imperial Masjid himself used to offer special prayers for the well-being of Abdul Jabaar Sahib! Pah!'

His voice had risen in his distress and disgust; the other man touched his forearm lightly. The gatekeeper turned to look at him, blinked and drew in a deep breath. He shook his head like a bull shaking off pesky flies; still angry, but now more in control of his emotions. 'Ah, well. I shouldn't be bothering you. Where does your master have his haveli? Somewhere close by?'

The visitor's reply was evasive. 'No, not close. He – ah, here he comes.' And sure enough, stepping out of the haveli, accompanied by a sombre-looking man who bore a pronounced resemblance to the late Abdul Jabaar Khan, was Akram Khan. He wore an expression as grim as that of his host; and his farewell – a subdued one, uttered before the two men descended the short flight of wide stone steps down to the garden – gave the impression that he was distracted. The gatekeeper had hurried off in the direction of the stables, calling for the gentleman's horse; by the time Akram had arrived at the gate, both his horse and his servant were ready for him.

☙

Neither the gatekeeper nor Akram's servant looked at each other. The horse was handed over by the stable hand who had fetched it; the servant held the bridle while the amir mounted. Then they stepped out over the threshold of the gate, the servant leading the horse by its bridle.

The horse and the man walking beside it turned at the corner and into the maze of alleys that comprised Mohallah Abdul Jabaar Khan. When they were well away from the neighbourhood, the man on foot looked up at the rider and asked, 'Well? Did you remember to leave something behind?'

'Of course I did, Muzaffar. What do you take me for?' Akram scowled. He let the horse move on a few yards before he added, 'But there's bad news. Abdul Jabaar's sons suspect foul play. One of them noticed the marks on the dead man's neck. Before Abdul Jabaar was buried, they had already called in a hakim to examine his body. They sent for the local thanedar too. They say he has begun his investigations.' He gazed anxiously into Muzaffar's face. 'I would not be surprised if Khan Sahib were dragged into this before the sun sets today.'

Muzaffar cursed, more fluently than Akram had ever heard him.

☙

Having parted ways with Akram near Faiz Bazaar, Muzaffar made his way homeward, meaning to have a quick lunch before the afternoon's work that awaited him. As he rode, impatient at the slow-moving traffic on the road – the palanquins, the bullock carts, the men lugging sacks, the many pedestrians – he remembered that he had not had a chance to tell Shireen of Abdul Jabaar's death, or of the possible danger to Khan Sahib's career and position if the killer was not swiftly brought to justice. Shireen had been sniffing, her nose turning an inelegant red and her voice going hoarse, for the past couple of days. She had treated herself with various concoctions, blends of honey and milk and turmeric and Allah knew what else, but the cold had been intent on running its course. It had become a full-blown cold, bringing with it a low fever, by the time Muzaffar had reached home the previous night. He had not thought it kind to rouse her from her bed to tell her his fears.

She had been much better this morning, and he hoped she would be well enough to give him company at lunch.

He was not destined to have lunch at home that day.

He was in the neighbourhood of his haveli – passing the chowki – when he was hailed.

'Jang Sahib!' The thanedar, his foot now appearing to be healed, was standing in the doorway of the chowki, in conversation with the chowkidar. 'I thought it was you, Jang Sahib,' the thanedar said, his sharp eyes noting Muzaffar's very plebeian costume, 'but I could not have been sure had it not been for huzoor's very distinctive height. And your stallion, too. All is well, I trust?' His gaze darted again to the shawl draped around Muzaffar's shoulders, the plain jama and pyjama, the lack of anything that would identify the wearer as an amir.

Muzaffar refused to take the hint. He nodded, muttered that all, indeed, was well, and waited with increasing impatience for the thanedar to explain why he had halted Muzaffar in his tracks.

'I have been to meet Parvez,' the thanedar said. 'He mentioned to me that he has asked you to help.'

Muzaffar winced. He had hoped Parvez would have been more circumspect. 'I have full faith in your abilities, Thanedar Sahib,' he said. 'Parvez, I think – and natural it is, too – has been severely affected by his brother's death. He is too distraught to think reasonably at the moment.'

'No, no. That was not what I meant; the very last thing I would think, in fact. No, Jang Sahib; what I meant was that if you are taking an interest in his death – surely you would have come to some conclusions by now?' He paused, eyes gleaming in anticipation, waiting with ill-concealed eagerness to hear what Muzaffar might have learned. 'Parvez tells me you are certain that maid – Ameena? – knew the killer. That he probably entered the house with her help.'

'It all appears very clandestine, does it not? Have you questioned the maid, Ismat? She was the one who overheard that conversation of Ameena's.'

'Yes, she was the first person we went and questioned when Parvez Sahib told us what you had said. The girl seems to have been very observant indeed.' The thanedar glanced in the direction of Parvez's house; from here, at the chowki, only part of the front wall of the house could be seen. 'Parvez Sahib said he had wanted to discuss the matter with his begum; that missing woman, after all, was her maid since childhood. But Begum Sahiba had gone off to Chandni Chowk and nobody seemed to know when she would be back. So he came to me directly, and then I and the chowkidar went back to his house to talk to that girl, Ismat.'

'And?'

The thanedar sighed. 'She seems to be very certain of what she heard and saw. The conversation, the packet thrown in, everything. It does appear that this Ameena was involved in Basharat's killing.' He harrumphed in sudden annoyance. 'Why could this girl not have spoken up the day Basharat was found dead?! We spent a good three hours there' – he turned towards the chowkidar, who nodded vigorously and murmured something about it having been closer to four – 'and she did not utter a word when we asked if anybody had seen or heard anything suspicious. Do you remember?' – another appeal to the chowkidar – 'outside the mahal sara, with Begum Sahiba sitting behind that screen and her maids lined up in front of her. All of them denied any knowledge. Even this one. The liar!'

His face had gone red, and his eyebrows had drawn together in a dark scowl.

A moment passed, and another. The thanedar seemed to recollect that he was standing with an amir. An amir, too, who was brother-in-law to the thanedar's own boss, the Kotwal. It was perhaps unseemly to air one's grievances in such company. He swallowed. 'However, that is neither here nor there, now that we have spoken to her.' A large bullock cart trundled past them, raising a cloud of dust, and he jumped at the chance of venting his suppressed annoyance. 'You! You, there! In the cart – what are you carrying? What's in those sacks? This is no thoroughfare, don't you know?' He turned to the chowkidar, who was already moving forward, running towards the cart with one of his men at his heels. The cart driver would be stopped, his wares examined, his permit to transport goods through the city scrutinized. Muzaffar felt sorry for the man; he was almost certainly a poor and ignorant driver, unaware of the rules that governed the transportation of goods through Shahjahanabad. Now, if the thanedar had his way, he may well get fined.

The thanedar's attention had suddenly shifted, his gaze turning from enraged to curious. 'What on earth – ' he began to say as he stepped forward. Muzaffar turned, looking to see what had caught the thanedar's eye.

ঙ

Just a few yards from the chowki, a man was approaching at a fast clip, impeded though he was by a young woman whom he was holding by the elbow and dragging along. They came to a halt in front of the chowki. The man was panting, whether from exertion or agitation, Muzaffar could not tell. The girl's skirts, the hem muddy from dragging in the damp earth of the lane, whipped momentarily around the man's legs and then fell into place. She was, thought Muzaffar as he looked down at that tear-streaked face, probably not even sixteen years old.

'Rahim,' said the thanedar, fisted hands on his hips. 'That is your name, is it not? And, if I recall correctly, this is Ismat.' He transferred his gaze to the girl. She was staring straight down at her feet, the worn leather of her shoes – certainly cast-offs, for servants and slaves did not wear shoes, unless possibly they worked for the Emperor – smeared with mud. She did not look up, but Muzaffar heard a whisper of assent, 'Yes, huzoor.'

'Well?'

Rahim looked down at the bowed, dupatta-covered head of the girl with contempt. 'Begum Sahiba has sent her apologies. Tell Thanedar Sahib, girl. It is for you to explain yourself.'

There was an audible gulp – or a sniff, Muzaffar could not tell – from beneath the dupatta.

'Hurry up,' snapped the thanedar. 'We have other work to do. What is it? Did you remember something else?'

The girl did not respond until Rahim gave her a sharp nudge. She winced at that, and then, after what sounded suspiciously like a sob, began to speak. It was all a lie, she confessed. She had not seen Ameena Bibi that night. Not in the courtyard, not whispering at the door leading outside, nowhere. There had been no one in the courtyard that night. It had been empty. She had not seen Ameena Bibi. Not at all.

Her words were running into each other, colliding and getting garbled in her distress.

'She is sadly childish, huzoor,' Rahim said, cutting Ismat short. 'And her imagination is too active for her own good. Begum Sahiba had not been at home when you came to question Ismat a while ago, as you well know. Begum Sahiba came back less than a quarter of an hour ago, only to find that Ismat had so terribly misled you – Begum Sahiba begs your forgiveness. Had she known – '

The thanedar, to his credit, looked sceptical. 'It does not make any sense to me. Why tell such tall tales when there is no need to do so? Why unnecessarily cook up a story?'

'I told you, huzoor; she imagines things – '

'I asked the girl, not you. Speak up, Ismat – that is your name, is it not? Why did you concoct that story?' His gaze, stern and disapproving, switched briefly to Muzaffar, and then back to the girl. Muzaffar, from the corner of his eye, saw that, some fifteen yards away, the chowkidar, till then busy inspecting the cart and talking to its driver, had turned to look towards the chowki. Obviously Ismat's forced visit to the chowki was of more interest to him than an errant cart. He glanced ruefully back at the cart, then with a word to the soldier who had accompanied him, turned away and headed back towards the chowki. The soldier, somewhat at a loss, stood beside the cart. He prodded one of the sacks with the end of his lance, and said something to the cart driver.

A few minutes more, thought Muzaffar, and the soldier would lose interest too and return to the chowki.

The thanedar was addressing Ismat. 'Jang Sahib here has already told me that you recounted the same story to his Begum Sahiba's maid, too, yesterday. Why?'

The girl had glanced up hurriedly at this allusion to Ruqayya; she coloured and looked down again. 'I – I thought she was looking for gossip.' Her voice fell, to a barely audible mutter. 'I thought it would be fun to give her some.'

'And you thought it would be fun to give the law some

gossip, too?!' The thanedar rasped out the words, flinging them at her so loudly that she flinched. 'I have a good mind to clap you in prison!'

'No, huzoor,' she babbled – Muzaffar could hear panic in her voice now, not just fear – 'that was not it. I did not know – ' she gulped, took a deep breath, and carried on. 'I hated Ameena Bibi. She was not a nice woman. I wanted her to get into trouble. That was why I said – '

The thanedar cut her off in mid-sentence. 'Not a nice woman? Why do you say that?'

There was utter silence. Ismat appeared to have turned to stone. Rahim nudged her. 'Thanedar Sahib is asking you a question. Don't make him wait!' He shook her slightly, and Muzaffar was tempted to tell him to desist; the girl was scared enough as it was.

'Well?' The thanedar sounded impatient.

'She – she was nasty.' The girl was barely audible.

'What did she do that was so nasty? And did not your mistress reprimand for it, if that were so?'

Ismat looked up, taken aback. Her astonishment had, for the time being, overtaken her fear of the thanedar. 'Begum Sahiba would not – she would not scold Ameena Bibi,' she said, in an awed whisper, as if the very thought was unspeakable. 'Ameena Bibi knew it too. She was always preening herself and boasting about how Begum Sahiba relied on her so much. She used to shout at the rest of us, say that she would get us dismissed or flogged or – or – ' She paused for breath, then seemed to give up on that sentence, unable to think of the punishments the much-dreaded Ameena had threatened them all with. 'None of us liked her.'

The soldier who had been stationed next to the cart had abandoned his post and returned to the chowki. To Muzaffar's amused astonishment, the cart driver had come too, more curious than prudent. They were not the only ones. Inquisitive passersby had slowed their steps; a few had stopped and were making no attempt to disguise their curiosity. In the few minutes since Rahim had dragged Ismat from Parvez's house into the presence of the thanedar, the chowki had become an exciting place. A place where something interesting was happening. Muzaffar, watching from the corner of his eye, could see faces filled with curiosity, could already hear the low hum of gossip. 'Go,' the thanedar snapped. 'Take her away, Rahim. And you, girl! Listen well. If I hear one more word of your gossip-mongering, I shall make sure you regret it for the rest of your life!'

ɞ

The thanedar's shoulders slumped. 'And so we run up against another blank wall,' he murmured. He looked into Muzaffar's eyes, his own disappointed. 'We are back where we began. With no clues to go on.'

He glanced over his shoulder at the chowkidar. 'Have you met Parvez? Did he give you a list of men who knew Basharat? Associates, other traders, buyers?' He waited for the chowkidar's quick nod of assent, and carried on. 'Start questioning them, if you haven't already.'

'I have begun, huzoor. I met five of them last evening.' The chowkidar rattled off some names. Muzaffar recognized them all. There was the man whose sister Basharat had refused to marry. And Bansi, the clerk whom Basharat had accused of embezzling funds. There were some others. 'All of them denied it.'

'Of course they would. But could they provide evidence of their innocence?'

There had been that, too. Two of the men – both merchants, like Basharat and Parvez – had been attending a wedding. They had participated in the festivities, feasting and singing till late into the night. That too at a haveli near Mehrauli; they had supplied the chowkidar with the names and addresses of a long list of reputable people, including several amirs, who had been present at the function. They could be vouched for.

They had not said so, but Muzaffar, the chowkidar and the thanedar had also noticed the other implication. Mehrauli was well outside the city walls, and a good way south. Even if the men had started out from the haveli in Mehrauli before dark – as they had not – they would not have made it to Dilli before the gates slammed shut for the night.

Bansi, who had greeted the news of Basharat's death with a look of unholy glee, had had an equally good explanation of his whereabouts on the night of Basharat's murder. He was now employed with a merchant who dealt in human wares: midgets, dancing girls, slaves from exotic lands. On that night, Bansi had accompanied a group of dancing girls to perform for a certain nawab. The chowkidar had taken the initiative to visit the nawab. Bansi had told the truth.

'The others,' said the chowkidar, with quiet satisfaction, 'could offer no proof of their innocence. They were all in the city on that night, and other than family members – who, of course, may be expected to hide the truth – nobody can say that they did not indeed sneak away.'

'Ah,' said the thanedar, the chowkidar's triumph reflected in his own expression and voice. 'That is good. Very good. What do you think, Jang Sahib?' he asked, turning to Muzaffar. 'Some rigorous interrogation, and I think we can possibly make one of them confess.'

Muzaffar, inwardly repulsed at this calm and matter-of-fact allusion to torture, shook his head. It did not take him long to repeat what he had said to Parvez: that the man who had killed Basharat had been in league with Ameena. 'You would do well, I think, to seek an interview with Ameena's mistress, Parvez's Begum. She might be able to cast some light on which of these men Ameena is likely to have known. I suppose Nilofer Begum would have kept tabs on her maid: where she went, whom she visited – I suppose she might have gone on errands now and then on behalf of her mistress; Begum Sahiba could hardly have sent a mere chit like Ismat – ' he broke off, his eyes suddenly alert, his nostrils thinning as if he sniffed something in the air.

'Allah,' he whispered, half to himself.

'Huzoor? Jang Sahib?'

Muzaffar stared, his gaze riveted on the wall of Parvez's house, across the street. The chowkidar and the thanedar exchanged glances, puzzled. They probably thought him an eccentric, he realized. But they would not say so. He was, after all, the brother-in-law of their boss. The boss, Muzaffar remembered with a sudden twinge of conscience, who might be in great danger if Muzaffar did not quickly return to his investigation. He had to get back to that.

'No,' he said briskly, turning back to the thanedar. 'No, don't go to Parvez's Begum. Don't you see, she must be on Ameena's side? She returned home, to find that Ismat had blurted out everything to you, so she sent Ismat here with that man to tell you that it had all been a lie' – the two officers of the law were now looking wide-eyed and bewildered; Muzaffar had to explain. 'Ismat had not been lying when she first recounted that conversation she had overheard. There were too many details in her narrative, things she could have no logical reason for dreaming up, even if she wanted to get Ameena into trouble.'

'Basharat had already been murdered when Ismat was questioned,' the thanedar said. 'And even when she spoke to your Begum Sahiba's maid, Jang Sahib. Just saying that she had heard Ameena talking to someone, telling him to come the following night, to look for the burning lamp, all of that – it would be enough for us to immediately suspect Ameena.'

'Ismat could have that much foresight,' Muzaffar conceded. 'But if you credit her with so much cunning, then credit her also with the intelligence to realize what would happen if she was found out. As she would, sooner or later, considering she was testifying to the law, not just sharing gossip with someone else's maid. You would take that seriously, would you not? She would not be let off with a mere scolding if she had cost the thana time and money and effort in trying to trace Ameena – and it had turned out be a wild goose chase.

'And there is the fact of her shoes,' he added. 'When narrating the incident of Ameena, Ismat had mentioned that she had taken off her shoes, which tended to squeak, because she wanted to listen without being detected.' He gave a soft smile. 'A little while back, when that man had brought her here, I noticed that her shoes do squeak. Quite terribly. Small details like that tend to get left out if they aren't really true.' He shook his head. 'No, Thanedar Sahib; I think you should take Ismat's testimony seriously.'

'Which implies that Nilofer Begum is not to be trusted?'

Muzaffar shrugged. 'I do not know. Perhaps she is blindly devoted to her old servant. Ameena had brought her up, had she not?' He had been moving as he spoke, reaching for the horse he had tethered to a spindly young fig tree beside the chowki. Now, as he untied the reins and prepared to mount, a thought came to him. He stopped and looked back. 'Ameena had also brought up Nilofer Begum's brother, Shamsuddin. It might be useful, Thanedar Sahib, to write to the Kotwal at Surat and ask about Shamsuddin's whereabouts. Parvez says they have not had any contact with him for a long time; I am curious. Could it be that Ameena has kept in touch with Shamsuddin? Could she have gone off to him?'

The thanedar looked flummoxed, but nodded. Muzaffar clicked his tongue at his horse, urging it on. He had gone a mere ten paces when he drew rein and returned. 'It might be a good idea to arrange a meeting between Parvez and Suraj Bhan, in your presence,' he said, addressing the thanedar. 'They are already acquainted with each other, so I do not think that will pose a challenge. And they both wish to get to the root of the matter; Suraj Bhan for Aadil's sake, Parvez for his brother's.' He had seen the bewilderment that had made the thanedar glassy-eyed, and though he was in a hurry, stopped long enough to add a few words of explanation. 'Surely you see? Aadil and Basharat – both merchants, and living in neighbouring houses – were stabbed to death in the middle of the night, and their documents searched through, though nothing was stolen? It seems very likely to me that the hand that killed Basharat was the same that had murdered Aadil. It might be useful if Suraj Bhan and Parvez were to compare notes about Aadil and Basharat's associates, possible enemies they may have had in common. It will narrow down the scope of your investigation somewhat, I think.'

'Especially as Ameena Bibi is nowhere to be – ' the thanedar began to say, but Muzaffar had already turned away. His horse galloped off down the road, a little faster than might have been considered prudent.

Muzaffar, keeping a sharp eye on the road and a firm grip on the reins, wondered what would come of this investigation. There seemed to be suspects, but no concrete evidence. And no very good motive. Then there was Ameena, with her macabre interest in Aadil's killing, and then her implication in Basharat's killing. Hers, Muzaffar was certain, could not have been the hand that had wielded the dagger in either case; that had required, surely, a stronger arm, younger. But she was involved. Why? How?

But he had other things on his mind, and they occupied it to the exclusion of all else as he rode away.

CHAPTER 13

Half an hour later, Muzaffar was back at the gate of Abdul Jabaar's haveli. Whatever visitors there had been had long gone. The haveli was quiet, and the gatekeeper sat on one of the stone benches in the gatehouse, his chin resting on his chest, his eyes closed. Muzaffar, clearing his throat, tapped the man gently on the shoulder. The gatekeeper woke with a start, disoriented for a moment.

Akram Sahib hated to bother the family, especially on a day such as this, said Muzaffar, apologizing on behalf of his 'master'. On his visit to the house earlier that day, Akram Sahib must have left his jade ring behind. Accidentally dropped, perhaps, or slipped off – huzoor was in the habit of slipping it on and off, playing with it, when distressed. And Allah knew he had cause for distress, what with the news of Abdul Jabaar Sahib's death – the gatekeeper received this last bit of information with a sarcastic smile, and was favoured with a similar smile from Muzaffar.

The essence of the request was simple: would a servant of the household please be deputed to search for the ring? It was bound to be in the dalaan where Akram Sahib had sat. There were many apologies for the trouble caused. Had it been anything else, it could have been overlooked without a second thought. But this was no mere trinket. It was an heirloom that could not be simply left to lie. A thorough search had been conducted in Akram Sahib's own house – but in vain. Sahib would be eternally grateful.

The steward, summoned to listen to this plea, looked annoyed, but nodded in a curt way and returned to the house. Muzaffar turned back to his old friend the gatekeeper, who was looking on with amusement. 'Come and sit down,' the man said. 'You wouldn't have any of that supaari still on you, would you?' When Muzaffar, chuckling, retrieved the pouch from his pocket, the man added, 'you may as well sit here a while. If I know the steward, he won't be in a hurry to set men to searching for your master's ring. The thanedar's in there now, with his men, talking to the master. Abdul Jabaar Sahib's elder son,' he added, by way of clarification. He was leaning so close that Muzaffar could see the fine crimson threads of blood vessels spreading through his eyes, like cracks in fragile glass.

Muzaffar raised an eyebrow. 'Does that mean they are convinced it is murder? Not suicide?'

'That's what your sahib's friend thought too, didn't he? Perhaps he knew what he was talking about.'

Muzaffar sat back, his expression thoughtful. The gatekeeper chewed on his mouthful of areca nut. Muzaffar had returned the pouch to his pocket; he watched the gatekeeper in silence for a while before asking, 'What do you think?'

'Me?' The man turned, startled. 'What do you mean? What would I think?'

'Do you think anyone would have wanted to murder Abdul Jabaar Sahib?'

The man looked sideways at Muzaffar and said nothing. His eyes were level, his gaze watchful, as if he were trying to size Muzaffar up. 'Why do you ask?'

Muzaffar shrugged. 'It is nothing to me. I wondered, that is all. When we were sitting here earlier, from what you said, I gathered he wasn't a good man. That all that goodness was a farce, a façade to fool others.'

The gatekeeper looked on, silent.

'It seems somebody wasn't fooled,' Muzaffar said softly.

The gatekeeper chuckled, in wry appreciation of the end Abdul Jabaar had come to. The suspicion in his eyes had dulled, replaced now by some of the camaraderie he had shared with Muzaffar earlier that day.

'Was he corrupt?' Muzaffar asked.

'Corrupt? In what sense? Women?' The gatekeeper glanced – perhaps involuntarily – towards the mahal sara, the women's quarters, of the haveli. From the gate, all that was visible was a single-storied blank wall, plastered with a coat of lime to a pristine white. All the windows would be on the inside, overlooking the inner gardens, safe from the gaze of every wanderer who happened to come through the gate. 'He wasn't interested in corrupting any women. He had three begums, you know. The gossip is that he never did pay them much attention, anyway. They gave him his heirs in the first few years of their marriages, and that was it. No more visiting them – or any other women, actually – after that.'

'That wasn't quite what I meant,' Muzaffar said. 'I meant corrupt in another sense. Bribery, embezzlement, things like that.'

'I'm a gatekeeper, not a bloody minister of the Baadshah's!' the gatekeeper snapped. 'How am I supposed to know whether he took bribes or got up to other unsavoury business?!' He sat up, ramrod stiff and bristling with annoyance. Muzaffar held his tongue, waiting for the man's anger to subside. His mind wandered.

What conclusion had the thanedar come to, he wondered. Had Abdul Jabaar Khan been murdered, or had he really killed himself? The dead man's sons seemed to have convinced themselves that it was, indeed, murder. Some would say that was natural; they would want to keep the family's honour intact, and it was far from honourable for a man to kill himself. What would the thanedar have decided?

He wondered if it was a thanedar he knew. He had been introduced to some of them in the course of his visits to the kotwali. He searched mentally through the list of thanas, trying to remember the jurisdictions of each thanedar. Under whom would Mohallah Abdul Jabaar Khan fall? Would the man come striding out, and recognize in the gatekeeper's companion a nobleman of Dilli? Would Muzaffar have the time and the opportunity to make his escape before that happened?

The gatekeeper harrumphed, a sound Muzaffar took to mean that he was being forgiven for having annoyed his host. And that the host was offering an apology, if not in words, for having lost his temper at what was a trifling matter. He looked back at the gatekeeper with an expression carefully schooled to a bland mildness.

'Mind you,' said the gatekeeper, now a little more in command of himself, 'I don't blame you for thinking all this luxury is the result of ill-gotten gains. But not from what I've heard. Of course, perhaps the poor peasants back at his estates in the countryside are paying for it with their blood, sweat and tears, as they say... I wouldn't be surprised at all.' He dragged the toe of his sandal along a flagstone, as if marking out a line. When he looked back up at Muzaffar, he shook his head. 'Maybe he was corrupt. I don't know.'

He had forgotten his anger at his inquisitive visitor, but the gatekeeper's resentment against his former master still festered. Muzaffar wondered what it would take to draw out the reason – and, just as importantly – how long it would take. 'And yet you say he was not really a good man,' Muzaffar prompted.

'He was not. Would you call a man good who could have men killed for the smallest of faults? A man who would not flinch from whipping someone – for stealing a roti, or for forgetting to feed a horse. Or something equally trivial?'

'He did that?'

The gatekeeper's head dipped. When he spoke, he did not sound annoyed or indignant, just weary. His voice dragged, so slow and so soft that Muzaffar had to strain to catch the words half-mumbled into the speaker's beard. 'He was a cruel man. Your master seems like a lenient sort. You look well-fed, well looked after. You don't what it is to be starved or flogged, do you?'

'You don't look as if you've been ill-treated either.'

'I just sit at the gate; all I can be faulted for are minor offences. Not opening the door quickly enough when the master arrives. Not opening it wide enough. Not closing it soon enough after he's passed through. Those are the offences for which I've merely been kicked, if Sahib happened to be in a good mood. Or, if he was already irritated and had the time, I've been taken aside and whipped.'

Muzaffar blinked.

'There was a whipping here last month,' the gatekeeper mumbled. 'Here, just here.' He pointed to where a rose bush grew, only about three yards along the paved path connecting the gatehouse to the haveli. 'Wahid, the son of one of the stablehands. Just ten years old.'

'A child? Whipped? But why?'

'He came running out of the stables just as Sahib's horse was being led in. He ran straight into the path of the horse. It was startled and reared up. Broke free of the stable hand who had been leading it, and raced off into the trees, there.' He gestured in the direction of the grove that spread along the western half of the haveli's grounds. 'When they got to the horse, they found it had run straight into a low branch.'

Muzaffar winced. The gatekeeper's face was wiped clean of all emotion. 'Oh, the horse wasn't wounded seriously. Just a gash on the shoulder. It was sewn up. There'll be a scar, but no more.'

'And the boy was flogged for it?' It was no small matter, of course, and Muzaffar knew of men so devoted to their horses, men who spent more on their steeds than on their families, who would have been furious had it been their horse that had been scarred so. He did not think, however, that any would have been so cruel as to have had a child whipped. For something, too, that was not his fault. Mere accident, from what he could tell.

'Abdul Jabaar Sahib and his two sons saw it happen.' The gatekeeper heaved a deep sigh, and Muzaffar watched as a tear made its way down the man's seamed old cheek. He seemed oblivious of it; he carried on speaking. 'The two sons caught Wahid and dragged him back to Sahib. A grown man might have been able to break free. What chance was there for a child? He struggled and cried. Even bit the elder son.' He gulped, his voice finally cracking, the half-contained sorrow bubbling up. 'Wahid's father, Faraaz, got down on his knees and caught hold of Sahib's feet. He wept – I have never seen him wail like that – and begged for his child to be forgiven. Said that he would sell even the clothes off his back, would do whatever it took to replace the horse.'

A forlorn hope, imagined Muzaffar. A pauper, pledging to replace a nobleman's best horse? It was laughable.

The gatekeeper's voice had trailed off. There was an unreal moment of silence. Not a bird chirped in the trees around, not a voice called within the haveli, not a utensil clanged inside. 'Sahib used his own whip to flog Wahid,' the man said, after a few moments had slipped by. 'He got his sons to hold the boy down, his arms and legs outstretched so that he was spread-eagled all over the path. And then he flogged him till Wahid stopped crying.' Another tear trickled down his cheek, and another.

cЗ

'Have you seen how the bark peels off some trees?' he said softly. 'That was what Wahid's back looked like when Sahib had finished with him. Faraaz would have ended up the same way as his son, if I and two of his colleagues from the stables hadn't held him back. When Sahib and his sons had gone inside, we helped Faraaz take the child into the huts behind the stables. We got a hakim too. But it was no use.'

'Wahid died?' Muzaffar asked quietly. It sounded an unnecessary question, even to his own ears. From what the gatekeeper had recounted, it seemed hardly likely that the child would have survived.

The gatekeeper did not answer the question. He did not even acknowledge that he had heard it. Instead, he continued his tale. 'Sahib would not even give Faraaz leave to go fetch the rest of his family. When Faraaz asked, he simply said, "You and yours have cost me enough. I cannot afford to have you go gallivanting all over the countryside."'

'Why? Did Faraaz have to go far?'

The man nodded regretfully. 'To Kanauj. He has an uncle there, and cousins. Now that Wahid is dead, Faraaz has nobody but them. From what I've heard him say, they would have been a great comfort to him at this time. He had a letter writer pen a note to them, and sent it through one of those men in the marketplace, who act as public couriers. That was all he could do. He wasn't allowed to go.'

He straightened up, blinking the tears away and hurriedly swiping at his cheeks with gnarled, knobby knuckles. 'Don't look so appalled. We have grown used to this. We must; there is no other way to survive. At least not if one is to remain sane.' He wiped his hand on his jama. 'I've been at this post since I was half your age – we lived in Agra then. I grew up in the household of Abdul Jabaar Sahib's father. They are all alike, the men of this family. Abdul Jabaar. His father. His sons.'

Muzaffar thought of asking more about the sons of Abdul

Jabaar, but the gatekeeper was still lost in his memories. Haunting, terrible memories to take to one's bed at night, thought Muzaffar as he listened.

'Years ago, I remember a barber who accidentally nicked Sahib while shaving him. It was no more than a scratch; we all saw it later that day, on Sahib's jaw. Do you know what Sahib did? Grabbed the blade from the man's hands, forced him down onto the mattress, and – and gelded him.

'Then there was this cook – Mustaqil – whom Sahib summoned because the limes he had served up at a banquet weren't juicy enough. Sahib liked to squeeze lime juice over the kababs, and those limes had proven unworthy of being presented on Sahib's table. When the guests were gone, Sahib called for Mustaqil. He had three men hold him down, and then he called one of the kitchen servants to bring fresh, ripe limes. Each of those he halved with his own hands and squeezed into the cook's eyes.'

He shut his eyes, squeezing them hard as if experiencing that long-ago cook's agony for himself. 'I could hear Mustaqil's screams from here. He moaned all night, until Sahib had him thrown out of the house because his cries were not letting the family sleep.'

Muzaffar swallowed. He had not realized how dry his throat was, constricted and choked, as if he had been one of those lying awake in Abdul Jabaar's haveli that night, listening to the cook's screams.

They sat there in the gatehouse, the two men. A gatekeeper and his visitor, one lost in the grief he was reliving, the other thinking over what he had been told. There was a sudden flurry of wings as a small flock of pigeons, roosting on the dripstone overhanging the entrance of the haveli, took off in fright. Somebody had emerged. Muzaffar looked up, squinting against the sunlight.

It was a servant, bearing a ring of carved jade. 'Is this your master's?' he asked, when he reached the gate. 'That's the only thing we could find in the dalaan which didn't belong to anybody in the household.'

Muzaffar took it – he had seen it often enough on Akram's hand to recognize it as belonging to his friend – and, with a subdued farewell to the gatekeeper, took his leave.

It took him half an hour to make his way to Akram's haveli, where he changed into his usual, more refined attire. It took him just as long to recount to an impatient Akram all that he had gleaned from the gatekeeper at Abdul Jabaar's house. 'He was not a kind man,' Muzaffar said quietly, hunched over bent knees, as he sat in Akram's dalaan. He was shaken. What the gatekeeper had told him had come as a shock. Muzaffar had never thought he had lived a sheltered life. Now he realized how wrong he had been. 'No,' he said, shaking his head. 'What am I saying? Abdul Jabaar was not merely unkind; he was cruel. A tyrant. Vicious. And men like that make far more enemies than they can ever imagine.'

'It is one thing, however,' he added, 'to know that a man has enemies, and to find him murdered in a closely-watched room. I wonder if Ilyas had been at the receiving end of one too many of Abdul Jabaar's cruelties?'

'How do you mean to find out?'

'By asking him.' Muzaffar looked up. His face was wiped clean of emotion. 'I think I know how to lead him into revealing how he actually felt about Abdul Jabaar. Perhaps he may also slip up and let fall a hint of what really happened that day at the hamaam.'

'What if he's too cautious? What if you aren't able to find out?'

'I shall try other means,' Muzaffar said. 'It will not be the first time I have had to don a disguise and follow a man about.' He got to his feet. 'Do you want to come with me?'

ꟲ

'There could be other reasons for Abdul Jabaar's murder, could there not?' Akram asked, in a hesitant voice, as they mounted their horses and started off for Hamaam Abdul Jabaar Khan. 'I know you said the gatekeeper ruled out women and corruption – and I know for a fact that Abdul Jabaar was generally not known to be a corrupt man; he could afford to be honest. But there could be other reasons. What if he was killed for his wealth?'

'He was a high-ranking amir, Akram. The only beneficiary from his death will be the state.'

Akram nodded, his expression morose. 'Escheat? Yes, you're right, of course. I had forgotten.'

The principle of escheat applied to all the possessions of the Mughal nobility who happened to be Muslims. The Rajput aristocrats were exempt, but the Muslims, whether they liked it or not, had to bow to the law. On a Muslim nobleman's death, all his wealth – his lands, his mansions, whatever he possessed – became the property of the state. The Baadshah could choose to distribute a dead man's wealth as he saw fit. One palace may be gifted to a loyal amir; another mansion may be handed over as a sop to a petty princeling who might prove a useful ally in a future tussle for power and wealth. A fertile stretch of land may be given to a favourite royal offspring. And perhaps a few lakhs' worth may be given, if the Emperor was in a generous mood, to the sons and daughters of the man who had died.

It was not feasible to keep an eye on every single Muslim nobleman in the empire, so the lesser nobility died without anyone taking any note. Their possessions – such as they might be – passed on unhindered to the man's own heirs. That was how it had been with Muzaffar himself. His father, Burhanuddin Malik Jang, while an able general and a well-respected one, had been relatively low in the hierarchy. He had passed away when Muzaffar was a gangly fifteen year-old, and his modest lands and equally modest store of wealth had come to Muzaffar with no obstacles posed en route by the exchequer.

With Abdul Jabaar, the case would be very different, thought Muzaffar. This was a man not just powerful and high-ranking, but also very much in the public eye. And, most important of all, fabulously wealthy. That mouth-watering wealth would attract the attention of the exchequer like syrup draws ants.

'No wonder he went around building hamaams and sarais and laying out gardens,' Akram said. 'Those works – his philanthropy – are the only property his family can lay claim to.' Muzaffar nodded, half-lost in his own thoughts, but aware enough of the laws governing escheat. Yes, assets created for the public good, or to glorify the Almighty, remained with a family despite the death of the man who had created them.

'I doubt if Abdul Jabaar's sons will be particularly pleased about being saddled with a whole lot of sarais and gardens and whatnot,' Akram said. 'After all, they will be expected to maintain them, if not for anything but to uphold their father's name. And what is the point of inheriting something that will only be a drain on your wealth?'

Muzaffar was brooding. 'If he was not murdered for his wealth, could there be another reason? While I was gone, were you able to find anything out? Some gossip?'

Akram nodded. 'I paid a couple of visits to some amirs, men who knew Abdul Jabaar better than I did. Some who did not hold him in high esteem, either.'

'You didn't tell them that you suspected the man had been murdered, did you?'

'Of course not. Do you take me for a fool? I went along with everybody's assumption that it was suicide. Not that that notion will last long; Abdul Jabaar's sons have called in the thanedar and convinced him it was a murder, after all. How long before that becomes common knowledge?'

'Go on, go on.' Muzaffar nodded, impatient. 'What did you learn?'

'Not very much. Nothing that could provide a clue to why anybody would want to kill him, I think. He was not greatly involved in court politics any more, so it isn't as if anybody would have gained a mansab or other political power from killing him off. ' He turned his horse leftward, towards the hamaam. Muzaffar followed suit. 'But who knows? Every man has secrets. Abdul Jabaar had lived a long and eventful life. Perhaps he had made enemies along the way. An enemy for some obscure reason, letting revenge fester in his heart – ' Akram saw the pained look on Muzaffar's face, and cut himself off in mid-sentence. 'I mean,' he said, with a sheepish grin, 'there could be something nobody even knows about. He was not a man who paraded his every deed for the world to see, you know: only the good ones, the philanthropy. Perhaps he had a very tainted past.'

'There has to be not just motive, but opportunity too,' Muzaffar said. 'It is not easy to find a means of killing a man like Abdul Jabaar, who is almost always surrounded by others, whether servants or family – the man who killed him that day must have laid his plans very carefully.'

'"The man"?' Akram repeated. 'Do you not think it was Ilyas, any more?'

'I did not say so. And who knows, Ilyas's may only have been the hands that throttled Abdul Jabaar. Perhaps he was hired by someone else. One of these men whom, as you say, Abdul Jabaar might have antagonized years ago. Might have.'

'You don't sound convinced.'

They were nearly at the hamaam. The bath house, after the sobering lull imposed by the death of its owner, was back in business. Men were climbing the short row of steps up to the entrance, chattering between themselves; the doorkeeper was busy bending, dropping salaams, accepting with suitable gratitude the tips left by pleased and benevolent patrons.

'I am sceptical,' Muzaffar admitted. 'For a man to kill another, the provocation must be great indeed. And provocations like that have a way of making themselves known; few men can hide the anger or the resentment they feel so well that nobody is aware of it. You say you met men who knew Abdul Jabaar well, for many years too, is that right?'

Akram nodded.

'And they knew of nothing in his past that could have provoked a man to kill him?'

Akram shook his head. They had dismounted at the entrance to the stable; Muzaffar handed over the reins of his horse to the stable hand on duty. Akram followed suit.

'Let us go into the hamaam,' Muzaffar said quietly. 'And talk to this Ilyas. It really all hinges on him, because he was the only man there – besides that vanished patron, whom Ilyas claims discovered the body.'

☙

Akram was taken aback to find Muzaffar asking the attendant in the central vestibule if the bathing chamber that had been Abdul Jabaar Sahib's private hot bath was now available to the public. Could they use it? Or had the new owners, Abdul Jabaar Sahib's sons, barred it to visitors? Did they use it?

The man looked surprised; no one, it seemed, had come asking to use the bath in which a man had bled to his death. 'Sahib's sons do not use the baths here, huzoor,' he said. 'The bathing chamber is open, if you should wish to use it. Not many do.'

'Ah, good. We shall be on our own then. Does Ilyas still look after the chamber?'

Yes, he did. It was not unusual; a servant who had spent so many hundreds of working hours within the confines of a bathing chamber and its dressing area knew every nook and cranny of the space. He would know where to look if water began welling up from a pipe under the floor. He would know how long it took for fresh hot water to flow in from the pipes, how long for the tank to be cleaned and readied for a new entrant. Abdul Jabaar's sons, their feet too firmly on the ground to be sentimental about making this room a secluded shrine to the memory of their father, had decided to keep it open for business; the obvious choice as attendant would be the man who knew it best.

He recognized Muzaffar immediately, even though Akram – a few steps behind Muzaffar, and half-hidden behind his taller, broader friend – had not yet come into sight. He greeted them, courteous but unobtrusive. The perfect hamaam attendant, thought Muzaffar, as Ilyas went to open the pipes to let in the hot water. The perfect servant, too: quiet, melting into the walls, almost. Leaving you to think you were all alone, even when you were not. He slipped off his choga and began untying the strings of his jama, wondering how much this very silent attendant had heard and seen that fateful day.

The two noblemen had lowered themselves into the hot water and Ilyas had turned to leave the room when Muzaffar called out to him, 'Did you ever see that man again?'

'Huzoor?'

Muzaffar scooped up warm water in his cupped hand and poured it over the back of his bent neck. He repeated the question, in as offhand a voice as when he had first asked it. He did not raise his head, look up at Ilyas, or show the slightest indication that he was interested in the man's answer. Akram, sitting immobile nearby, the water sloshing gently about his waist, looked nervous.

It was a few moments before Ilyas replied. 'No, huzoor,' he said, and then – before Muzaffar could say anything – 'I – I mean – you do mean the man who found Abdul Jabaar Sahib, that day? I suppose that is whom huzoor meant?'

Ah, thought Muzaffar. So that was the conclusion Ilyas had jumped to. Was it because the incidents of that day were still preying on his mind? Was that guilt speaking? Or – a sobering thought, a reminder of the many times Kotwal Sahib had cautioned him to not apportion guilt to a suspect without knowing all the facts – was it just a result of a shocking incident in which he had been closely involved, the only known witness?

He had finished dousing his neck; he moved his hand to his chest and began scrubbing. 'Yes,' he said, his voice neutral. 'I did mean that man. I wondered if he came back. One would think he would. Just out of curiosity, perhaps? On the other hand' – he stretched, flexing his shoulders, wincing as stiff, tired muscles ached in protest – 'it may well be that he is haunted by his memory of finding that dead body and all the blood here. It could scare off a man forever.'

Ilyas shrugged. 'I think it has scared off even those who did not see the room that day, huzoor. Very few people come to this chamber to bathe, even though it is now open to all.'

He had to tread carefully, thought Muzaffar. No sudden moves, no overtly probing questions, nothing that might make Ilyas retreat into the shell from which he seemed to be tentatively beginning to poke his head out. 'You must be right. That man must have been scared out of his wits when he found the dead body. And dead in such a gruesome way, too.' He had begun to, awkwardly, knead his own shoulders. 'Most men, though, would have been curious enough to hang around and see what came of it,' he added, in a conversational tone. 'This one must have been one of those timid sorts, I suppose? Or squeamish? One of those oversensitive fops who faint away at the mere mention of blood? '

Ilyas had walked a few steps across to the stone bench on which lay a low pile of folded towels, each of them of fine, absorbent cotton. He picked up two. 'He did not look the type to do that, huzoor,' he said. 'Far from it.' He had arrived at the edge of the pool of water, the towels laid neatly across his outstretched palms, folded edges hanging neatly off either side of his hands. A precise man, thought Muzaffar, and a neat one. He stretched out a hand to take a towel from Ilyas. Akram did likewise.

'Ah? "Far from it"? How so?' He moved to the edge of the water tank and deposited the towel on the well-scrubbed floor beyond before placing his palms on the floor and hauling himself up out of the water. He stood beside the bench there and towelled himself down.

'He was a broad, burly man, huzoor. Built like a wrestler. Not a sensitive bone in that body, I would have thought.' Ilyas had gone to the other side of the pool to help Akram out. 'He did smell, though. Reeked like a woman. All flowers and pretty things.'

Muzaffar could not resist a grin as he reached for the fresh loin cloth he had left on the bench before entering the water. 'An amir? A thickset amir with a love for attar? Perhaps you should not hold his build against him, Ilyas; there are many such men who have inherited far from perfect bodies and equally imperfect faces, but why hold their love for fine jewellery or expensive attar against them?' He had, behind the shield of the towel – draped loosely but discreetly around his hips – changed the soaked loin cloth he had been wearing for the fresh one.

Akram too was now drying himself off, and Ilyas turned to look at Muzaffar. 'No, no, huzoor,' he said, his voice urgent, earnest. 'He was not an amir; I am sure of that. His speech was not that of an educated man. His hands were rough, calloused. And his clothes were a common man's clothes. He was no amir, huzoor, even if he used attar so liberally.'

But that was all he could say about the man; there was nothing else that was exceptional about him. Just the smell of him. And after he had raised the alarm and Ilyas had rushed off to inform Altaf of Abdul Jabaar's death, he had been forgotten.

Just another man, a patron who had been unlucky enough to have stumbled upon a gory corpse. Some might have said he had been inauspicious, ominous; that the one time he had come to the hamaam, the owner had died.

Muzaffar left the bathing chamber not so certain any more of Ilyas's guilt.

☙

'I do not know what to make of it,' he confessed to Shireen, when he sat with her in their private chamber inside the mahal sara that evening. The worst of Shireen's cold was behind her. Pepper, turmeric, ghee and milk, she had informed Muzaffar. With a dose, too, of chickpea flour. All of it cooked together under the supervision of Zeenat Aapa, who had come calling and had been horrified to see her young sister-in-law so under the weather. She had not spent very long in the house – she was headed home, and had time to spare only to have the cook prepare a concoction to soothe Shireen's throat and her cold – but she had left a brief message for Muzaffar: Come some day. Your quarrel is with your brother-in-law, not with me.

It was a verbal message, not written, and Shireen had passed it on in what Muzaffar had recognized as the same quiet, solemn tone in which Zeenat Begum must have said it in the first place. He had nodded, but had refrained from commenting. He would go to Zeenat Aapa's someday soon, and not just to meet her. He had to meet Khan Sahib too. But when that would happen, he did not know. He did not look forward to it, and yet – yet there was that sword dangling over Khan Sahib's head, the anger of Abdul Jabaar's sons if the murder of their father was not solved quickly enough for their liking.

'The murders of Aadil and Basharat?' Shireen had asked, puzzled. 'And the disappearance of Ameena? I thought you had made up your mind to distance yourself from those cases, Jang Sahib.'

Muzaffar had groaned. 'I had forgotten about them.' He had squeezed his eyes shut for a moment. 'Would you believe it, Shireen? Even though that had been on my mind this morning – not when I set out, but later, when I ran into the thanedar – it had slipped away, right out of my thoughts, until you mentioned it.'

Her eyes narrowed. 'Then what did you mean when you said you did not know what to make of it?'

So Muzaffar poured it all out, holding back nothing. He told her of his suspicions, of his fears for Khan Sahib, of the mysterious patron who had come out of nowhere and vanished into thin air. 'I may not be the best judge of character,' he confessed ruefully, 'but I do not think I am mistaken in thinking that Ilyas is, after all, innocent. His hesitation was the hesitation of a nervous man, I am almost certain of it. And he seems as baffled as we are. He was certain Abdul Jabaar had killed himself. Do you know – no, of course you wouldn't – but when we were leaving the hamaam, we brushed past Ilyas again. He was standing and chatting with the doorkeeper, and he didn't see us until we were nearly upon him. But I overheard what he was saying. "I would not have had the nerve to lift a finger against Abdul Jabaar Sahib. He was so strong, and so very ill-tempered; he could easily have cracked my spine with one blow of his fist. Can you imagine what would have happened if one tried to attack him and failed to kill him at the first go?" That man was not joking, Shireen. I truly do not think he could have killed Abdul Jabaar, even if he had wanted to.'

'What was his reaction when he saw you and Akram Sahib go past? He must have realized you would have heard him.'

Muzaffar pulled at a bolster, old and misshapen with age and much use, but an obvious favourite. He tugged it into place behind his back. 'He looked embarrassed. But he said nothing.'

'And I am stuck, even worse than before,' he added, with a sigh of frustration. 'At least earlier – even if I was headed down the wrong path – I had a definite suspect in mind. Now that suspect is no longer under suspicion, and I have no clue about where to turn. There can be motives aplenty when a man is as ruthless as Abdul Jabaar, and it could well be that the 'patron' Ilyas spoke of was the very man who killed Abdul Jabaar. It sounds increasingly plausible, does it not? He could well have slipped inside the bathing chamber while Ilyas was away – ' he broke off, and sat up straight, the bolster forgotten. His eyes had gone very wide.

'That is it, Shireen,' he breathed. 'Of course. That is it. Why did I not see it before?' The frustration of a minute before had gone, evaporated. 'Ilyas said the man had stripped down to his pyjamas when Ilyas emerged from the bathing chamber, after Abdul Jabaar had instructed him to send for the masseur and to have the cold bath prepared.' He cleared his throat. 'Imagine this. Abdul Jabaar has sent Ilyas off to fetch the masseur. Obviously, the masseur will not massage Abdul Jabaar in the bath; so Abdul Jabaar prepares by climbing out of the pool and perhaps lying down prostrate on one of the benches. He's waiting for the masseur, a hamaam attendant who will be wearing what the hamaam attendants wear: just a pair of common pyjamas.'

Shireen inhaled so sharply that she was seized by a fit of spluttering, and spent the next couple of minutes trying to regain her breath. Muzaffar rubbed her back, drawing her closer to him, and offered her a sip of water. Her eyes were still red and watery when she finally straightened, drew back, and looked at Muzaffar. 'You mean – that other man? The "patron"?'

Muzaffar's smile was wry. 'Yes. At least to attendants like Ilyas, or the doorkeeper. To Abdul Jabaar, he pretended to be an attendant. If he knew that Abdul Jabaar came daily to the hamaam, at a fixed time to use his own exclusive bathing chambers, he surely would know more. For example, he would probably be certain that there would only be one attendant on duty outside Abdul Jabaar's bathing chamber. Also that there would be little chance of other customers being around, because everybody knew that Abdul Jabaar was not expected to emerge for a while yet.'

'And this man strangled Abdul Jabaar?' Shireen's usually mellifluous voice was scratchy.

'I suppose that was how it happened. Abdul Jabaar was not expecting an attack, and from what Ilyas told us, it seems this man was a powerful one. He would have had the upper hand, I suppose. Abdul Jabaar did not look especially fit to me.'

'But why all that blood, then? Why cut Abdul Jabaar's wrists? He was already dead.'

'When Abdul Jabaar's corpse would be found, choked to death, the first assumption would be that he had been murdered, wouldn't it? But to find a man with his wrists slit, and the knife lying beside him in the pool – that would make everybody assume that the man had taken his own life. Of course, if one stopped to think, one would wonder how a man, clad only in a loincloth, could smuggle in a knife before the very eyes of the bath attendant.' Muzaffar grinned, a cynical grimace as he mulled over that possibility. 'It would have been dangerous. One might just end up a eunuch rather than a corpse. Most humiliating.'

'Jang Sahib!'

Muzaffar's eyes twinkled. 'I beg your pardon, Shireen. This far, I have mostly had to relate my experiences only to men – it will take me time to learn to guard my tongue.' He paused long enough to gather his thoughts, then continued. 'A knife can be hidden in a pair of pyjamas – especially if all the knife is needed for is to cut open the veins of a corpse. A small knife will do, small enough to fit into a pocket sewn into the pyjamas.'

'Yes – but then what?'

'Abdul Jabaar's killer, having murdered his man, drags the dead body and dumps it in the pool. Then he quickly slits Abdul Jabaar's wrists; the man has been dead a matter of mere moments, so his blood flows easily and dramatically around him in the pool. The knife is dropped into the pool, too. Our man is intelligent enough to realize that people will look about for the weapon with which Abdul Jabaar was killed. He provided one, within easy reach.'

Shireen shuddered. 'It sounds so very cold-blooded.'

'It was. That was why he managed to get away with it. He must have plotted it well, long and carefully.'

Shireen cleared her throat, and poured some water into the goblet. She raised it to her lips and looked up into his face as she swallowed, nodding slightly to indicate that she was waiting to hear more. Muzaffar obliged.

'He must have bloodied his hands in the process. Even a little, noticed by someone with sharp eyes, could have brought suspicion his way. He had to wash it off right then, and the water in the pool was too bloody for that. So he went to the water chute which brought hot water into the chamber. He washed there; and because he was in a hurry, he failed to see the bloodstain he left behind.'

'And then he came out and raised a hue and cry, pretending he was the one who had found Abdul Jabaar's corpse?'

'An easy way to draw attention to the fact that Abdul Jabaar was dead – and to draw suspicion away from himself. Which murderer, after all would draw attention to a crime he had committed? It helped, too, to reinforce the impression that Abdul Jabaar had committed suicide. Just a few minutes earlier, Ilyas had seen Abdul Jabaar alive and well; had spoken to him, in fact. Now, this man was screaming that Abdul Jabaar was lying dead inside the bathing chamber. And nobody had gone in. What was everybody to think? Especially when they saw the knife, and Abdul Jabaar's slit wrists. Suicide. That was what everybody was meant to believe.'

'But who is the murderer? You say he came to the hamaam, pretending to be a patron – but who is he? Why did he kill Abdul Jabaar?'

Muzaffar's shoulders slumped in dejection. 'That is what I do not know.'

ଓ

He came awake sometime in the dead of the night. Because the night was not quite as bitingly cold as it had been two weeks earlier, Shireen had insisted on removing one of the quilted curtains at a small window and replacing it with a lighter one of white cotton. 'Let some moonlight in, at least,' she had said. 'Since you will not allow even a small lamp to be kept lit at night for fear of fire, the least we can do is this. I hate waking up to a pitch dark room.'

Through the cotton curtain a faint grey wash of moonlight lit up part of the room. Just enough to let him see a blur of shadows and silhouettes, of the cusped arch at the doorway, the small niches in the wall, the chests. Beside him, the slim form of Shireen, burrowed deep into the quilt. Her hair cascaded all over her pillow, spilling over her cheek.

Muzaffar lay still, the back of his head resting on his hands. He had taken long to fall asleep, and his last thought had been the one that had kept him awake: who was the man who had murdered Abdul Jabaar? And where was he to be found? Ilyas had been certain he had never seen the man before, or since. It was not surprising, either, seeing the shrewdness with which the man had murdered Abdul Jabaar. Such a man, so cunning, would not loiter about unnecessarily in a place where he could be recognized as having been present at the time of a murder.

And why had he killed Abdul Jabaar?

Someone – he did not remember who, did not even remember whether it was in connection with Abdul Jabaar's death, or Basharat's, or even Aadil's – had said that a man could make many enemies in the course of a lifetime. Abdul Jabaar had lived a long life. A long life, and for all his philanthropy, not a blameless one, either. Not as far as those who had served him were concerned. And a man who could be so cruel to his servants, who was to know what else he had done in his past? To whom?

There could be hundreds of men nursing grudges against Abdul Jabaar, thought Muzaffar with a silent groan. True, few men would be able to summon up the courage to actually kill a man, no matter how grievous the hurt caused. Fewer men would nurse a grudge for long. And Akram, from his conversation with Abdul Jabaar's sons, had gathered that they could not think of anyone who had threatened Abdul Jabaar. Anger and resentment so deep-seated that it could lead a man to murder invariably found some expression: not many men would stay absolutely silent. There would have been some disquiet, some murmur of discontent.

Unless Abdul Jabaar and his sons had not been listening. Or the man had been too frightened.

Muzaffar's brows drew together as he inhaled sharply. His mind was racing, looking for ways to find out more about Abdul Jabaar, the man he had been. Who would have known him better than his sons? His associates? But Akram had already spoken to some of them.

He must have disturbed her sleep, for Shireen stirred. 'Are you all right?' he heard her murmur, her voice sleepy and only half-audible.

'Yes,' he whispered back. 'Go to sleep.'

Obediently, Shireen turned over. A whiff of jasmine, sweet and elegant, floated on the air. Muzaffar remembered: an attar, received as a gift...

The next moment, he was scrambling out of his bed and hurrying to change into clothes suitable for a trip out of his haveli.

CHAPTER 14

The first flush of dawn was beginning to tinge the eastern sky when Muzaffar clucked gently to his horse, pulling it to a stop. This was not the usual chestnut stallion he rode; that was too magnificent a horse, too noticeable. He had, instead, chosen a subdued roan mare, one few people would remember. He had dressed himself in accordance: even more sedately than was his wont. A middling merchant, a passerby would have thought him; not too wealthy. Certainly not an amir. Anonymity was what Muzaffar wanted right now.

Mohallah Abdul Jabaar Khan was still asleep. Stray dogs still lay curled up against the outer walls of houses, sheltering from the wind. Birdsong floated on the air, but other than a sleepy-eyed watchman resting under a tree, there was nobody to be seen. Perhaps half an hour from now, there would be more. The lowest of the low, the men who cleaned the streets and picked up the refuse, carried away the waste – bodily and otherwise – from the grand havelis around. The faceless, the nameless, the men who were not.

Society was cruel, he thought, as he dismounted. It set up its rules to favour a certain class, and then enforced those rules with not a single thought for even basic humanity.

But you could crush a man only so far. So much cruelty, and then no more.

The heavy wooden gate to Abdul Jabaar's haveli stood shut, barred and solid. The squat tower-like turrets on either side of the gate had held torches in their sconces, but the torches had long flickered out. In the grey light of the morning, Muzaffar saw a figure sitting slumped against one of the turrets. A thin grey blanket muffled the man from head to knee, revealing only the haggard oval of his face. Near his feet were the ashes of a small but dead fire. Leaning against the wall beside him was a tall, solid bamboo, the thickness of a man's forearm, and as tall as Muzaffar himself.

Muzaffar stepped forward. He would have imagined that any respectable household would have had two gatekeepers, one for the day and another for the night. It was not merely human; it was a matter of common sense. A man could stay awake and alert only so many hours at a stretch.

Abdul Jabaar's family seemed to lack both sense and humanity.

Muzaffar glanced about him to make sure he was not being watched. Reassured, he bent and touched the man lightly on the knee, shaking him. The man must have trained himself, over long years of service in this unfeeling household, to come awake in a hurry; in the wink of an eye, he was awake, reaching for his bamboo, blinking away the sleep from his eyes, pulling the blanket down over his shoulders, mumbling a salaam and an apology to this strange visitor who had arrived at such an odd hour.

And then he actually looked up into Muzaffar's face. There was sudden recognition, a moment when his eyes widened in horror. He shrank back against the wall, beginning to speak. Muzaffar knew, even before the man had finished one incoherent sentence, what was coming: expressions of disbelief, profuse apologies for the unforgivable familiarity with which he had treated a man who had now revealed himself to be an amir.

'Shh. Quiet. Don't arouse the household.' Muzaffar swung about, seating himself beside the man, pushing him firmly back into his place with a palm on the shoulder. The man stared at him, wide-eyed.

'When do the servants inside start stirring? Or the members of the family?' Muzaffar whispered.

The man gulped. 'N – not for a while, huzoor,' he whispered back, his voice hoarse with fear. His gaze did not shift from Muzaffar's face. 'Not the family, at least. Some of the servants will be up already, beginning the day's work.'

Those wary eyes were assessing Muzaffar. Wondering why Muzaffar had turned up at the haveli at so unearthly an hour. Wondering if Muzaffar would enter the haveli only to go straight to Abdul Jabaar's sons and convey to them all the tales their gatekeeper had told of his masters. Or wondering if Muzaffar was indeed not all he seemed.

There was no time to waste. Not just because he wanted to get away without being noticed by anyone else, but also because justice was at stake. Muzaffar shifted his hand to the gatekeeper's forearm. 'Listen to me, and carefully,' he said. 'This Faraaz, the man whose son was killed – he is a friend of yours, isn't he?'

The gatekeeper's face remained still, eyes scared. 'Don't waste time!' Muzaffar hissed. 'If he is your friend, you wouldn't want him getting into trouble, would you?'

'He is my friend, huzoor. Yes.' A drop of perspiration dripped down his forehead, past his cheek and into his beard. It was incongruous in the chill of the morning.

'And that evening – the day Abdul Jabaar died – Faraaz went out? Perhaps about half an hour before Abdul Jabaar died?' The man looked confused; Muzaffar added, 'Around sunset. Or a little before.'

The man swallowed. His nod was almost imperceptible, but Muzaffar saw it.

'And how long was he gone? Long enough to run to the hamaam, deliver a message, and hurry back?'

Again the nod, barely there.

Muzaffar drew in a long, deep breath and straightened, removing his hand from the man's arm. 'Go inside,' he said. 'Go and call Faraaz. Bring him out here, so that I can talk to him. Go, and do not let anyone see or hear you. Or him. Understand? Go, hurry.'

ଓ

'A man does not commit suicide on a sudden whim, does he?' Muzaffar said, placing his goblet on the salver Akram's servant had placed before him. 'There has to be a reason – a dire and pressing reason – to make a man so desperate that he will take his own life. And from all we heard of Abdul Jabaar, he seems to have been a man more inclined to take others' lives. Not a troubled man, perhaps.'

'There were rumours that the servant who had come to Abdul Jabaar while he was in the hamaam might have brought bad news,' Akram pointed out. 'Though that, of course, is probably only a matter of academic interest now, considering you have unearthed the truth. And heard a confession too?' There was admiration in his tone, in the expression.

Muzaffar shrugged, self-conscious and embarrassed at this unexpected adulation. 'Hardly a confession, since it came not from the murderer but from the man who knew him. Who helped him. Because of whom the murder was committed.' He picked up his goblet again, which Akram had discreetly refilled with sherbet. 'As for the servant having brought bad news from the haveli – well, that would have to be very bad news, wouldn't it, to have made Abdul Jabaar kill himself?' He took a sip of lemon-scented sherbet. 'In which case, someone at the haveli – Abdul Jabaar's own sons, or whoever sent that servant – would have guessed the possible consequences of sending a message so earth-shattering. In any case, you forget: Ilyas said that Abdul Jabaar had not appeared distressed by the message. The only result of it was to make Abdul Jabaar hurry, as Ilyas told us. And there are other things you have to remember. Abdul Jabaar, even if the message should have driven him to suicide, is unlikely to have known that it was coming. And if he had not known, then why should he have taken a knife into the bath with him, ready to cut his wrists?' He paused for breath. 'And you forget; Abdul Jabaar did not bleed to death; he was strangled. The finger-marks were there on his throat. A man, as far as I know, cannot throttle himself like that; as soon as he presses hard enough, he will lose consciousness and his grip will relax.'

'That's all very well.' Akram sounded dubious. 'But how did you arrive at the culprit? How did you discover who killed Abdul Jabaar? And you don't even know the man's name.' The note of doubt in his voice had changed to one of utter bewilderment.

'It was a chance fragrance,' Muzaffar said. 'Shireen's attar, a jasmine one. It's lovely. Even I, who know little about such things, could tell that it was a very fine perfume, elegant and' – he broke off, with a grin. 'No, Akram; I am not going mad. Truly. I caught a whiff of Shireen's attar, and was reminded of where she had got it. Someone had given it to her as a wedding present, brought all the way from Kanauj. The best attars come from Kanauj, do you know? You do? Yes, I should not be surprised. I didn't know. But that fact made things fall into place. Kanauj.'

Akram was regarding Muzaffar with something between admiration and bafflement.

'What is it? Why do you stare at me so?'

Akram shook his head so vigorously, the knotted strings on the right side of his jama danced. 'There is obviously some method to your madness, but I fail to see what. Why this sudden rambling about attar? You are the last man I would have thought interested in attar. And yet, you are not given to chattering on and on about something with no rhyme or reason. How your Begum Sahiba's perfume is connected to this case escapes me, but apparently you know more than I do.'

Muzaffar responded with the ghost of a grin, a forced one. He did not feel like smiling. All that he had seen and heard these past few days, the strained relationship with Khan Sahib and the horrors of what the gatekeeper had divulged about Abdul Jabaar Khan, had drained him of happiness, left him tired in mind and heart. It was a relief, at least, he thought with a private sigh, that he had Akram for a friend and Shireen for a wife, two people whom he could confide in, two people he could trust and be himself with.

'Do you not remember?' he asked. 'I remember having told you. Faraaz, the man whose child was whipped to death? His relatives are from Kanauj.' He saw a glimmer of enlightenment in Akram's eyes. 'And the gatekeeper told me that they were his only kin, people he was very close to. They would have been a comfort to Faraaz; that was what the gatekeeper said.' He stared at a lovely blue and white porcelain vase, crammed a little too full of red and pink roses, that stood in a niche in the wall opposite, a vibrant splash of colour that lit up the wall. 'And you remember what Ilyas told us? That the man – the "patron" who supposedly discovered Abdul Jabaar's corpse – smelled very strongly of flowers, but did not look fashionable? A common man, a worker, but smelling not of sweat but of attar.'

'A man can smell of flowers if he works with them all day, all week, all the months of a year. He does not need to be a nobleman, dabbing himself with attar' – Muzaffar ignored the indignant look Akram directed his way – 'all he needs is to be distilling the attar, working with those roses and jasmine and whatnot. The smell probably settles in his very pores, so that when he's away from his work, even away from Kanauj, it never really goes.' He took another swallow of sherbet from the goblet; his throat was parched from all the talking. 'When the thanedar begins questioning people, it will come out sooner or later that Faraaz's son had died because of Abdul Jabaar. And if the thanedar perseveres – and if he is smart enough – he might decide to bring Ilyas to Abdul Jabaar's haveli and parade all the servants before him. Ask him to identify which man had come to the hamaam that day, bearing a message for Abdul Jabaar.'

Akram frowned. 'I still do not know who that was.'

'Faraaz. It had to be him. It was, by the way; I checked with the gatekeeper of the haveli, and Faraaz later admitted it when I spoke to him.' The befuddled expression had still not left Akram's face. Muzaffar drank down the last mouthful of sherbet in his goblet and said, 'I must go now, Akram – no, don't get angry at me, please – I must go and talk to Khan Sahib; there is so much I need to tell him.' He was already getting to his feet, shaking out his choga, straightening his jama. 'Faraaz is not an exceptionally strong man, you know. Not strong enough, at least, to strangle a man of Abdul Jabaar's girth. That needed a more powerful man, and one who would not be recognized at the hamaam.'

Akram, eager to get as much information out of Muzaffar as he could before his friend left, escorted him out of the dalaan. 'Why a relative? It could have been a paid killer?'

'Paid killers must be paid. And they do not come cheap, I believe. One willing to risk his neck to kill an amir like Abdul Jabaar – no, he would demand a price commensurate to the risk.' Muzaffar turned the corner, into the corridor which led to the row of wide steps at the foot of which spread the neat square garden in front of Akram's haveli. 'No, it had to be someone who was ready to side with Faraaz, even kill for him, because of his relationship with Faraaz. Possibly also because he hated Abdul Jabaar as much as Faraaz did.'

Akram followed Muzaffar down the steps and onto the path, paved with slabs of red sandstone, which led to the gate. At the gate, a figure moved forward, then responding to a gesture from Akram, changed direction and hurried away towards the stables. 'What now, Muzaffar?' Akram said softly. 'You may have sent Faraaz off to your lands, into relative obscurity. He will – hopefully – be safe. But what happens now? Abdul Jabaar's sons aren't going to sit quiet. They won't accept that their father's murderer has vanished into thin air.' When Muzaffar did not say anything, he persisted. 'What will you do? You said you're going to meet Khan Sahib? What will you tell him?'

Muzaffar heaved a sigh. 'I won't tell him about Faraaz, not now. I will tell him only why and how I know it was murder. I will tell him my reasoning. How I came to the conclusion that the man who raised the alarm was actually the murderer. I shall focus on that. I will sneak in a word regarding Abdul Jabaar's true self. Not a philanthropist or a truly noble nobleman, but a cruel bastard who should have long ago been done away with – ' Muzaffar broke off, aware that he had let his emotions run away with him. 'I hope Khan Sahib will be convinced that there would be no dearth of men – especially among those who worked for Abdul Jabaar, whether here in Dilli, or on his estates, or in his kaarkhaanas – who hated the man. Enough to murder him.'

Akram nodded, looking a little pensive. And a little doubtful. 'What if Khan Sahib learns about Faraaz?'

'It won't be so easy. Faraaz has already left the haveli. At my suggestion, he begged leave to go to Ajmer, to offer up prayers for the soul of his son. Abdul Jabaar's sons are too preoccupied and excited over the death of their father to worry over petty matters like a stable hand going on a pilgrimage. They let him go. Some weeks may pass before they realize that Faraaz has not returned.' From the stables, Muzaffar's horse, its coat well-brushed, had been led out by the man who had gone to fetch it. Muzaffar turned to Akram. 'And Faraaz has an alibi, does he not? Even if Ilyas identifies him – which he cannot, now that Faraaz is nowhere around – what would come of it? Abdul Jabaar was still alive when Faraaz left; that was the whole point of Faraaz's visit to the hamaam: it was a mere pretext to draw Ilyas away, leaving Abdul Jabaar alone and vulnerable. And yet to have Ilyas be a witness to the fact that Abdul Jabaar was alive when Faraaz left him.'

They had reached the gate, and Muzaffar reached for his horse. He mounted up, and looked down at Akram. 'I will need your prayers, my friend,' he murmured, with a smile. 'I go to beard the lion in his den.'

Akram nodded, his hand on the neck of Muzaffar's horse, caressing. 'It will be all well,' he said. 'Khan Sahib will understand. You know him, Muzaffar, far better than I could ever do.'

'From your lips to God's ears,' murmured Muzaffar.

Akram's hand shifted to the horse's bridle, detaining Muzaffar for a few moments more. 'Abdul Jabaar's sons,' he said, in a low voice, even though it was not necessary – the servant and the gatekeeper had moved out of earshot, leaving the two friends to themselves – 'they will perhaps soon be more worried about whether or not they will inherit any of their father's wealth. It may just be possible that they will call off the hunt for his killer.'

'Let us see. I must go, Akram.'

'Yes. Of course. May Allah keep you safe.' Akram stepped back, and Muzaffar could not resist a laugh at his parting words. Common words, a well-used farewell, but singularly appropriate at this moment. 'I hope he will,' he said, and dug his heels into the flanks of his horse.

ଓ

The kotwali, the headquarters of the Kotwal, the man in charge of the law and its administration in Shahjahan's Dilli, stood at one of the main squares down the length of road popularly known as Chandni Chowk – though the actual 'Moonlight Square', the Chandni Chowk, was technically only part of this stretch. It was a crowded, glittering market, the shimmering canal known as the Nahar-e-Bihisht, the 'Stream of Paradise', running down the centre and reflecting, at night, the moonlight. Trees stood on either side, and the awnings of shops selling a million different wares stretched bright and colourful.

Muzaffar galloped past it all without giving it a second glance, and drew rein in front of the kotwali.

'But Kotwal Sahib is not in, huzoor,' said the officer on duty, who – having seen Khan Sahib's young brother-in-law often enough during Muzaffar's many visits to the kotwali – had recognized him. 'I thought he had gone to meet you.' He hesitated, his forehead crinkling in thought. 'Perhaps – will you wait for a moment, huzoor? I shall find out; he will have left word. I could have sworn Khan Sahib said he was headed towards Dilli Darwaza, but I might have been mistaken.'

As it turned out, the man was not mistaken about Khan Sahib having gone to Dilli Darwaza. But his destination had not been Muzaffar's haveli. He had received a message from the thanedar of the area. A message borne personally by the chowkidar, and begging Kotwal Sahib, if he could spare the time, to come immediately. There had been an incident at the house of the merchant Parvez.

CHAPTER 15

There was a small crowd hanging around outside Parvez's house, but it was being kept in check and at a prudent distance by a quartet of soldiers. Except for one – in whom Muzaffar recognized the local chowkidar's assistant – none were armed with anything more dangerous than a stout bamboo each, but Muzaffar knew, as no doubt did the crowd, that a cleverly-wielded bamboo could do a good deal of harm.

Muzaffar wondered whether to go home and call on Khan Sahib later in the evening. In the seclusion of Khan Sahib's haveli, in the quiet dalaan where Khan Sahib could be as blunt or as cutting as he felt when Muzaffar tendered the long-due apology and begged to be allowed back into Khan's good graces. Muzaffar's shame would at least be private.

On the other hand, something momentous enough to have the thanedar send the chowkidar for Khan Sahib had happened at Parvez's house. Muzaffar had followed the events in this house over the past few days with erratic but intense interest. He could not help but wonder what had occurred now. A murder? Nothing less, he thought, could bring Khan Sahib here.

A decision made, he turned his horse and rode to his own haveli, where he left the beast at the gate in the care of the gatekeeper and made his way back on foot to Parvez's house. In the few minutes he had been away, the crowd had thinned a bit. There were still the hangers on, the men with nothing better to do, and too much curiosity for their own good. Two of them – a thin old man with half his teeth missing and a leg in a splint, and a fat woman holding a reed basket full of dried cow dung cakes – were in the forefront, pestering the soldiers for news of what had happened.

'This house is jinxed,' the old man was saying. 'First that other brother was killed. Then someone kidnapped their maid – '

'No, no,' the woman with the dung cakes said, hoisting her basket up on one hip. 'The maid was abducted first. Why, I don't know: a hag, if you ever saw one.' A few of the people standing around her sniggered, and she flashed an angry eye at them. 'I ask you! What would anybody want to do with someone old and decrepit, and poor on top of it? Nobody would even bother to pay a ransom for her!' A few heads around nodded, acknowledging – if grudgingly – the sound logic of this statement.

If Muzaffar had recognized the chowkidar's assistant, the man too had recognized him in return. He bobbed his head in greeting when his gaze encountered Muzaffar's. 'Huzoor! Sahib will be glad to see you.' The woman with the dung cakes swivelled her head and stared with unabashed curiosity at Muzaffar; beside her, the old man too turned to look, but with some deference mixed in his glance.

Muzaffar hesitated. No matter how much the chowkidar or the thanedar might be glad of his presence, Khan Sahib, he felt, would not welcome him with open arms. Far from it.

But he had to meet Khan Sahib anyway, and the chowkidar's man was already moving forward, shoving aside those of the bystanders who stood in the way. And, thought Muzaffar, as he followed the man into Parvez's house, he knew something of what had happened here. Not all, but something. Besides, he was eager to know what had befallen the household to bring upon it not just the local guardians of the law, but the Kotwal too.

The inside of the house was contained chaos. The thanedar had deputed more men, and they were ranged through the main areas of the house: the courtyard, the corridors leading from it, the dalaan. There were herds of servants, clustered in whispering, excited groups. There were people going to and fro, rushing away into the depths of the house, emerging from it. Somewhere deep in the belly of the house, a woman was wailing loudly.

'You?' Khan Sahib said when Muzaffar stepped into the small inner courtyard – one of several in the house – where he stood with several other men. The chowkidar was there, as was the thanedar; the other two men Muzaffar did not recognize. They looked at him with curiosity. The thanedar moved forward a step, with a smile of relief on his face. Muzaffar acknowledged him with a quick nod, and turned to his brother-in-law.

'Khan Sahib,' he said, in a soft but urgent tone. 'I need to talk to you, please. It is important.'

As he had guessed, Khan Sahib's dignity and his sense of honour – both his own as well as Muzaffar's – did not let him berate Muzaffar in public. He led the way into one of the small rooms adjoining the courtyard – a storeroom, thought Muzaffar, stacked with large bundles wrapped in sacking. Jute, perhaps, or bales of cotton.

'You have been poking your nose in this,' Khan Sahib hissed as the curtain fell into place behind the two of them.

'The thanedar told you?' Muzaffar grimaced. 'I had not meant to, Khan Sahib; it just so happened – ' he stopped; it was apparent that Khan Sahib did not believe him. And Muzaffar himself knew the truth: had he really wanted to, he could have stayed well clear of the goings-on in this house and the one next door. That he found himself embroiled in these investigations was a result of his own curiosity, his own insatiable need to get at the truth. 'I came looking for you,' he admitted. 'I – I know something, Khan Sahib, that you should know too. As soon as possible. Well, before someone asks you,' he added, lamely.

'Stop blabbering,' Khan Sahib snapped. 'I don't have the time for this, or for you.' He glowered, cleared his throat. 'What is it?'

'I know why Abdul Jabaar was killed,' Muzaffar replied. 'And why.'

☙

Khan Sahib blinked, caught off-guard. He had been expecting, thought Muzaffar, something about Basharat or Parvez or his jinxed household of theirs.

'Abdul Jabaar?' Khan Sahib's eyes had narrowed. 'How is it that you should know anything about that? Don't tell me you – '

'Please. I happened to be in the hamaam with Akram when Abdul Jabaar's body was found. I did not mean to get involved,' Muzaffar was rushing on, eager to get this over and done with. He had to tell Khan Sahib about Abdul Jabaar, and yet he did not have the luxury of time; there was, pressing in on them both, the incident that had occurred – 'what happened here – ' he began to say, then, realizing that Khan Sahib was beginning to look apoplectic, hurriedly changed tack.

It did not take him long to give Khan Sahib the bare essentials of why Abdul Jabaar had been done in. He did not mention Faraaz or his relative from Kanauj; he did not talk about the brutal killing of Faraaz's child. He spoke only of the bloodstain on the water chute; of the marks on Abdul Jabaar's neck, which proved he was killed; of the mysterious patron who had vanished so completely after having raised the alarm. Khan Sahib heard him out, and with lessening annoyance.

'You realize, do you not, that this story you have told me lacks a motive?' Khan Sahib said, when Muzaffar fell silent. 'I agree that the rest of it fits in, how it was done, and by whom – not, of course,' he added, pointedly, 'that you have told me the identity of this strange man – but still. What will I tell Abdul Jabaar's sons when they demand an explanation of why their father was killed?'

A chill crept up Muzaffar's spine. 'They – have they been threatening you, Khan Sahib?'

'Threatening me?' Khan Sahib frowned, puzzled. 'Of course not. Why should you think they would?' He regarded Muzaffar with grave eyes, now free from anger. When Muzaffar merely looked uncomfortable, he nodded. 'Ah. I see. So you have been told about them? That they're a vindictive lot? Was that why you went poking your nose in this business?' There was gruff affection in his tone now.

He shook his head as he turned back towards the doorway leading into the courtyard outside. 'No. They have not been threatening me, and they will not. They know that I have a certain amount of influence. I have assured them that my men will do what they can to find Abdul Jabaar's murderer, and they have understood that they will have to be satisfied with that.' He drew the curtain open, squinting as he looked out on the bright sunshine pouring into the paved courtyard. 'Later sometime, you can tell me whom you are protecting in Abdul Jabaar's case. I assume it is with good reason. Right now, we need to find another murderer.'

'Parvez? Is – was he killed?'

'Yes. It does not surprise you, it appears.'

Muzaffar shook his head as he followed Khan Sahib back into the courtyard.

ᴄᴕ

Of the two other men, one was the steward of the household, an elderly man with an air of quiet efficiency about him. The other was the doorkeeper. 'Aslam,' said Khan Sahib to the thanedar – it was the first time, Muzaffar realized, that he had heard the thanedar's name – 'tell Jang Sahib what has happened here. Quickly.' As the thanedar bobbed his head, Khan Sahib turned to the doorkeeper and the steward. 'And you. Come with me. I want you to show me around the entire house, all the doors and windows that look out onto the street outside. I want to examine for myself the condition of each of them.'

Not, it seemed, that nobody had attended to that already. Aslam the thanedar, out of earshot of the Kotwal, whispered to the chowkidar to accompany Khan Sahib and the two servitors. 'Make sure they don't leave anything out, even by mistake. And you had seen everything carefully the first time around, had you not?' Apprehension made his eyes widen, his voice quiver. The chowkidar, he murmured to Muzaffar by way of explanation, had been the first to be summoned when the crime had been discovered, and while he had sent a man off to alert the thanedar, he had looked around for clues. The corpse, the room in which it had been found. Signs of disturbance. Signs of the entrance and exit of the intruder.

They had found no signs of how the killer had made his entrance, but once in, he had wreaked havoc in the room where Basharat himself, a few days earlier, had been found dead. Parvez, as was his wont – and now even more of a necessity, considering his dead brother's share of the work had also fallen on his shoulders – had been burning the midnight oil. A servant had gone to him with refreshments – a pitcher of sherbet, some nuts – an hour before midnight, and had been told to leave the salver there. Parvez, buried in his papers and with his hands inkstained, did not want to be disturbed, not even to have the salver cleared.

No other member of the household – not Nilofer Begum,

and not any of the other servants in the house – had come to the room until the early hours of the morning. Then, Nilofer Begum, waking and seeing that her husband had apparently not come to his bed all through the night, had arisen and gone to search for him. She had supposed that he had drifted off to sleep over his work, and had made her way to the room where Parvez worked.

She had found him slumped over his slope-topped desk, stabbed in the chest, but with no sign of the dagger. There had been blood all around, soaking through the mattress on which Parvez sat, through every inch of his clothes, even forming great gory splashes on the carpet. It was all over the documents he had been working on. There had even been blood on the wall. It was a gruesome sight.

'It sickened me, Jang Sahib,' the thanedar said, with a shudder. 'Imagine what effect that sight would have had on a woman. She screamed and nearly fainted.' But Nilofer was probably made of even sterner stuff than the thanedar could imagine, for despite the trauma of discovering her husband murdered so bloodily, she had had her wits about her – and had realized, even as she made the discovery, that the intruder was there too.

'There? In the room?' Muzaffar gaped.

The thanedar nodded. 'In the room. He was there, crouching in a corner, half-hidden by the dark shadow of one of the chests. He must have been looking through the things in the room, searching for something to steal, when she came by.'

'Do you truly believe that?' Muzaffar asked, but before the thanedar could respond to that, Khan Sahib was back.

The Kotwal had returned, after what had been a quick but disappointing tour through the house. There had been no signs of forced entrance. The doors and windows had been barred and locked the previous night, and had been found in the same condition. Nobody had forced one open, or broken a lock. The steward explained that ever since the murder of Basharat, they had taken special pains to secure the house at night: he had personally gone around every night when the household shut itself in, making sure that all was secure. All had been secure the previous night. And he had found it in the same condition this morning.

'Except, of course, the staircase leading upstairs,' added the chowkidar, with a note of triumph in his voice, as if priding himself on having taken the initiative to go around and examine the house well before his superiors had arrived.

Muzaffar lifted an eyebrow. 'Meaning?'

The thanedar, having been the narrator of events for Muzaffar's benefit all this while, took it upon himself to explain. 'He means the staircase to the mahal sara,' he said. 'At the top of the staircase is a door which leads out onto the terrace. Beside it is the corridor leading into the women's quarters.' He caught Khan Sahib's eye, the Kotwal now looking impatient. His voice speeded up, hurrying to impart information. 'When Begum Sahiba began screaming, the man shot out of the room and ran straight up the staircase. By the time the rest of the household arrived, he had already unbolted the door to the terrace and fled. Begum Sahiba saw him race up the staircase, but he was gone by the time the others arrived.'

And, having raced across the terrace, had climbed down the outer wall, using a rope which was found hanging there – 'one of those wandering acrobats, perhaps' surmised the thanedar. He was gone, vanished into thin air, by the time the steward and the other menservants of the house had reached the terrace.

଼

'It is not so very straightforward, is it?' whispered Muzaffar to Khan Sahib as the thanedar, with the steward beside him, led the way to the room in which Parvez's dead body had been found. The doorkeeper had been sent back to his post.

Khan Sahib had instructed the chowkidar to go to the crowd milling about outside the front door – growing increasingly shrill in its curiosity – and to find out, if he could, whether any among them had any information to impart. 'Tell them, otherwise, to not waste their time and ours by hanging about here and making a racket. And if anybody insists on making a nuisance of themselves, arrest them.' The chowkidar had blinked in surprise, and the thanedar had looked taken aback – the Kotwal they knew had tended to be lenient about such things. 'Go on,' Khan Sahib had snapped. 'I can barely hear myself think, what with the noise. If nothing else, they should show some sensitivity for the people who mourn in this house.'

Then, accompanied by Muzaffar and the thanedar, Khan Sahib had made his way once again to the scene of the crime. It was a middle-sized room, which put Muzaffar in mind of the room he had sat in at Lakshminarayan's house: in essence, a dalaan, but furnished in a way that made it obviously functional. The mattresses were thick, the bolsters heavy, well-padded. There were niches and shelves and chests to accommodate the many ledgers, documents, and some of the goods that the two merchants had dealt in.

The corpse had been removed and taken to a small room nearby, where it had been covered with a sheet of white cotton. Muzaffar peeped in at Khan Sahib's invitation, and was repelled by the metallic stench that pervaded the space. The blood had dried on the man's clothing before he had been covered, so the sheet was as spotless as when it had come back from the washerman's. Below that, Parvez's body was a wreck.

'He's been savaged,' Khan Sahib said wearily, looking on with his arms folded across his chest as Muzaffar bent down to look at the corpse. 'The man made very sure Parvez was dead. He must have stabbed the man again and again, long after he had died.'

'I suppose a hakim has been sent for?'

'Yes. He should be here soon. I doubt if he will be able to add anything to what we already know. There appear to be no signs of any poison, or strangulation, or anything else – he obviously died of these multiple wounds. See? Chest, stomach, face – his murderer must have hated him with a vengeance. But we shall see what the hakim has to say.'

It was as they walked away from the makeshift mortuary back to the room where Parvez had been found that Muzaffar put his question to Khan Sahib. 'I mean,' he added, 'this does not appear to be a simple breaking in and entering, or a man killed because he interrupted a thief.'

Khan Sahib looked at Muzaffar, an expression of sarcasm in his eyes. 'What did you expect?' he asked. 'After what happened to Basharat? And to Aadil, next door? Surely these incidents are not each of them unique? There are too many similarities, are there not?'

Muzaffar did not answer until after he had stepped into the room and looked around once, a brief but intense stare. 'Yes,' he agreed. 'There are too many similarities. But there are differences, too, are there not?' He tilted his head in the direction of the room they had come from. 'Parvez's body, for instance, and the way he was hacked about. Aadil and Basharat were stabbed too, but stabbed to kill, not to – to decimate. It seems almost as if the murderer vented all his – ' he frowned, his eyes suddenly narrowing as he fell silent in mid-sentence.

'What is it, Muzaffar?'

Muzaffar shook his head. 'Something occurred to me. Just a thought; it needs to be examined further before I even dare voice it.' He stepped closer to the place where the man had been sitting when he had been killed. A frown furrowed his brow as he examined the place, the blood-soaked mattress and sheet, the splashes of congealed blood on the velvet covers of the bolster. The great clots of blood on the piles of papers at Parvez's desk.

'The papers,' Muzaffar observed. 'They have been tossed about, of course, as one would expect if a struggle of this sort occurred. And,' he grimaced as he lifted a few of the sheets, holding them gingerly by the corners, 'there would not be much point trying to make any sense of what was written here, would there? They're well-nigh illegible, obscured by the blood.'

'What do you mean, Jang Sahib?' the thanedar asked. 'Do you think the killer came to look at the documents in this room? Why would he?' Sudden comprehension dawned even as he spoke. 'Oh,' he breathed. 'You mean as he did when he killed Basharat? And Aadil? It was the same man, I take it.'

'It seems to be the same man,' Khan Sahib butted in. 'It would be too much of a coincidence to expect that Aadil, Basharat and Parvez would all be murdered within days of each other, by three different men. Well,' he conceded, 'one could, I suppose, expect that since Parvez and Basharat were brothers and worked together, they could have a common enemy – but there has been no evidence so far, has there, that they shared an enemy in common with Aadil?'

The thanedar nodded. 'Early last evening, Aadil's clerk Suraj Bhan came with me to meet Parvez. They talked it over. Parvez mentioned all the men he could think of who might have wanted to harm Basharat; Suraj Bhan recognized some of the names, but apart from one man, did not think that Aadil had ever had any sort of association with any of them. And even that one man – well, it had been a completely amiable dealing over some goods. There had been no cause at all for enmity.'

'Perhaps we should have Suraj Bhan in again,' Muzaffar suggested, his face grave. 'It may be that he knows of a man who could be an enemy of Parvez's. Perhaps that is what we should have been looking for all along.'

Khan Sahib, who had been bending over, peering closely at the mattress on which the dead man had been found, straightened up so suddenly and sharply that he winced and clutched at his spine. With a scowl – directed at himself, for the incautious movement – he asked, 'And what makes you say that?'

'The day Parvez came to meet me, he said something odd just as he was leaving. He told me that had it not been for a sudden headache, he would have been in the room with Basharat the night Basharat was murdered. It did not occur to me till just a little while back that Ameena, after all, had not mentioned who would be working late, when Ismat eavesdropped on her conversation that night. Both brothers used to work late in this office. She could have meant either one. We assumed that she meant Basharat, because Basharat was the one who was found dead.

'But what if it was all a mistake? What if the killer had meant to murder Parvez all along?'

'Why would he have killed Basharat then?' Khan Sahib said. He turned, even as he spoke, to the thanedar. 'You saw the body. Did Basharat resemble Parvez to such an extent that he could have been mistaken for Parvez?'

The thanedar shook his head. 'They were of a similar build, but that was all. Basharat was more jowly, not as fine-featured as Parvez.'

'The similarity in build might have been what got him killed,' Muzaffar said. 'He was stabbed in the back. The murderer may have entered the room, expecting to see only Parvez here, and he did not bother to see who the man sitting here was.'

Khan Sahib, hands clasped behind his back, mouth pursed into a contemplative moue, nodded slowly. 'That sounds plausible to me, especially since there seems to be nobody to whom we can ascribe a motive and an opportunity to kill Basharat. That his murder was a result of mistaken identity is unfortunate, but believable. However,' he looked at Muzaffar, his eyes now piercing, 'that still does not account for the other two deaths we have to deal with. Who killed Aadil and Parvez, and why?'

ଔ

'I would think Aadil was killed for the same reason as Basharat was,' Muzaffar said, after a long pause. 'It was a mistake.'

'A mistake?! Muzaffar, this is no time to be flippant!' Khan Sahib exploded. 'What do you take this man to be? A blunderer? A man who goes from one house to another, killing any man he happens to come upon? I conceded your point about Basharat's killing, but Aadil – '

'Hear me out, Khan Sahib,' Muzaffar said soothingly. The thanedar, standing beside Khan Sahib, was looking startled and curious. The steward, just outside the doorway, wore an identical expression. 'I met Ameena one day, you know, when I was passing by. She was standing outside, and we began a conversation.' He saw Khan Sahib's raised eyebrow, correctly interpreted it as a mild reprimand for Muzaffar's prying, and gave a small smile by way of apology. 'She mentioned to me that she had not been in Dilli in Dhul-kadah, when the family shifted households and the old house was sold off to Aadil.' He glanced towards the steward, addressing him. 'Is that correct? Was Ameena not here when the family moved?'

The man shook his head. 'She was not, huzoor.'

'And the house was sold without her knowledge? So she left Dilli when the family still lived in the house next door? And when she returned, it was to find that the family had shifted here?'

'Yes, huzoor. That was how it happened.'

There was silence. Khan Sahib was regarding Muzaffar with interest, and with a glimmer of understanding in his own eyes. The thanedar was looking baffled. The steward looked wary, uncertain of what was happening. Muzaffar turned back to

Khan Sahib. 'And we know, of course, that Ameena knew the murderer – had helped him, even, if only with information. The night Ismat overheard their conversation, Ameena was trying to tell the man when and where to find his victim. And do you remember what Ismat repeated of Ameena's words? "How could I have known?" and something about "you knew what he looked like". What does that indicate?'

It was a rhetorical question, and Khan Sahib recognizing it as such, merely gave a small smile of amusement. The thanedar did not venture an answer; he appeared to be all at sea.

'Could she have meant that she would not have known about Parvez and Basharat having moved out of the house and shifted next door – because she had not been in Dilli when that happened? And that she was berating the killer for taking her to task? I can imagine he must have said something to the effect that she had given him incorrect information, and as a result, he had killed the wrong man. She was pointing out that he knew what his victim looked like.'

'Or that he knew what Aadil looked like. Or both,' Khan Sahib said.

Muzaffar inclined his head, conceding the point. 'There was, of course, the fact that Aadil had been killed in the courtyard, on a dark and rainy night when he could not possibly have been carrying a candle or lamp that would have illuminated his face and made it possible for the killer to recognize him as not the intended victim. But the fact of the matter is that the killer did not recognize Aadil; he took him to be – who? Parvez? It seems like it – and stabbed him as soon as Aadil had opened the door and admitted the man into the courtyard.'

He paused for breath. The thanedar's expression had changed to one of deep reverence; a look that made Muzaffar feel a little awkward. He shrugged and hurried to finish. 'The important point is that Ameena said she had not known of the shifting of the household. I take that to mean that she had told the man the address at which Basharat – or Parvez, whoever – was to be found. So did the man not know already where his victim lived? But he knew Ameena? How could that be? And if Ameena told him the wrong address – the old address – then it could only have been that she met him before she left Dilli in Dhul-kadah. Or while she was gone.' He swallowed, trying to wet his parched throat. 'If she told him the address before she left Dilli: the question arises – why did she need to tell him the address? If he was in Dilli too, what need was there? Couldn't he have come? Or, if he could meet her, why did he not know the address already?'

Khan Sahib opened his mouth to speak, and Muzaffar stalled him. 'Yes, I know what you will say, Khan Sahib: that she might have met him outside the house. It is possible; I agree. What seems to me more likely is that she met this man while she was away – during that trip she made out of Dilli in Dhul-kadah. She told him where Parvez and Basharat lived, little aware then that while she was away they had sold off their house and shifted here.'

'And so he turned up in Dilli, went to Aadil's house and murdered the poor man,' Khan Sahib murmured. 'Yes, that fits together, except that it indicates a murderer who is too impulsive for his own good, perhaps – barging into a house and murdering a man without even seeing his face?'

'Yet, cool-headed enough to then head into the man's house and search through his belongings, his documents,' Muzaffar pointed out.

'I wonder why.'

'It is also,' Muzaffar said, 'one of the things that distinguishes Parvez's murder from those of Aadil and Basharat. Not only was Parvez slashed and hacked in a far more brutal fashion than were his neighbour and his brother; his documents, too, were not examined. At least, not that I can see.'

'Which is odd. If Parvez, all along, was the intended victim

– and if the murderer wanted to look at his papers – why not do so? Especially when he had had no luck with either Aadil's or Basharat's papers.'

Muzaffar lifted a shoulder and let it drop in a gesture of helplessness. 'I cannot hazard a guess, Khan Sahib. That is what puzzles me.' He heaved a sigh of frustration. 'Who is to say, too, whether Parvez was the intended victim and not – not a mistake?' In the very next moment, he shook his head. 'No, I think not. I think we can safely assume he was the man the murderer had been looking for.'

'Stabbed in the chest, Muzaffar? And in a lighted room? Which meant his assailant saw his face? And was so angered that he stabbed Parvez again and again?'

Muzaffar nodded. There was something thoughtful in his expression. 'Talking of a lighted room,' he murmured. 'I wonder – ' he left the sentence at that, and turned his attention back to the room, his gaze wandering from the triple-arched doorway screened by quilted curtains, at which they stood, right around the room. 'Were there lamps or candles still burning here in the morning when Begum Sahiba entered the room?' he asked the steward.

The man's forehead furrowed as he tried to remember. 'I arrived here – maybe a minute or two – after Begum Sahiba raised the alarm. I do not recall any light here then. No,' he said, in a decisive voice. 'I am quite sure, huzoor; the lamps had gone out by then. They would have; the oil would have been exhausted before dawn.'

They lapsed back into silence. Silence, too, had fallen over the rest of the haveli. The chowkidar and his men had succeeded in dispersing the crowd, it seemed, for here inside the house, they could no longer hear any of the incessant chatter of when Muzaffar had arrived. The inhabitants of the house itself had fallen silent: the woman Muzaffar had heard wailing – was it Nilofer, he wondered? – had gone quiet too.

A thought struck Muzaffar. 'Where had Ameena gone,' he asked the steward, 'in Dhul-kadah?'

The man blinked, caught momentarily not at his most alert. 'I – Surat, I believe,' he replied. 'One of her grandsons was getting married. Yes, it was definitely Surat.'

There was a discreet cough outside the curtains. 'Huzoor?' said a voice. 'The hakim is here.'

ʗЗ

'Nilofer is lying,' said Shireen in a firm little voice. 'That is what you think, do you not, Khan Sahib?'

She was sitting at lunch with Muzaffar and Khan Sahib. The Kotwal had been initially reluctant to accompany Muzaffar to his haveli for lunch; it had taken persuasion and logic – Muzaffar had insisted that a man could not think well if he was hungry. In any case, he had added, one could think as well in a haveli a few minutes' ride from Parvez's house as one could in the dead man's house itself. And Parvez's house was in reliable hands: the chowkidar and his men were on duty while the thanedar had returned to his own office.

The hakim had examined the corpse, and had – as Khan Sahib had predicted – not been able to add anything to what they already knew. There were no signs of poison or throttling or any cause of death other than the most obvious. Yes, he said: Parvez had been killed by being stabbed, again and again. He could not say, with any certainty, how long the man had been dead. Looking at the state of the body – still stiff – he thought the man had not been dead more than eight hours. There was no way of knowing for sure, he had emphasized.

Khan Sahib had harrumphed, made a quick calculation, and had wondered aloud if that meant the man had died somewhere about – well, four hours after midnight? The hakim had nodded nervously. 'Or thereabouts, huzoor,' he had said. 'You will appreciate that this is not something we can be absolutely certain about.'

'And what time was it that Begum Sahiba discovered her husband's body?' Khan Sahib had asked the steward. 'All I have heard is that it was a little before dawn. Is there any more precise way of knowing what time it was?'

There was. It was a stroke of good luck, Muzaffar was to realize later. The steward admitted that he had woken up just moments before he heard Nilofer Begum begin to scream – and what had woken him up was the call to prayer, resonating from the minaret of the nearest mosque. A devout man, he was in the process of getting out of bed, preparing for his morning namaaz, when the alarm had been raised.

'Which means,' Khan Sahib had said as he went with Muzaffar to the younger man's haveli, 'that Nilofer Begum must have found the body sometime around – what? – five hours after midnight? An hour after he had been murdered?'

Muzaffar had nodded silently, but there had been a deep furrow between his brows. 'There is something wrong here, Khan Sahib,' he had said. And Khan Sahib, his own face tense and his mouth thin-lipped, had agreed. 'One hour after the murder, and the murderer was still in the room? I wonder what he can have been doing.'

They had gone on their way in silence, and when they had reached Muzaffar's haveli, the first quarter of an hour had gone in this and that. Shireen had been pleased – more than pleased, for she knew how much Khan Sahib meant to her husband – to welcome the Kotwal after the recent bitterness between the two men. Like Zeenat Begum, she did not stand on ceremony. Khan Sahib had made a half-hearted suggestion that he and Muzaffar have their meal in the dalaan, but she had overruled him. 'Of course not, Khan Sahib,' she had said as she led the way into the mahal sara. 'You may not be related to me by blood, but you are like a father and a brother to my husband. Of course you must come into the mahal sara. You would not have me sitting here and eating my lunch all by myself, consumed by curiosity about what the two of you have been about?'

Over the kababs and naans, the lentils and the various vegetables – and a ghee-scented khichdi which was Shireen's favourite – Muzaffar had told her what had happened. The morning expedition to Abdul Jabaar's haveli he said nothing about; that was something he would explain later, when Khan Sahib was gone. At night, perhaps, before they went to sleep.

And Shireen had, in the uncanny way she had, voiced the very thought that had been going through his head.

'Nilofer Begum, lying?' Khan Sahib said, raising an eyebrow. 'Why do you say so, Shireen?'

She had not covered her face, though her ice blue dupatta, embroidered along the edge in fine silver thread, was draped decorously over her head. Muzaffar saw a dull flush rise to her cheeks. She hesitated. 'I think Jang Sahib knows, too,' she murmured. 'The – the incident with Ismat, Jang Sahib? And now – this?'

Khan Sahib turned a quizzical eye on Muzaffar. 'The "incident with Ismat"? She is the girl who overheard that conversation between Ameena and the murderer?'

'When Nilofer discovered that Ismat had testified before the thanedar, she forced Ismat to retract her statement. Said that she was pulling a prank. But Ismat wasn't lying when she told us about Ameena; I am sure of it.' He explained his reasons, and Khan Sahib nodded. 'So Nilofer tried to defend her old servant. Misplaced loyalty, but I do not see what bearing it has on this case. Unless, of course, one continues with the assumption that the same man killed both Basharat and Parvez. And Aadil.' He sighed. 'I am getting old. Yes, of course. We are continuing with that assumption, are we not? But is that your only reason for being wary of Nilofer Begum?'

Shireen glanced at Muzaffar, as if urging him to speak. 'I shall tell Khan Sahib why I think Nilofer Begum is lying, Shireen,' he said, 'but you know her better than I do – at least you have met her; I have not. If you have reasons other than mine that make you think her guilty of something, you will have to speak up.' He acknowledged her nod with one of his own, and continued. 'There are two things I see here, both stemming from the time Nilofer Begum says she found the body. The hakim says Parvez is likely to have been killed about four hours after midnight. That is only approximate, of course; but if that is indeed the case, then what was the killer doing lurking in the room for the next one hour?'

'He could have decided to try and search the place for himself, to see if there was anything there that he could steal,' Khan Sahib said, with little conviction. 'Or he could have spent the time searching carefully through Parvez's papers, as he did for Aadil and Basharat. Looked them over at his leisure and so carefully that he left no trace there.'

'But,' Shireen blurted out, so caught up in the excitement of what they were discussing that she forgot her reticence, 'the lamps in the room would have gone out by then, wouldn't they? It would be dark in the room by the time the aazaan for the first namaaz was called. It always is here, I know; and that is why I have one candle lit just as we go to bed, in case one needs to get out of bed at night –' she broke off. 'Forgive me; I am rambling.'

'No, go on,' Khan Sahib said. 'Tell us what you think, Shireen.' His tone was gentle, genuinely respectful. A man who respected a woman who could think, as his wife Zeenat Begum could. Perhaps it came of spending a lifetime with a woman like that, thought Muzaffar; perhaps there was, too, an innate appreciation of wisdom, no matter whom it belonged to.

Shireen inclined her head, graciously accepting Khan Sahib's request. 'I meant that the room would almost certainly be dark by the time the aazaan was called. What would the murderer be doing in a dark room? Even if a lamp had been burning in the room an hour earlier – say, at four hours after midnight, when he killed Parvez – it would probably have been close to the end of its wick. Unless Parvez himself trimmed it and replenished the oil... no? He was not the man to do so?' She nodded when Khan Sahib shook his head. 'Yes, I did not think he would. And he had not called anybody from the household to do it? Not a lampman, a mashalchi?'

She fell silent, and looked up at Muzaffar – who smiled gently, encouragingly, at her. Then at Khan Sahib, who was looking pensive.

'You are right,' he said. 'And if the room had been dark –' his eyes narrowed, as he thought it out, 'and it would have been, at that hour of the morning, with the curtains of the room drawn, too – then how did Nilofer Begum see her husband's body?'

Shireen deserted her demureness and smiled triumphantly at Muzaffar. He grinned back at her. 'Yes,' he said, 'And we have only Nilofer Begum's word for it that her coming into the room made the murderer run up the staircase and onto the terrace. None of the servants who came in response to her screaming saw the man.'

'I hate to waken the two of you from your dreams,' Khan Sahib said, his voice dry. 'But when I went around the house, the bloody footprints going up the staircase were clear to the eye. Leading from the room where Parvez had been murdered, down the corridor, and up the stairs. The steward led me up the stairs, too. They were there, crossing the terrace, more faint – almost smudges, at the end – but they were there. Right up to the rope.'

Shireen's face had fallen. She looked down, her fingers beginning to make small, precise pleats in the edge of her dupatta. A sign, Muzaffar recognized immediately, of confusion.

'Tell me, Khan Sahib,' he said, 'Were there signs of blood on the rope?'

Khan Sahib frowned, thinking back. 'The chowkidar had pulled it up and formed it into a coil. He had left the end knotted around one of the columns of a small rooftop pavilion. A chhatri – I suppose you've seen them; there are two of them on the terrace at Parvez's house. Can be seen from the road.' He groaned. 'I really am growing old, far too old for this work. Look at the way I'm rambling!' He shook his head in a self-deprecating sort of way. 'No, Muzaffar; I had a look at that rope myself, from one end to the other. There were no signs of blood on it.' He scowled again. 'Yes,' he murmured to himself. 'There should have been, shouldn't there? A man who had committed a murder – and that too a murder so very bloody – would have blood on his hands. If his sandals could leave bloody footprints, why did his hands not leave any marks?'

'Unless he had washed them. If one believes that he did indeed potter about in Parvez's room, with the corpse cooling all the while there, searching for things to steal or documents to examine – well, perhaps he did not like to do so with sticky hands? Even if he wiped his hands on a piece of cloth, it would have helped.'

'There was no such cloth in the room, Muzaffar. What was there was either clean or soaked through with blood: there was nothing that had anything resembling handprints.' He squeezed the bridge of his nose between the tips of his thumb and forefinger. 'And there had been no water in the room, not even a goblet. Some sherbet in a pitcher, but Parvez had obviously drunk most of it in the course of the night; there was barely a swallow left.'

A silence fell across the room. 'I think – ' Muzaffar began to say, when there was the sound of soft footsteps outside the curtain that hung across the doorway. 'Begum Sahiba?' said a feminine voice, stopping at the threshold but not entering the room. 'A man has come to meet huzoor and Kotwal Sahib. He says Thanedar Sahib has sent him.'

Khan Sahib exchanged a glance with Muzaffar. Shireen too had looked up, curious. 'Who is it, Ruqayya?' Muzaffar called out.

'He says his name is Suraj Bhan, huzoor.'

CHAPTER 16

Aadil's former clerk looked shaken. 'This has come as a shock,' he explained as he sat down in Muzaffar's dalaan. 'To think I was in that room, talking to Parvez Sahib just the other day – and that he should now be dead. Stabbed, too, I was told, like Aadil Sahib was. And Basharat Sahib.' The look of distress in his eyes deepened. 'They are connected, are they not, Jang Sahib? Kotwal Sahib? We were not able to think of any enemies that my late master and Parvez Sahib's brother might have had in common, though we talked for nearly two hours. But this third murder makes me certain that there is, in fact, someone who wished all of them ill.'

Khan Sahib looked on, watchful. It was Muzaffar who spoke. 'During your conversation with Parvez, did he mention anybody who knew both him as well as Basharat? I realize, of course, that there must be dozens of such men – after all, they both worked together here – but perhaps a mention? Perhaps' – and he sent up a silent prayer, knowing that this was an arrow shot into pitch dark – 'perhaps a man who may have not liked Parvez himself?'

Suraj Bhan's eyes narrowed in sudden interest. 'A man who may have been Parvez Sahib's enemy?' He chewed on his moustache. 'Let me think... it seems to me that all the men he spoke of were those Basharat Sahib had known while he was in Dilli, and Parvez Sahib –' he broke off, his eyes agleam as a thought came to him. 'There was a man named Ghulam Mustafa,' he said. 'He had been very eager to have Basharat Sahib marry his sister, I believe.'

'I remember Parvez telling me of this man. Basharat refused, and Ghulam Mustafa was most annoyed about it. But do you say that Ghulam Mustafa knew Parvez too? And had reason to hate him?'

'Not hate,' Suraj Bhan corrected. 'I got the impression that it was more a form of disappointment than anything else. Parvez Sahib gave me to understand that Ghulam Mustafa had initially approached Parvez Sahib and asked him to marry the lady. Parvez Sahib declined. Basharat Sahib's refusal added insult to injury, I suppose.'

Muzaffar nodded, unsatisfied. 'It seems little reason,' he said, doubtfully. 'Not, at least, to hack the man to death in such a way.'

'Yes, I suppose so.' Suraj Bhan's voice was gloomy. 'I think what irked Ghulam Mustafa was that he had known Parvez Sahib in Surat, and felt slighted that when Parvez Sahib came to Dilli, he did not think it necessary to even call upon Ghulam Mustafa. Parvez Sahib was amused – in a contemptuous sort of way – when he told me about it the other day.'

'I don't understand. Do you mean to say that both Parvez and this Ghulam Mustafa knew each other in Surat, and then both of them came to Dilli?'

'Yes, huzoor; that was how it was. Parvez Sahib said that there had been some misunderstanding regarding the closeness of their relations: he considered Ghulam Mustafa a mere acquaintance, but Ghulam Mustafa had obviously been looking upon him as a prospective brother-in-law, even in Surat. When Parvez Sahib came to Dilli and bumped into Ghulam Mustafa one day at Daryaganj, Ghulam Mustafa expressed hurt that

Parvez Sahib, despite having come to Dilli, had not thought fit to call on him.'

Khan Sahib glanced towards Muzaffar. Muzaffar was staring fixedly down at the intricate pattern of vines and leaves woven in shades of muted green into the carpet spread on the floor. After a few moments of gazing, he looked up, first at Suraj Bhan and then at Khan Sahib. 'Khan Sahib,' he said, 'I had suggested to the thanedar that he write to the Kotwal at Surat and ask him about Parvez – just some information about the man's sojourn in Surat. It is impossible that the information would have arrived already, or will arrive even within the next few days. But perhaps this Ghulam Mustafa might know something of Parvez's stint in Surat?'

'Perhaps. But why are you so keen on finding out what Parvez did in Surat? Do you think it has a bearing on this case?'

'It may. I did not initially suppose it might, but – well, Ameena Bibi appears to have met a man in Surat and passed on the Dilli address of Parvez's house to him, isn't it? And that man came along, some months later, and killed off Aadil and Basharat, in addition to Parvez... perhaps there is – or was, he is probably now in Dilli – a man in Surat who was a sworn enemy of Parvez's.'

Suraj Bhan's face wore a look of utter bewilderment. 'Killed off Aadil Sahib?' he echoed. 'Do you mean – no, but how could it be? Aadil Sahib barely knew the two brothers.'

'I'll explain it to you,' Muzaffar said, getting to his feet in a sudden surge. 'I think Suraj Bhan had better take us to this Ghulam Mustafa as soon as possible, don't you, Khan Sahib?' He was already heading for the doorway, looking back over his shoulder to ask the clerk, 'Ghulam Mustafa is in Dilli, I gather? Or Parvez would not have suspected him of having killed Basharat.'

ೞ

Ghulam Mustafa was a man with small eyes that looked like polished jade, that same uncanny green, and very bright too. The rest of his face took away from the astonishing beauty of those eyes: it was jowly, pock-marked, with a bulbous red nose, and a grey moustache that had gone untrimmed far too long. Suraj Bhan knew him only by reputation, so it had taken the clerk an hour or so to first find someone who knew where Ghulam Mustafa lived, get the address from the man, and then escort Khan Sahib and Muzaffar to Ghulam Mustafa's somewhat slovenly house near Kashmiri Darwaza.

'Allah watches over the blameless,' Ghulam Mustafa said, every syllable dripping sanctimony. 'Had it not been for him – what if my sister had married either of those two brothers? She would have been a widow today! But no; the Almighty was watching over us. That is why she is safe today, safe and married to a decent man, not like those two.'

He had known already – through the traders' grapevine – about the murder of Basharat. Parvez's death was far too recent for him to know about, but Khan Sahib, having introduced himself and his two companions, had imparted the information. It had made Ghulam Mustafa's bushy eyebrows rise nearly up to the edge of his turban. And it had elicited this torrent of self-righteousness.

'"Not like those two"?' Khan Sahib repeated. 'Do you mean they were not good men? Of course,' he added, 'Both Suraj Bhan as well as Jang Sahib' – he had refrained from mentioning that Jang Sahib was anything other than a neighbour and one-occasion confidant of Parvez's – 'were told by Parvez that you had been eager for a match with either of the brothers.'

'Eager! Hardly.' The man had been sipping from a goblet of sherbet – he had a pitcher beside him, but had not bothered to have a servant fetch any refreshment for his guests. 'I was not eager, Kotwal Sahib. By no stretch of imagination. Let us say I felt sorry for Basharat. He was a widower; I thought he must be a lonely man, and in need of companionship, stability.' He took a deep gulp from the goblet, draining it, and swiped the back of his hand across his mouth. 'I had been told that Basharat was not a bad man, you see, Kotwal Sahib. And when he started visiting me now and then – well, I was given the impression that he was interested in a match.'

'But that was not the case, I take it?'

'No.' Ghulam Mustafa shook his head sadly and poured himself another goblet of sherbet. 'He wasn't a bad man, not from what I had heard. I suppose it was my fault, too, to some extent. I should not have jumped to the conclusion that he wanted to marry my sister.'

'And when Basharat refused, you turned to Parvez?'

'That!' Ghulam Mustafa, lifting his goblet to his lips, put it down on the salver so abruptly that sherbet sloshed over the edges and onto the salver, creating a pool of ruby red. 'There I was not to blame; not in the least. I had known Parvez when we both lived in Surat, you see, and he had indicated then – this was ten years back, perhaps nine – that he would not be averse to marrying my sister. She was young then, of course, and I had hopes of finding a far better match for her than Parvez. So when I moved to Dilli – '

'When?' Muzaffar, besides a brief greeting when they had entered Ghulam Mustafa's house, had been silent so far. His question appeared to startle his host. He blinked. 'When?'

'When did you move to Dilli? And why?'

The man scratched his beard. 'About eight years ago – no, nearer to seven. My forefathers were originally from Dilli, you see. My uncle died eight years ago, and since I was his only living relative, he left this house to me. I thought it appropriate to come back here.'

'Ah. And you met Basharat here? Had Parvez told you about him? Yes? That was why you cultivated his acquaintance?'

Ghulam Mustafa nodded. 'Parvez had given me to understand

that he was a good man. Seemed like it, too, to me. It was only later that I realized.' He shook his head in a gesture of disillusionment and disappointment. 'Still, Basharat wasn't as bad as Parvez! I was badly deceived in that case. Imagine, he didn't even have the decency to come and visit me when he arrived in Dilli. And when he did come – after I happened to bump into him – he didn't tell me anything about the Shamsuddin episode! I would have thought he would have said something to me. I was one of his nearest and dearest in Surat – '

Muzaffar's ears had pricked up. He leaned forward, eyes alert. 'The Shamsuddin episode?' he asked. 'What was that about?'

ଓଓ

Ghulam Mustafa had been picking his front teeth with a fingernail as he spoke. He had given Muzaffar a look of indignation at being interrupted, but let it pass. 'Shamsuddin was – is, I suppose I should say – Parvez's brother-in-law. His wife's brother. I didn't know, then, of course. I didn't even know Parvez was married. That was why I approached him with my sister's match. I would not like my sister to marry a man who already had another wife; she was used to running the household ever since Ammi died, you know, and it would be terrible for her to have to be at the beck and call of a senior wife. No – what? Ah, yes, yes, I'm coming to it.'

And, in his rambling style, punctuated now and then by reiterations of how very used and deceived he felt, and how unreliable a man Parvez had turned out to be, Ghulam Mustafa told the story of Shamsuddin. Shamsuddin had been a merchant too, in Surat, along with Parvez and Ghulam Mustafa. He had not traded on as extensive a scale as his two colleagues, but the three of them had still been on good terms with each other. 'I would even have called us friends, in a formal sort of way,' Ghulam Mustafa clarified. 'But who was to know?'

Ghulam Mustafa at least, had not known. News had arrived that his uncle had died, and he had moved, along with his sister, to Dilli. Oblique references and hints from Parvez – bolstered by a letter of introduction to his brother in Dilli – had led Ghulam Mustafa to comfort himself with the thought that even if he had been unable to broach the topic of a marital alliance between his sister and Parvez, he may well succeed with Parvez's brother.

Then, a few weeks after Ghulam Mustafa had moved to Dilli, the Shamsuddin episode occurred. Ghulam Mustafa first caught a glimmering of it when he confronted Parvez, many months later, in Dilli, only to discover that the man had married in the meantime. 'And that too, Shamsuddin's sister! Of course, I do not intend to besmirch the lady's name, not when she is widowed now too – but, really.' An incensed Ghulam Mustafa, unable to extract more information from a reticent Parvez, had written letters of enquiry to some of his more gossipy acquaintances in Surat, and the story had emerged, in bits and pieces. Some were garbled, some definitely more flight of fancy than hard fact. But from them, Ghulam Mustafa had been able to piece together what had happened.

Parvez had gone to the Kotwal of Surat and reported a theft, one involving consignments of goods worth many thousands of rupees. No petty thievery, this, but something to be taken very seriously indeed. An investigation had been carried out, and Parvez – who had had his own suspicions, it appeared – had cooperated with commendable eagerness. He had taken the Kotwal's men around his warehouses, had shown them where carpets, bales of silk, indigo, and other valuable goods had been stored. He had given them details of all the men who had means of access to the warehouse. He had even volunteered the information that Shamsuddin had been present when the goods, now stolen, had been delivered. He had, with what seemed a childlike innocence, mentioned that Shamsuddin was, financially, in dire straits. And that Shamsuddin had looked longingly at the carpets and wondered what one would fetch...

The Kotwal, no fool, had immediately led a small group of his men to search Shamsuddin's house and the attached warehouse. In the warehouse, tucked away in a corner, they had found some of the material reported as missing by Parvez. Parvez had been called, and had identified it. So had his clerk and the labourers who worked for him. Shamsuddin had denied any knowledge of how the goods had made their way from Parvez's warehouse to his own. He had insisted that he was innocent, and after his pleas had proved ineffective, he had resorted to accusations: Parvez had conspired against him. Parvez had hired thieves to break into his, Shamsuddin's, warehouse and plant the stolen items there.

When the Kotwal had raised the question of motive, Shamsuddin had supplied one. A disgraceful one, a scandalous secret that not many men would have revealed to the world even in circumstances such as this. Parvez had one day come to Shamsuddin's home, only to discover that Shamsuddin – who had not been expecting the visit – was not at home. A servant had seated Parvez in the dalaan, where he had expressed a desire to wait for Shamsuddin to return. But Parvez had not stayed long in the dalaan. He had wandered about the corridors, somehow managing to avoid the few servants who were in the house, and had boldly gone into the khanah bagh of the mahal sara – where Shamsuddin's sister, Nilofer, had been lying on a stone bench, unveiled and wearing only the most minimal clothing, for it was the height of summer, and Surat, of course, was known for the sultriness of its summers.

'Utterly crass,' Ghulam Mustafa said, having called a servant to fetch him another pitcher of sherbet. 'Had I known he was capable of something like that, I would never have even dreamed of my sister marrying his brother, let alone him!'

The voyeur had not gone undetected; in fact, it seemed he had made no attempt to hide his presence. The lady had seen him, had tried to raise an alarm, and had found herself being cajoled and coaxed by the man, who tried to tell her how hopelessly he had fallen in love with her, and how he would do anything for her, if only she would let him.

Muzaffar, listening to Ghulam Mustafa's detailed but long-winded narrative, found himself feeling repulsed. Shireen's opinion of Nilofer – her single-minded devotion to the decoration of her person; her extravagance; her seeming disinterest in her husband and her household – had seemed to mark the woman as a selfish, unfeeling sort. They had known, he now realized, only one side of the story.

Ghulam Mustafa hurried towards the end of his story, encouraged by a snappy 'What happened, eventually?' from Khan Sahib. Parvez's unwelcome attentions had been nipped in the bud by the arrival of some maids, come rushing in response to Nilofer's shrieks. Later, Nilofer had recounted the incident to her brother, and Shamsuddin had gone off, hot-headed, to Parvez's house to confront him. Parvez had offered to marry Nilofer, but his tone, his very demeanour, had reeked of lecherousness. Shamsuddin had lost control. Blows had been exchanged, and Parvez had been told never to come near Shamsuddin's house ever again.

That, Shamsuddin has insisted, had been the reason for Parvez's attempt to implicate him in this theft. He was innocent.

He had not been believed, even though Nilofer and her maids had testified to the truth of the incident in the khanah bagh. Parvez's servants, on the other hand, had sworn that Shamsuddin had come barging into the house, threatening their master, whom he ended up hitting. There were other witnesses, passersby and neighbours, who had seen Shamsuddin storming out of Parvez's house, still yelling curses.

'And there were the goods that had been found in Shamsuddin's warehouses. He could not account for them.' So Shamsuddin had been tried. The usual penalty – a heavy fine – had been imposed. In addition, he had been imprisoned for several years.

'But how did Nilofer Begum end up marrying Parvez, after all?' Muzaffar asked.

'Who knows? Shamsuddin was her only close relative, you see; they were orphans, and if they had any aunts or uncles or anybody else to fall back upon – well, I don't know. I never heard Shamsuddin mention anyone. Perhaps after Shamsuddin was imprisoned, she found that she really couldn't manage on her own without a man to look after her. She did have that maid of hers, an old woman who'd almost brought up the two of them – but what support could an old hag, one foot in the grave, offer? And perhaps, with Shamsuddin out of the way, Parvez could' – he looked uncomfortable, twirling the squat stem of the goblet between his thumb and forefinger as he harrumphed. 'Perhaps – hmm – Parvez was able to persuade her.'

☙

'What do you think?' Khan Sahib asked. He was looking up into the branches of an old fig tree, its new leaves dappled with sunshine. They had left Ghulam Mustafa's house a quarter of an hour earlier, three men shaken and shocked by what they had heard. They had wandered on, the two noblemen leading their horses while Suraj Bhan walked alongside, until they had reached a small public garden. It had, from the small pavilion, the grove of mango trees, and the modest but now dry water channel down the centre, been once laid out with care. Now it was neglected, home to a pair of large goats that nibbled at the tall grass near the far wall. Khan Sahib, noting the seclusion of the place, had elected to stop there for a quick conference. Muzaffar and Suraj Bhan had raised no objections.

Muzaffar glanced at Khan Sahib, the faraway look in the older man's eyes not disguising his anxiety. 'Shamsuddin, I think,' Muzaffar said. 'He had good reason – very good reason – for killing Parvez. And if, as Ghulam Mustafa said, Shamsuddin was due to be released seven or six months back: well, then. It would be very likely that he would have emerged from prison just as Ameena herself arrived in Surat. I can well believe that she would have told him all that had happened, if he already did not know it: Nilofer's marriage to Parvez, their moving to Dilli.'

'And where they lived in Dilli,' said Suraj Bhan in his soft voice. 'Only, she did not know that Aadil Sahib had bought the house by then and moved in.' His words were uttered in a level tone, but Muzaffar could hear the underlying distress.

A noisy flock of rosy starlings came flying into the garden and alighted on a pair of mulberry trees nearby. The flowers had just started to turn to plump white fruit; the pickings would be slender. But the birds, their creamy-pink and black feathers flashing against the green fuzz of flowers and fruit, were enthusiastic in their foraging. Their loud chattering washed over the three men as they sat, brooding.

'The problem,' said Khan Sahib after a while, heaving a sigh of frustration as he did so, 'is that we have not the faintest idea of where to find Shamsuddin.' He glared, irritated, at the starlings in the mulberry trees. 'What irks me is that we know who the culprit is, why he did it, how he did it – '

'Do we, Khan Sahib?' Muzaffar murmured. 'Do we really know how he did it?' He nodded in response to the sharp look Khan Sahib directed at him. 'There is something fishy about Parvez's murder. If he was killed about four hours after midnight, and Nilofer Begum raised the alarm an hour later…

well, that makes me think Nilofer Begum was involved in it all.' He paused, gathering his thoughts. 'I think Nilofer Begum perhaps did not know what was planned until fairly recently. It seems to me that Shamsuddin and Ameena planned Parvez's murder all those months back in Surat, but did not tell Nilofer; perhaps they hoped to keep her out of it – after all, it is often the members of the household who are first suspected when a man is murdered.

'But when Aadil was killed by accident, and Shamsuddin came to talk to Ameena that night, he threw something into the courtyard for the maid to pick up. Could it have been a letter? A letter for Nilofer, explaining it all? That her brother had come to Dilli, to get rid of the unwanted husband?'

'But he killed Basharat Sahib the very next night, did he not?' Suraj Bhan said.

'Again by mistake. And Ameena had gone by then – fled, I suppose, to wherever Shamsuddin was staying. Or wherever he had made arrangements for her to stay. Ismat overheard her asking whether he had left word; that they would not turn her away? – I have a feeling Ameena suspected she had been seen or heard; that could be why she ran away that very night, to evade questions from the law.

'I think, though, that either she or the letter explained a lot to Nilofer; not just what Shamsuddin had done or planned to do, but also where he was staying, and how to reach him. After Basharat was killed, Nilofer probably sent a message to Shamsuddin. Or visited him; I don't know. But I suspect that when he finally entered the house last night – or early this morning, as you will – he knew exactly what he was going to do. And Nilofer was there to help him.'

'Help him murder her husband? Or escape?' Khan Sahib asked. 'Though, if I were in Nilofer Begum's place, I would have been more than happy to help Shamsuddin put an end to Parvez's existence.'

Muzaffar grinned. 'Hardly the sort of thing I would have expected the Kotwal to say, Khan Sahib!' The grin faded as quickly as it had appeared. 'I meant, though, that Nilofer helped him get away. I think she helped him into the house – that rope on the terrace? It had been knotted around the pillar; if Shamsuddin had indeed come up the rope – and I see no other way he could have entered the house – then someone must have knotted the rope there in the first place. Nilofer, I suspect.'

The starlings, having fed as much as they could on what mulberries they could find, flew away, chattering as they went. Muzaffar glanced up at them. 'Just a few more weeks,' he said absent-mindedly, 'and then they will be gone. They visit Dilli only in the spring, you know.' He blinked, flushed. 'I beg your pardon. Where was I?' And he came back to his theory; of how Nilofer, after quietly letting her brother into the house, had perhaps retreated into the mahal sara while Shamsuddin went downstairs and murdered Parvez. How Shamsuddin, the injustices against him and his sister avenged, had then come upstairs, leaving a trail of bloody footprints.

'Which would not have mattered, if they did not intend to hide the fact that the killer had escaped by way of the terrace. But they forgot that a killer, fleeing in a hurry from a room where he had murdered a man so bloodily, would have very bloody hands – and those hands would leave their mark on the rope.' Shamsuddin would have gone up the stairs, to be met by Nilofer, who would have taken him silently inside the mahal sara, for him to wash his hands, clean himself so that he would not draw attention in the streets when the sun arose.

'All of it done in silence,' Muzaffar said. 'The man lying dead in his room, while his widow and her brother, his killer, carried out the rest of their plan. Shamsuddin must have been long gone, well away to safety, when Nilofer came downstairs and pretended to raise the alarm, using the bloodied footprints on the stairs as proof of how the killer had escaped.'

'Unless we arrest her and beat the truth out of her, there is little hope that she will tell us where he is,' Khan Sahib observed, in a strained voice. 'And that does not appeal to me. I could never sanction anything more than questioning, when it comes to a woman.'

'I don't think it will come to that, Khan Sahib,' Muzaffar said. 'Perhaps we can use Nilofer to take us to Shamsuddin.'

ꕥ

A particularly vivid sunset had gilded the outer walls of Parvez's house. The crowd that had hovered outside through much of the morning and afternoon had dispersed, gone at last to homes and businesses neglected through the day. The thanedar had left one man on guard at the front door of the house. Another was patrolling the area, making it a point to keep an especially keen eye trained on the house. Inside the chowki, huddled around a small lamp that was too dim to even illuminate their faces to any great extent, were four men: the Kotwal, the thanedar, the chowkidar, and Muzaffar. The thanedar had arrived less than a quarter of an hour earlier, in response to an urgent summons from Khan Sahib. The chowkidar had been there, or at Parvez's house, all through the day. The stress showed in his face, but mingled with it now was excitement.

The soldier who had been put on guard outside the chowki – with explicit instructions to watch for a particular palanquin that had entered Parvez's house less than half an hour earlier – shifted restlessly. Then, with a sudden jerk, he whirled round and ran to the doorway of the chowki. 'Huzoor! Begum Sahiba's palanquin is coming back!' He had not even finished what he was saying when Muzaffar, already tense as a coiled spring, leaped to his feet and rushed out. The guard moved away just in time to avoid a collision.

The kahaars bearing Shireen's palanquin were still a few

yards away, but the young woman who had accompanied the palanquin came running forward on light feet. 'Huzoor!' Ruqayya panted, 'Begum Sahiba begs you to hurry – '

Muzaffar hurried. He ran forward, indicating to the kahaars to set the palanquin down. He glanced towards Parvez's house as the palanquin was placed on the ground, by the side of the lane. The house was quiet; he could see the thanedar's man on guard outside, but that was all.

A slim hand, wearing a slender bracelet of gold studded with pearls, had made its way between the curtains of the palanquin, and if Muzaffar was not mistaken, Shireen would have stepped out, regardless of the fact that this was the open street. She would be veiled, of course, but still. He reached the palanquin, caught her hand in his, and drew it inside even as he looked in.

She had thrown back her dupatta from her face. Her eyes were wide with excitement. 'Jang Sahib! Hurry, please – I believe Nilofer means to leave as soon as she can. She nearly shoved me out, making excuses about a sudden headache – '

Muzaffar directed another quick look towards Parvez's house. It was still silent. Behind him, Khan Sahib had stepped out of the chowki too; Muzaffar recognized the familiar clearing of the throat that signified his brother-in-law's presence. 'Khan Sahib,' he whispered, pulling his head out of the palanquin. 'It is time.' And, while Khan Sahib turned to give instructions to the men waiting for them – instructions to fetch their horses, instructions to alert men on foot – Muzaffar turned back to his wife.

'You are sure, Shireen? You're sure you told her – '

'Of course I did!' This time it was Shireen who cut him off in mid-sentence. 'I told her that my brother-in-law, the Kotwal Sahib, had had a stroke of luck and found a witness who had actually seen the murderer fleeing the house an hour before Nilofer had surprised whoever it was in the room. I gave her to understand, just as you had instructed me,' she added with a touch of sarcasm, 'that Khan Sahib had deduced that the murder had been committed about four hours after midnight, not when Nilofer raised the alarm. So she knows that Khan Sahib is indeed close to the truth. Now will you please hurry?!'

Muzaffar gave her a quick smile and drew back just as he heard Khan Sahib say behind him, 'There she is. Come on!'

Khan Sahib was already mounting up, spurring his horse forward. Muzaffar, turning for his own horse, glanced over his shoulder. The front door of Parvez's house had opened wide, wide enough to allow four kahaars, wrapped in heavy shawls, their sinewy legs bare below their dhotis, to carry out a palanquin. They stepped over the threshold, smoothly lifting their burden above it, and slipped into a smooth, quick stride as they headed down the street, in the direction opposite the chowki.

Khan Sahib had drawn his horse up next to Muzaffar's. 'Too few riders in this part of town,' he muttered. 'We will stick out; she is a clever woman, that one, and if she realizes she is being followed – we had best string ourselves out. You go on ahead, Muzaffar; I do not think she has ever seen you, has she? I will follow. You, Aslam,' he said to the thanedar, who had also mounted up, though somewhat gingerly – his foot was perhaps still not completely healthy – 'you bring up the rear. Your man is with you?'

The thanedar nodded. Riding pillion behind him was a soldier, a man the chowkidar had identified as being a particularly swift runner, and one, importantly, with considerable stamina. A distance Nilofer's kahaars could cover, the man could cover just as easily on his two feet. Anywhere along the way, if the horse riders needed a message sent quickly back, either to the chowkidar, or to the local thana – where instructions had been left – he could be relied upon.

Flinging one last look over his shoulder to ensure that Shireen's palanquin was headed back in the direction of his own haveli, Muzaffar moved his horse forward, following the kahaars who carried Nilofer's palanquin.

☙

Muzaffar frowned in consternation. When he had concocted this plan with Khan Sahib and Shireen, he had assumed that Nilofer, lured out by the supposed threat to her brother's freedom and life, would head for the teeming, busy markets in the vicinity of the Qila Mubarak. Chandni Chowk, he had imagined, or the many tiny lanes and alleys that crisscrossed the area surrounding it. In one of those, perhaps holed up in a nondescript little shack, would be Shamsuddin. That was the part of town Muzaffar had feared they would have to follow Nilofer's palanquin into: a maze into which a man on foot – or a woman, if she were resourceful and unafraid – could easily vanish.

But Nilofer's kahaars were carrying her palanquin south, not north. South, and – to Muzaffar's greater surprise – west. He could see them, perhaps twenty yards ahead, weaving their way between passersby, roadside sellers of vegetables and fruit, the occasional rider, the even more occasional palanquin. Where could she be headed?

Then, suddenly, they were moving with the unbroken stone bulk of the city wall to their left. Muzaffar, one eye on the kahaars, glanced about, noting the buildings he passed. Yes, there, piercing the wall, was the Turkman Darwaza, the stumpy stone gate named for Shah Turkman Biyaban, the long-ago hermit saint whose tomb was next to the gate. Tucked away near the saint's nondescript tomb was another tomb, even more nondescript, and with less reason: the tomb of the only woman who had ever sat on the throne of Dilli, the redoubtable Razia Sultan. Sultan was what she had been called, not Sultana, as a Sultan's wife or mother would be traditionally addressed. Sultan, as brave and as capable as a man.

Muzaffar smiled to himself as he edged his horse past Razia's tomb. His contemporaries may think of women what they felt, but Muzaffar had known some exceptionally strong-willed women. Women of far greater wisdom than most men. Women who knew what they wanted from life, and were not afraid to say it. Women who did not cower and let the world ride roughshod over them. His sister Zeenat Begum was one of them. Shireen was another. There had been that courtesan, Mehtab, and even – to an extent, though he had discovered it only later – her young companion and apprentice, Gulnar. And here, he thought, as he saw Nilofer's palanquin go past Turkman Darwaza and straight on, was another.

Off to the right, looming high above its surrounding houses, he noticed the Kalan Masjid, the 'large mosque', built by the prolific mosque-builders, Khan-e-Jahaan Junaan Shah Telangani, father and son, in Firoz Shah Tughlaq's reign. Large mosque, indeed, and almost fortress-like, in the forbidding bastion-like shape of its façade, its stark and undecorated symmetry.

The kahaars moved on. Muzaffar glanced over his shoulder; well behind him, within sight but keeping his distance, was Khan Sahib. He raised his hand briefly to Muzaffar in a gesture Muzaffar interpreted as enquiring. Muzaffar gestured back, shrugging. They could only wait and see.

'Ajmeri Darwaza,' he muttered to himself a few minutes later, as the next gate along this stretch of city wall came into view. This, the gate facing the direction of Ajmer, was more prominent than Turkman Darwaza. A busy gate, too, right now open and letting in a stream of bullock carts and horses. The kahaars paused briefly, waiting for a gap in the crowd. Muzaffar lined up his horse, suddenly tense. There was too much coming and going – too much dust, too many animals and people, too much shouting and neighing. If, in all the confusion, he should lose track of that blue-painted palanquin...

And he had. Even as the deluge coming in through the gate passed him, another caravan headed out. There were camels in this one, too, besides bullock carts, both carts and animals loaded with goods. A large caravan, this one, and probably bound for distant lands. And in a hurry to get out through Ajmeri Darwaza, too. Muzaffar, impatient and anxious, trying to push his way through, found his way barred by two merchants, along with their assistants, a camel driver and a string of laden camels. An altercation had erupted somewhere down the line, between one of the guards at the gate and a camel driver. Angry shouts rang out, arguing, some urging on others. 'Move on, move on! Let him be!' someone called, the panic rising in his voice. 'If we don't get out within the next half hour – '

'I presume you've lost her,' said a quiet voice behind Muzaffar.

Muzaffar looked over his shoulder. 'Look at this,' he said, annoyed at his own helplessness, and frustrated. 'A rat could not get through to the other side, Khan Sahib.'

'But Nilofer's palanquin seems to have made it through.'

Muzaffar shrugged, embarrassed, but said nothing.

The thanedar drew up beside them. The man sitting behind him slid off the horse and moved purposefully forward on foot. 'No,' Khan Sahib said, moving his horse ahead and blocking the man's path. 'Do not reveal our identities. I do not want word to spread that we are here.'

There was not much chance of any word spreading here, thought Muzaffar bitterly. The clamour showed no sign of abating. Neither did the crowds, which seemed to have grown. Yes; there were certainly more people now, jostling and pushing, bellowing and arguing to get through the gate. 'We will be locked in!' a man was yelling. 'A good half day's journey, gone down the drain!'

Of course. The jostling and shoving was not mere impatience;

it was far more urgent. As Muzaffar had heard someone mention earlier, Ajmeri Darwaza would be shut and barred within half an hour. Like all the other gates – Turkman Darwaza, which he had passed a while back; Dilli Darwaza, further east; and the others which pierced the city walls. Shahjahanabad would be shut in for the night, safe behind solid stone. The gates would not open until late the next morning.

For anybody setting out on a journey, it was pointless to leave Dilli in the morning. Pointless, and foolish. In the summer, leaving just two hours before noon meant that the coolest hours of the day had already been wasted. In winter, to leave at first light meant to take advantage of considerably fewer hours of sunlight.

No wonder, then, that it was usual for travellers to leave the city the evening before they meant to set out. Leave the city before the gates closed for the night, and take shelter at one of the many sarais that stood just outside the city walls, in close proximity to the gates. From the sarais, it was an easy matter to leave as early or as late in the morning as one wished.

'The sarais,' Muzaffar whispered to himself. 'Yes, that must be it. Of course!' He turned to Khan Sahib, drawing his horse in close to the Kotwal's. 'Where better?' he added, after he had told Khan Sahib his theory. 'A travellers' inn; nobody will know him, nobody will question his coming or going. And, as long as he paid up, he could stay as long as he wished.'

'Let us go,' said Khan Sahib. 'As soon as we can get through. How many sarais are there outside Ajmeri Darwaza, do you remember?' He was already plunging into the crowd, pushing, using his horse to carve a path.

It was impossible to hold a conversation in a melee such as this. Muzaffar tried to remember how many sarais there might be outside the Ajmeri Darwaza, and could not. Several, he was certain of that; to which one would Nilofer have gone? He followed in Khan Sahib's wake, weaving his way through the surging mass of humanity and cattle, wondering which of the sarais they should go to. Perhaps, he thought, as he slid his horse quickly between one bullock cart and the next, they might split up. Khan Sahib could go to one sarai, Muzaffar to another, the thanedar and his man to others. They could cover at least four sarais that way. He hoped it would not be too difficult. A palanquin, after all; and a lady's palanquin at that, a distinctively coloured one: the gatekeepers at the sarais would be certain to have noticed one like that, if one had entered.

And, even as he broke through and out into the fresh air outside the gatehouse, there it was. Its poles held on the shoulders of four kahaars. A blue palanquin, bobbing jerkily along towards Ajmeri Darwaza from the direction of one of the sarais, off to the left.

Khan Sahib had seen the palanquin too; he whirled his horse round, heading for it. Muzaffar, looking over his shoulder to check on the thanedar's progress, was relieved to see that his horse, too, had come through – and that the thanedar, showing commendable initiative, had made his man dismount and race towards the sarai. It was an intelligent thing to do, to inform the gatekeeper. Even as Muzaffar drew rein in front of the palanquin, he saw the heavy wooden gate of the sarai swing shut. There would be protests, of course, from those who had been hoping to enter, but it could not be helped. The official in charge of the sarai's security – there was one in every sarai – would be hurrying to the gate even now, to find out from the approaching Kotwal the reason for this sudden shutting of the gate.

'Halt!'

It was, Muzaffar realized, not even necessary for Khan Sahib to have said that. He had swung down from his horse right in the path the palanquin had been taking, and the kahaars could only have gone around him. And that had become well-nigh impossible. The crowd milling about Ajmeri Darwaza, whether just emerging from the city or impatient to enter it, had sensed that something exciting was happening. They had seen the three horsemen struggling to get through the mob; they had noticed the slamming shut of the sarai's gates; they had seen the imperious Khan Sahib – few would know that he was the chief law officer of the city, but they would probably recognize the air of authority he bore about him. They stopped, clustered around. Waited to see what would happen. And they blocked, unwittingly, the further passage of the palanquin. Whether Nilofer's kahaars liked it or not, they could go no further.

From the direction of the sarai, a stout man came bursting through the crowd. In his wake trotted six men, not uniformed, of course – even the foot soldiers in the Baadshah's armies rarely wore a uniform – but clearly soldiers. Two of them carried flaring torches; all of them bore lances. Khan Sahib nodded as the portly man leading the contingent arrived. 'You are in charge of the sarai's security?'

'Huzoor.' The man nodded. The thanedar's man had, even in the short while it had taken to pass on the order to shut the gates of the sarai, informed those at the sarai of whom the order had come from. This man knew he was speaking to the Kotwal of Dilli, even if he had never seen Khan Sahib before.

'This palanquin came from your sarai?'

The man looked to his left, and waved forward one of his soldiers. 'I was stationed at the gate, huzoor,' the soldier volunteered, addressing Khan Sahib. 'I saw it enter, and I saw it leave.'

'How long was it inside the sarai?' Khan Sahib's voice was a low but startlingly audible rumble, loud enough to be heard for yards around, especially since the crowd surrounding them had fallen silent. Waiting, thought Muzaffar, with bated breath, to see what would happen next. The sarai official's men, at an indication from Khan Sahib, had spread out. They surrounded the palanquin now, in a rough circle inside which stood Khan Sahib, Muzaffar, the thanedar, the sarai officer, and the four kahaars. Four men, stoop-shouldered, their heads and shoulders draped in shawls. Faceless men, nameless men, to those who sat in their palanquins. They stood now, grateful perhaps for the unexpected opportunity to take a rest.

'Where was the palanquin carried in? Where was it set down?' Khan Sahib darted a glance at the kahaars, but his question was addressed to the sarai guard who had answered his first question.

'In the main yard, huzoor, near the well.'

Khan Sahib looked taken aback. Muzaffar certainly was; it was unusual that a woman – and that too a wealthy upper class woman like Nilofer – should have had her palanquin set down in such a very public space.

'And? Was one of the kahaars sent in, with a message?' A thought seemed to strike Khan Sahib. 'Or was there someone accompanying the palanquin? A maid, perhaps?'

'None but the kahaars, huzoor.' The man paused. Even in the dimness of the torch-lit night, Muzaffar could see that he flushed. 'I do not know what happened; I was distracted. Some travellers came by – '

Khan Sahib silenced him with a brisk wave of his hand. 'But you did see this same palanquin leave the sarai – after how much time inside?'

'A few minutes, huzoor. Not more than that. A few maids had come to the well to fill water when the palanquin arrived; I remember they were still there when it left.'

The crowd around them, regardless of the presence of the Kotwal, had started to turn restless. There were murmurs, whisperings, signs of people growing impatient. There were few here who were really idle; most, after the first flutter of excitement and curiosity, would be eager to carry on, either into the city or further out. Once the crowd began to disperse, there would be confusion. And confusion could allow the palanquin's kahaars to make a quick getaway. It would be difficult, but it could be done. And if it happened, Khan Sahib would be not merely the Kotwal of Dilli, he would be the laughing stock of the city too.

He had been trying to get at the truth without having to resort to searching the palanquin, but he had been left with no option. Muzaffar saw Khan Sahib square his shoulders and step up to the palanquin. A sudden hush fell across the crowd.

'Begum Sahiba,' Khan Sahib said, looking towards the heavy cloth that formed a curtain for the palanquin, 'you have heard what I have asked. You know, too, I think, why you have been stopped. Will you climb out of your palanquin, please? I will not force you, but if you refuse to do so, I can call on one of the ladies here to look inside your palanquin. What would you prefer?'

☙

She must have been shocked, thought Muzaffar. He certainly was; he had not expected Khan Sahib to confront her so boldly.

There was silence for a few moments. The crowd, even those who had started drifting away, froze. Muzaffar wondered if Nilofer would call Khan Sahib's bluff. She could well refuse to emerge from the palanquin, and if Khan Sahib did ask one of the very few women in the crowd to step forward and look inside the palanquin – to verify that the only person inside was actually Nilofer, and not her criminal brother – she could probably find a way out of that too. A gold coin, a precious ring pressed into the hand of the woman, and the way would be clear. Short of Khan Sahib himself parting the curtains of the palanquin and looking in, there seemed no sure way of determining whether it was Nilofer in the palanquin. And whether she was alone.

'There is no need to inconvenience the women here, Kotwal Sahib,' said a rich, clear voice, attractively deep for a woman's. Simultaneously, the curtains of the palanquin were parted by a slender hand, hennaed and beringed, its wrist heavy with a striking bracelet of coral and gold. A beautifully adorned hand, at odds with the stark brown of her garments, revealed as she stepped out of the palanquin and stood beside it. Covered from head to toe, as faceless as the kahaars who stood well away from the palanquin. With her sleeves down to her fingertips, she looked as proper a new widow as one could have expected.

'You recognize my voice, Kotwal Sahib?' she asked. 'Or shall I unveil myself so that you may convince yourself of my identity? Ah, but you have not seen my face – but Jang Sahib's Begum Sahiba? Perhaps she can be fetched?' Nilofer's head turned towards Muzaffar. She was audacious, and her audacity, no doubt, was what she was depending upon to carry her through this. Almost any other woman would have kept silent until questioned further. A frisson of excitement rippled through the crowd; this was turning out to be far more interesting than they could have imagined.

'No, Begum Sahiba,' Khan Sahib said through gritted teeth. 'I do not need you to unveil yourself.' And, paying her no more attention, he moved forward towards the palanquin. 'Muzaffar, if you will come here, please. And you, Aslam.' When the others joined him, Khan Sahib bent forward, clasped one of the horizontal poles of the palanquin and hefted it. 'It seems empty to me. What do you think?'

By turn, Muzaffar and the thanedar lifted the palanquin. 'Empty, yes.' Muzaffar murmured. The thanedar agreed. They stepped back. 'Just to be certain,' Khan Sahib whispered, and drawing back the curtains of the palanquin, peered inside. He withdrew his head and shoulders a moment later. Only someone who knew him as well as did Muzaffar would have seen past the wooden expression to the disappointment, the puzzled look in the eyes.

'You may go now, Begum Sahiba,' Khan Sahib said.

'Go, Kotwal Sahib? Have you no questions for me?' The voice held a distinct note of sarcastic incredulity in it. Muzaffar would have warned Nilofer Begum against baiting Khan Sahib. People might side with her, as a gentlewoman who had been asked to emerge from her palanquin in the midst of a crowd, but Khan Sahib had enough evidence – and Muzaffar and the thanedar, possibly even the sarai officer and his men – as witnesses to prove Nilofer's complicity in at least one murder.

'If there are any questions for you, Begum Sahiba, I will send for you at your home,' Khan Sahib replied, tight-lipped. 'You may go now.'

Nilofer inclined her head slightly, and with the same dignity that she had shown in climbing out of the palanquin, re-entered it. The curtains settled into place behind her. The kahaars, at a signal from Khan Sahib, moved back into their places and lifted the poles of the palanquin onto their shoulders. The sarai's soldiers moved back, allowing the palanquin to pass through; and the crowd, both baffled as well as disappointed – they had hoped for more – parted. People were beginning to drift away. Muzaffar could hear snatches of whispered conversation, guesses about what the incident had been all about. The brief glimpse of the veiled lady, her stilted conversation with the Kotwal, his obvious suspicion of her yet his allowing her to go: surely there was something there? And why had the Kotwal not put his foot down?

'Aslam,' said Khan Sahib, drawing the thanedar and Muzaffar aside, out of the way of the now moving crowd, flowing about them like the rushing waters of a stream around rocks. 'Listen carefully. Aslam, I want you to take the sarai officer with you' – he indicated the man, now standing looking a little forlorn, by the side of the road – 'and search through the sarai. Nilofer must have managed to get there only long enough to warn Shamsuddin; she obviously wasn't able to get him out. So he should still be there, unless he was able to escape over the wall or by some other means before the sarai was alerted – '

She was a smart woman, Muzaffar was thinking. Shireen had come away from their first meeting with the impression that Nilofer was all beauty and no brain. That impression had had to be amended as they had got to know Nilofer better. She was not a woman to stand up to the Kotwal so brazenly for no rhyme or reason. Any other – man or woman – cornered by the law, even if innocent, would have tried to be gentle, polite. Most would have been subservient.

He glanced in the direction her palanquin had taken, following the path by which they had come. To his surprise, he could still see it. The crowds had shifted, thinned perhaps, and there, not more than twenty yards away, was the palanquin, bobbing jerkily along. An odd movement, not that brought on by uneven ground – which it was not; this was good level road. The movement, rather, of a kahaar who was perhaps nursing a wounded shoulder, or an injured leg.

'Khan Sahib!' Muzaffar grunted, turning and vaulting onto his horse as he spoke. 'The kahaars!' And without adding anything to that, he swung his horse about. The chestnut stallion raced forward, the clatter of its hooves scattering passersby, clearing the road faster than a slower, more prudent pace could have achieved.

Muzaffar swooped down on the palanquin. In the flickering lights from roadside torches, he had seen, even as he bore down on the quartet of kahaars, that the one in front, carrying the pole on the right, was a taller, more well-built man than the others. It was he, with his longer stride, who was ruining the careful rhythm the team had maintained on its way to Ajmeri Darwaza.

'You!' Muzaffar yelled, bending over his horse's neck, pulling off the man's heavy shawl with one hand even as he reached for the dagger in his cummerbund. If he was right about this man, he could be in danger of his life. The shawl went flying and the palanquin overbalanced, the other three kahaars struggling in vain to keep a hold on it. The air was suddenly filled with screams, the sound of running feet, the neighing of Muzaffar's horse as he slid off it, one hand still grasping the kahaar by his throat. The man had recovered from the shock of the assault, and he was fighting back now, kicking, trying to get his hands around Muzaffar's neck, hitting out.

They tumbled to the ground, the other man on top of Muzaffar. He was bent over, his face contorted and so close that Muzaffar could see the gap where one tooth was missing. Could smell the stale, cloying smell of lemons. An attar. This was the scent, overpowering and nauseating, that had filled Aadil's room, because a tiny vial of attar had been knocked over when the merchant's house was ransacked by his murderer.

He relaxed, and then, the very next moment, as soon as he could sense that his opponent had been lulled into a sense of security, he put all of his strength into his shoulders and pushed upwards, hard. The heel of one hand caught the man under his chin. The other hand, balled into a fist, flew a little off its intended mark, landing on the man's shoulder. He was flung back, but only momentarily. He scrambled to his feet, and Muzaffar was up, too, dagger in hand.

'Shamsuddin,' he panted, even as he heard the clatter of hooves behind him and Khan Sahib's voice calling to them to stop, 'I know who you are. And we know what you have done. There is no hope. Give up.'

EPILOGUE

'I should have realized long before,' Muzaffar said, shaking his head in a gesture of self-reproach. 'As soon as Nilofer stepped so obediently out of the palanquin, actually. She is fiercely loyal to her brother, that one. She would not have come away from the sarai without ensuring that Shamsuddin was safe. And if she thought there was a chance that he was still stuck in the sarai, liable to be caught and arrested – well, she would not have been so bold as to confront Khan Sahib.' He glanced towards Suraj Bhan, who was smiling to himself. 'What?'

'Had I been in her place, I would not have had the courage to speak in those words to Kotwal Sahib even if I were innocent. She must be quite a woman. What will happen to her now?'

They had met at the kotwali, summoned by Khan Sahib to give their testimonies. Khan Sahib had been in a hurry and had not bothered to tell Suraj Bhan anything of what had happened except that Shamsuddin had been arrested. Their testimonies recorded, Muzaffar and Suraj Bhan had left the kotwali, only to discover that they were both headed the same way: towards Dilli Darwaza, Muzaffar bound for his haveli and Suraj Bhan for Aadil's house. 'I have received instructions from Aadil Sahib's brothers in Kashmir,' Suraj Bhan had explained. 'They have told me to have all his possessions packed and sent to them, and to sell off whatever merchandise is there. I have to go to his house to separate his personal belongings from the stock.' He had paused. 'Will you allow me to accompany you till your mohallah, Jang Sahib? I am eager to know some of the finer details of this entire affair.'

Muzaffar was willing to comply. Suraj Bhan, after all, had been a part of this mad adventure from almost the very beginning, when Aadil had been killed. And in the course of their association – over the investigation of Aadil's and his neighbours' deaths, as well as the case that Suraj Bhan had brought his way, the abduction of Lakshminarayan's child Nandu – Muzaffar had realized that this was a man singularly astute. An intelligent man, a man sure of himself yet not arrogant, a man for whom he had developed a deep respect.

'I do not suppose anything very much will happen to Nilofer Begum,' Muzaffar said as they walked along, down one of the narrow winding lanes that led from Chandni Chowk towards Jama Masjid. They were nearing the great mosque now; he could see the three black-striped domes of it towering into the sky. 'All she is guilty of is helping her brother to escape. Compared to what he did, that is a minor crime. I suppose all that will happen to her is a fine. A penalty to be paid, and that is all.'

'And her brother? He appears to have had ample reason to kill Parvez Sahib; reason, perhaps, which any man aware of his own honour would consider valid. And he did find proof of his own innocence, did he not? I thought Kotwal Sahib mentioned that after he had been arrested, he confessed that after committing the murder, he had been looking for documents that proved that Parvez had actually hired someone to steal the merchandise and place it in Shamsuddin's warehouse.'

Muzaffar nodded. They had reached the end of the lane; ahead of them, sitting on the natural rise called the Bhojla Pahari, sat the Jama Masjid. A flock of pigeons, perhaps a few dozen birds, wheeled over the mosque before swooping down towards the main courtyard. 'Yes,' Muzaffar said. 'With Nilofer's help, he was able to lay his hands on those papers – they weren't among the papers Parvez kept in his office; they were in his personal correspondence.' He walked on in silence for a few yards. 'That will perhaps be in his defence when it comes to his killing of Parvez. But the fact remains that Shamsuddin did kill Aadil and Basharat. He will still be tried for that.'

'Hmm. I suppose Nilofer Begum would be best off returning to Surat.'

'Whenever Khan Sahib lets her go. I suppose he will, soon enough. And Ameena, who was also unearthed from the sarai, seems to be of the same opinion. Dilli is not a city either of the two women has liked much.'

'It can be a brutal city,' Suraj Bhan remarked. 'I wonder what is going on there,' he murmured, indicating, with a tilt of his chin, a small crowd at the foot of the Jama Masjid.

'Shall we see? Or do you have to reach Aadil's house soon?'

'I am in no hurry. Let us see; I am curious.'

Under a small square canopy of red cloth, held up at its four corners by bamboo poles, sat an old man, his arm resting atop a short stick. His hair was salt and pepper, his stringy body devoid of any clothing, even in the chill that still hung in the air. An old man, anywhere between fifty and seventy years of age, but – said his detractors – with the obstinacy and wilful evil of an adolescent.

'Sarmad,' said Muzaffar, with a brief nod. 'I should have guessed. He is often to be found here.'

They had ascended the first few steps up to the mosque, so that the naked mystic and the crowd surrounding him were ranged below. There were others here, too, looking on at the spectacle at the foot of the steps.

A step above them, a conversation was in progress. 'Sarmad

sits,' said a man to his neighbour, 'in the very shadow of the Jama Masjid, and blasphemes. Did you hear about his version of the kalima?'

There was an indistinct murmur, a muffled question.

'Not "There is no God but Allah",' answered the first man, in a low voice – a voice almost awed, as if fearful of being overheard repeating something so sacrilegious – 'he said, "There is no God." Can you believe it?' There was a moment of horrified silence, both listener and speaker shocked by the sheer unholiness of what had been said. 'And when he was asked how he dared to say such things, do you know what he said? That it was as far as he had reached in his quest for the truth.'

Sarmad, Muzaffar knew, had indeed laid claim to having devoted much of his life to that particular quest. From the gossip that was tossed about in the markets, Muzaffar had gathered that Sarmad's search for the truth had perhaps not been his primary motive in life for the first several decades. His early life, in fact, bore the signs of what some may well term hedonism.

There were stories galore about the man. Some were fanciful, others less so. Everybody seemed to agree that he had been born and brought up in Thatta, in faraway Sindh, the son of an Armenian merchant. A Jew, by all accounts, though how long Sarmad had adhered to the faith of his childhood nobody was willing to venture. Trained as a merchant, skilled in Persian, he was said to have fallen violently in love, as a young man – with a boy named Abhai Chand. Where another liaison such as this would have resulted in some lovelorn poetry or some clandestine meetings, Sarmad's torrid love affair with Abhai Chand had had startling consequences: Sarmad had left off wearing clothes, and the two lovers had run away, travelling all over the land, from Lahore to Hyderabad in the Deccan, and finally to Dilli.

'He believes there is no Allah? Truly? How can a man like that be allowed to go on like this? Unfettered. Unhindered? Preaching freely on the steps of the Jama Masjid itself?'

The irony of that last observation was not lost on Muzaffar. That Sarmad, the man who claimed no religion and seemed to fling scorn at every religion – Islam, Hinduism, and Judaism – should preach his irreligious theories at the very foot of the imperial mosque was certainly ironical. But Sarmad, odd though he was, and even downright blasphemous, had as his disciple the Shahzada Dara Shukoh. Dara may not be a fine general or an able administrator; and Muzaffar privately doubted that he would be an Emperor of the likes of his forefathers, whether the ambitious Babar or the farsighted and wise Akbar. But Dara's loyalty towards those he favoured or admired could not be faulted. And Sarmad, for all his eccentricities, had won the admiration of Dara.

'Let us go,' said one of the two men to his companion. 'This disgusts me. I had not imagined him to be so utterly past redemption.'

They stepped down, past Muzaffar and Suraj Bhan, and went their way. Muzaffar glanced at them briefly as he moved aside to let them pass. When he looked back, Suraj Bhan's face wore an enigmatic smile. Muzaffar raised an eyebrow in query.

Suraj Bhan's smile widened. 'Do you not find Sarmad's views blasphemous, Jang Sahib?' he asked, his voice low.

Muzaffar shrugged. 'I believe religion is a very personal thing. A man's views, as long as he does not try to shove them down the throats of others, are his own to hold. If Sarmad believes there is no Allah – well, he is entitled to that belief. It does not make me stop believing in a divinity that rules our lives, call it Allah or what you will.'

Suraj Bhan's smile did not change. It did not widen, it did not waver. A pensive look came into his eyes, though. 'You are one of the few who think this way, Jang Sahib,' he murmured. 'You, and this man, whom most people think mad.'

'Dara Shukoh does not,' Muzaffar pointed out.

'And I thank the Gods for it. I thank every single one of them that the man who will one day sit on the throne is a broad-minded man, a man who does not hold another man's religion against him. The Shahzada Dara Shukoh will be good for the empire,' he finished, his voice fervent.

'Amen,' Muzaffar said.

AUTHOR'S NOTE

In November 1656, the ruler of Bijapur, Mohammad Adil Shah, died. The succession – by the ruler's son, still a boy – caused questions and speculation on the child's paternity, and the Mughal Empire, eager to expand its territory and lay its hands on the immense wealth of Bijapur, moved into action. Mir Jumla, the Diwan-i-kul or prime minister of Shahjahan, was sent to the Deccan with a large army. Along with Aurangzeb (the governor of the Deccan), Mir Jumla's army began the invasion of Bijapur. Of this campaign, one of the most decisive battles was the siege of Bidar.

The garrison at Bidar was commanded by the doughty warrior Sidi Marjan, who – despite the fact that he had only a fraction of the military power at the disposal of the Mughals – refused to either submit or be bribed. The siege lasted for 27 days, with the Mughals pounding Bidar with cannon, grenades, and rockets. Bidar lost 2,600 soldiers (out of a total of 5,000, against the Mughals' 70,000). Sidi Marjan was wounded, and died as a result of these wounds, when a Mughal rocket caused the explosion of a gunpowder depot at Bidar. By March 1657, the Mughals held Bidar.

The annexation of Bidar helped boost (though only briefly, since the rot had already set in) the fortunes of the Mughal Empire.

The brief history of Sarmad, as mentioned in the epilogue, is as factual as can be guessed, considering the conflicting tales about his life. His mysticism and his influence on Dara Shukoh's way of thinking in spiritual matters are however widely acknowledged. Sarmad was beheaded in 1661 at the orders of Aurangzeb.

ACKNOWLEDGEMENTS

Many thanks to Nandita Aggarwal and Rohit Chhetri, former editors at Hachette, whose insights, suggestions and support were – as always – invaluable. Thanks are due, too, to the many fans who, by frequently asking, 'When is the next Muzaffar Jang adventure due?' have helped keep me going.

And, last but not least, my family, without whose unwavering support and love (even if often biased and blind beyond belief) this book might never have got written. Thank you, sweethearts.